Adventure Time™

Ice King

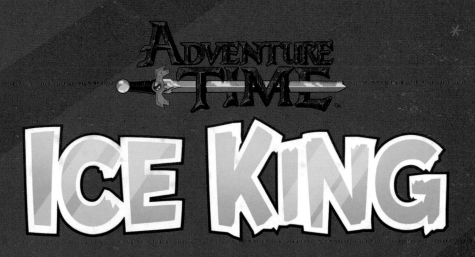

ADVENTURE TIME: ICE KING, December 2016. Published by KaBOOM!, a division of Boom Entertainment, Inc. ADVENTURE TIME, CARTOON NETWORK, the logos, and all related characters and elements are trademarks of and © Cartoon Network. (S16) Originally published in single magazine form as ADVENTURE TIME: ICE KING No. 1-6. © Cartoon Network. (S16) All rights reserved. KaBOOM!™ and the KaBOOM! logo are trademarks of Boom Entertainment, Inc., registered in various countries and categories. All characters, events, and institutions depicted herein are fictional. Any similarity between any of the names, characters, persons, events, and/or institutions in this publication to actual names, characters, and persons, whether living or dead, events, and/or institutions is unintended and purely coincidental. KaBOOM! does not read or accept unsolicited submissions of ideas, stories, or artwork.

A catalog record of this book is available from OCLC and from the KaBOOM! website, www.boom-studios.com, on the Librarians Page.

BOOM! Studios, 5670 Wilshire Boulevard, Suite 450, Los Angeles, CA 90036-5679. Printed in China. First Printing.

ISBN: 978-1-60886-920-6, eISBN: 978-1-61398-591-5

Created by
PENDLETON WARD

Story by
EMILY PARTRIDGE

Written by
PRANAS NAUJOKAITIS

Illustrated by
NATALIE ANDREWSON

Colored by
ANDY BRINKMAN (CHAPTERS 1-4)
NATALIE ANDREWSON (CHAPTERS 5 & 6)

Cover by
WYETH YATES

Designers KELSEY DIETERICH WITH GRACE PARK

Associate Editor WHITNEY LEOPARD

Editor SHANNON WATTERS

WITH SPECIAL THANKS TO MARISA MARIONAKIS,
JIM VALERI, NICOLE RIVERA, CONRAD MONTGOMERY,
MEGHAN BRADLEY, CURTIS LELASH AND THE WONDERFUL
FOLKS AT CARTOON NETWORK.

CHAPTER ONE

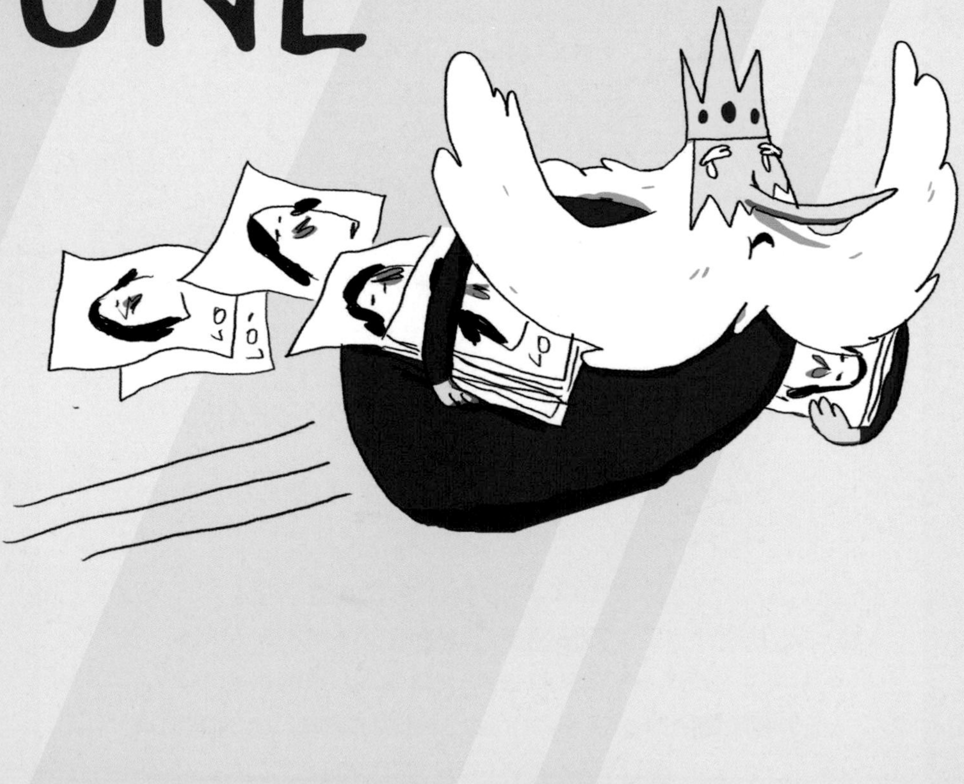

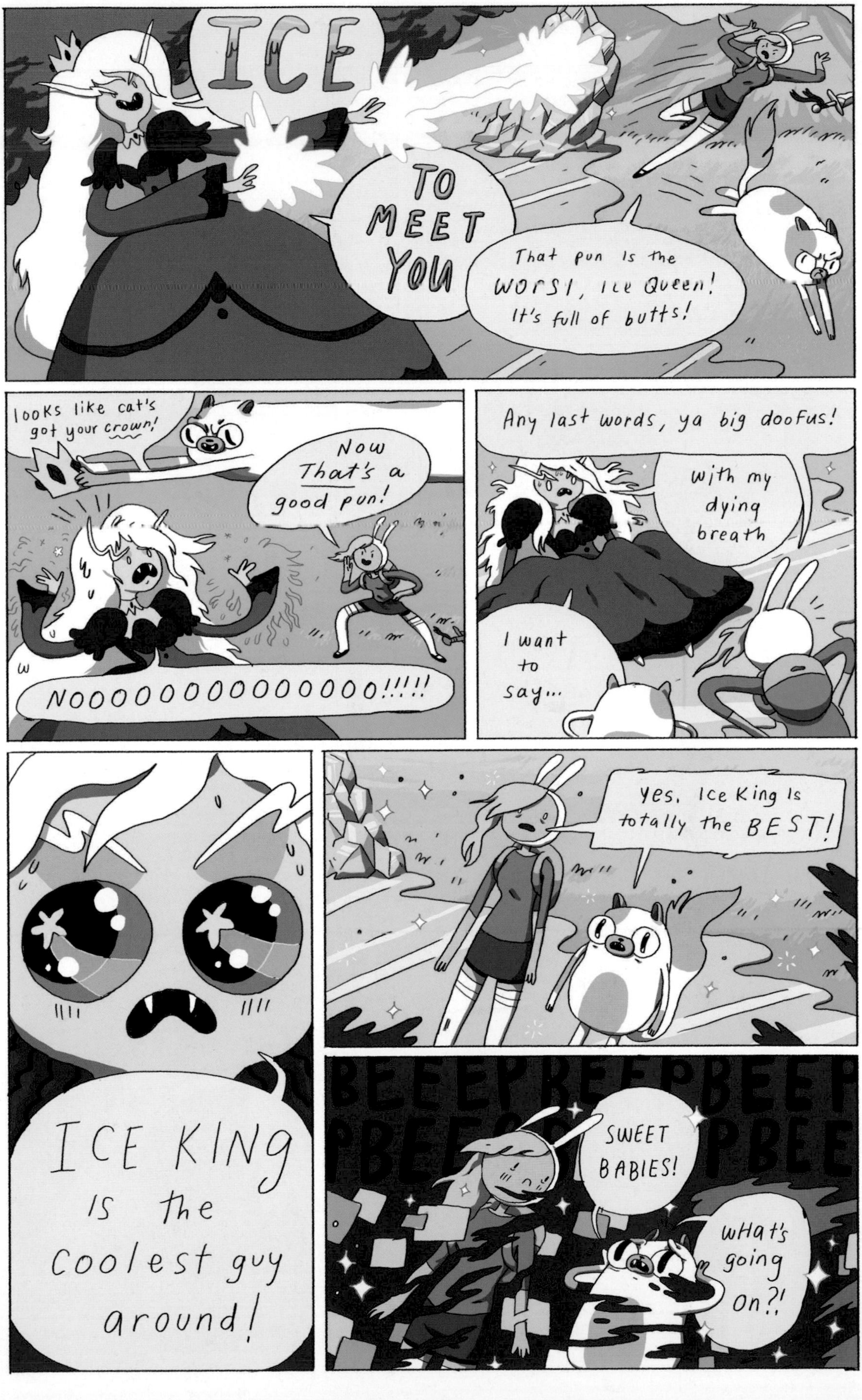
ICE
TO MEET YOU
That pun is the WORST, Ice Queen! It's full of butts!
looks like cat's got your crown!
Now That's a good pun!
NOOOOOOOOOOOOOOO!!!!!
Any last words, ya big doofus!
with my dying breath
I want to say...
ICE KING is the coolest guy around!
Yes. Ice King is totally the BEST!
BEEEPBEEEPBEEEP
SWEET BABIES!
wHat's going on?!

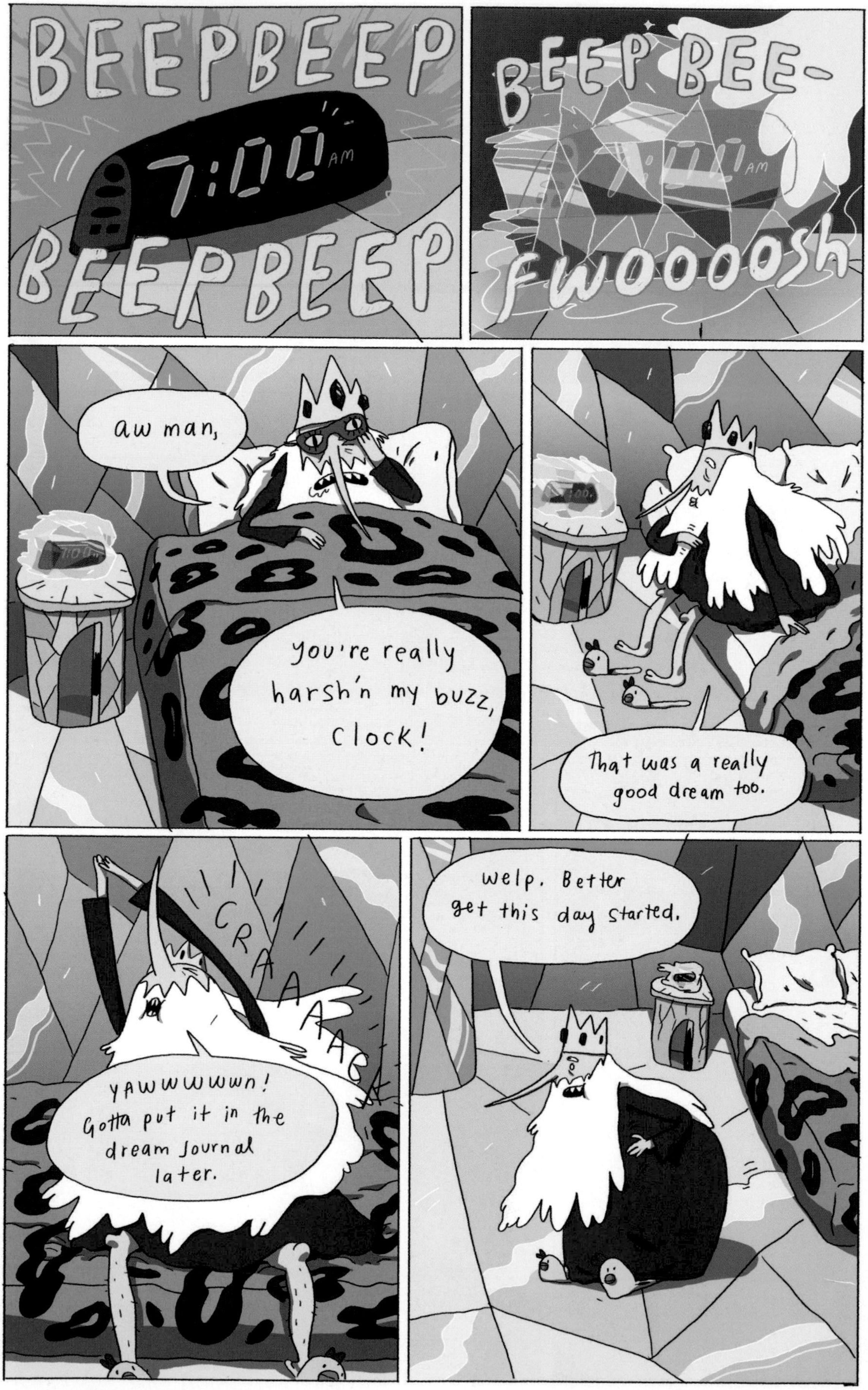
BEEPBEEP
7:00 AM
BEEPBEEP
BEEP BEE-
7:00 AM
FWOOOOSH
aw man,
You're really harsh'n my buzz, Clock!
That was a really good dream too.
CRAAAAAG
YAWWWWWN! Gotta put it in the dream journal later.
welp. Better get this day started.

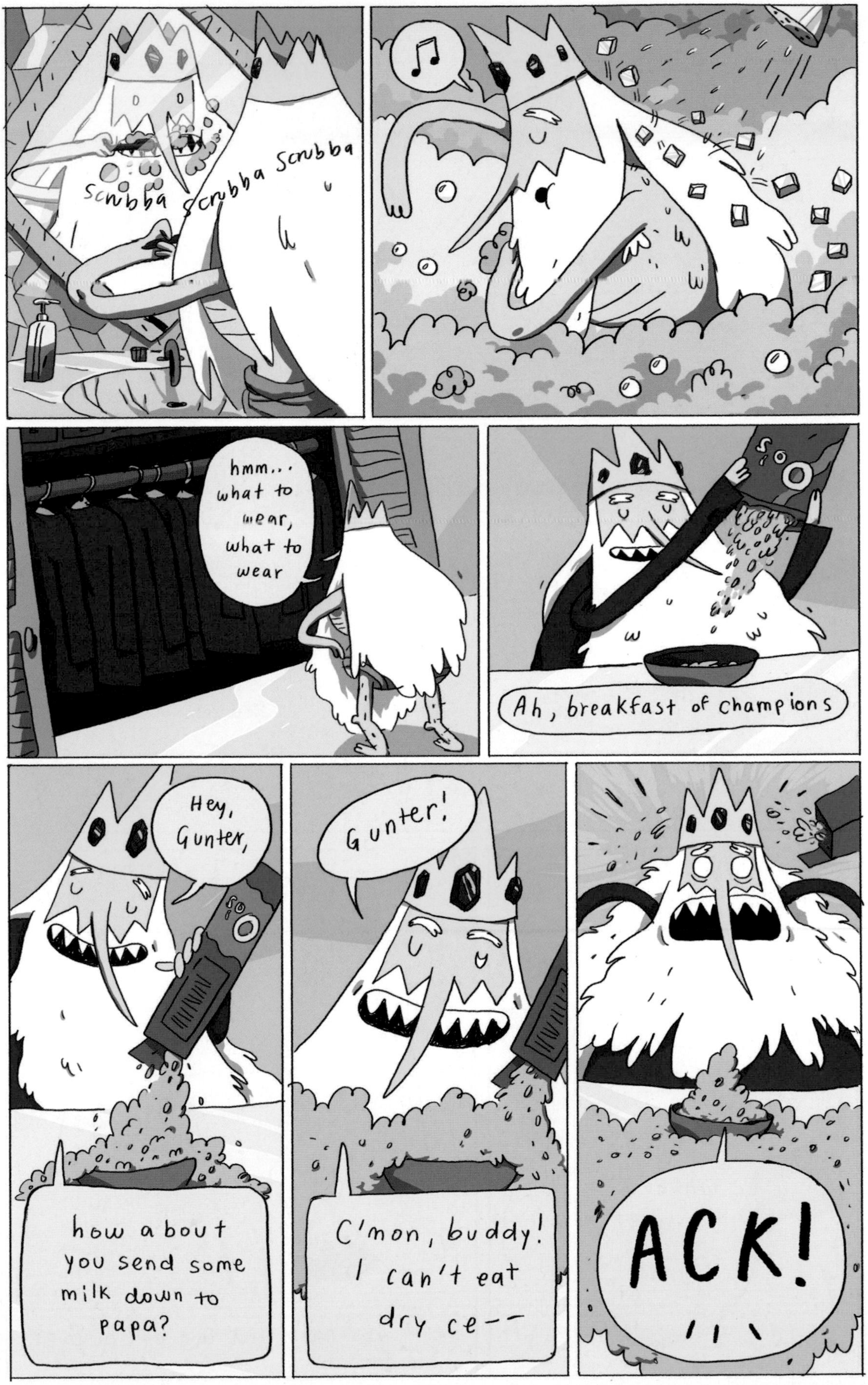
Scrubba Scrubba Scrubba
hmm... what to wear, what to wear
Ah, breakfast of champions
Hey, Gunter,
how about you send some milk down to papa?
Gunter!
C'mon, buddy! I can't eat dry ce--
ACK!

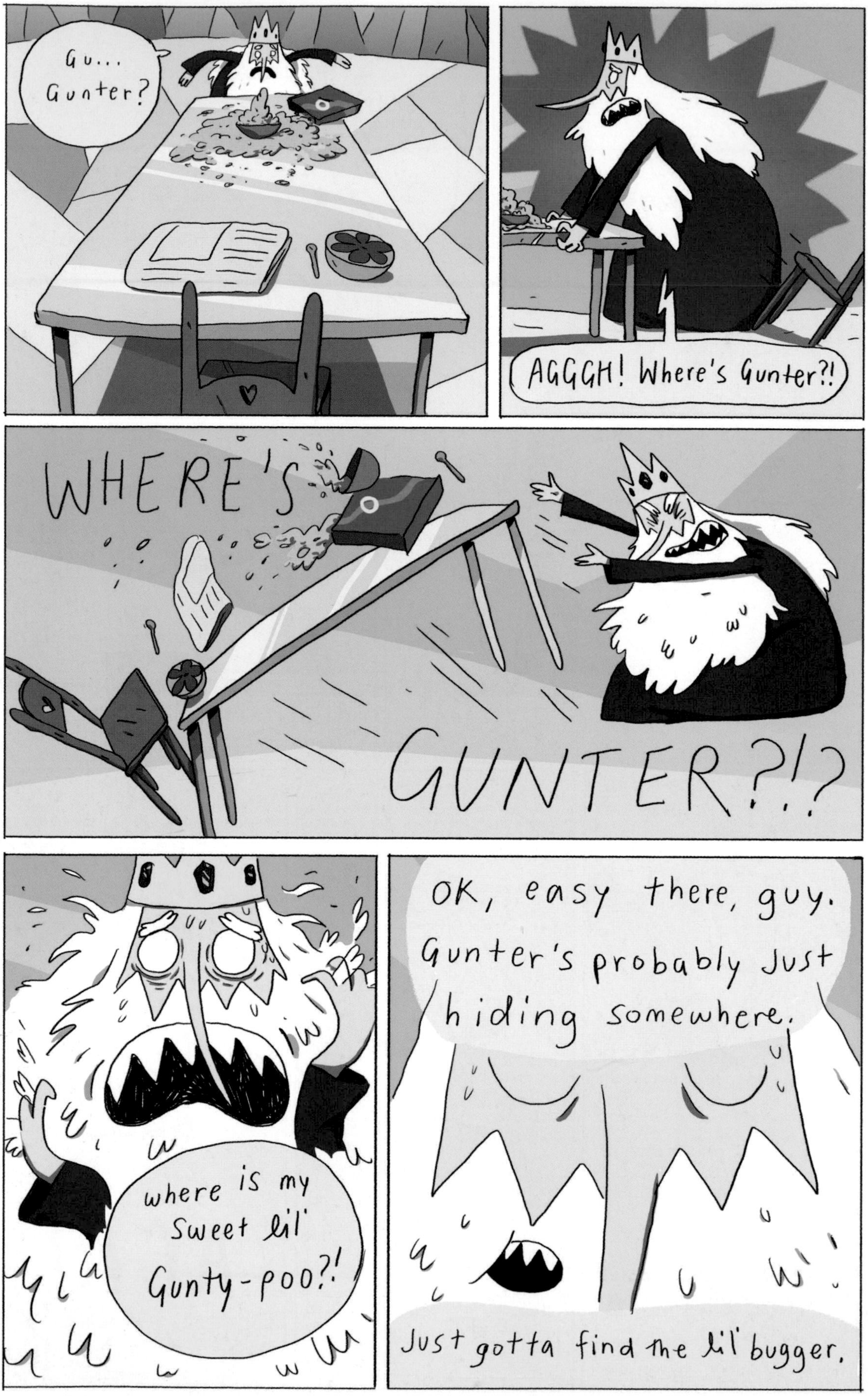
Gu... Gunter?
AGGGH! Where's Gunter?!
WHERE'S GUNTER?!?
where is my sweet lil' Gunty-poo?!
OK, easy there, guy. Gunter's probably just hiding somewhere.
Just gotta find the lil' bugger.

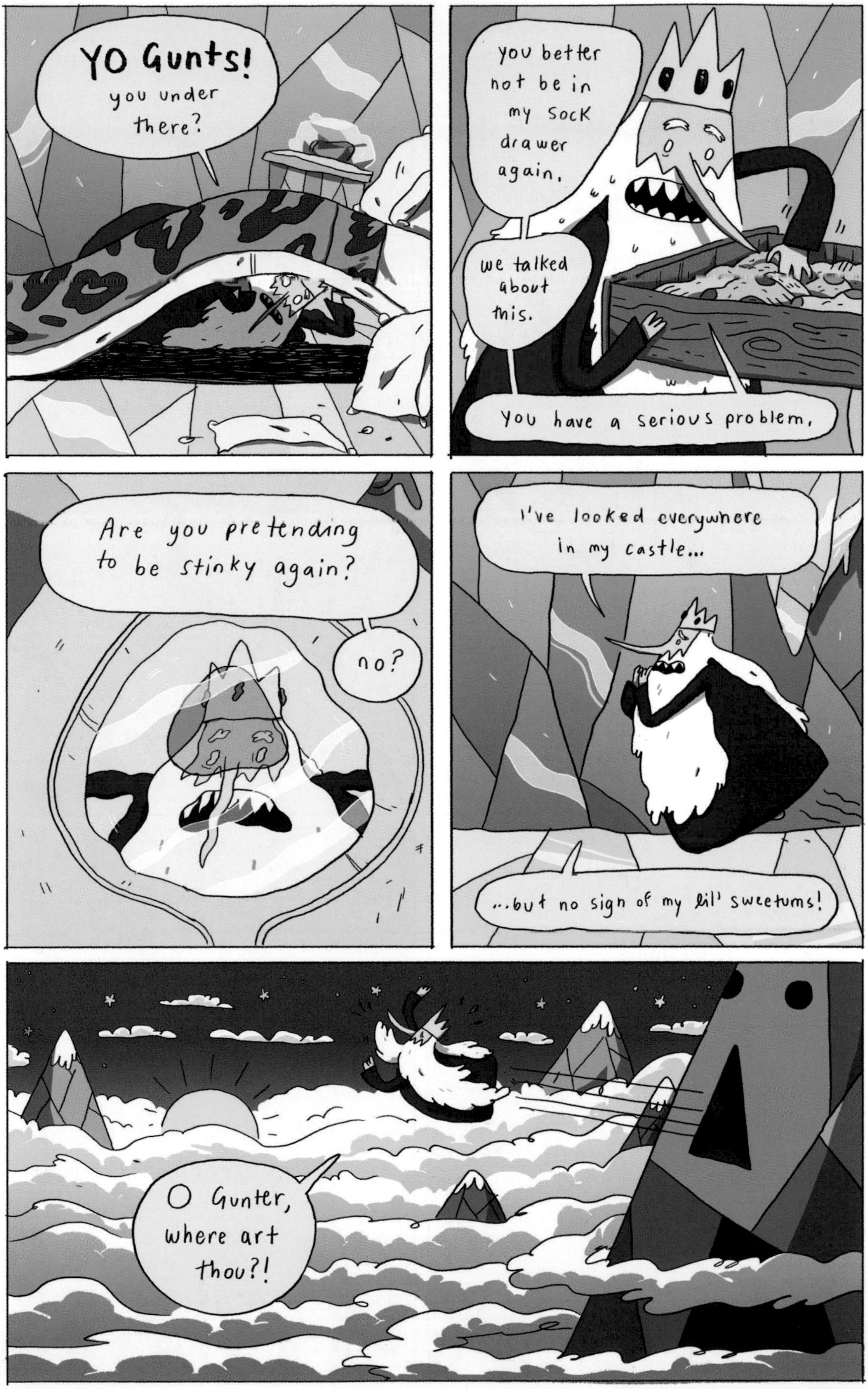
YO Gunts!
you under there?
you better not be in my sock drawer again.
we talked about this.
You have a serious problem.
Are you pretending to be stinky again?
no?
I've looked everywhere in my castle...
...but no sign of my lil' sweetums!
O Gunter, where art thou?!

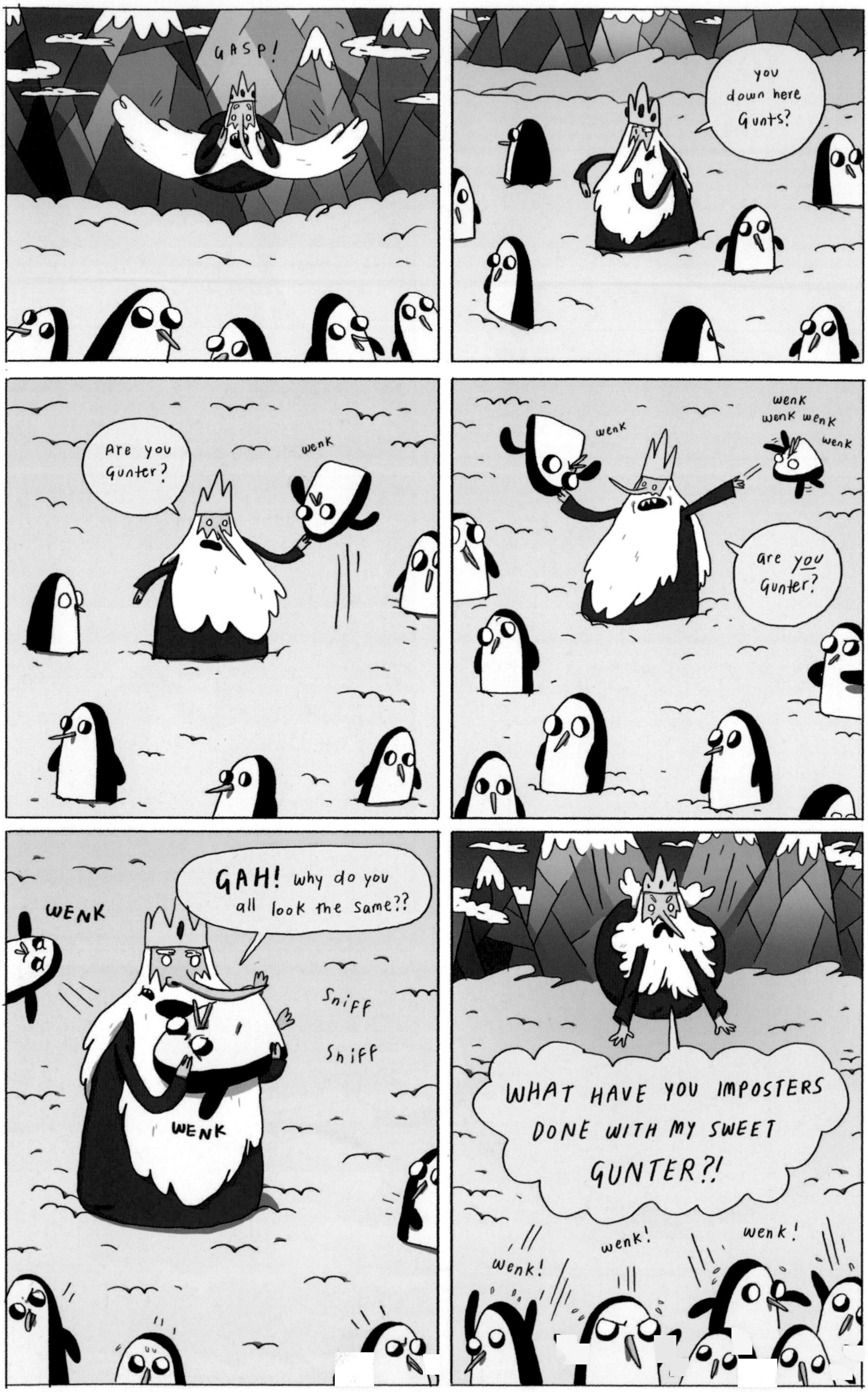
GASP!
you down here Gunts?
Are you Gunter?
wenk
wenk
wenk wenk wenk
wenk
are you Gunter?
WENK
GAH! why do you all look the same??
Sniff
Sniff
WENK
WHAT HAVE YOU IMPOSTERS DONE WITH MY SWEET GUNTER?!
wenk!
wenk!
wenk!

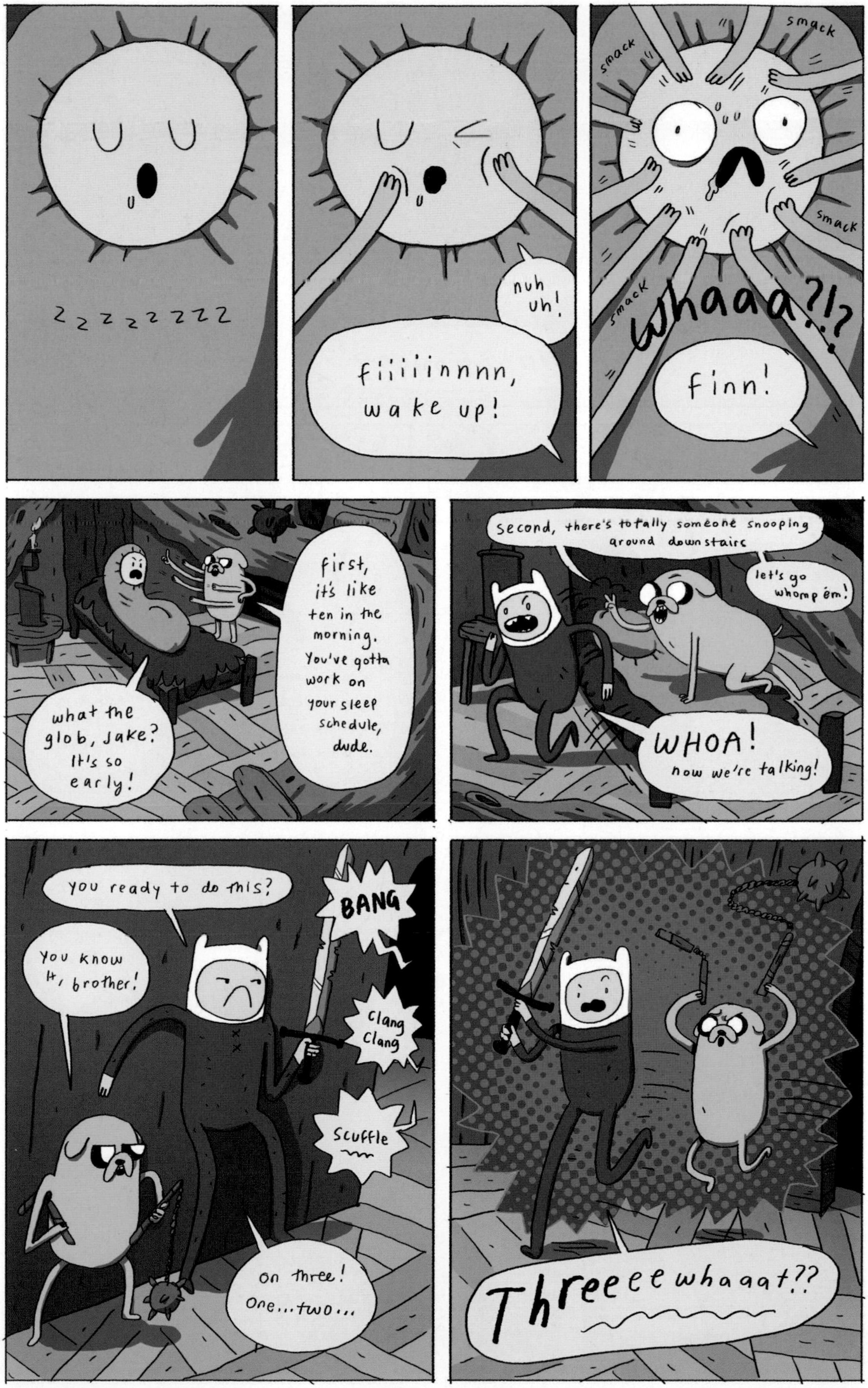
Z z z z z z z z
nuh uh!
fiiiiinnnn, wake up!
smack
smack
smack
smack
Whaaa?!?
finn!
what the glob, Jake? It's so early!
first, it's like ten in the morning. You've gotta work on your sleep schedule, dude.
second, there's totally someone snooping around downstairs
let's go whomp 'em!
WHOA! now we're talking!
you ready to do this?
You know it, brother!
BANG
Clang Clang
Scuffle
on three! One... two...
Threeeewhaaat??

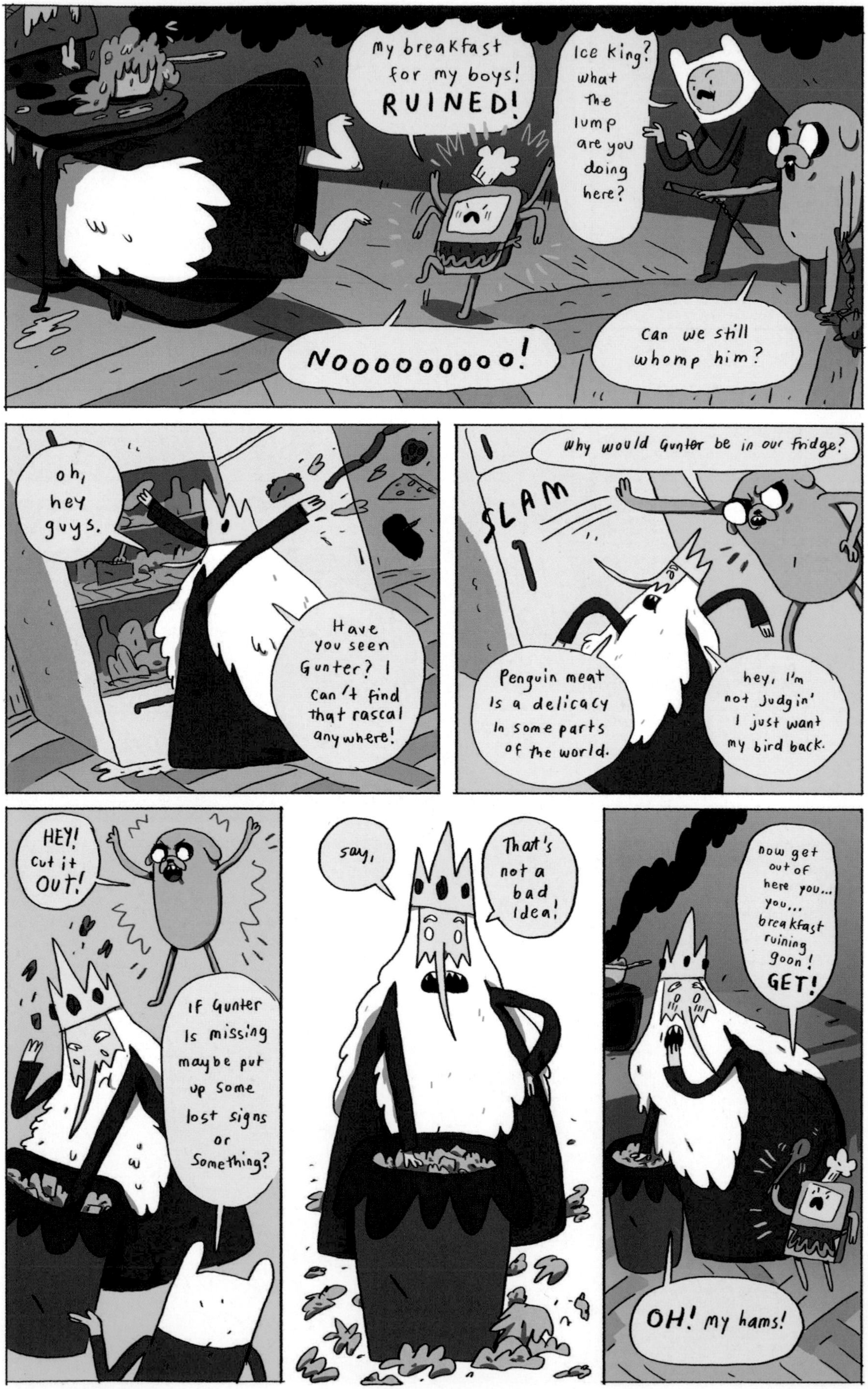
My breakfast for my boys! RUINED!
Ice King? what the lump are you doing here?
NOOOOOOOOOO!
Can we still whomp him?
oh, hey guys.
Have you seen Gunter? I can't find that rascal anywhere!
Why would Gunter be in our fridge?
SLAM
Penguin meat is a delicacy in some parts of the world.
hey, I'm not judgin' I just want my bird back.
HEY! cut it OUT!
If Gunter is missing maybe put up some lost signs or something?
say,
That's not a bad idea!
now get out of here you... you... breakfast ruining goon! GET!
OH! my hams!

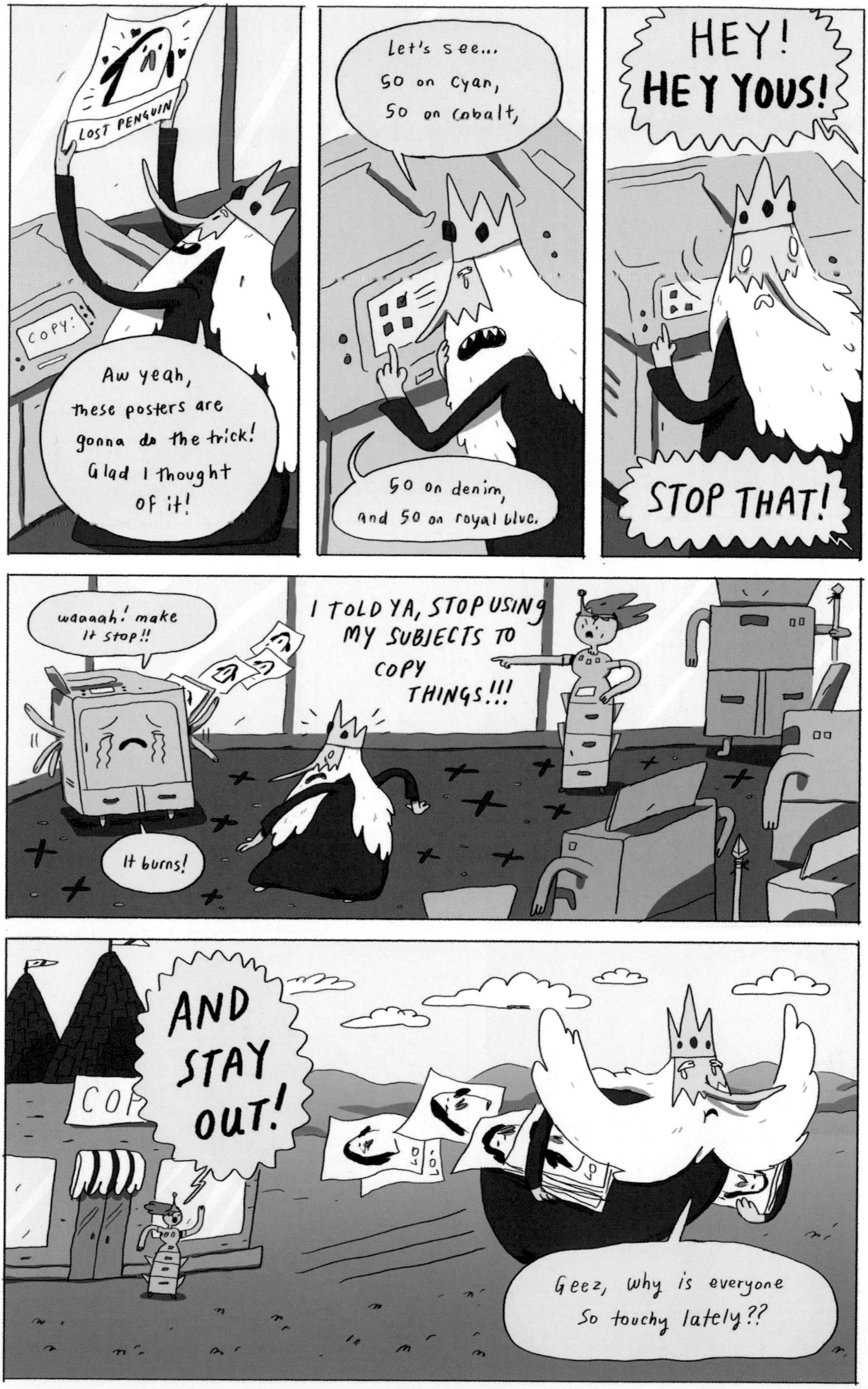
LOST PENGUIN
COPY:
Aw yeah, these posters are gonna do the trick! Glad I thought of it!
Let's see... 50 on cyan, 50 on cobalt,
50 on denim, and 50 on royal blue.
HEY! HEY YOUS!
STOP THAT!
waaaah! make it stop!!
It burns!
I TOLD YA, STOP USING MY SUBJECTS TO COPY THINGS!!!
AND STAY OUT!
Geez, why is everyone so touchy lately??

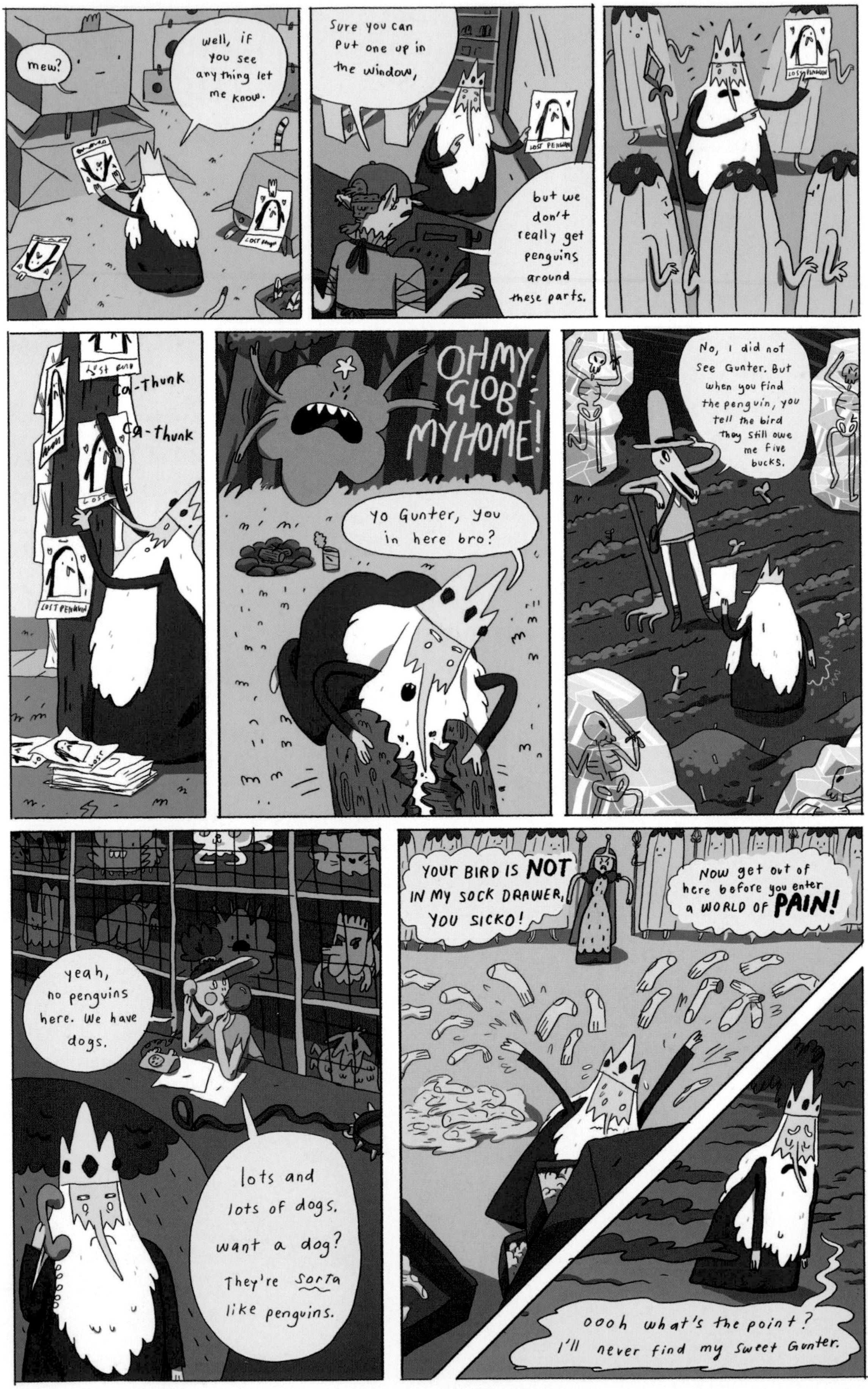
mew?
well, if you see anything let me know.
Sure you can put one up in the window,
but we don't really get penguins around these parts.
LOST PENGUIN
Ca-thunk
Ca-thunk
LOST PENGUIN
OHMYGLOB MYHOME!
Yo Gunter, you in here bro?
No, I did not see Gunter. But when you find the penguin, you tell the bird they still owe me five bucks.
yeah, no penguins here. We have dogs.
lots and lots of dogs. want a dog? They're sorta like penguins.
YOUR BIRD IS NOT IN MY SOCK DRAWER, YOU SICKO!
Now get out of here before you enter a WORLD OF PAIN!
oooh what's the point? I'll never find my sweet Gunter.

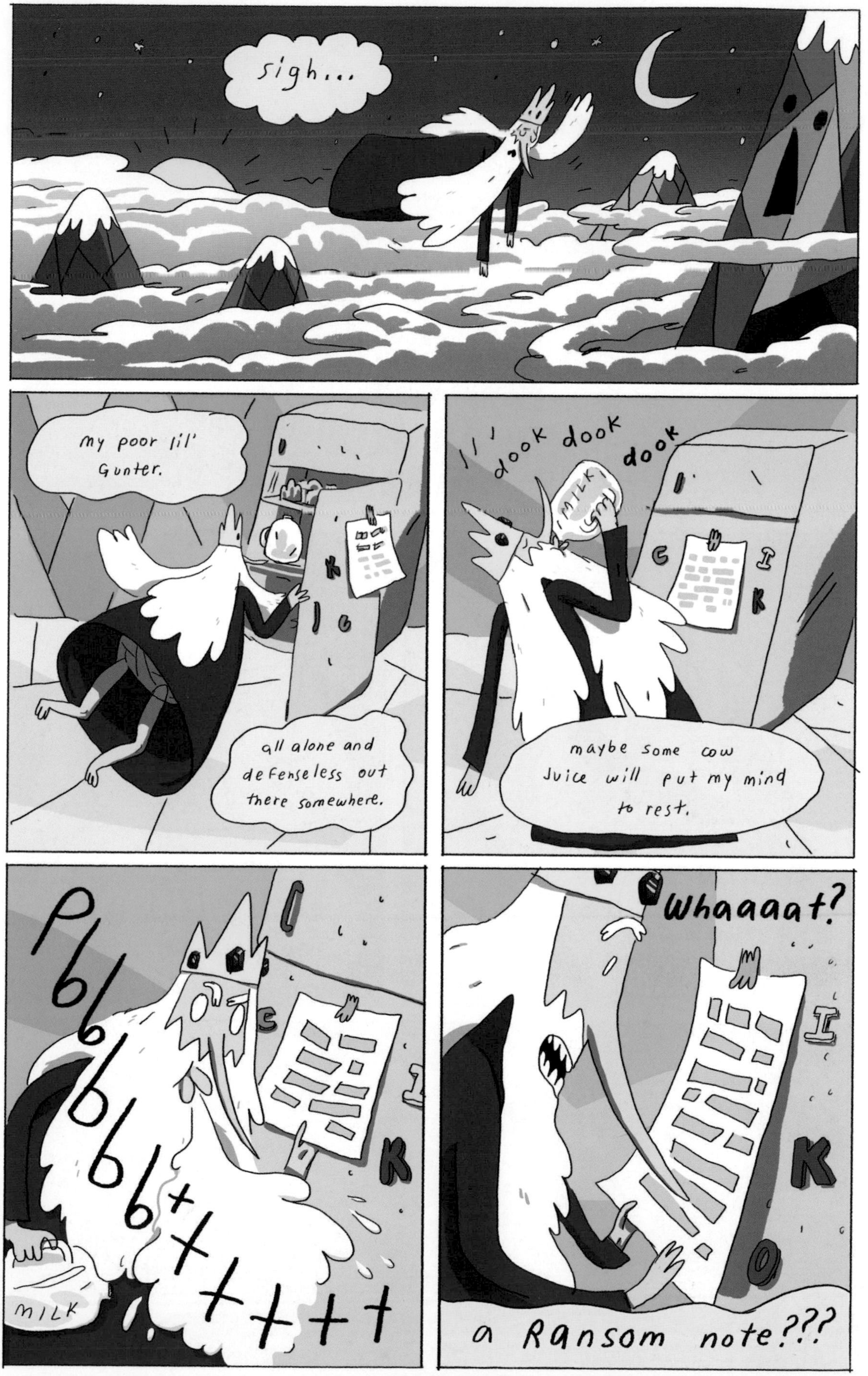

sigh...
my poor lil' Gunter.
all alone and defenseless out there somewhere.
dook dook dook
MILK
maybe some cow juice will put my mind to rest.
Pbbbbb+++++
MILK
Whaaaat?
a Ransom note???

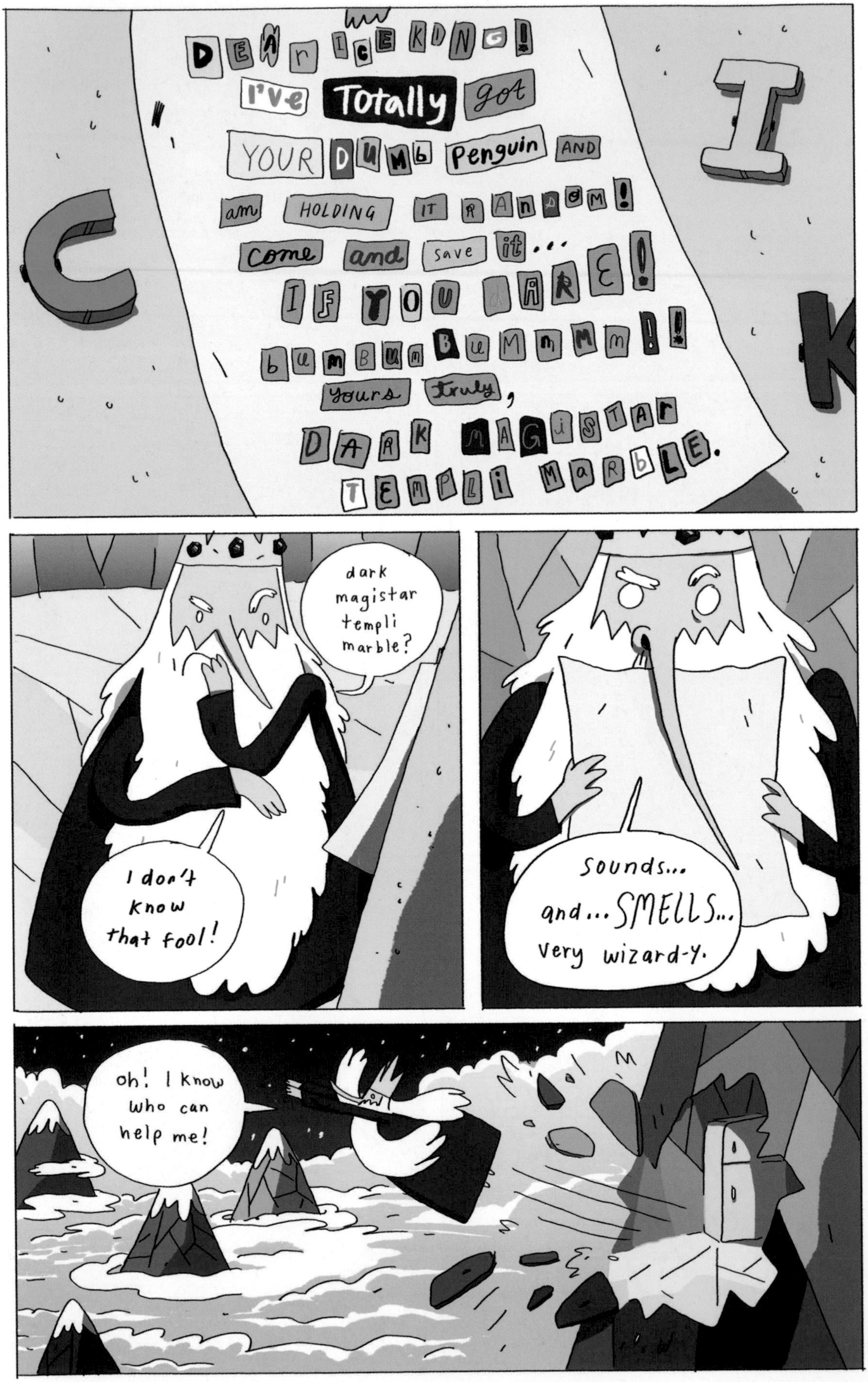

DEAR ICE KING!
I've Totally got YOUR DUMB Penguin AND am HOLDING IT RANDOM!
come and save it...
IF YOU DARE!
bumBumBumMMM!!
Yours truly,
DARK MAGISTAR TEMPLI MARBLE.
C
I
K
dark magistar templi marble?
I don't know that fool!
sounds... and... SMELLS... very wizard-y.
oh! I know who can help me!

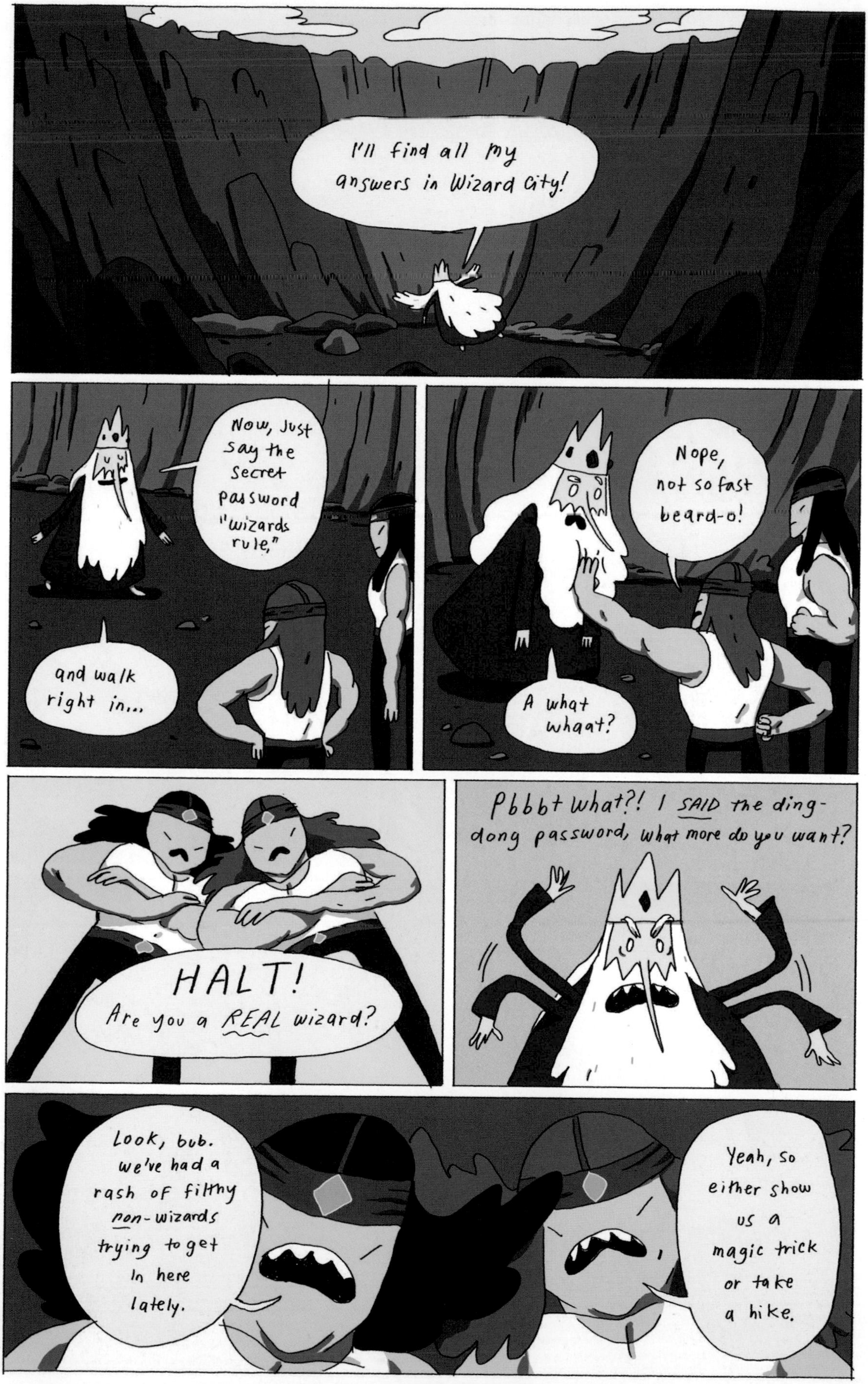
I'll find all my answers in Wizard City!
Now, just say the secret password "wizards rule,"
and walk right in...
Nope, not so fast beard-o!
A what whaat?
HALT! Are you a REAL wizard?
Pbbbt what?! I SAID the ding-dong password, what more do you want?
Look, bub. we've had a rash of filthy non-wizards trying to get in here lately.
Yeah, so either show us a magic trick or take a hike.

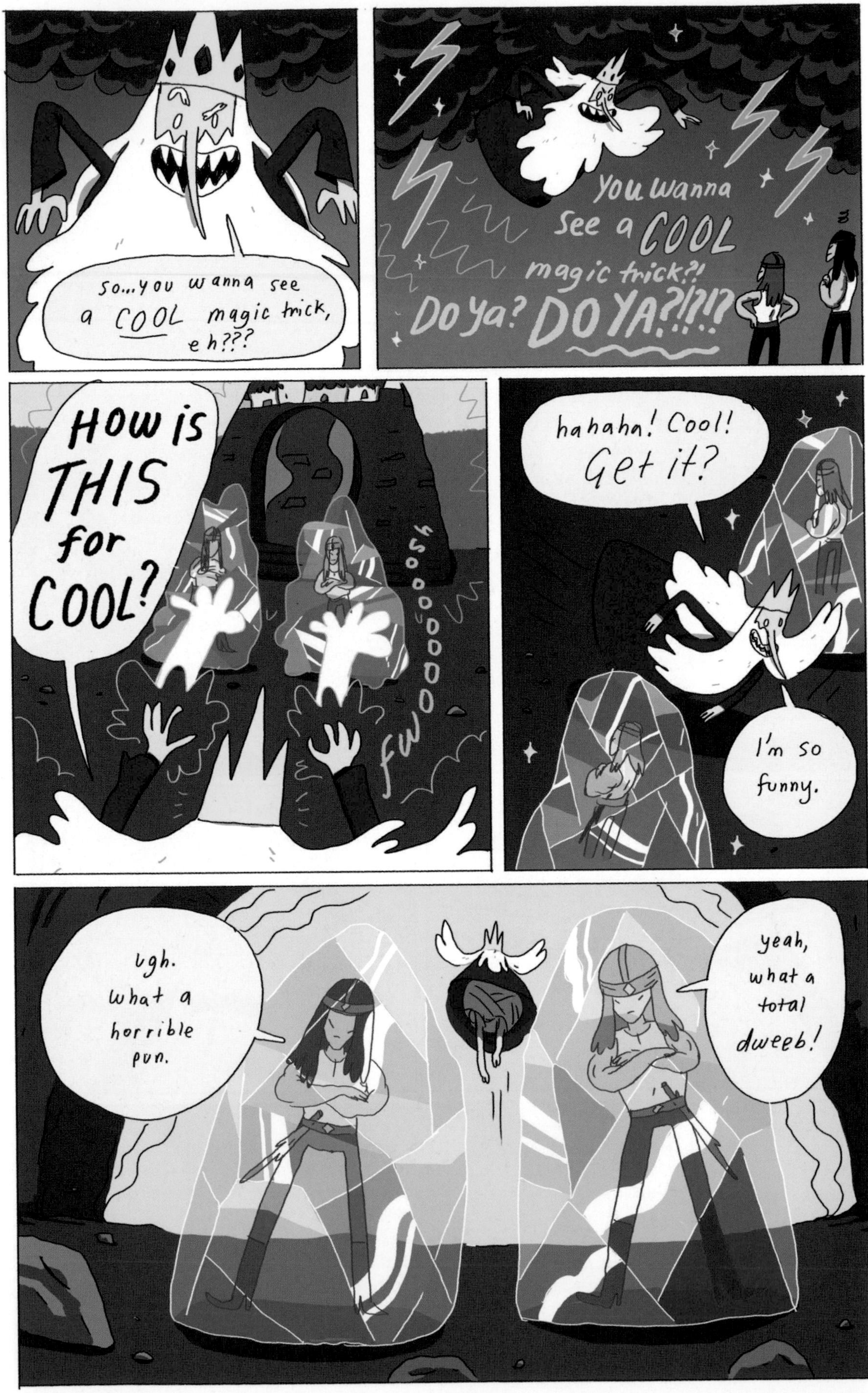
so...you wanna see a COOL magic trick, eh???
You wanna see a COOL magic trick?! Do ya? DO YA?!?!?!
How is THIS for COOL?
FWOOOOOOOOOSH
hahaha! Cool! Get it?
I'm so funny.
ugh. what a horrible pun.
yeah, what a total dweeb!

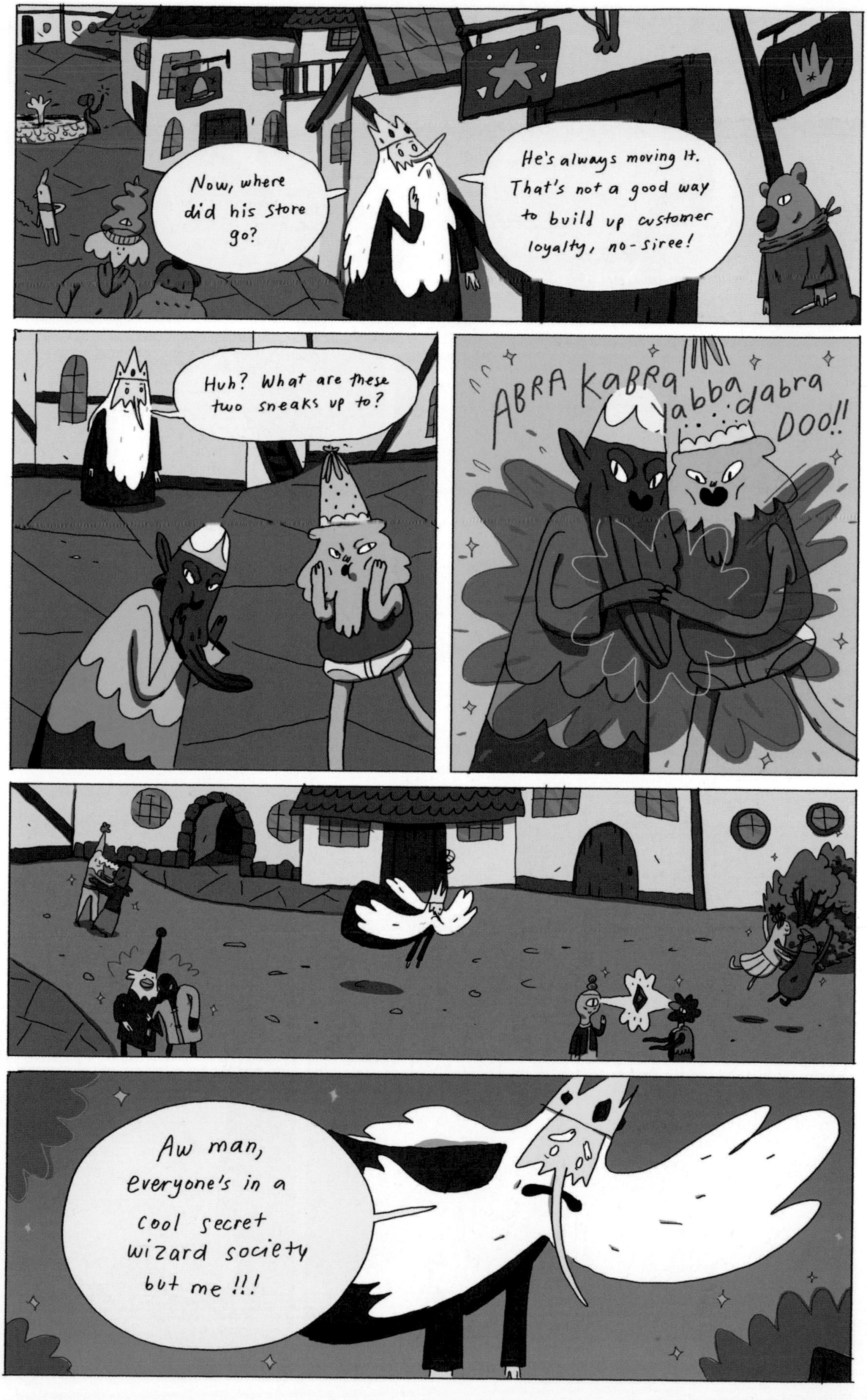
Now, where did his store go?
He's always moving it. That's not a good way to build up customer loyalty, no-siree!
Huh? What are these two sneaks up to?
ABRA KABRA yabba dabra DOO!!
Aw man, everyone's in a cool secret wizard society but me!!!

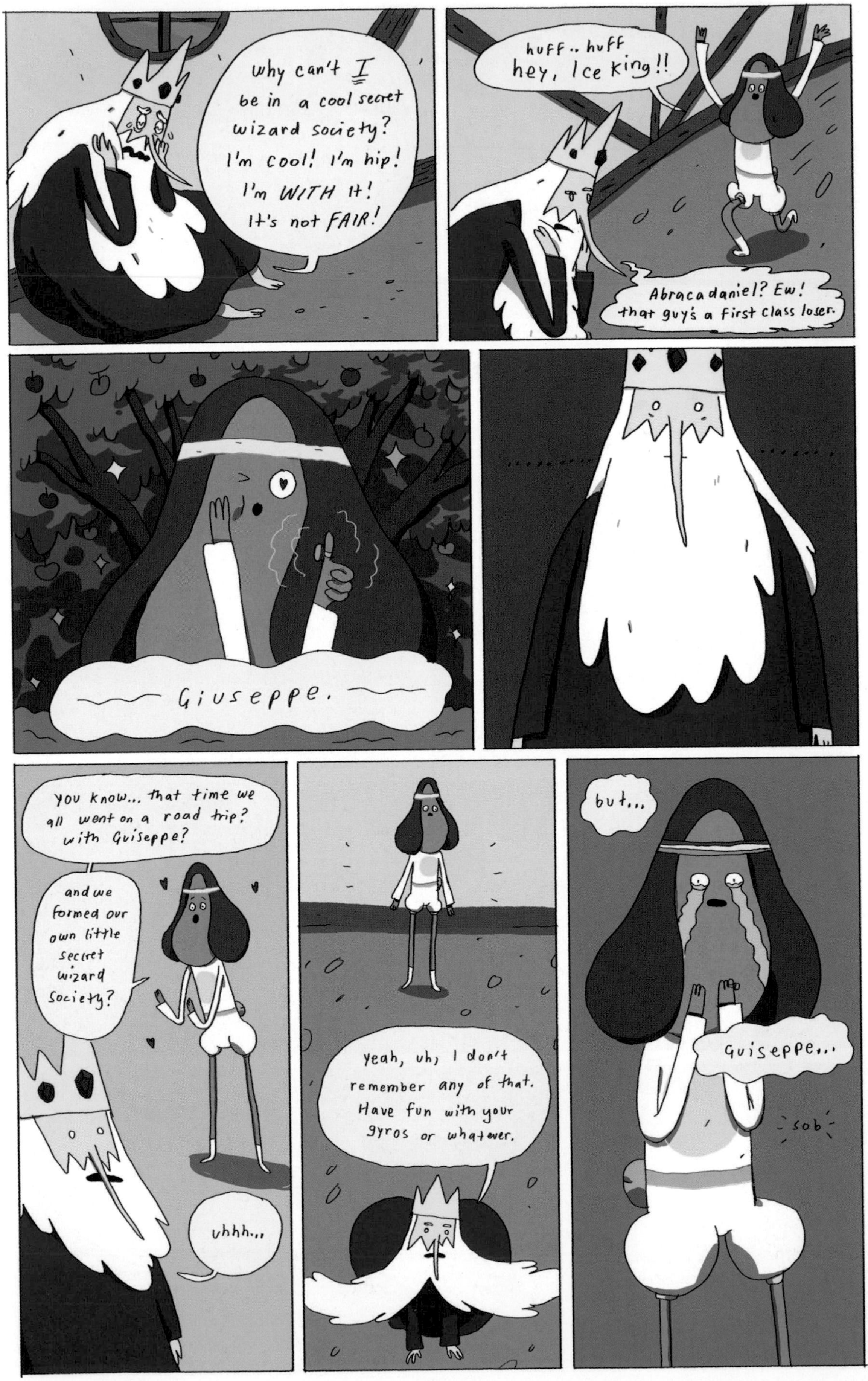

why can't I be in a cool secret wizard society? I'm cool! I'm hip! I'm WITH it! It's not FAIR!
huff.. huff hey, Ice King!!
Abracadaniel? Ew! that guy's a first class loser.
Giuseppe.
you know... that time we all went on a road trip? with Guiseppe?
and we formed our own little secret wizard society?
uhhh...
yeah, uh, I don't remember any of that. Have fun with your gyros or whatever.
but...
Guiseppe...
sob

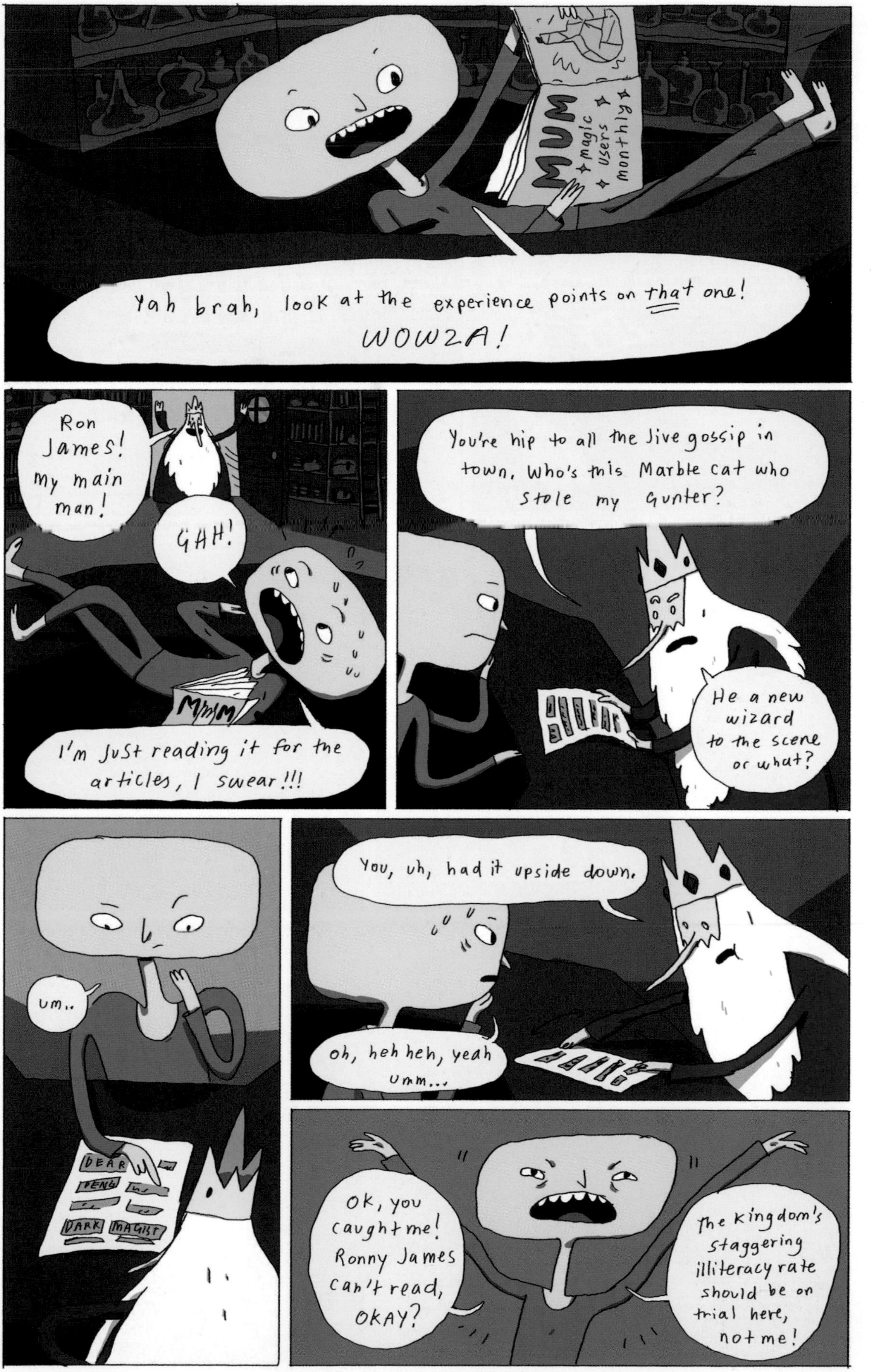
MUM
magic users monthly
Yah brah, look at the experience points on that one!
WOWZA!
Ron James! my main man!
GAH!
MUM
I'm just reading it for the articles, I swear!!!
You're hip to all the jive gossip in town. Who's this Marble cat who stole my Gunter?
He a new wizard to the scene or what?
um..
DEAR
PENG
DARK MAGIST
You, uh, had it upside down.
Oh, heh heh, yeah umm...
OK, you caught me! Ronny James can't read, OKAY?
The kingdom's staggering illiteracy rate should be on trial here, not me!

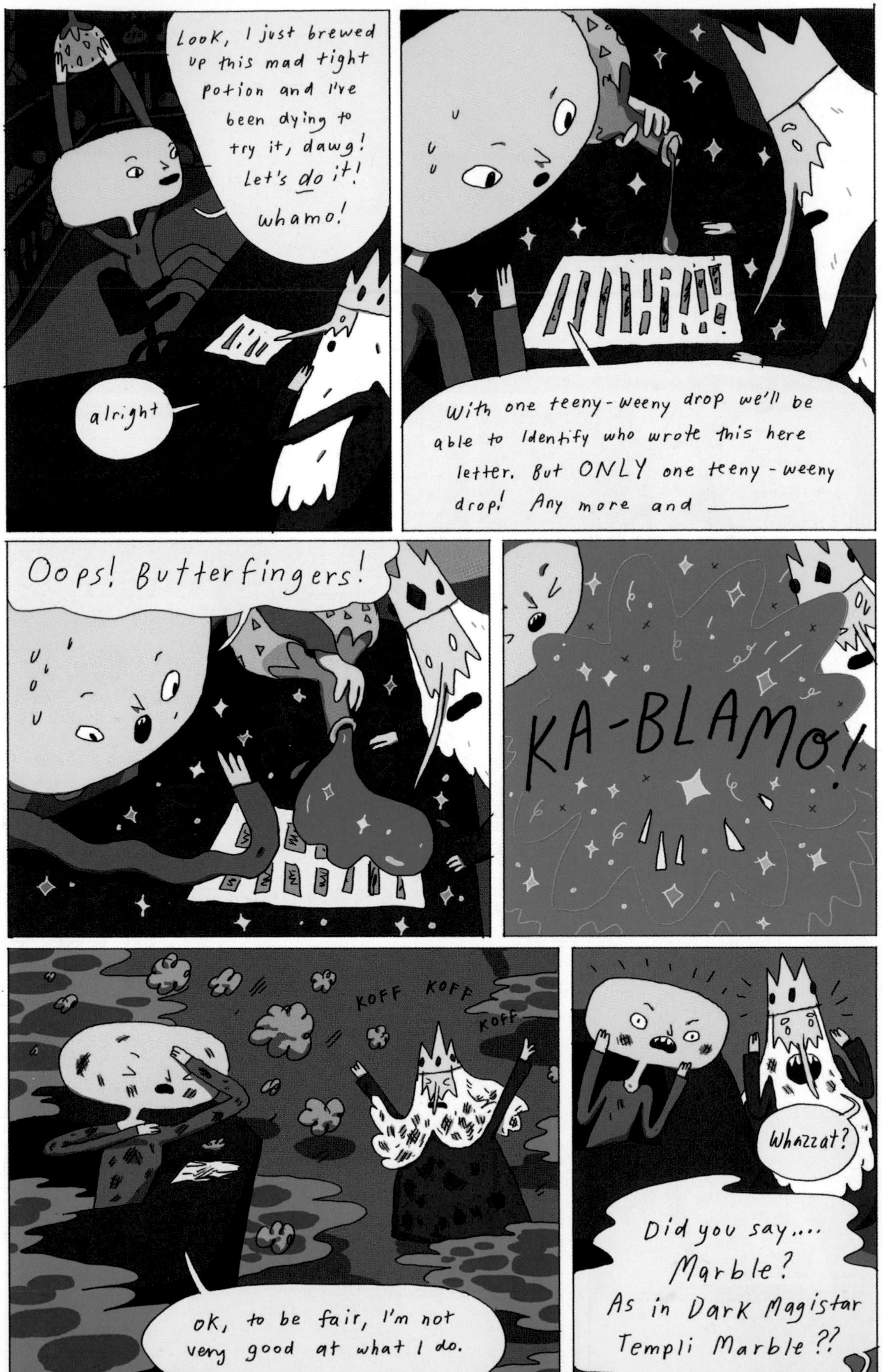

Look, I just brewed up this mad tight potion and I've been dying to try it, dawg! Let's do it! whamo!
alright
With one teeny-weeny drop we'll be able to Identify who wrote this here letter. But ONLY one teeny-weeny drop! Any more and ——
Oops! Butterfingers!
KA-BLAMO!
KOFF KOFF KOFF
ok, to be fair, I'm not very good at what I do.
Whazzat?
Did you say.... Marble? As in Dark Magistar Templi Marble??

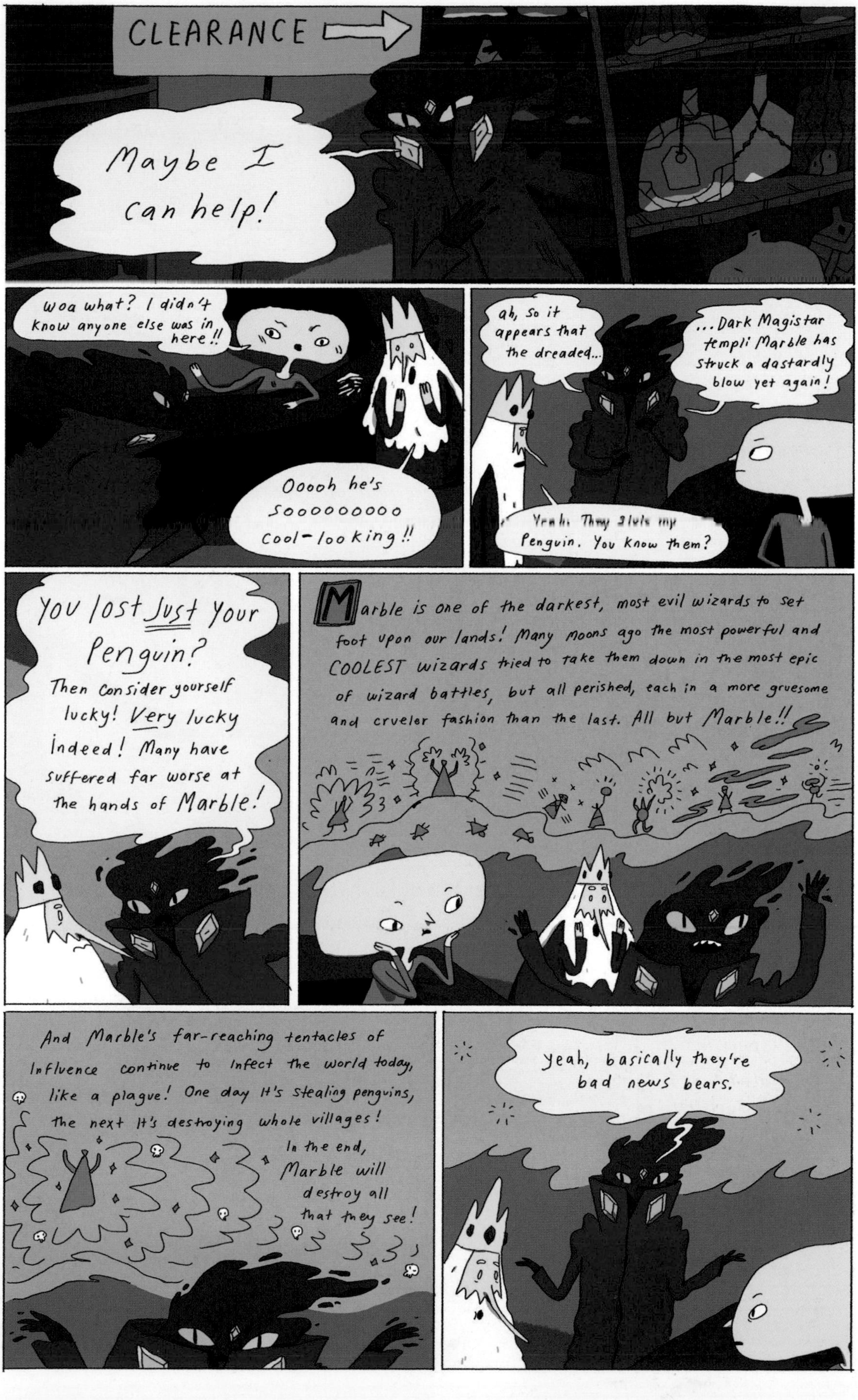
CLEARANCE
Maybe I can help!
woa what? I didn't know anyone else was in here!!
Ooooh he's sooooooooo cool-looking!!
ah, so it appears that the dreaded...
...Dark Magistar templi Marble has struck a dastardly blow yet again!
Yeah. They stole my Penguin. You know them?
You lost Just your Penguin? Then consider yourself lucky! Very lucky indeed! Many have suffered far worse at the hands of Marble!
Marble is one of the darkest, most evil wizards to set foot upon our lands! Many moons ago the most powerful and COOLEST wizards tried to take them down in the most epic of wizard battles, but all perished, each in a more gruesome and crueler fashion than the last. All but Marble!!
And Marble's far-reaching tentacles of Influence continue to Infect the world today, like a plague! One day It's stealing penguins, the next It's destroying whole villages!
In the end, Marble will destroy all that they see!
yeah, basically they're bad news bears.

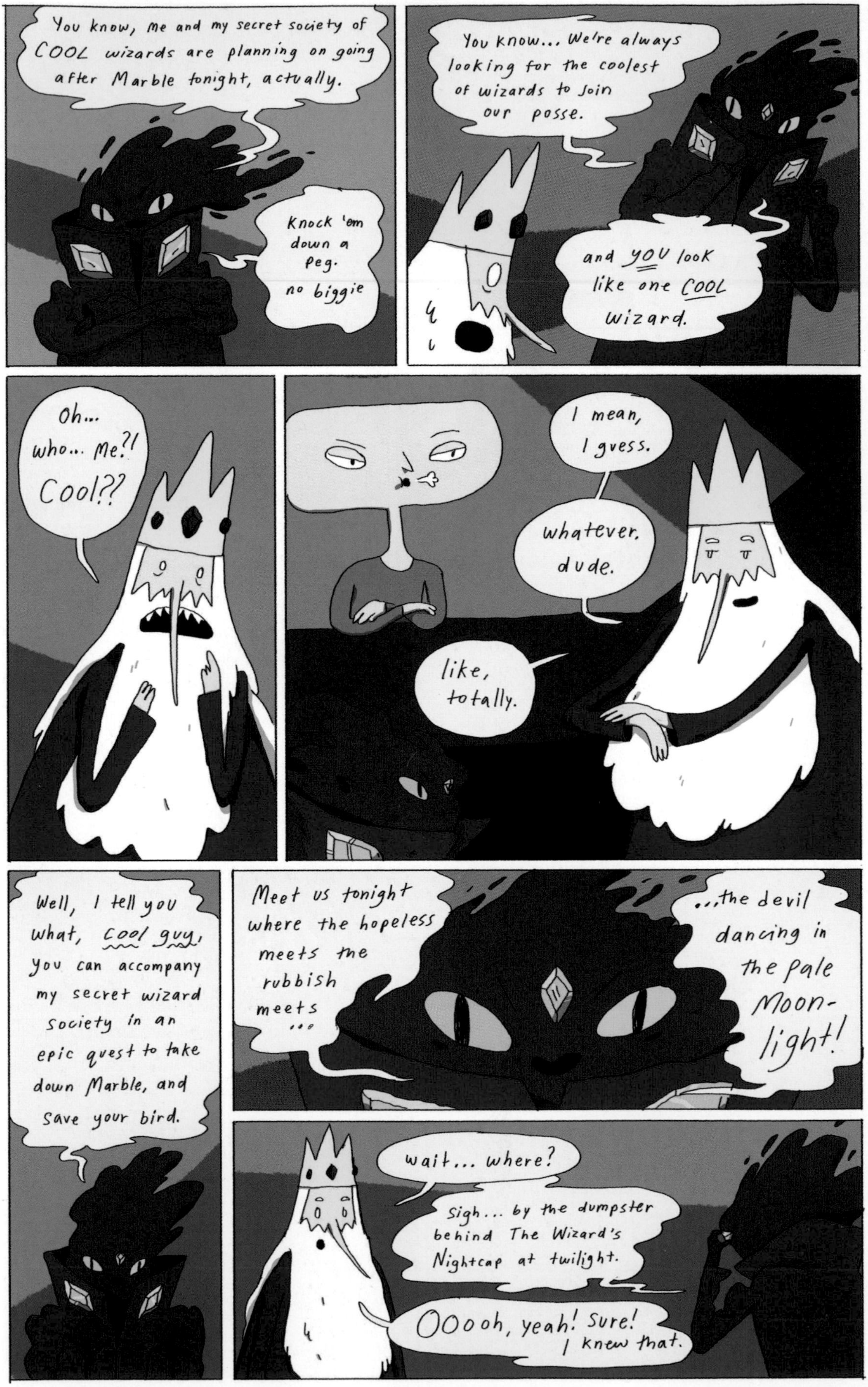
You know, me and my secret society of COOL wizards are planning on going after Marble tonight, actually.
Knock 'em down a peg. no biggie
You know... We're always looking for the coolest of wizards to join our posse.
and YOU look like one COOL wizard.
Oh... who... me?! Cool??
I mean, I guess.
whatever, dude.
like, totally.
Well, I tell you what, cool guy, you can accompany my secret wizard society in an epic quest to take down Marble, and save your bird.
Meet us tonight where the hopeless meets the rubbish meets ...
...the devil dancing in the pale Moon-light!
wait... where?
Sigh... by the dumpster behind The Wizard's Nightcap at twilight.
OOooh, yeah! Sure! I knew that.

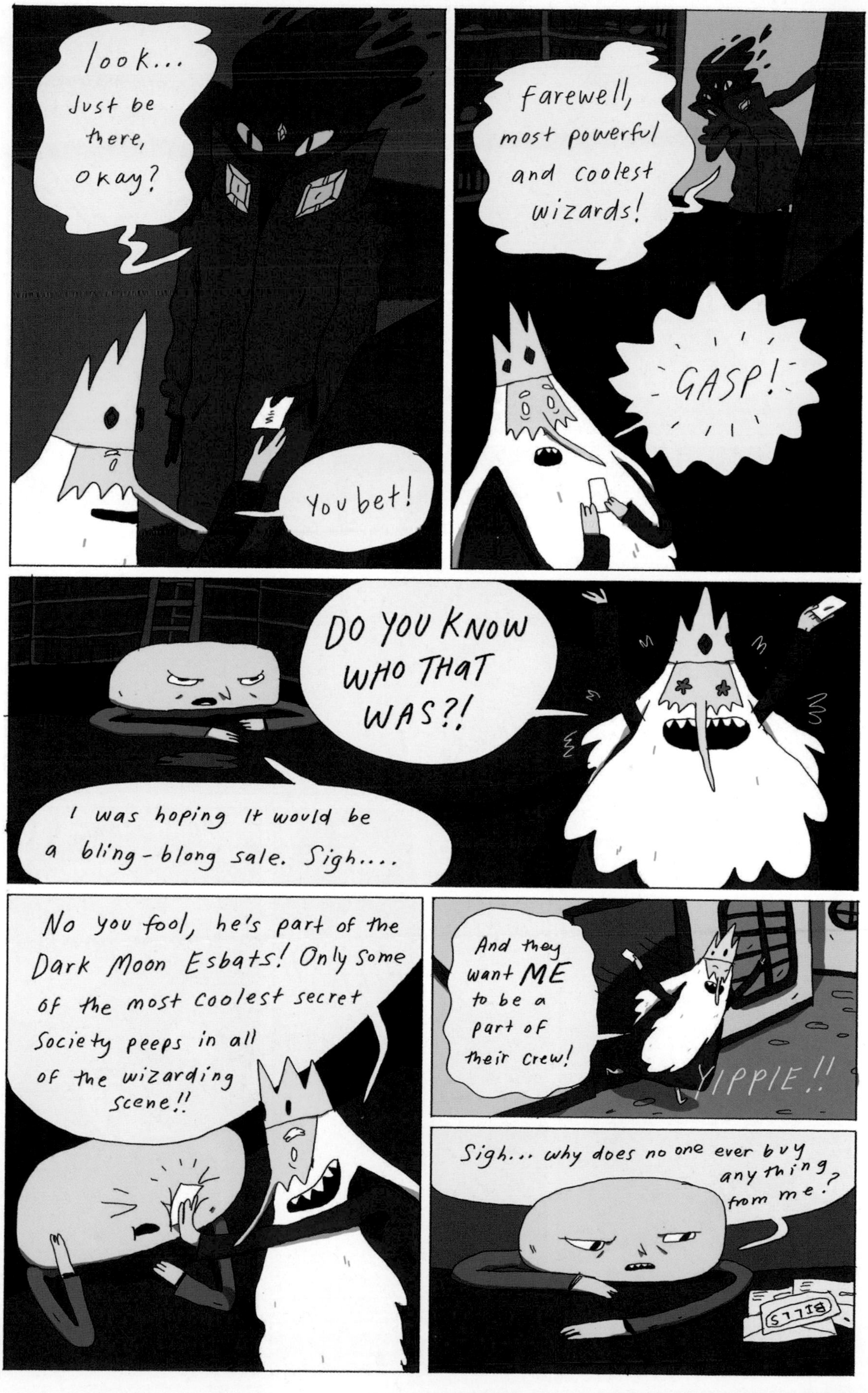
look... Just be there, okay?
You bet!
Farewell, most powerful and coolest wizards!
GASP!
DO YOU KNOW WHO THAT WAS?!
I was hoping It would be a bling-blong sale. Sigh....
No you fool, he's part of the Dark Moon Esbats! Only some of the most coolest secret Society peeps in all of the wizarding scene!!
And they want ME to be a part of their crew!
YIPPIE!!
Sigh... why does no one ever buy anything from me?
BILLS

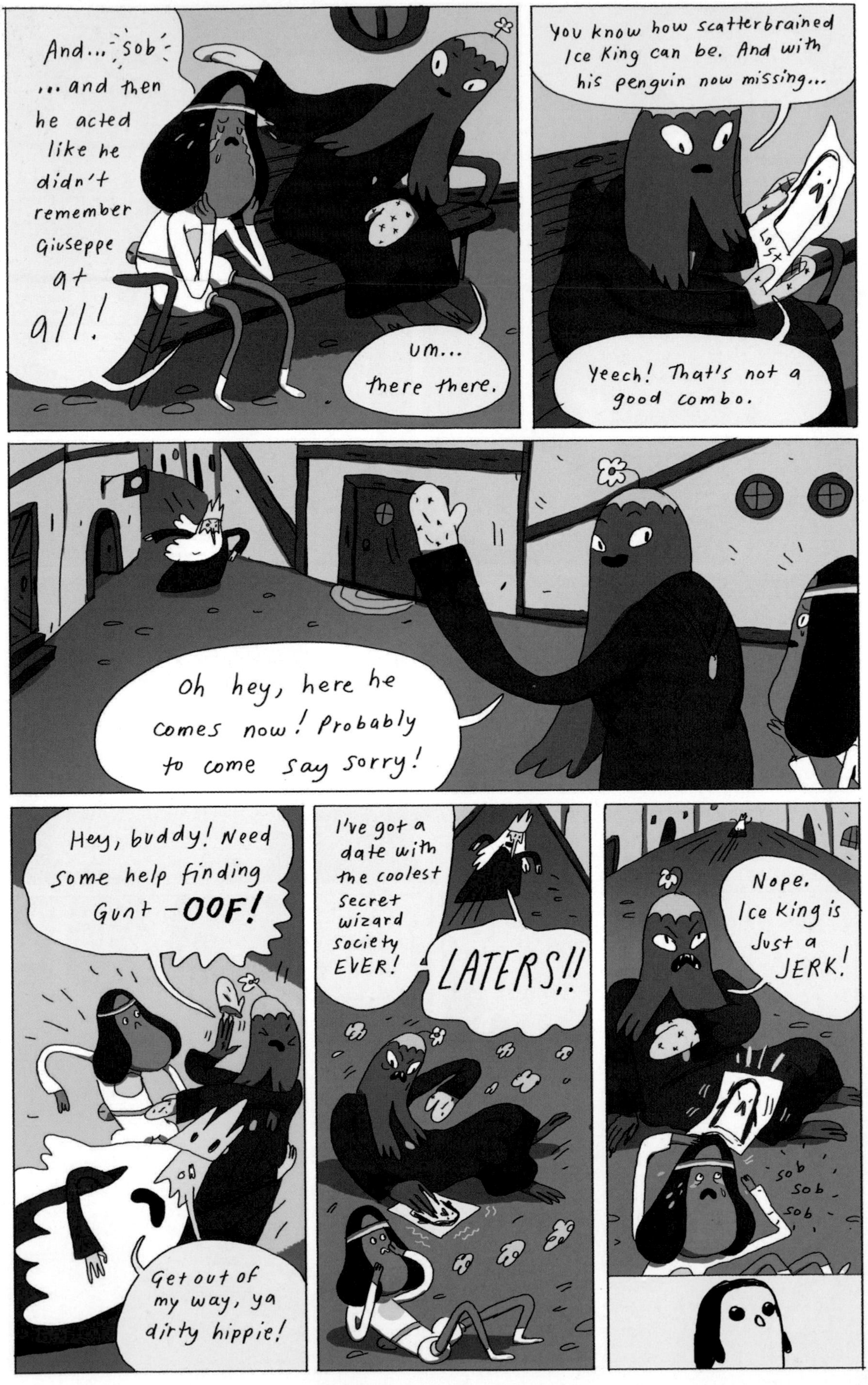
And... sob ...and then he acted like he didn't remember Giuseppe at all!
Um... there there.
You know how scatterbrained Ice King can be. And with his penguin now missing...
LOST
Yeech! That's not a good combo.
Oh hey, here he comes now! Probably to come say sorry!
Hey, buddy! Need some help finding Gunt -OOF!
Get out of my way, ya dirty hippie!
I've got a date with the coolest secret wizard society EVER!
LATERS!!
Nope, Ice King is just a JERK!
sob sob sob

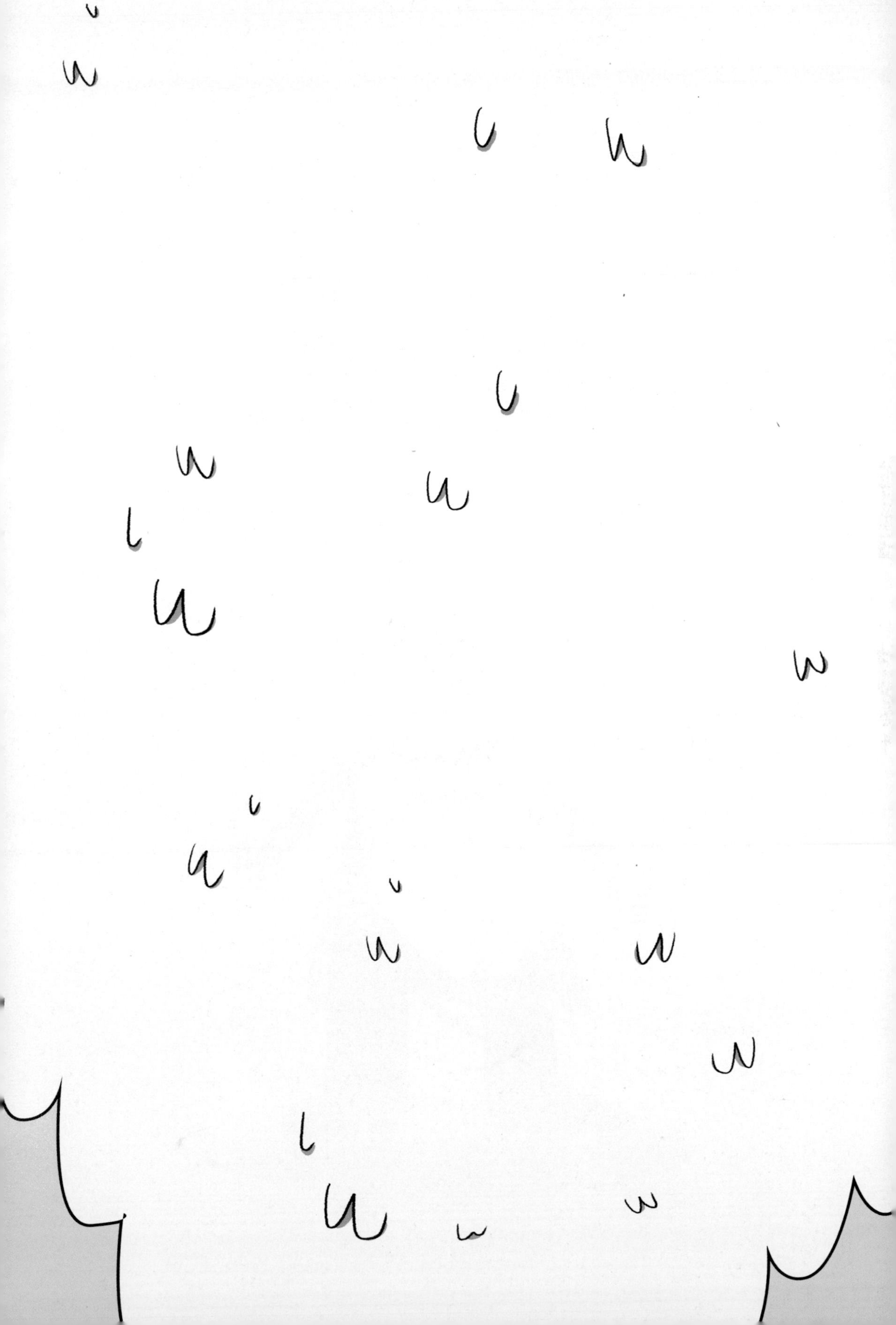

CHAPTER
TWO

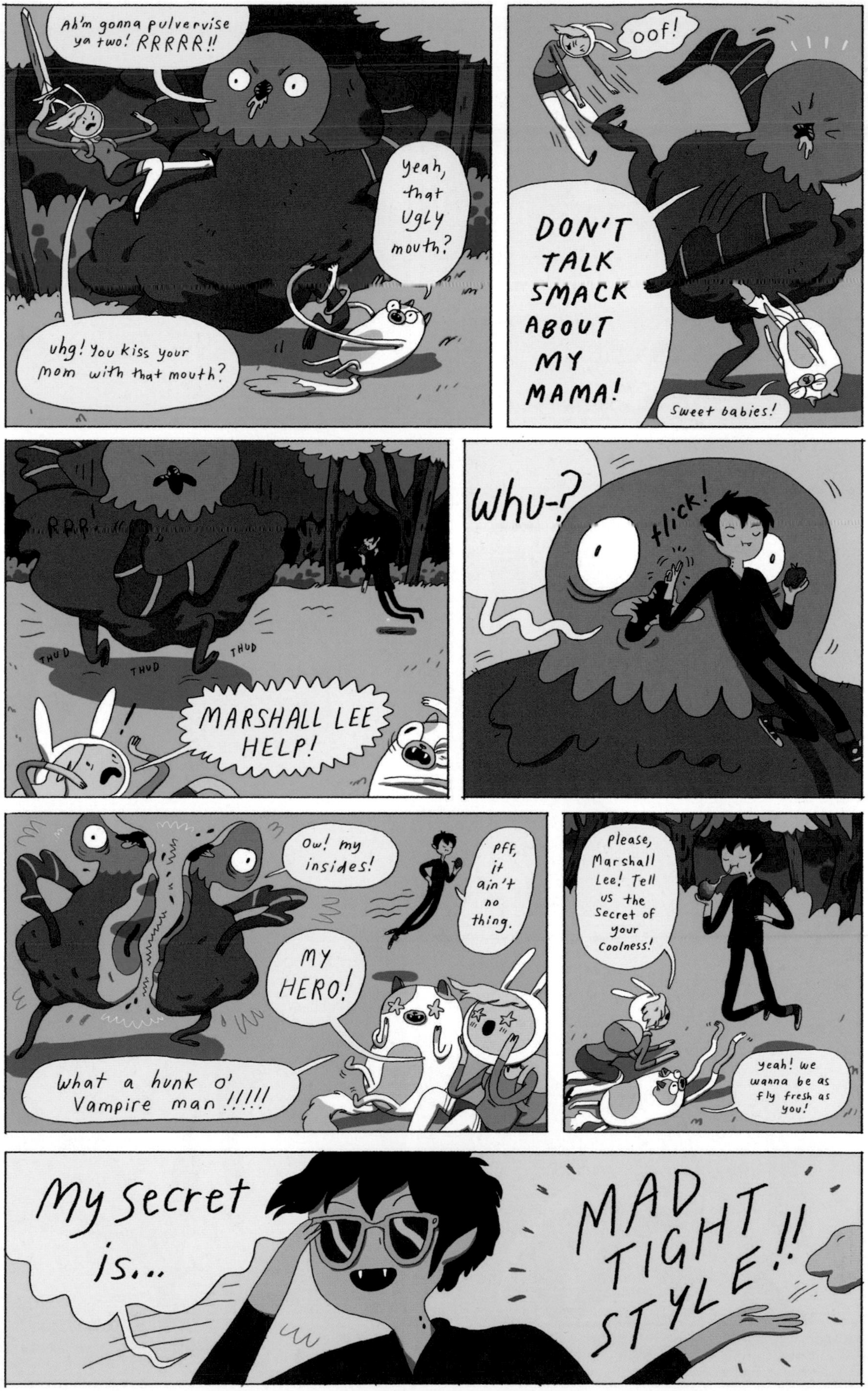
Ah'm gonna pulvervise ya two! RRRRR!!
yeah, that ugly mouth?
uhg! you kiss your mom with that mouth?
oof!
DON'T TALK SMACK ABOUT MY MAMA!
Sweet babies!
RRR
THUD
THUD
THUD
MARSHALL LEE HELP!
Whu-?
flick!
Ow! my insides!
PFF, it ain't no thing.
MY HERO!
What a hunk o' Vampire man!!!!!
Please, Marshall Lee! Tell us the secret of your coolness!
yeah! we wanna be as fly fresh as you!
My Secret is...
MAD TIGHT STYLE!!

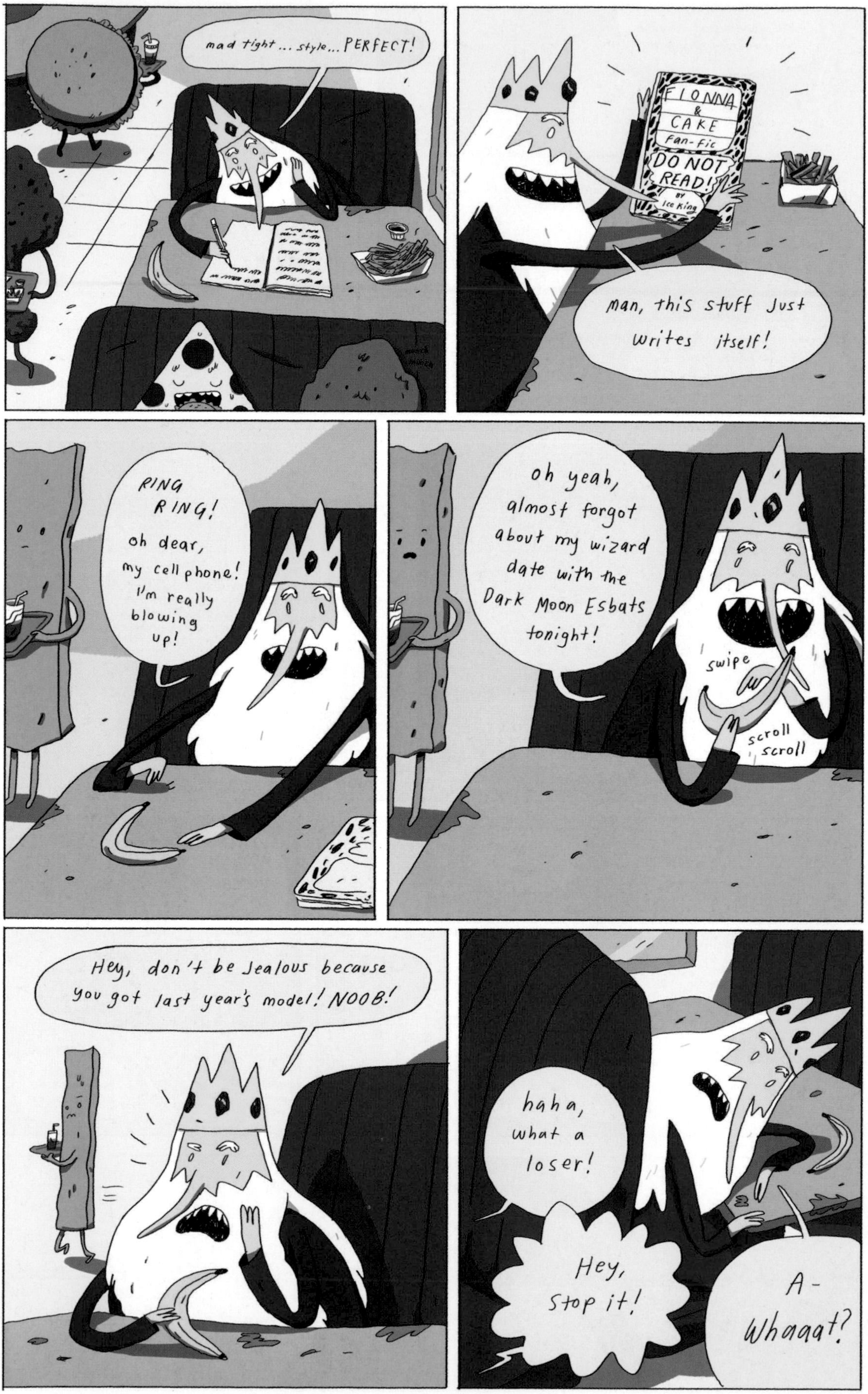
mad tight... style... PERFECT!
FIONNA & CAKE Fan-Fic DO NOT READ! BY Ice King
man, this stuff just writes itself!
RING RING! oh dear, my cell phone! I'm really blowing up!
oh yeah, almost forgot about my wizard date with the Dark Moon Esbats tonight!
swipe
scroll scroll
Hey, don't be jealous because you got last year's model! NOOB!
haha, what a loser!
Hey, Stop it!
A-Whaaat?

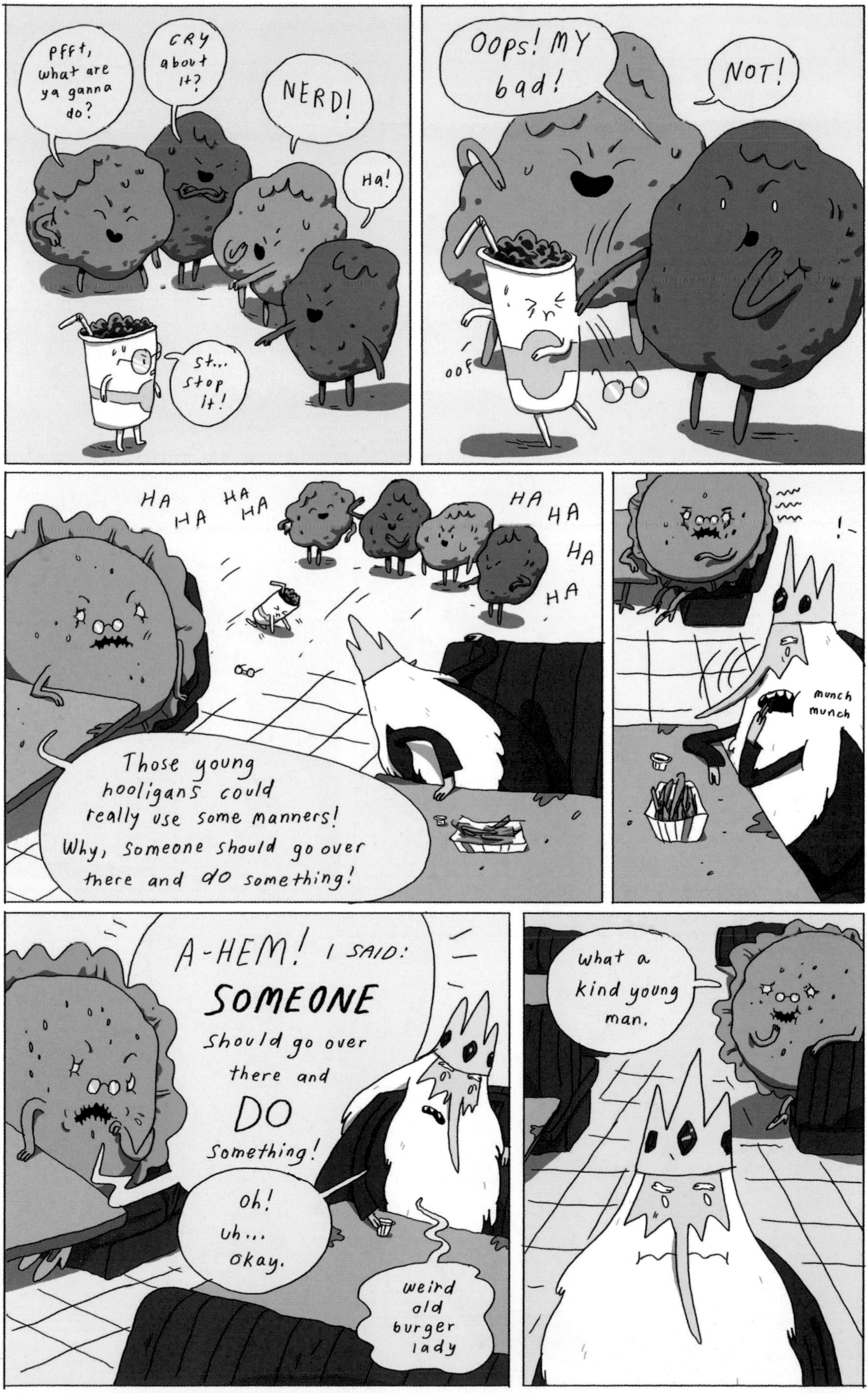
Pfft, what are ya ganna do?
CRY about it?
NERD!
Ha!
St... stop it!
Oops! MY bad!
NOT!
oof
HA HA HA HA
HA HA HA HA
Those young hooligans could really use some manners! Why, someone should go over there and DO something!
!
munch munch
A-HEM! I SAID: SOMEONE should go over there and DO something!
Oh! uh... okay.
weird old burger lady
What a kind young man.

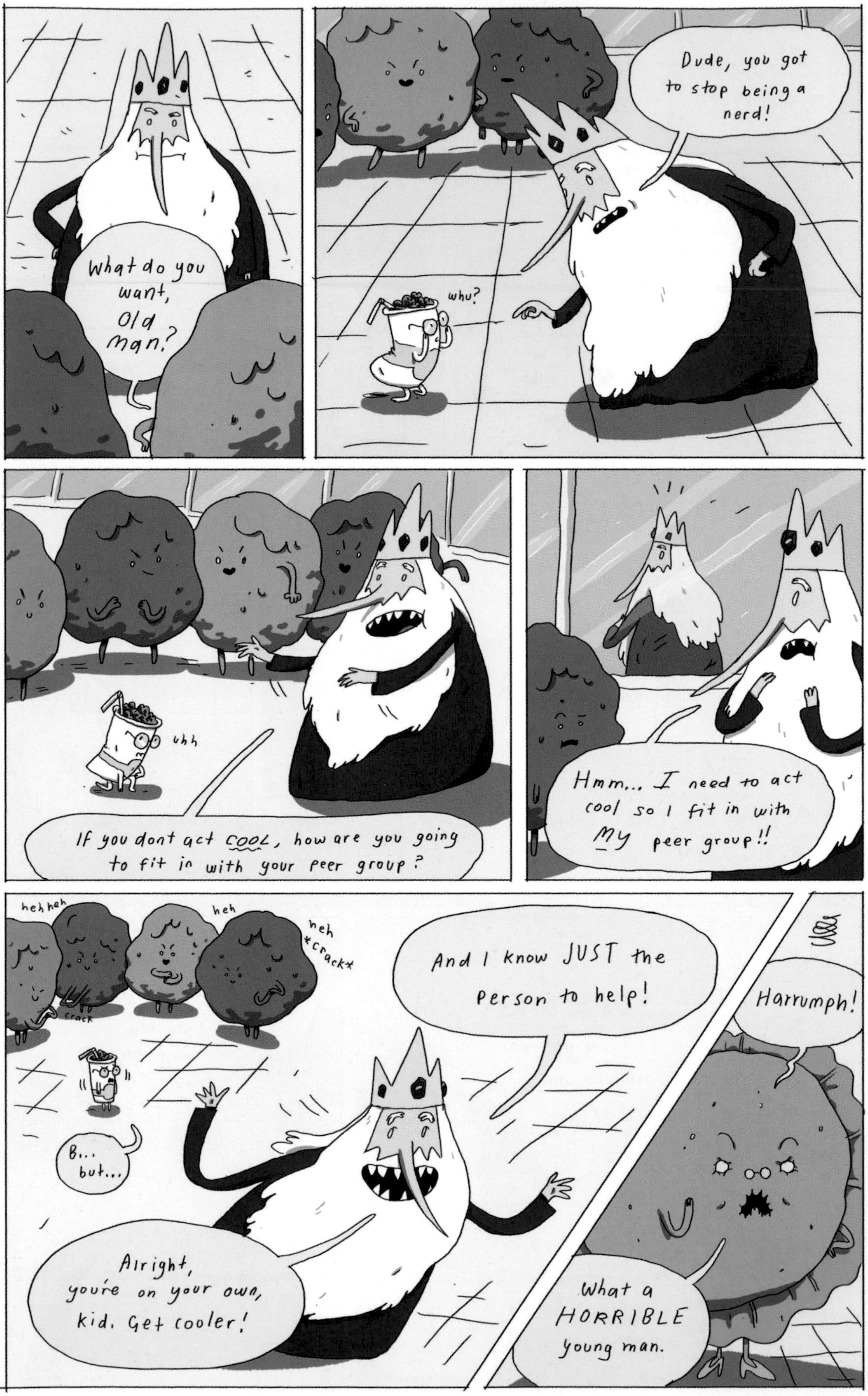
What do you want, Old man?
Dude, you got to stop being a nerd!
whu?
If you dont act COOL, how are you going to fit in with your peer group?
uhh
Hmm... I need to act cool so I fit in with MY peer group!!
heh heh
heh
heh
crack
crack
And I know JUST the person to help!
B... but...
Alright, you're on your own, kid. Get cooler!
Harrumph!
What a HORRIBLE young man.

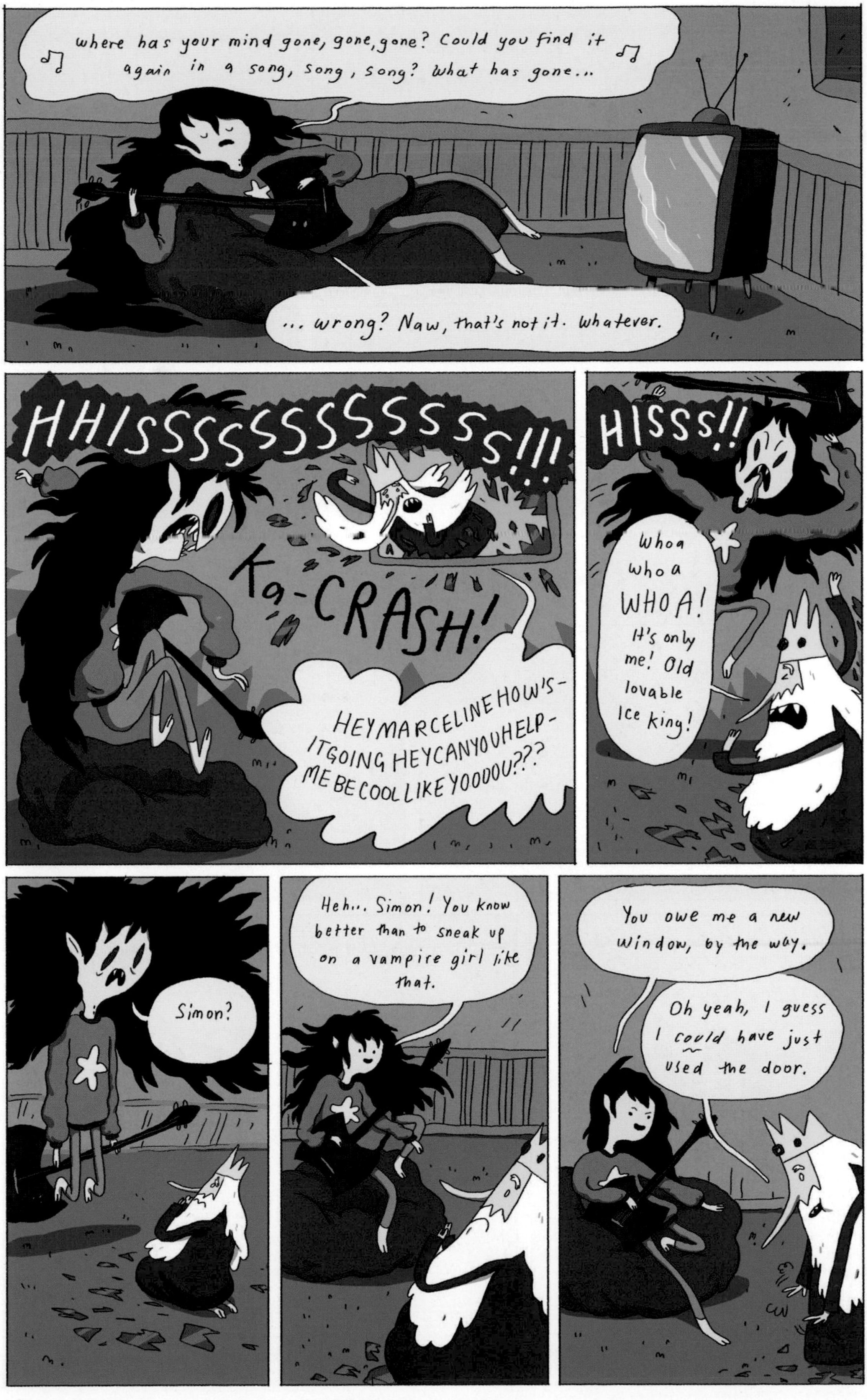
where has your mind gone, gone, gone? Could you find it again in a song, song, song? What has gone...
... wrong? Naw, that's not it. whatever.
HHISSSSSSSSSSSS!!!
Ka-CRASH!
HEYMARCELINEHOW'S-ITGOING HEYCANYOUHELP-MEBECOOLLIKEYOOOOU???
HISSS!!
Whoa whoa WHOA! It's only me! Old lovable Ice King!
Simon?
Heh... Simon! You know better than to sneak up on a vampire girl like that.
You owe me a new window, by the way.
Oh yeah, I guess I could have just used the door.

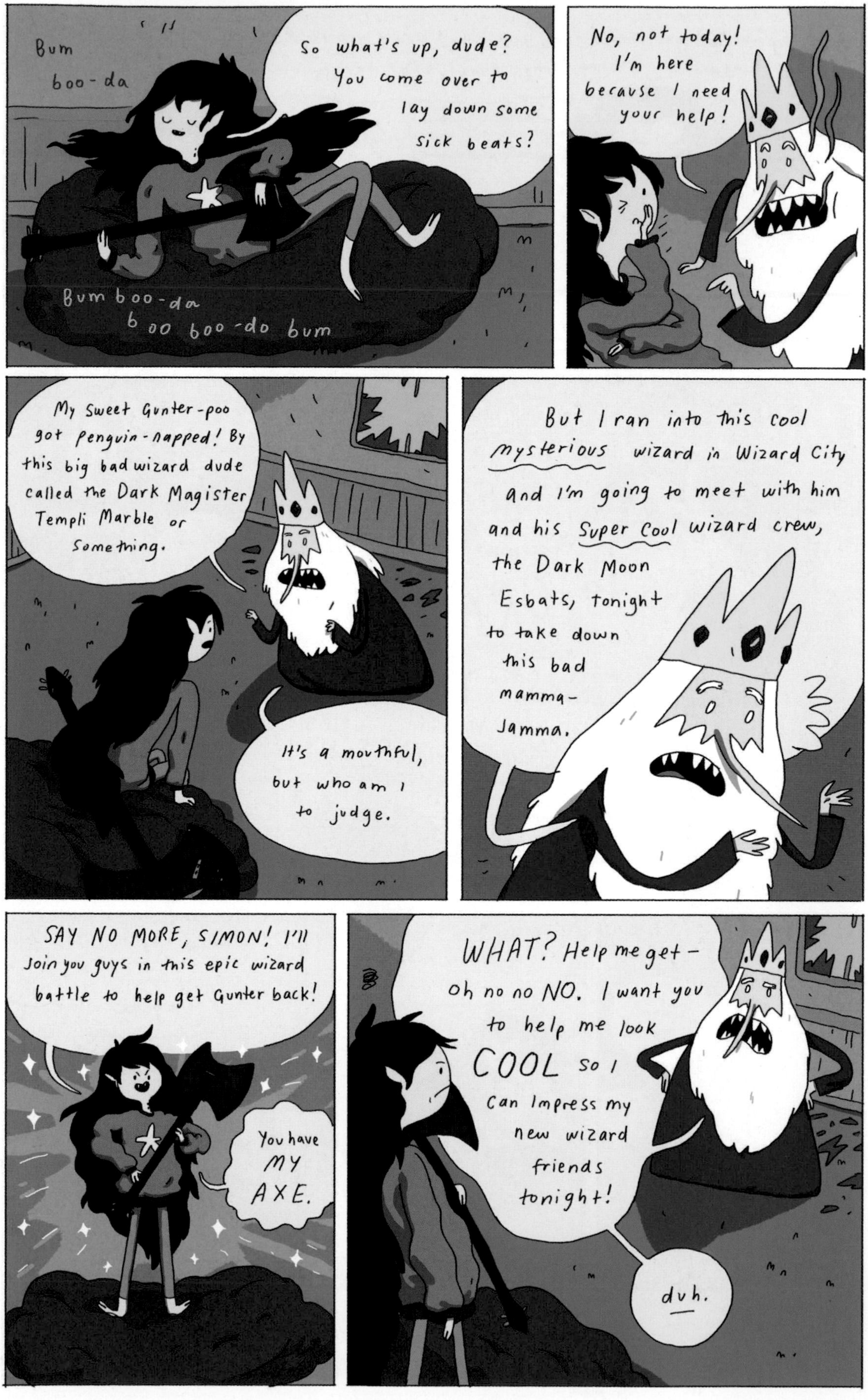
Bum boo-da
So what's up, dude? You come over to lay down some sick beats?
Bum boo-da boo boo-do bum
No, not today! I'm here because I need your help!
My sweet Gunter-poo got penguin-napped! By this big bad wizard dude called the Dark Magister Templi Marble or something.
It's a mouthful, but who am I to judge.
But I ran into this cool mysterious wizard in Wizard City and I'm going to meet with him and his Super Cool wizard crew, the Dark Moon Esbats, tonight to take down this bad mamma-jamma.
SAY NO MORE, SIMON! I'll join you guys in this epic wizard battle to help get Gunter back!
You have MY AXE.
WHAT? Help me get- oh no no NO. I want you to help me look COOL so I can impress my new wizard friends tonight!
duh.

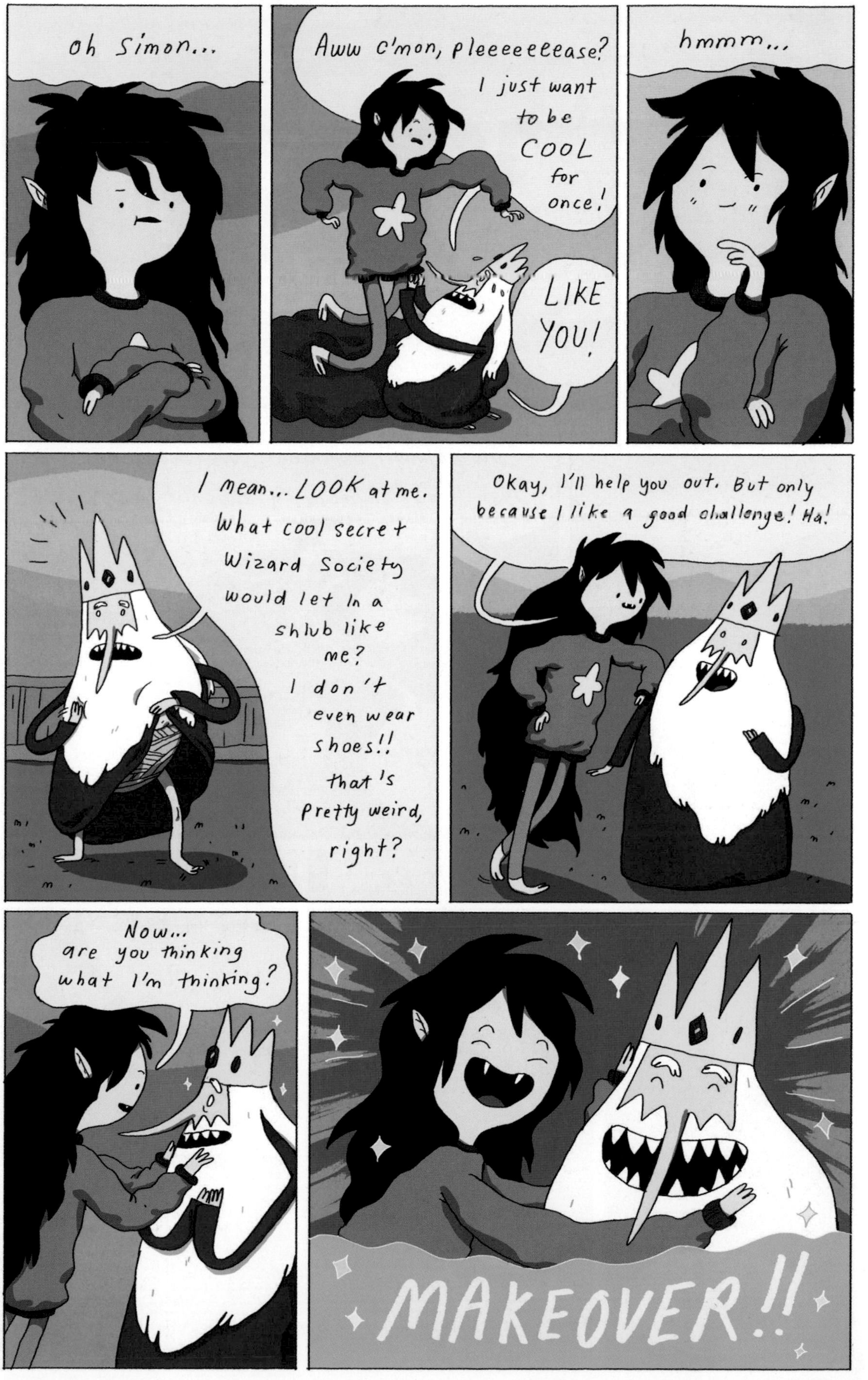

oh Simon...
Aww c'mon, pleeeeeeease? I just want to be COOL for once!
LIKE YOU!
hmmm...
I mean... LOOK at me. What cool secret Wizard Society would let in a shlub like me? I don't even wear shoes!! that's pretty weird, right?
Okay, I'll help you out. But only because I like a good challenge! Ha!
Now... are you thinking what I'm thinking?
MAKEOVER!!

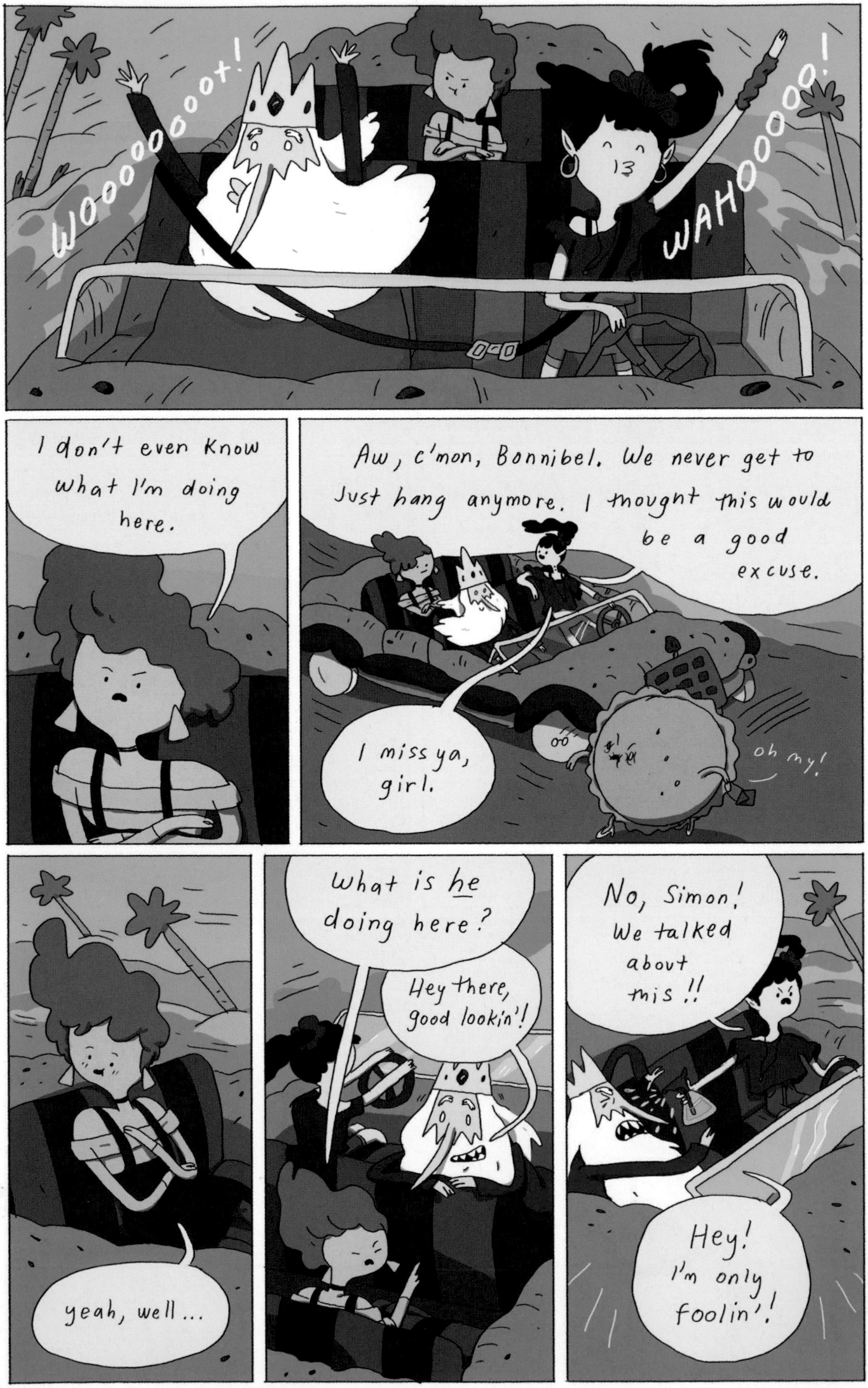
WOOOOOOOOOT!
WAHOOOOOO!
I don't even know what I'm doing here.
Aw, c'mon, Bonnibel. We never get to just hang anymore. I thought this would be a good excuse.
I miss ya, girl.
oh my!
yeah, well...
What is he doing here?
Hey there, good lookin'!
No, Simon! We talked about this!!
Hey! I'm only foolin'!

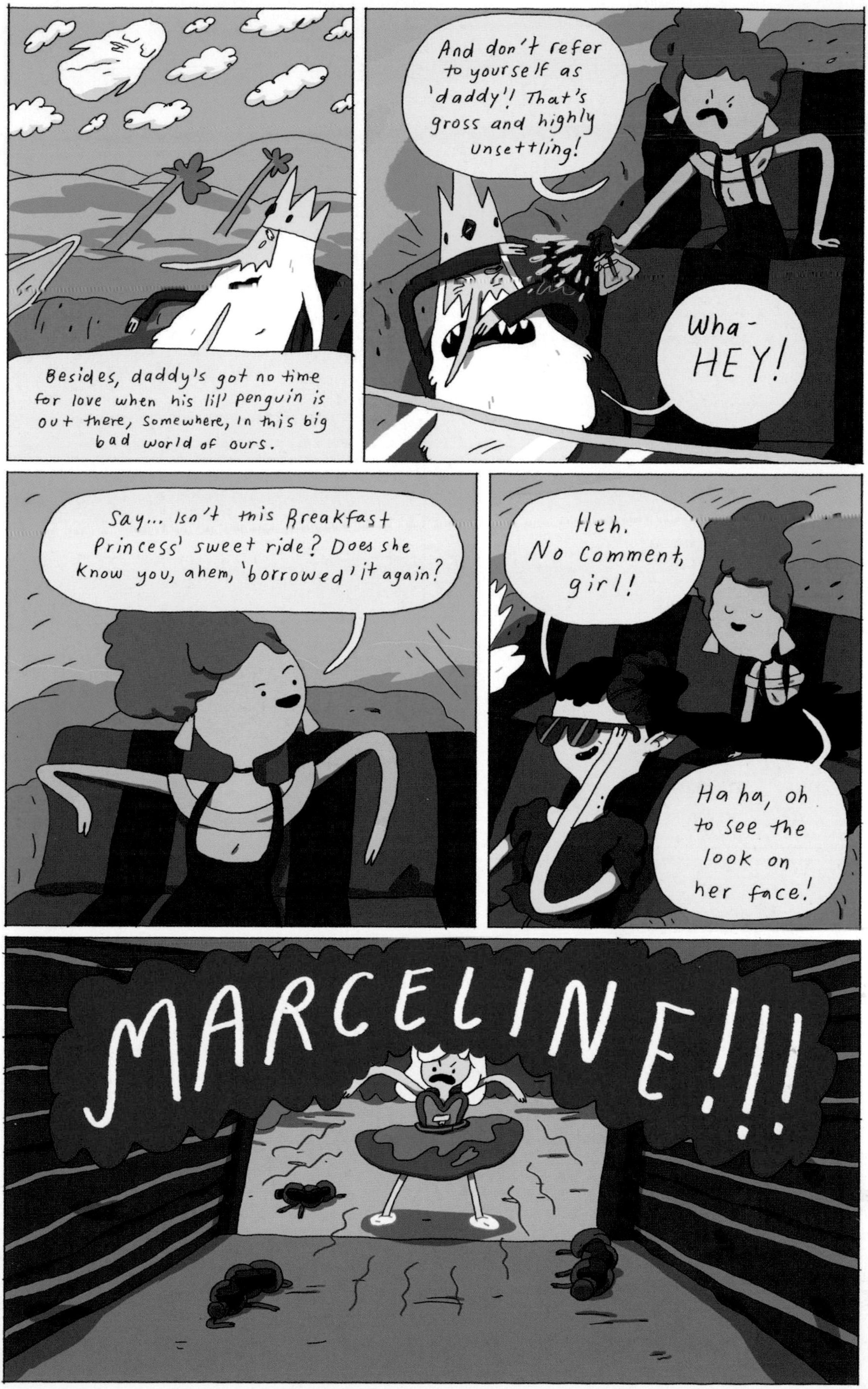
Besides, daddy's got no time for love when his lil' penguin is out there, somewhere, in this big bad world of ours.
And don't refer to yourself as 'daddy'! That's gross and highly unsettling!
Wha- HEY!
Say... Isn't this Breakfast Princess' sweet ride? Does she know you, ahem, 'borrowed' it again?
Heh. No comment, girl!
Ha ha, oh to see the look on her face!
MARCELINE!!!

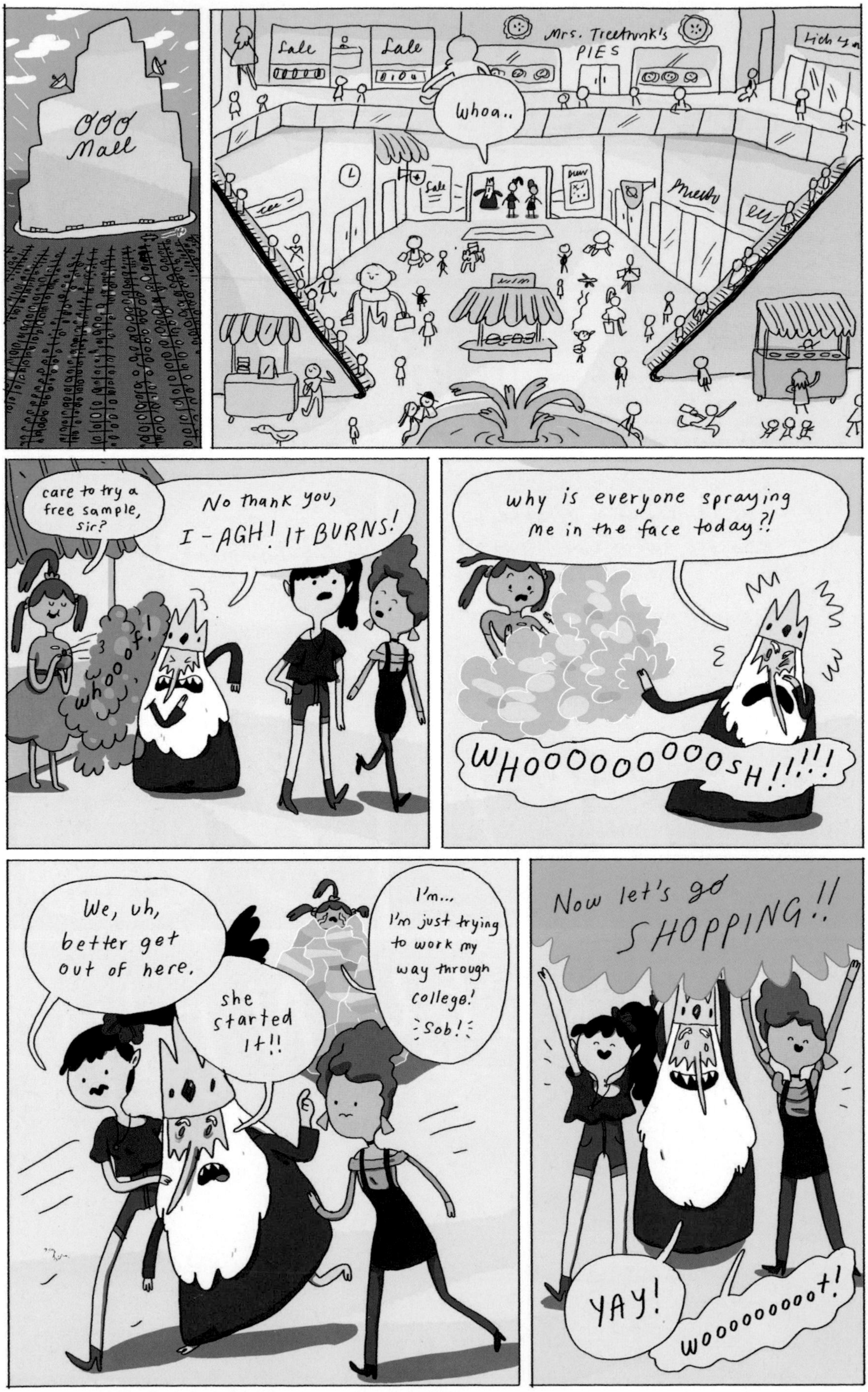
OOO Mall
Mrs. Treetrunk's PIES
Sale
Sale
Whoa..
care to try a free sample, sir?
No thank you, I-AGH! It BURNS!
whooof!
why is everyone spraying me in the face today?!
WHOOOOOOOOOOSH!!!!!
We, uh, better get out of here.
she started it!!
I'm... I'm just trying to work my way through college! Sob!
Now let's go SHOPPING!!
YAY!
wooooooooot!

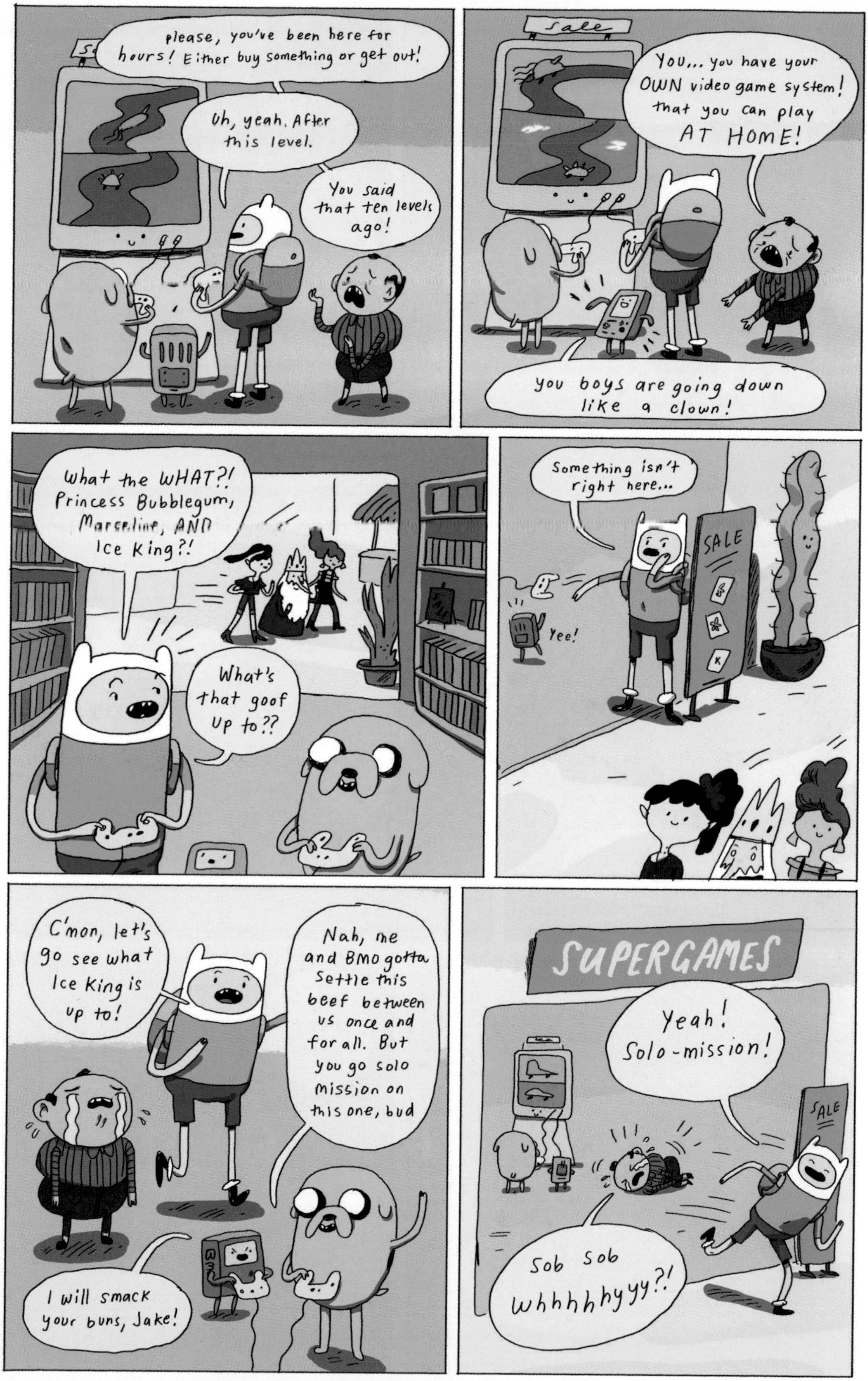

Sale
please, you've been here for hours! Either buy something or get out!
Uh, yeah. After this level.
You said that ten levels ago!
You... you have your OWN video game system! that you can play AT HOME!
you boys are going down like a clown!
What the WHAT?! Princess Bubblegum, Marceline, AND Ice King?!
What's that goof up to??
Something isn't right here...
SALE
Yee!
C'mon, let's go see what Ice King is up to!
Nah, me and BMO gotta settle this beef between us once and for all. But you go solo mission on this one, bud
I will smack your buns, Jake!
SUPERGAMES
Yeah! Solo-mission!
SALE
Sob sob whhhhhyyy?!

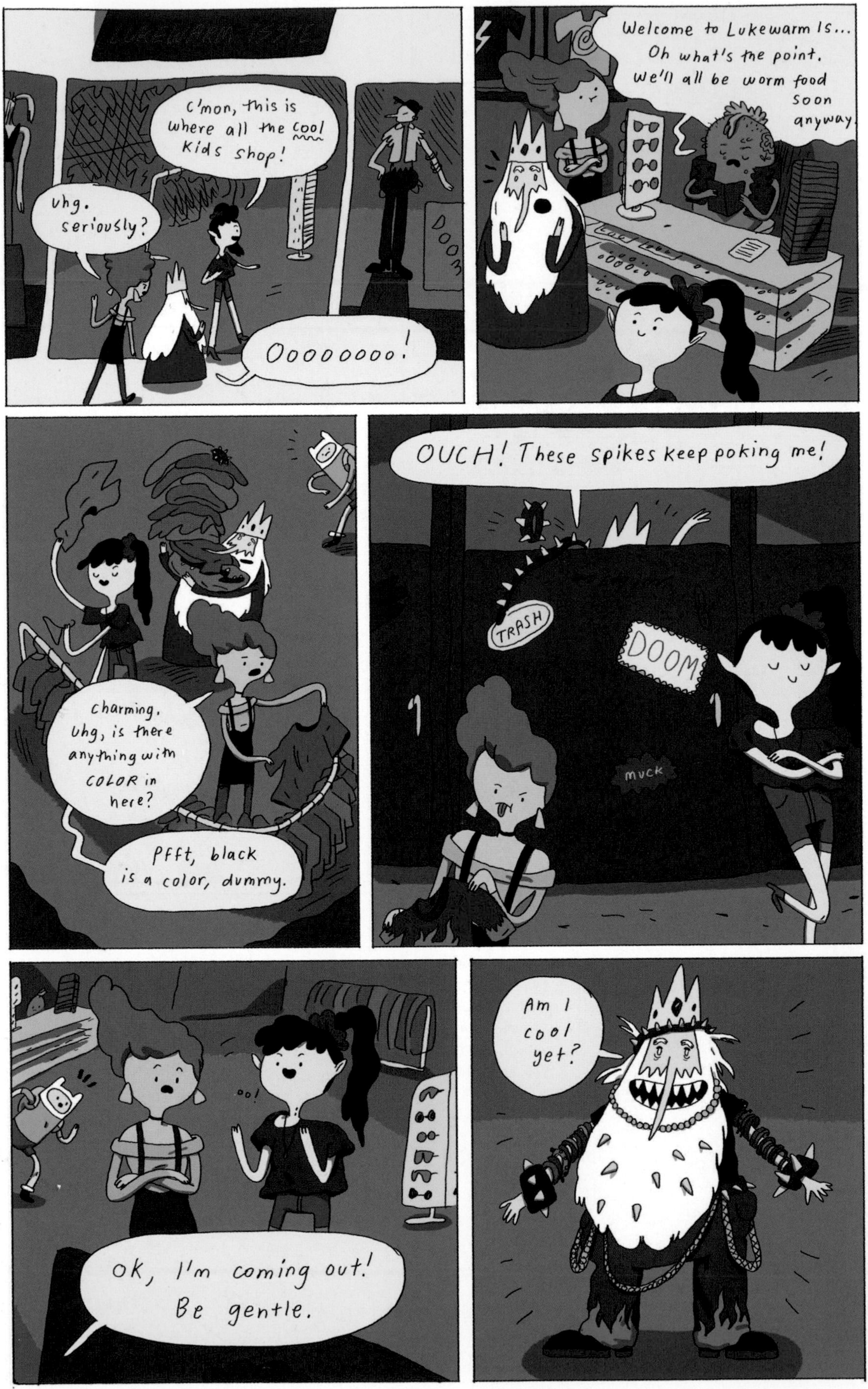
C'mon, this is where all the cool kids shop!
uhg. seriously?
DOOM
Ooooooo!
Welcome to Lukewarm Is... Oh what's the point. We'll all be worm food soon anyway.
Charming. Uhg, is there anything with COLOR in here?
Pfft, black is a color, dummy.
OUCH! These spikes keep poking me!
TRASH
DOOM
MUCK
Ok, I'm coming out! Be gentle.
Am I cool yet?

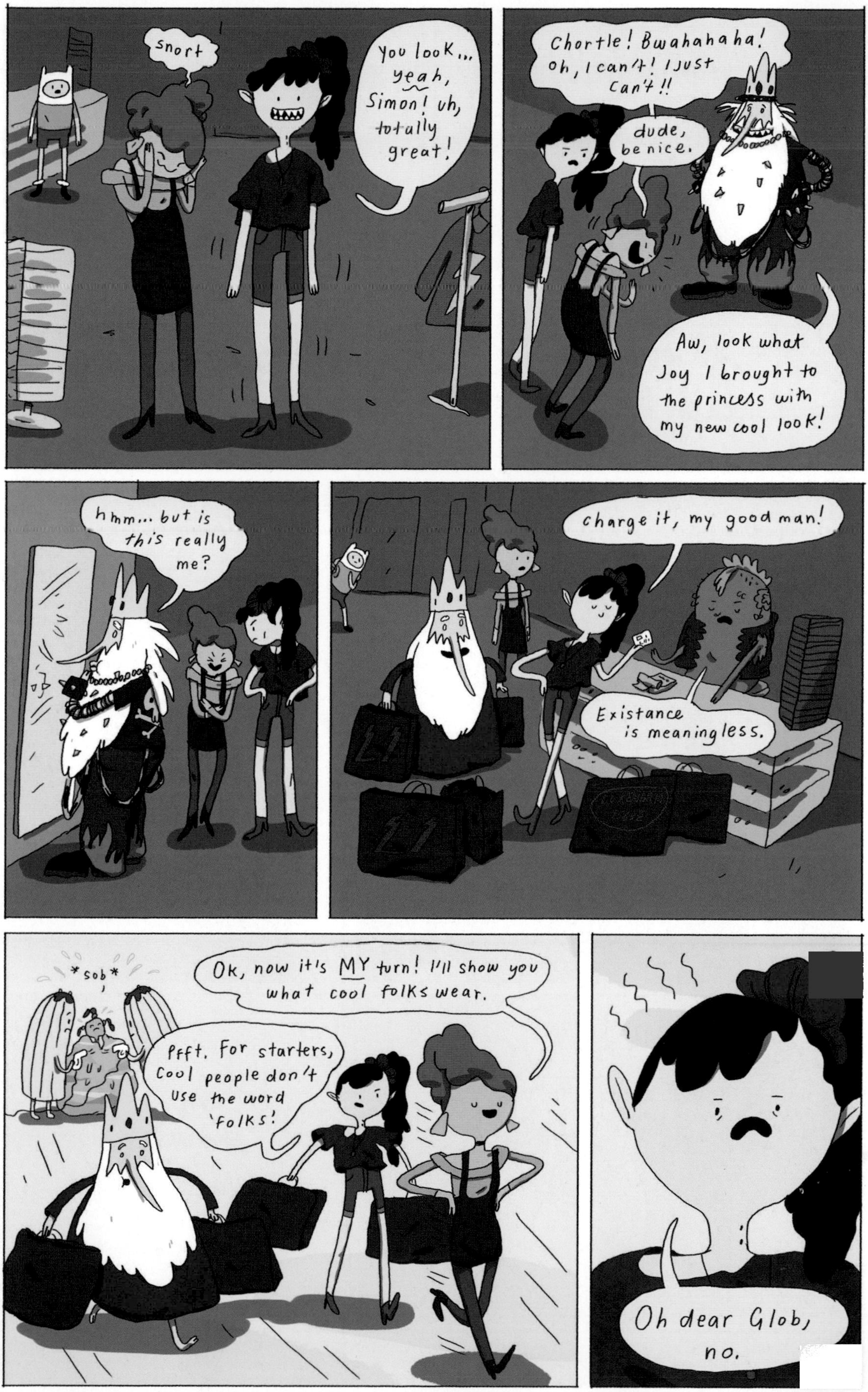
snort
You look... yeah, Simon! uh, totally great!
Chortle! Bwahahaha! Oh, I can't! I just can't!!
dude, be nice.
Aw, look what Joy I brought to the princess with my new cool look!
hmm... but is this really me?
charge it, my good man!
Existance is meaningless.
sob
Ok, now it's MY turn! I'll show you what cool folks wear.
Pfft. For starters, cool people don't use the word 'folks'!
Oh dear Glob, no.

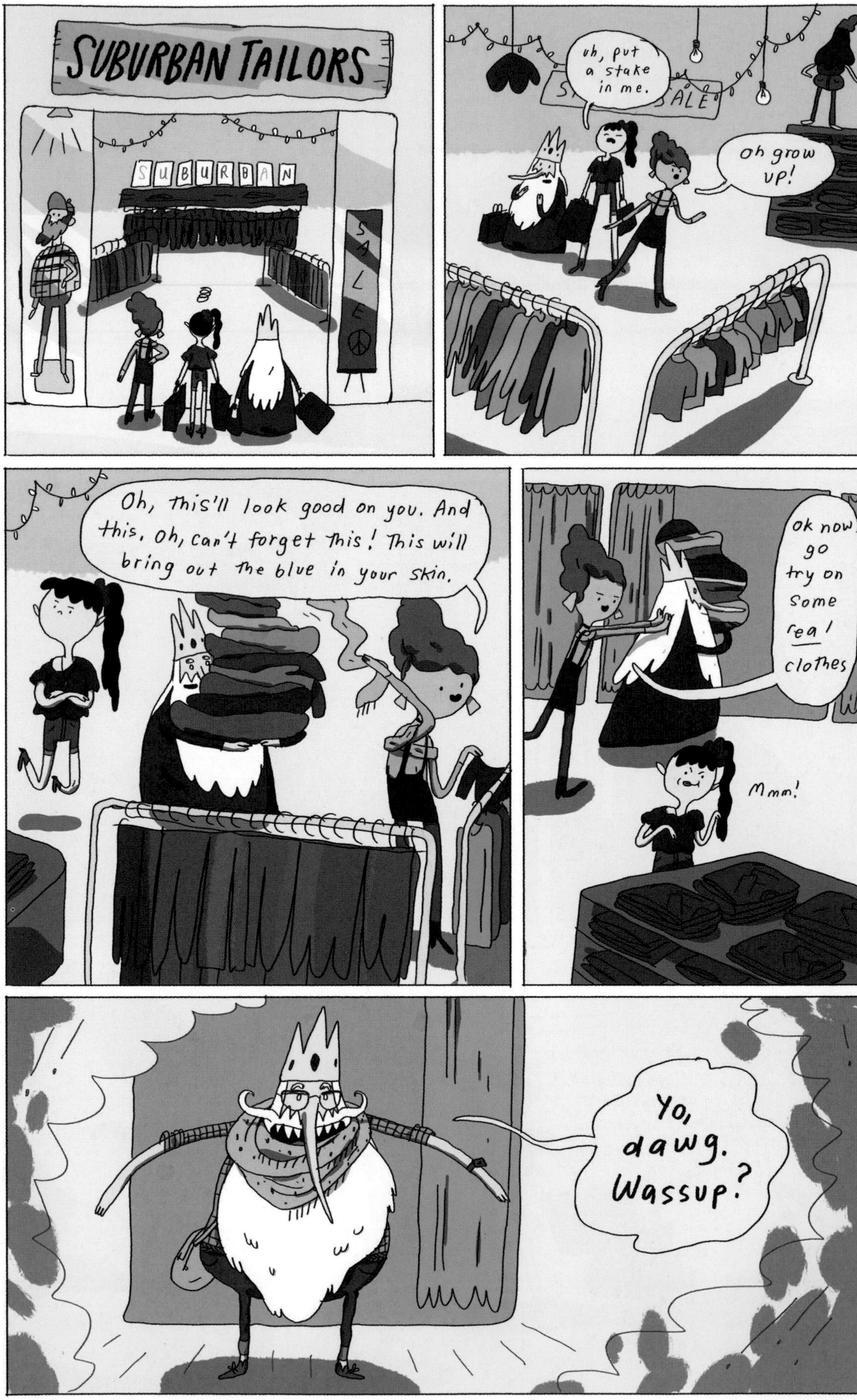
SUBURBAN TAILORS
SUBURBAN
SALE
uh, put a stake in me.
SALE
Oh grow up!
Oh, this'll look good on you. And this, Oh, can't forget this! This will bring out the blue in your skin.
ok now go try on some real clothes
Mmm!
Yo, dawg. Wassup?

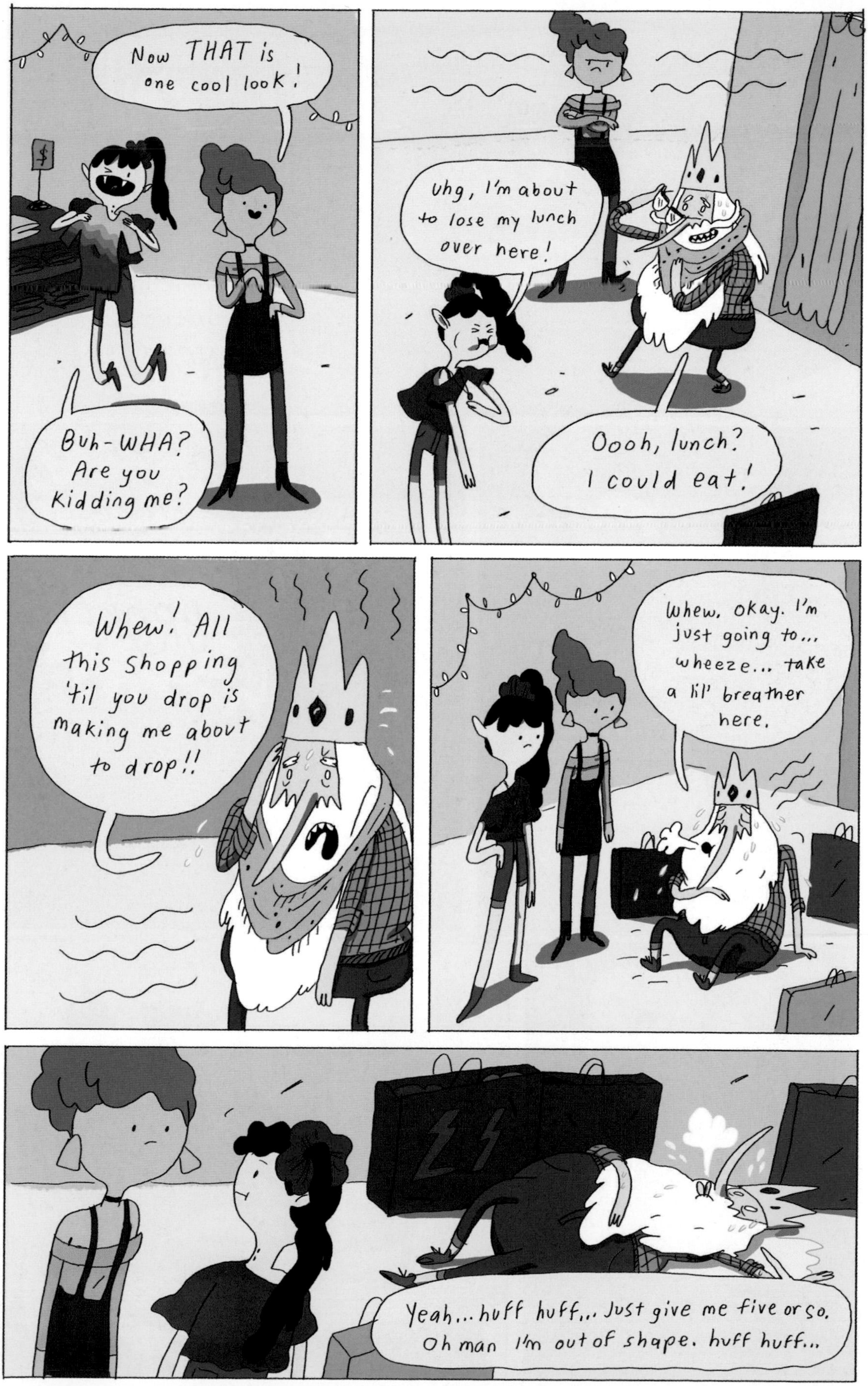
Now THAT is one cool look!
Buh-WHA? Are you kidding me?
Uhg, I'm about to lose my lunch over here!
Oooh, lunch? I could eat!
Whew! All this shopping 'til you drop is making me about to drop!!
Whew, okay. I'm just going to... wheeze... take a lil' breather here.
Yeah... huff huff... Just give me five or so. Oh man I'm out of shape. huff huff...

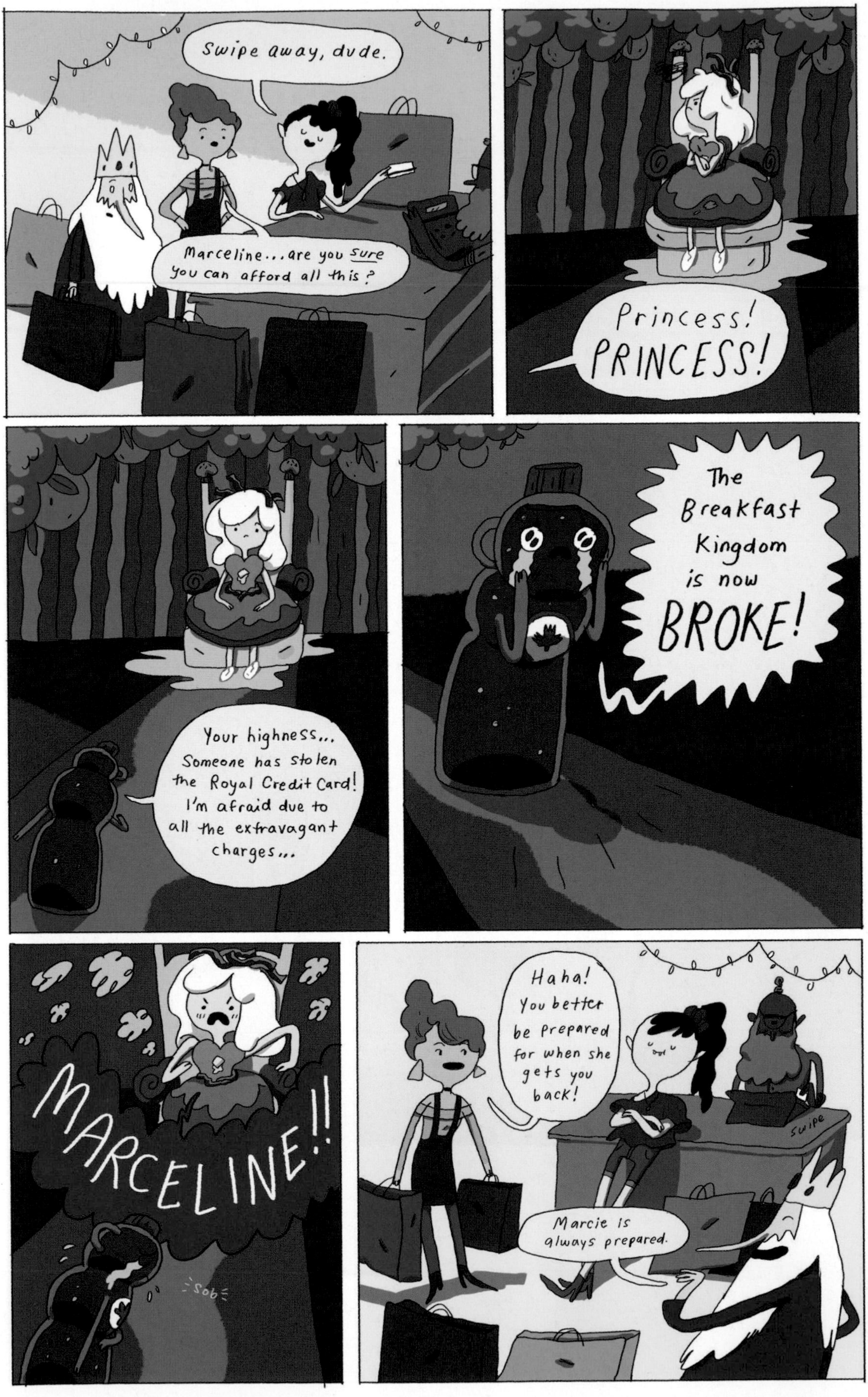
Swipe away, dude.
Marceline...are you sure you can afford all this?
Princess! PRINCESS!
Your highness... Someone has stolen the Royal Credit Card! I'm afraid due to all the extravagant charges...
The Breakfast Kingdom is now BROKE!
MARCELINE!!
sob
Haha! You better be prepared for when she gets you back!
swipe
Marcie is always prepared.

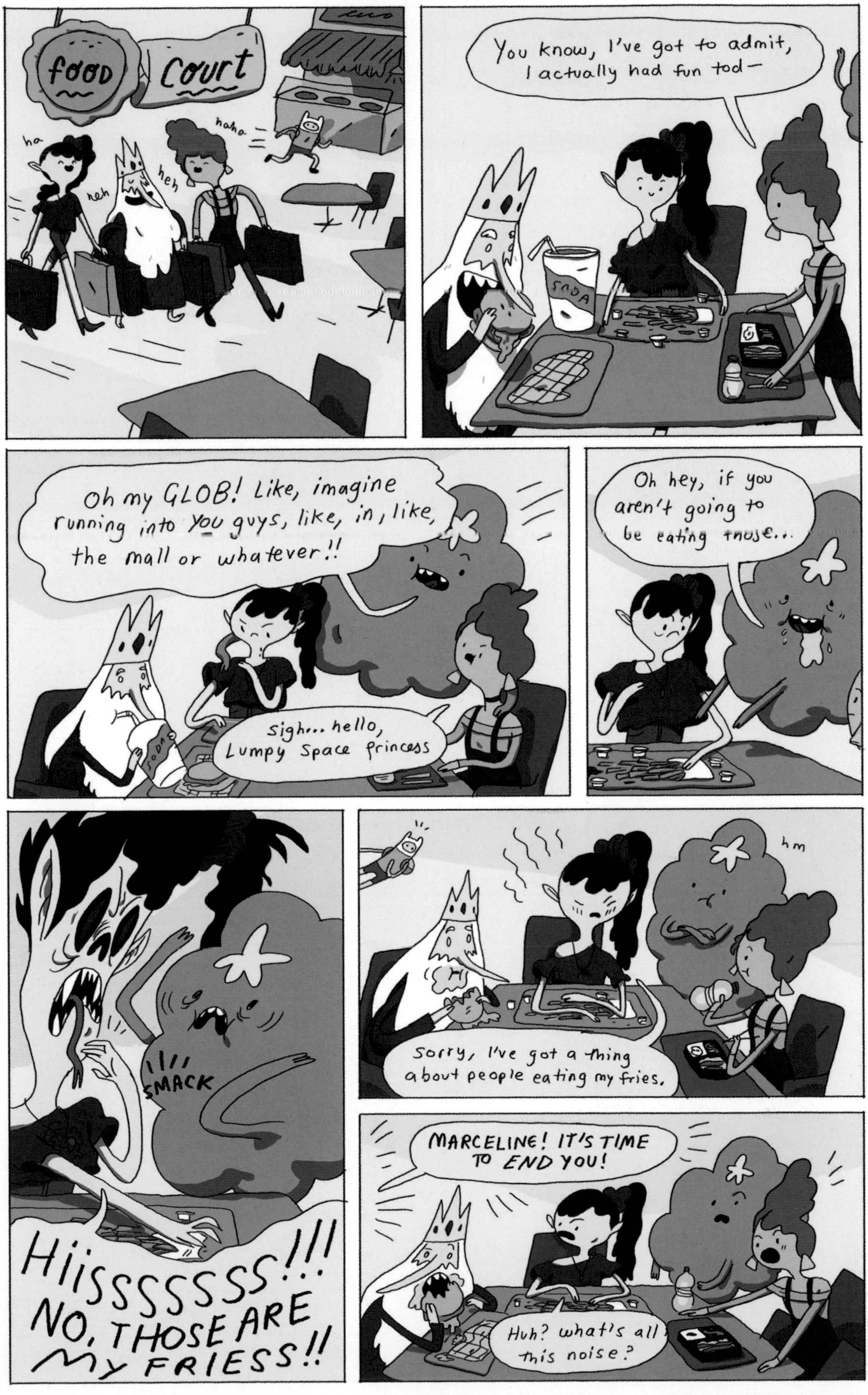

food
court
ha
heh
heh
haha
You know, I've got to admit, I actually had fun tod—
SODA
Oh my GLOB! Like, imagine running into you guys, like, in, like, the mall or whatever!!
sigh... hello, Lumpy Space Princess
Oh hey, if you aren't going to be eating those...
SMACK
Hiissssss!!! NO, THOSE ARE MY FRIESS!!
hm
Sorry, I've got a thing about people eating my fries.
MARCELINE! IT'S TIME TO END YOU!
Huh? what's all this noise?

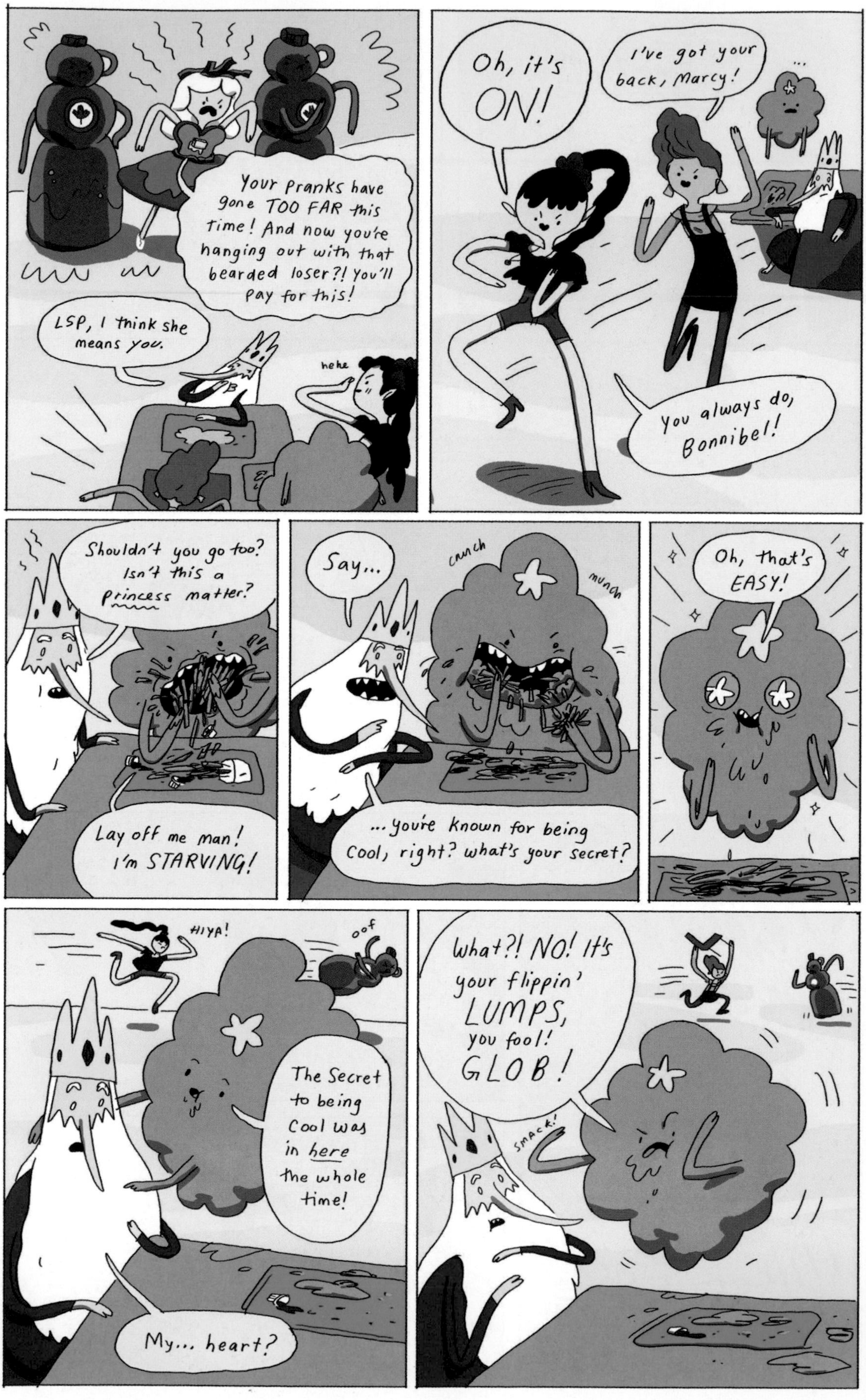

Your pranks have gone TOO FAR this time! And now you're hanging out with that bearded loser?! You'll pay for this!
LSP, I think she means you.
hehe
Oh, it's ON!
I've got your back, Marcy!
...
You always do, Bonnibel!
Shouldn't you go too? Isn't this a princess matter?
Lay off me man! I'm STARVING!
Say...
crunch
munch
...you're known for being cool, right? what's your secret?
Oh, that's EASY!
HIYA!
oof
The Secret to being Cool was in here the whole time!
My... heart?
What?! NO! It's your flippin' LUMPS, you fool! GLOB!
SMACK!

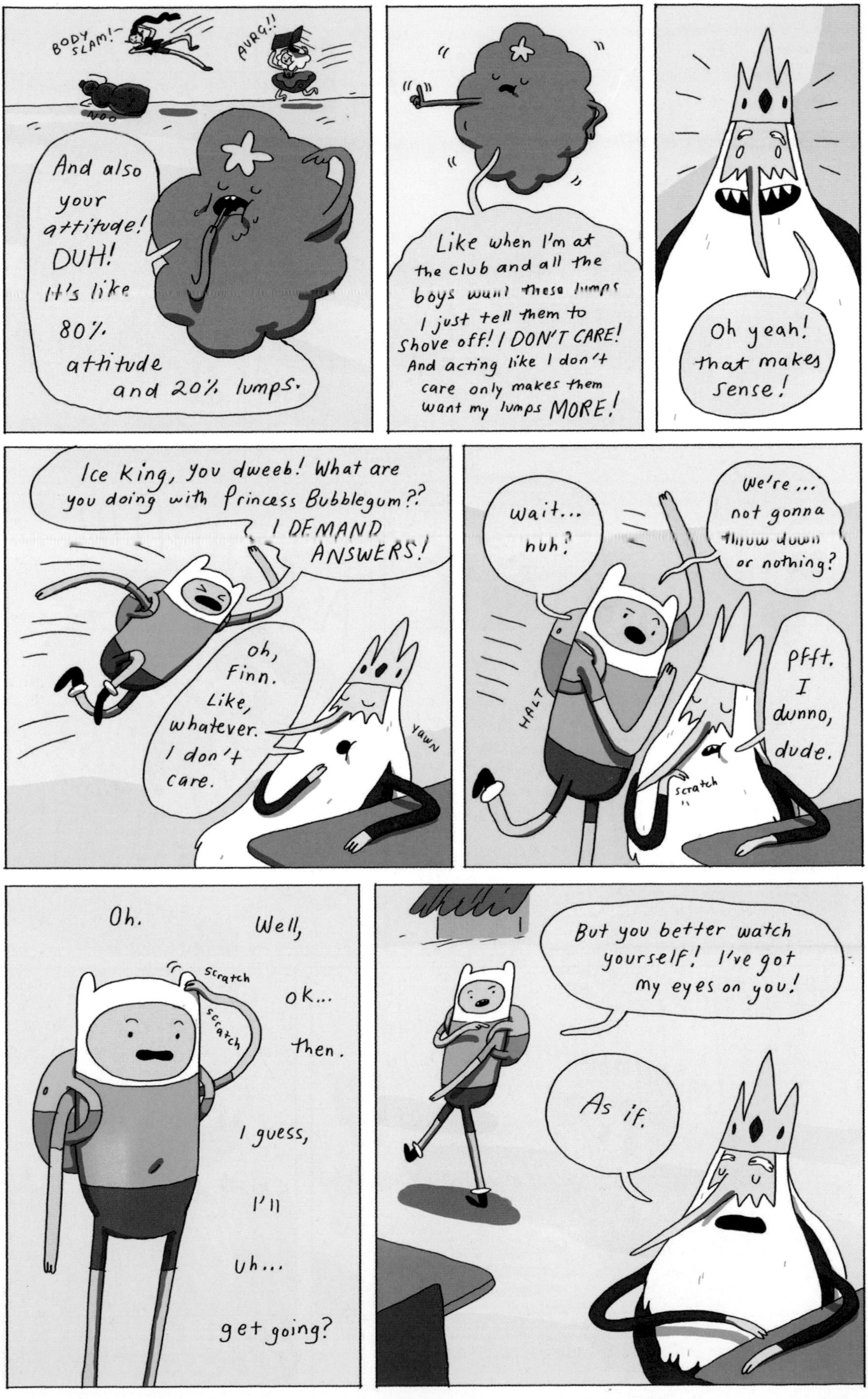
BODY SLAM!
AURG!!
NOO
And also your attitude! DUH! It's like 80% attitude and 20% lumps.
Like when I'm at the club and all the boys want these lumps I just tell them to Shove off! I DON'T CARE! And acting like I don't care only makes them want my lumps MORE!
Oh yeah! that makes sense!
Ice King, you dweeb! What are you doing with Princess Bubblegum?? I DEMAND ANSWERS!
oh, Finn. Like, whatever. I don't care.
YAWN
wait... huh?
We're... not gonna throw down or nothing?
HALT
pfft. I dunno, dude.
scratch
Oh.
Well,
scratch
scratch
ok...
then.
I guess,
I'll
uh...
get going?
But you better watch yourself! I've got my eyes on you!
As if.

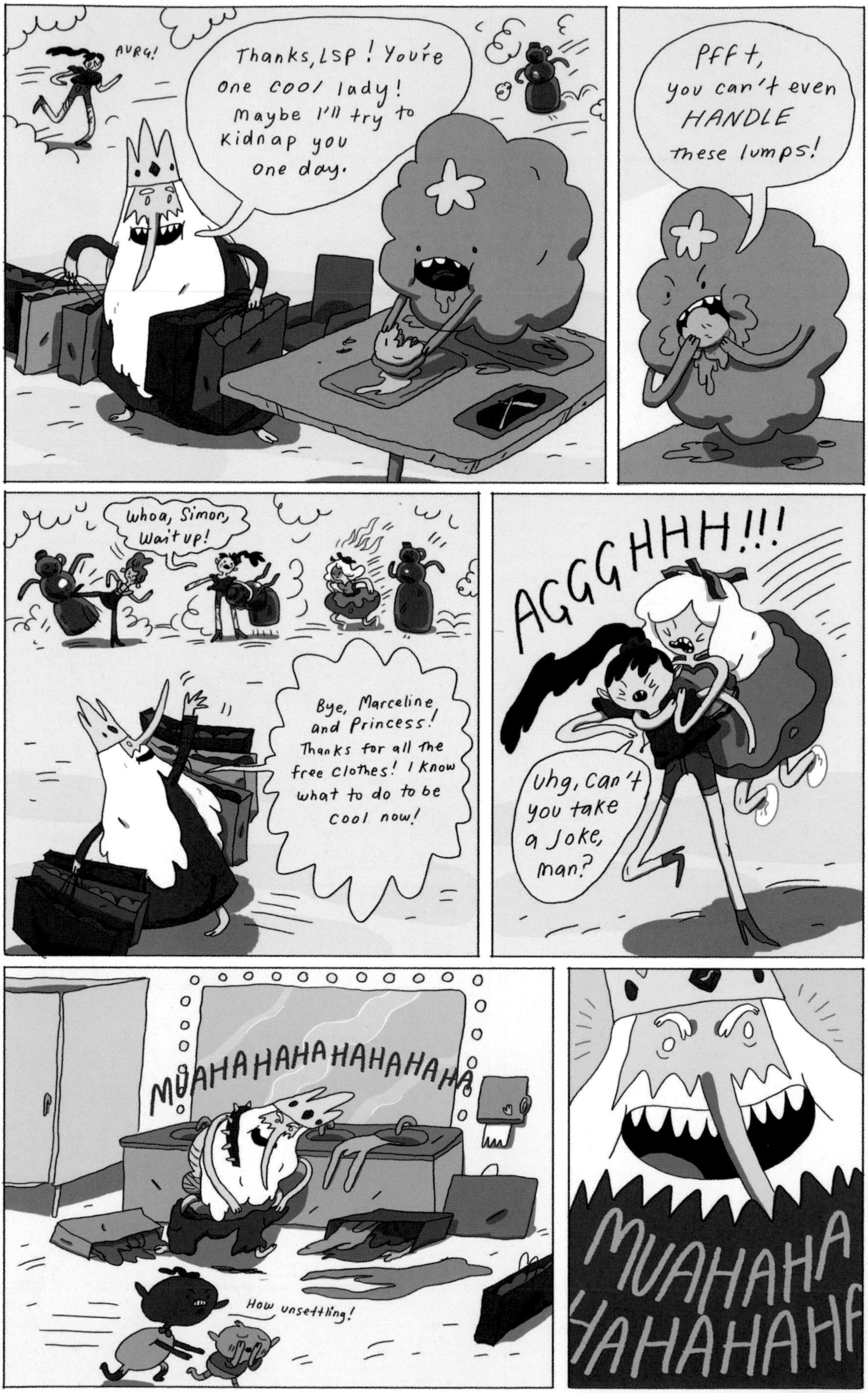
AURG!
Thanks, LSP! You're one cool lady! Maybe I'll try to kidnap you one day.
Pfft, you can't even HANDLE these lumps!
Whoa, Simon, wait up!
Bye, Marceline, and Princess! Thanks for all the free clothes! I know what to do to be cool now!
AGGGHHH!!!
Uhg, can't you take a joke, man?
MUAHAHAHAHAHAHAHA
How unsettling!
MUAHAHA
HAHAHAHA

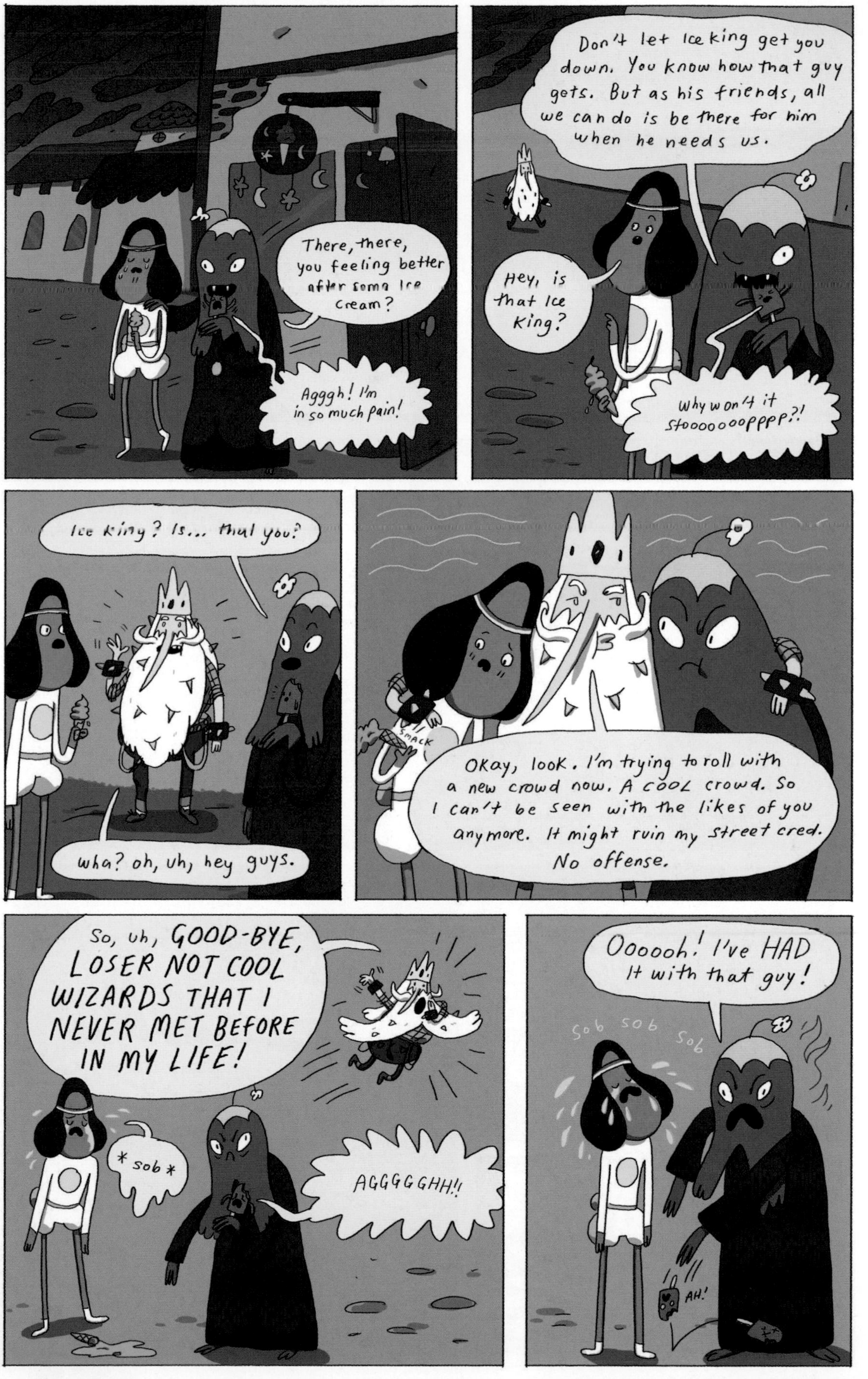
There, there, you feeling better after some Ice cream?
Agggh! I'm in so much pain!
Don't let Ice King get you down. You know how that guy gets. But as his friends, all we can do is be there for him when he needs us.
Hey, is that Ice King?
Why won't it stoooooooppppp?!
Ice King? Is... that you?
wha? oh, uh, hey guys.
SMACK
Okay, look. I'm trying to roll with a new crowd now. A COOL crowd. So I can't be seen with the likes of you anymore. It might ruin my street cred. No offense.
So, uh, GOOD-BYE, LOSER NOT COOL WIZARDS THAT I NEVER MET BEFORE IN MY LIFE!
* sob *
AGGGGGHH!!
Oooooh! I've HAD It with that guy!
sob sob sob
AH!

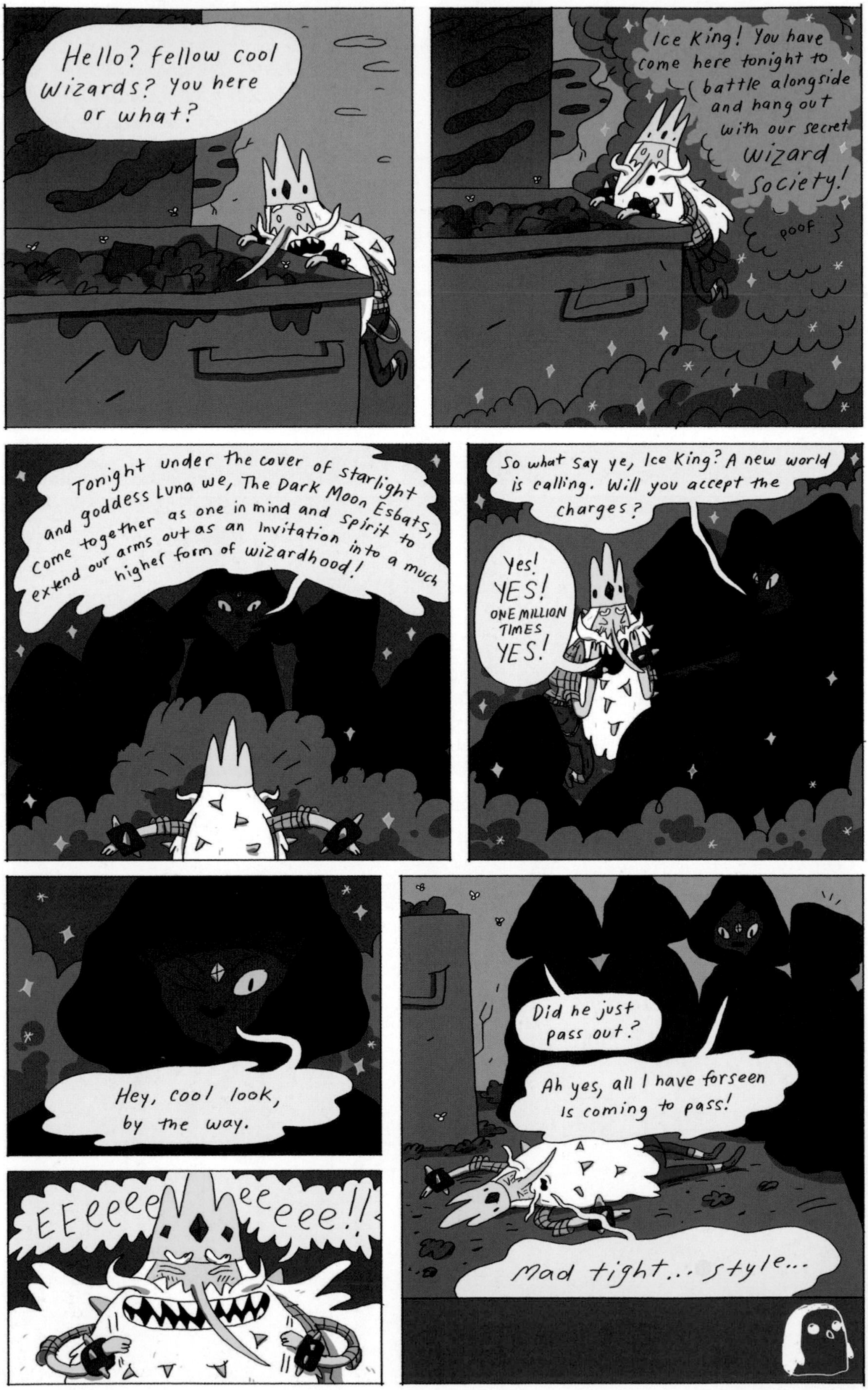
Hello? fellow cool wizards? You here or what?
Ice King! You have come here tonight to battle alongside and hang out with our secret wizard society!
POOF
Tonight under the cover of starlight and goddess Luna we, The Dark Moon Esbats, come together as one in mind and spirit to extend our arms out as an invitation into a much higher form of wizardhood!
So what say ye, Ice King? A new world is calling. Will you accept the charges?
Yes! YES! ONE MILLION TIMES YES!
Hey, cool look, by the way.
EEeeeeeeeee!!
Did he just pass out?
Ah yes, all I have forseen is coming to pass!
Mad tight... style...

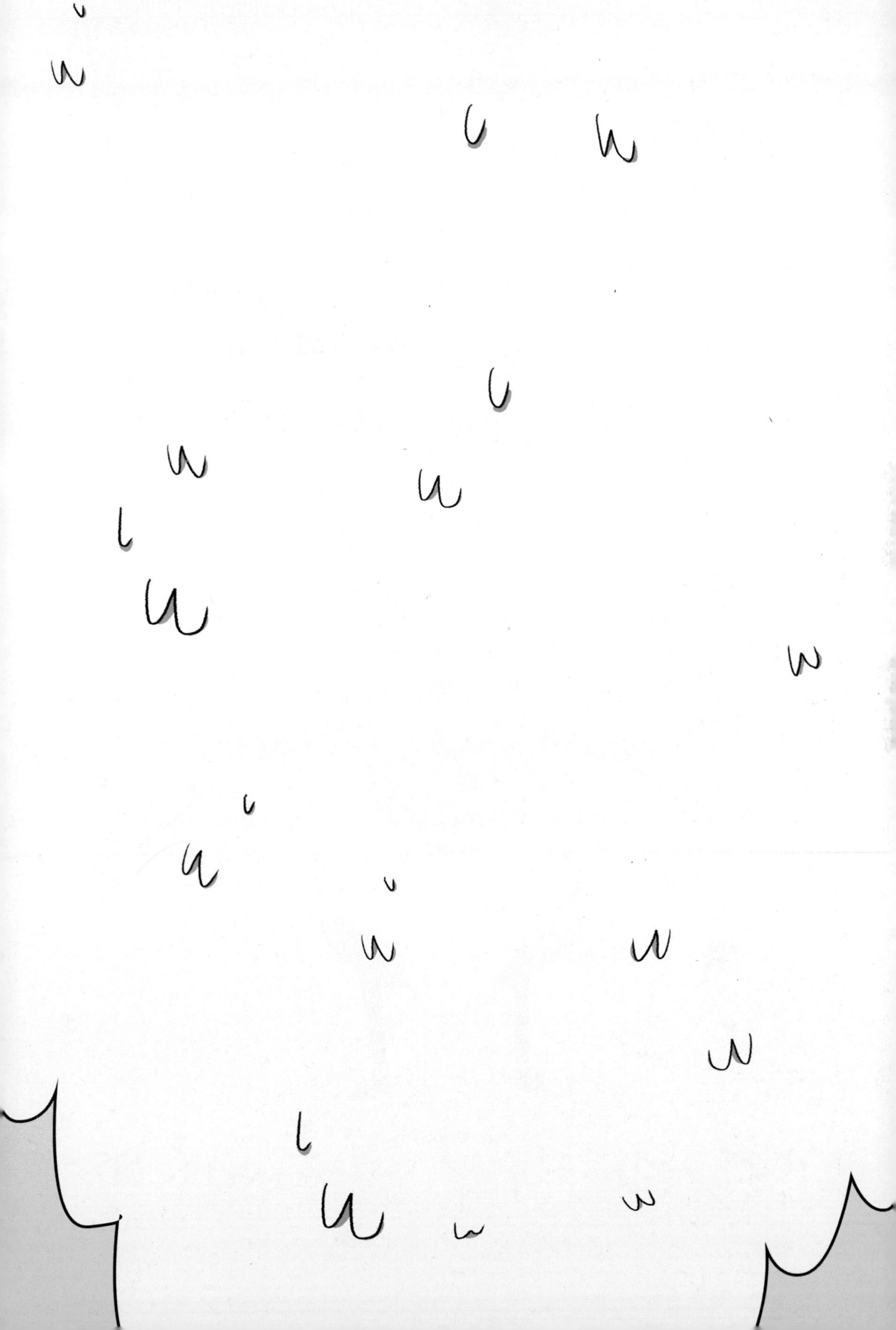

CHAPTER
THREE

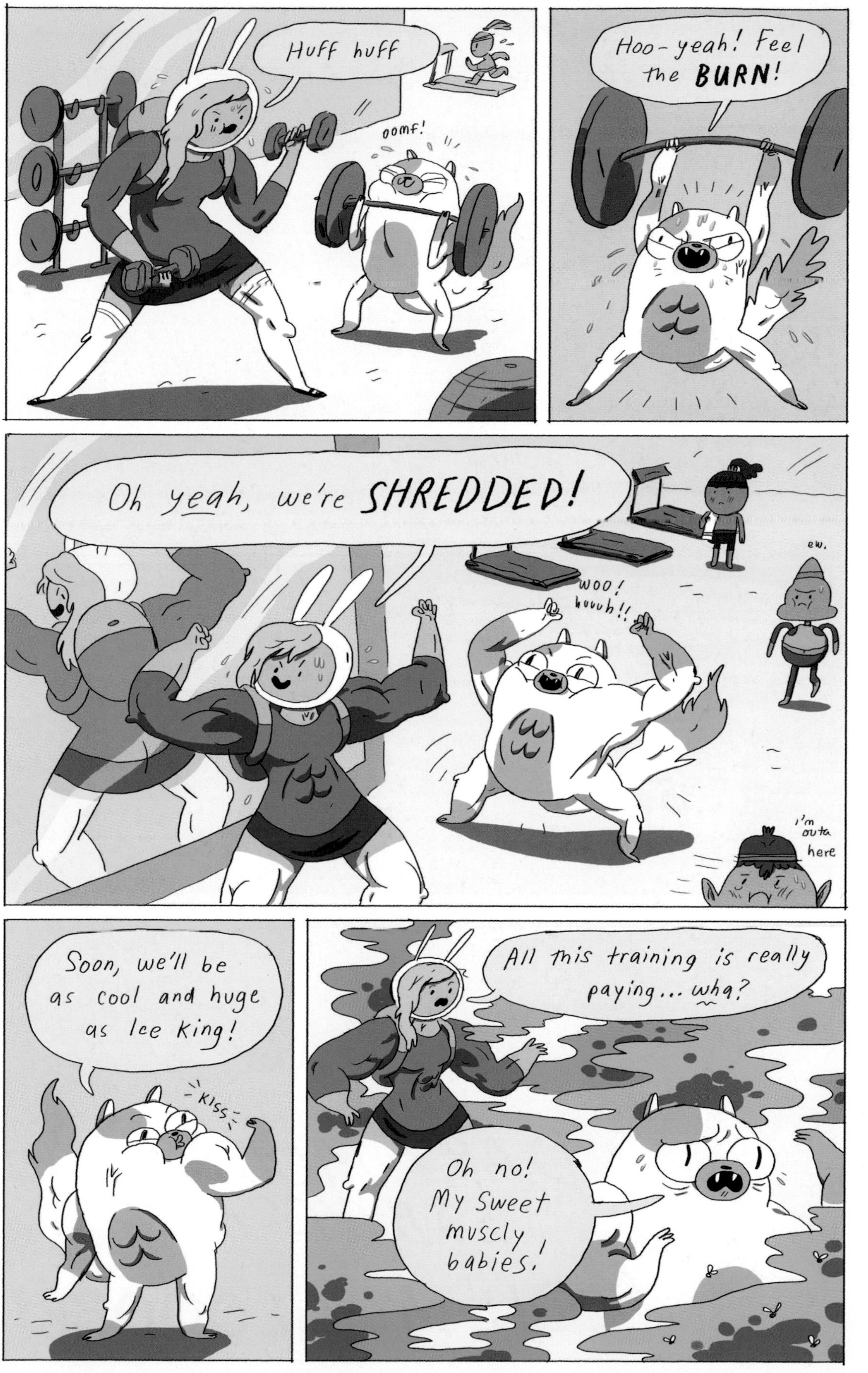

Huff huff
OOMF!
Hoo-yeah! Feel the BURN!
Oh yeah, we're SHREDDED!
ew.
WOO! hoooh!!
i'm outa here
Soon, we'll be as cool and huge as Ice King!
KISS
All this training is really paying... wha?
Oh no! My sweet muscly babies!

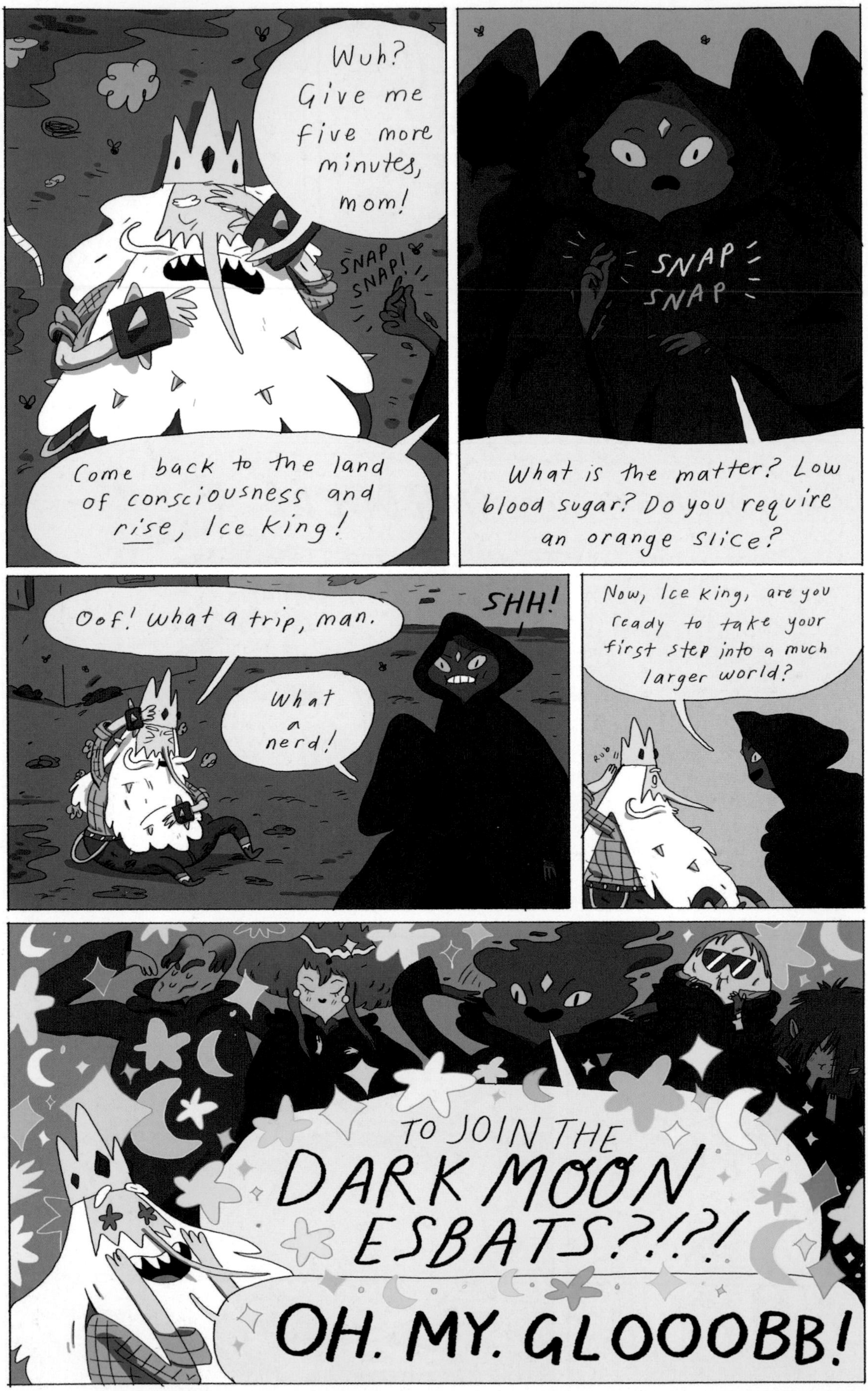

Wuh? Give me five more minutes, mom!
SNAP SNAP!
Come back to the land of consciousness and rise, Ice King!
SNAP SNAP
What is the matter? Low blood sugar? Do you require an orange slice?
Oof! What a trip, man.
SHH!
What a nerd!
Now, Ice King, are you ready to take your first step into a much larger world?
RUB
TO JOIN THE DARK MOON ESBATS?!?!
OH. MY. GLOOOBB!

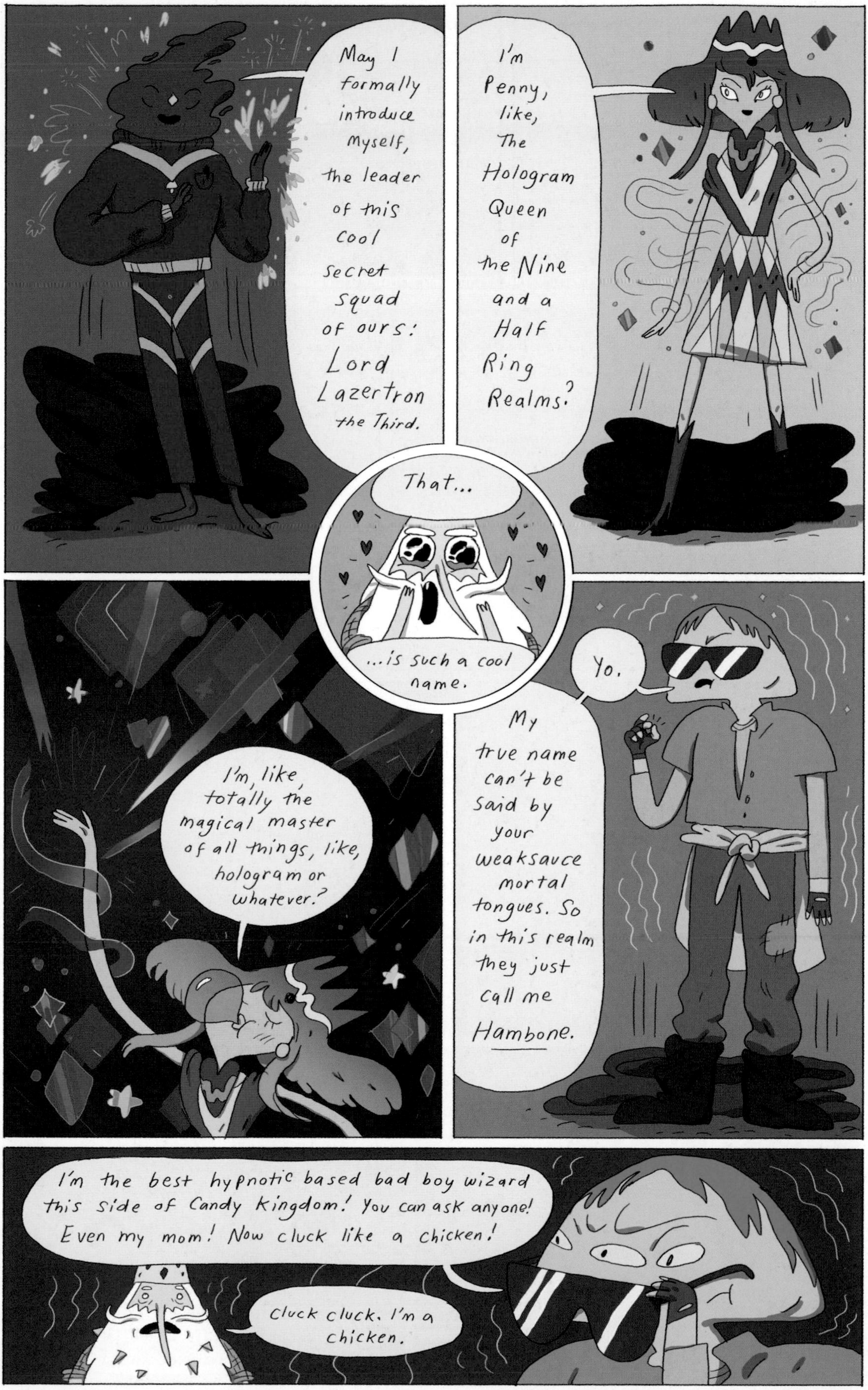
May I formally introduce myself, the leader of this cool secret squad of ours: Lord Lazertron the Third.
I'm Penny, like, The Hologram Queen of the Nine and a Half Ring Realms?
That...
...is such a cool name.
I'm, like, totally the magical master of all things, like, hologram or whatever?
Yo.
My true name can't be said by your weaksauce mortal tongues. So in this realm they just call me Hambone.
I'm the best hypnotic based bad boy wizard this side of Candy Kingdom! You can ask anyone! Even my mom! Now cluck like a chicken!
Cluck cluck. I'm a chicken.

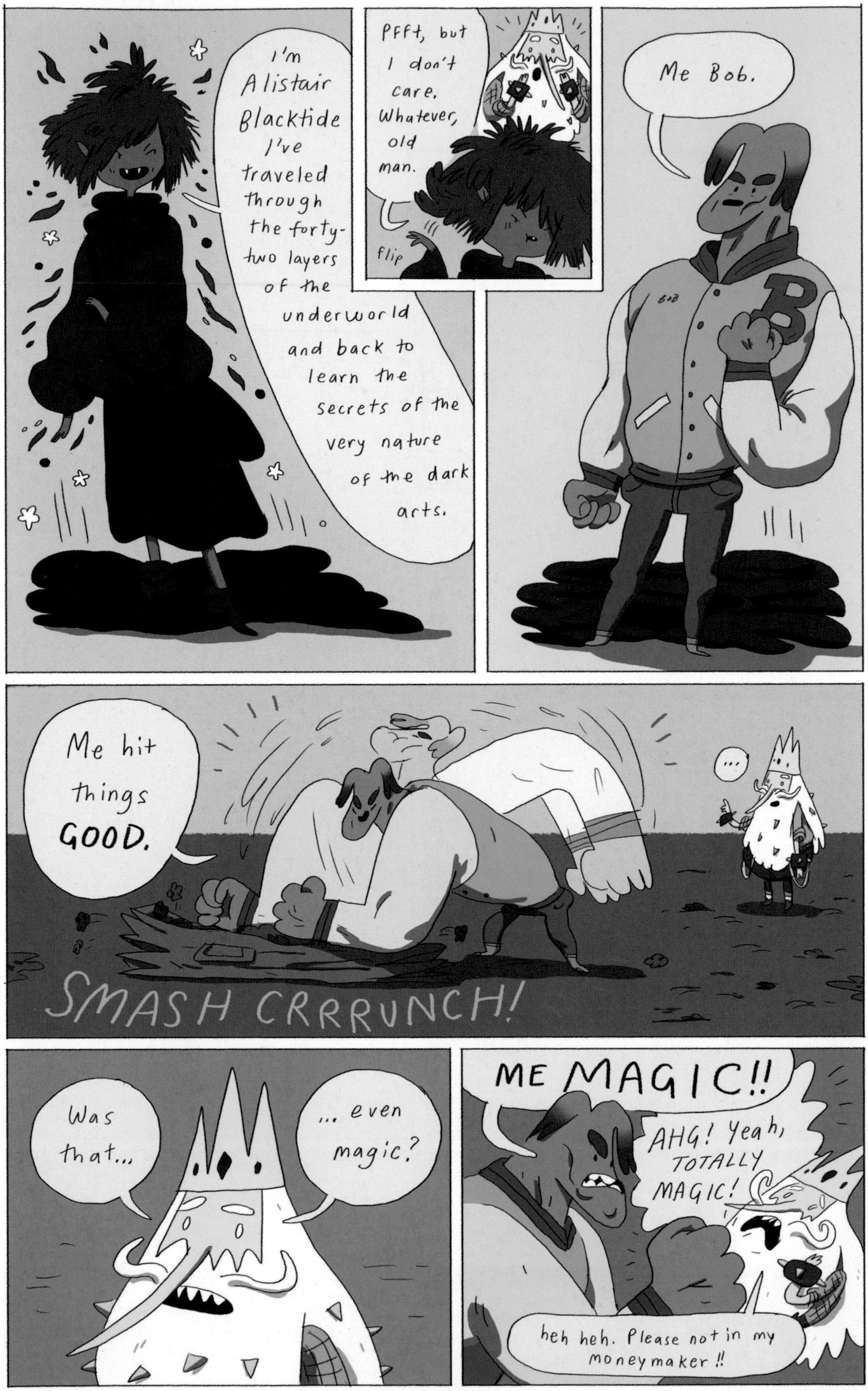
I'm Alistair Blacktide I've traveled through the forty-two layers of the underworld and back to learn the secrets of the very nature of the dark arts.
Pfft, but I don't care. Whatever, old man.
flip
Me Bob.
Me hit things GOOD.
...
SMASH CRRRUNCH!
Was that...
... even magic?
ME MAGIC!!
AHG! Yeah, TOTALLY MAGIC!
heh heh. Please not in my moneymaker!!

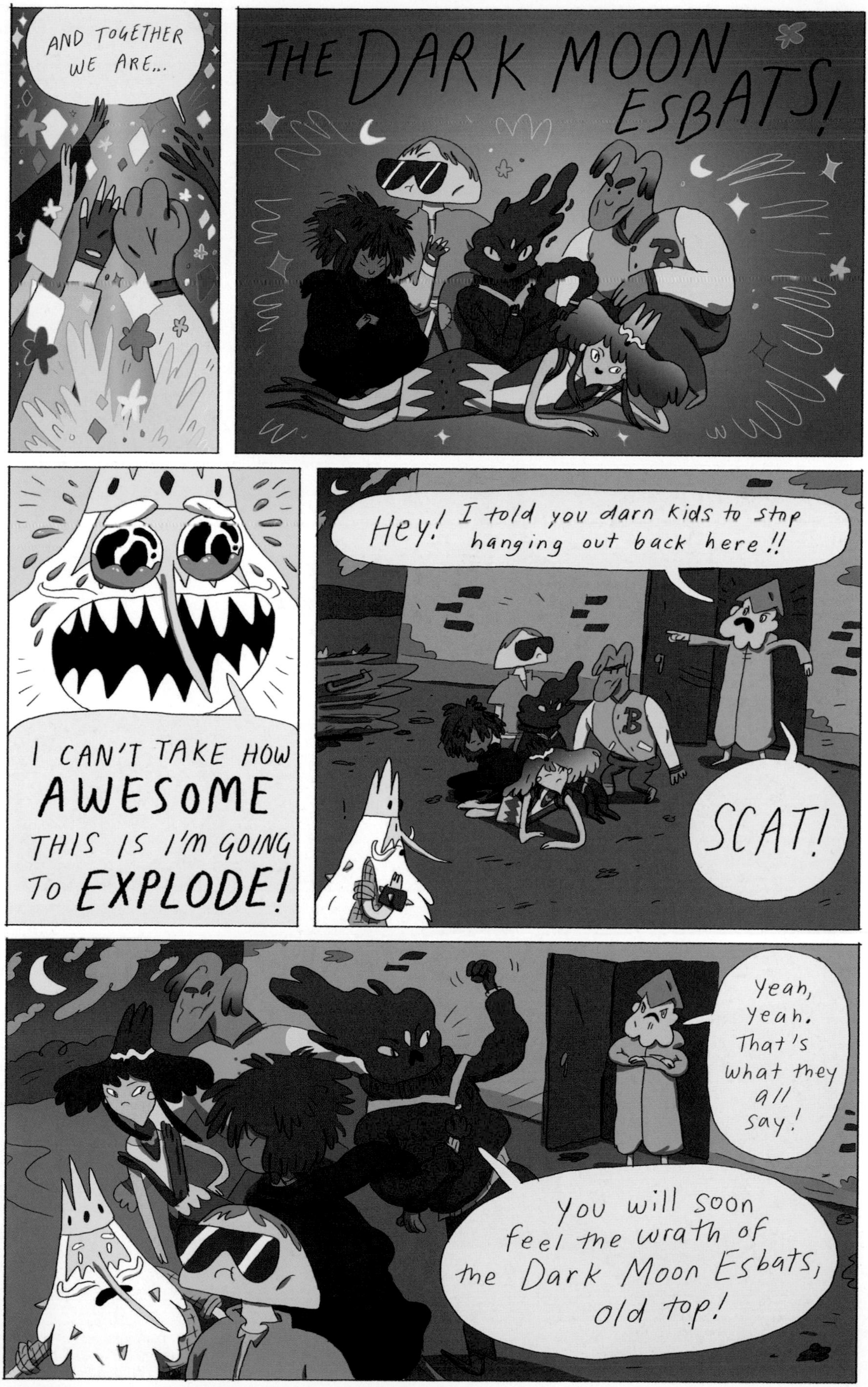
AND TOGETHER WE ARE...
THE DARK MOON ESBATS!
I CAN'T TAKE HOW AWESOME THIS IS I'M GOING TO EXPLODE!
Hey! I told you darn kids to stop hanging out back here!!
SCAT!
Yeah, yeah. That's what they all say!
You will soon feel the wrath of the Dark Moon Esbats, old top!

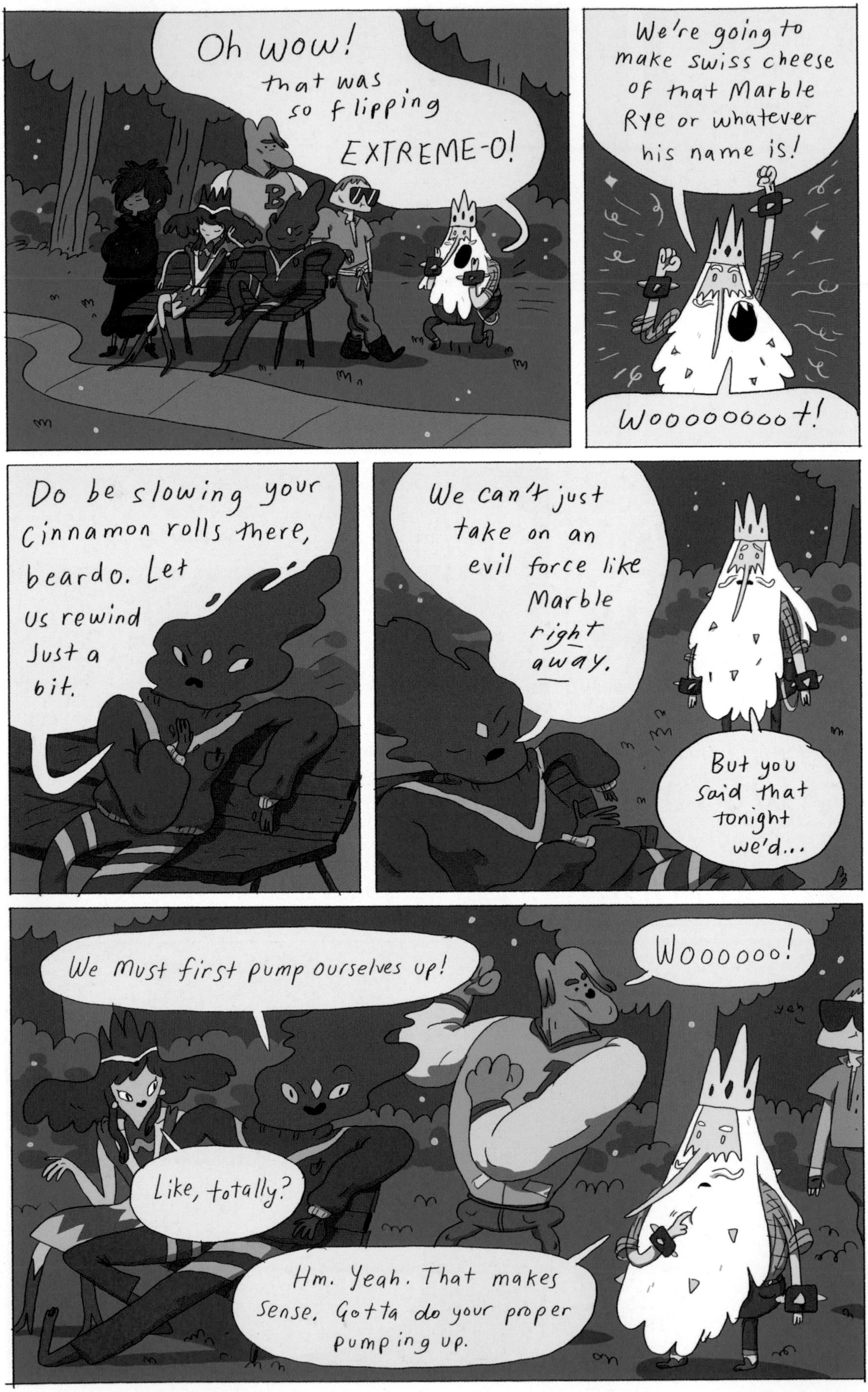
Oh wow! that was so flipping EXTREME-O!
We're going to make swiss cheese of that Marble Rye or whatever his name is!
Woooooooot!
Do be slowing your cinnamon rolls there, beardo. Let us rewind just a bit.
We can't just take on an evil force like Marble right away.
But you said that tonight we'd...
We must first pump ourselves up!
Woooooo!
yeh
Like, totally?
Hm. Yeah. That makes sense. Gotta do your proper pumping up.

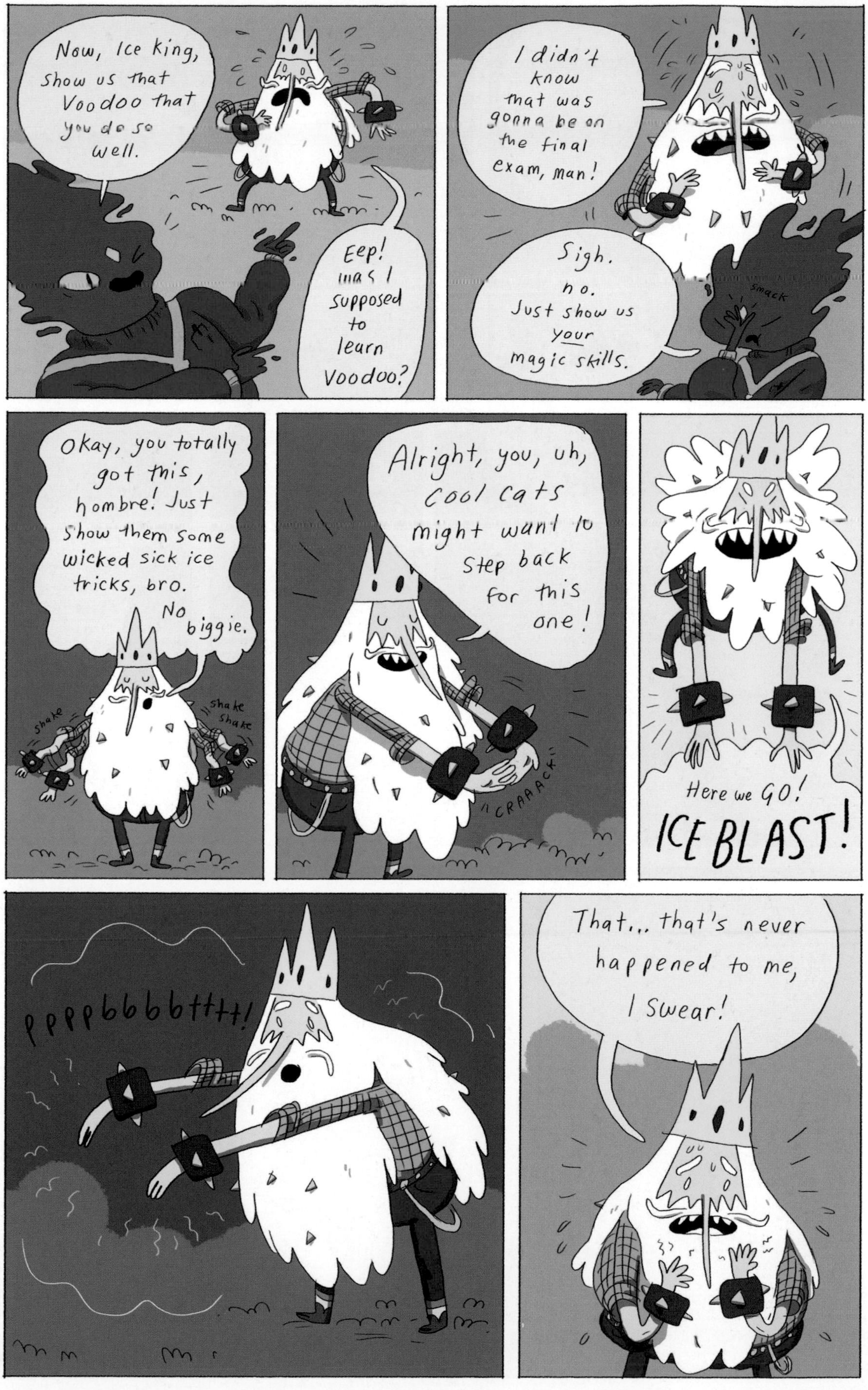
Now, Ice King, show us that Voodoo that you do so well.
Eep! Was I supposed to learn Voodoo?
I didn't know that was gonna be on the final exam, man!
Sigh. No. Just show us your magic skills.
smack
Okay, you totally got this, hombre! Just show them some wicked sick ice tricks, bro. No biggie.
shake
shake shake
Alright, you, uh, cool cats might want to step back for this one!
CRAAACK
Here we GO!
ICE BLAST!
PPPPbbbbtttt!
That... that's never happened to me, I swear!

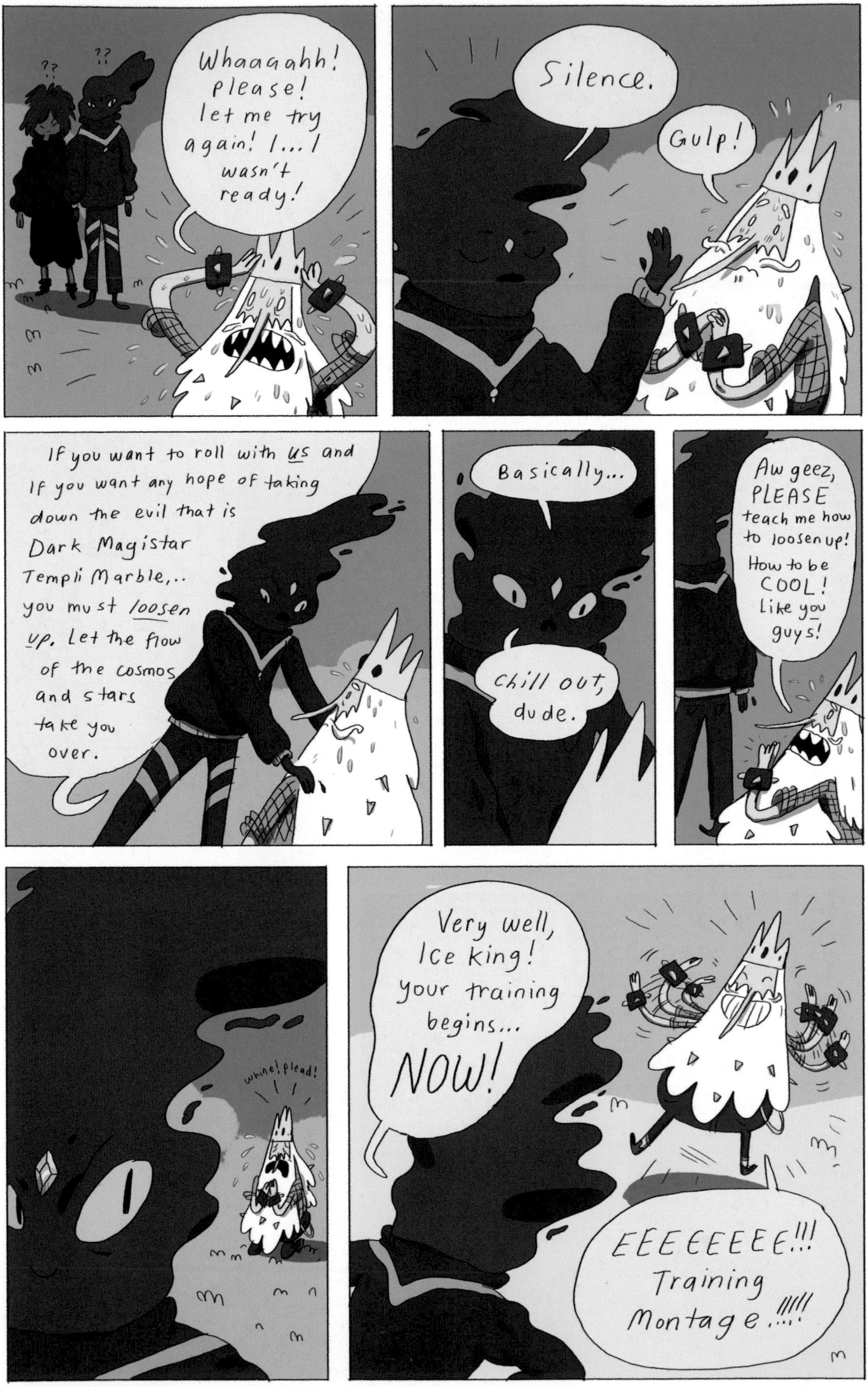
??
??
Whaaaahh! please! let me try again! I... I wasn't ready!
Silence.
Gulp!
If you want to roll with us and If you want any hope of taking down the evil that is Dark Magistar Templi Marble,.. you must loosen up. Let the flow of the cosmos and stars take you over.
Basically...
Chill out, dude.
Aw geez, PLEASE teach me how to loosen up! How to be COOL! Like you guys!
whine! plead!
Very well, Ice King! your training begins... NOW!
EEEEEEEE!!! Training Montage.....!!!!!

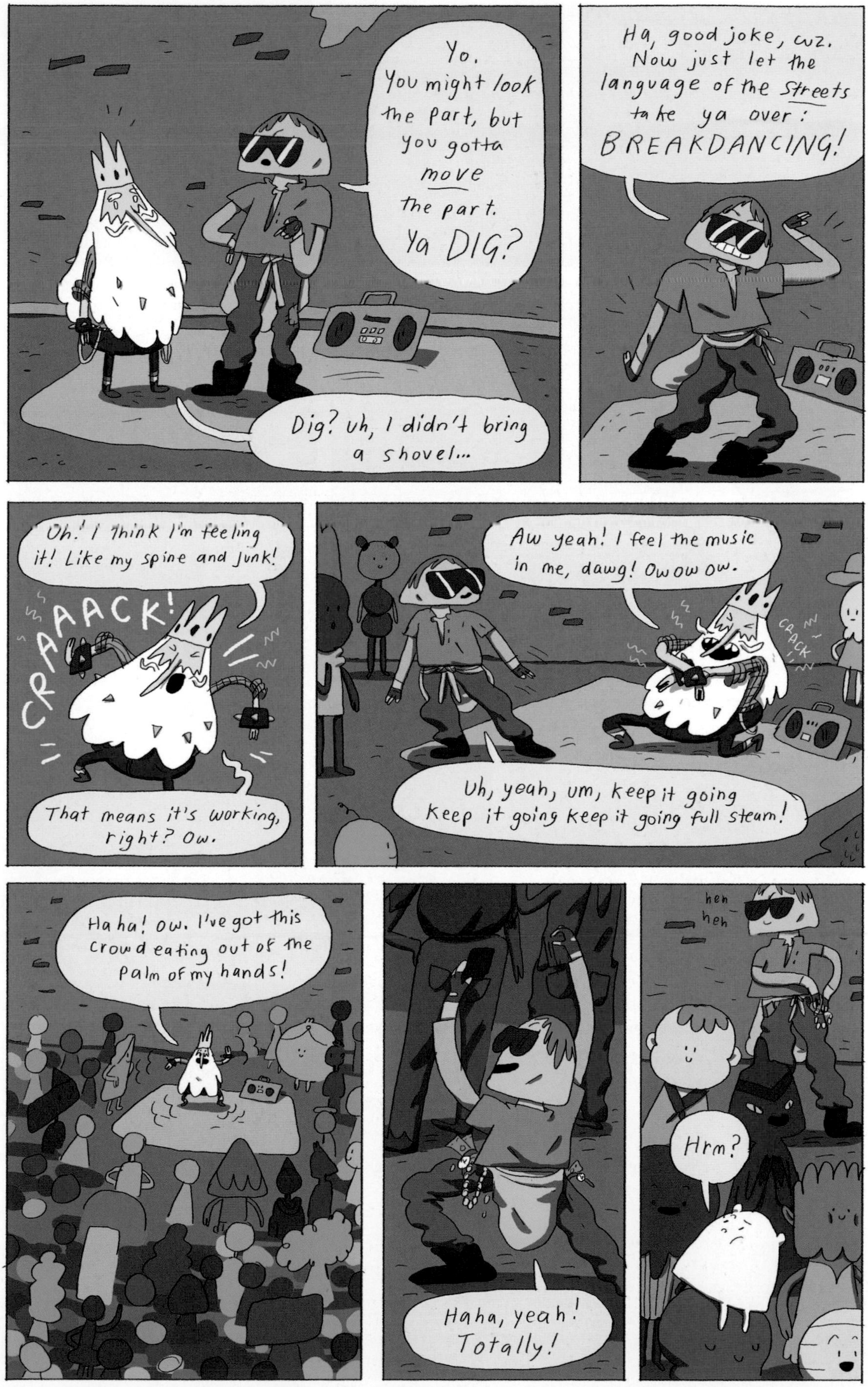
Yo. You might look the part, but you gotta move the part. Ya DIG?
Dig? uh, I didn't bring a shovel...
Ha, good joke, cuz. Now just let the language of the Streets take ya over: BREAKDANCING!
Oh! I think I'm feeling it! Like my spine and junk!
CRAAACK!
That means it's working, right? Ow.
Aw yeah! I feel the music in me, dawg! Owowow.
CRACK
Uh, yeah, um, keep it going Keep it going keep it going full steam!
Ha ha! Ow. I've got this crowd eating out of the palm of my hands!
Haha, yeah! Totally!
heh heh
Hrm?

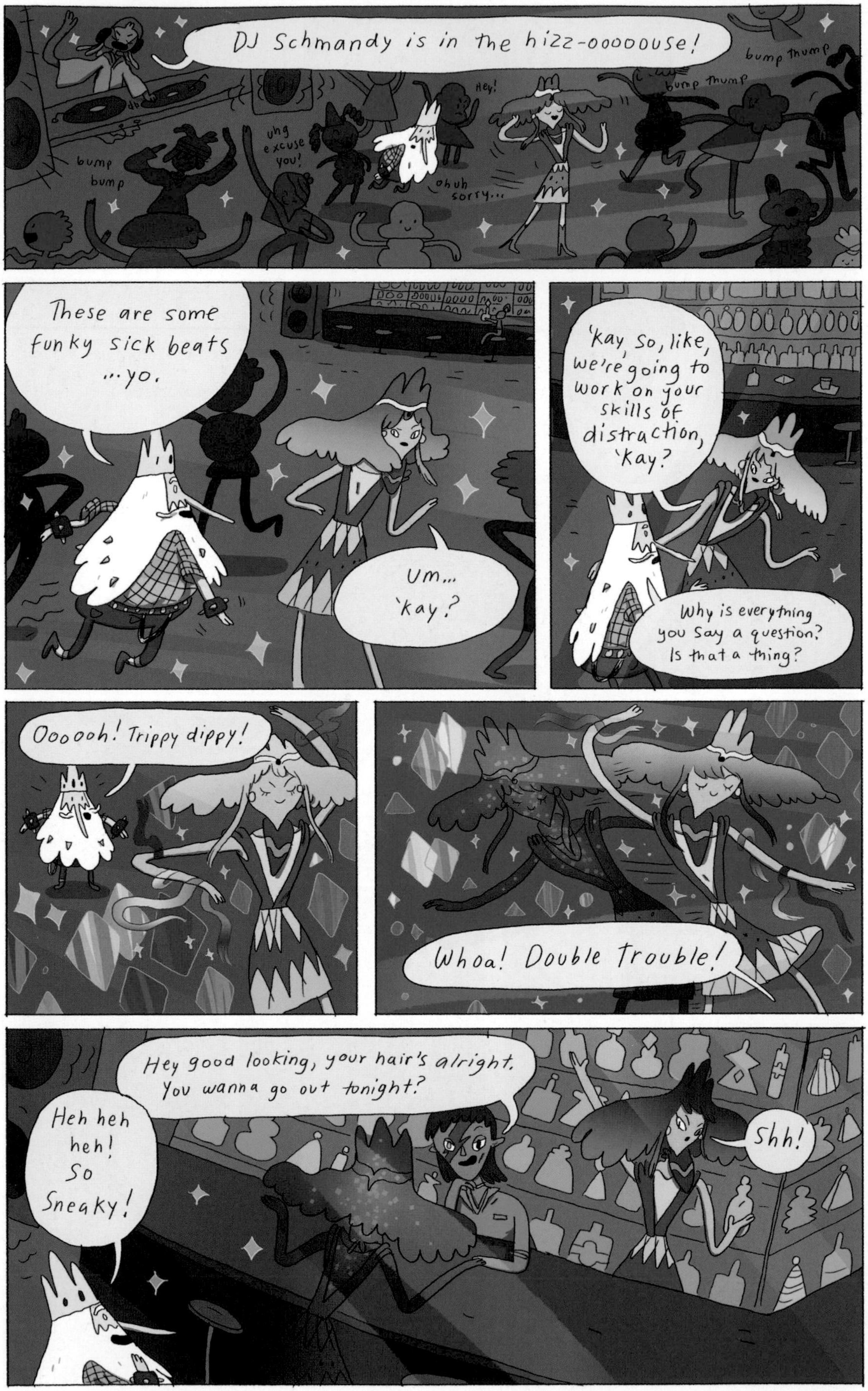
DJ Schmandy is in the hizz-oooooUSE!
bump thump
bump thump
Hey!
uhg excuse you!
oh uh sorry...
bump bump
These are some funky sick beats ...yo.
Um... 'kay?
'Kay, so, like, we're going to work on your skills of distraction, 'kay?
Why is everything you say a question? Is that a thing?
Oooooh! Trippy dippy!
Whoa! Double Trouble!
Hey good looking, your hair's alright. You wanna go out tonight?
Heh heh heh! So Sneaky!
Shh!

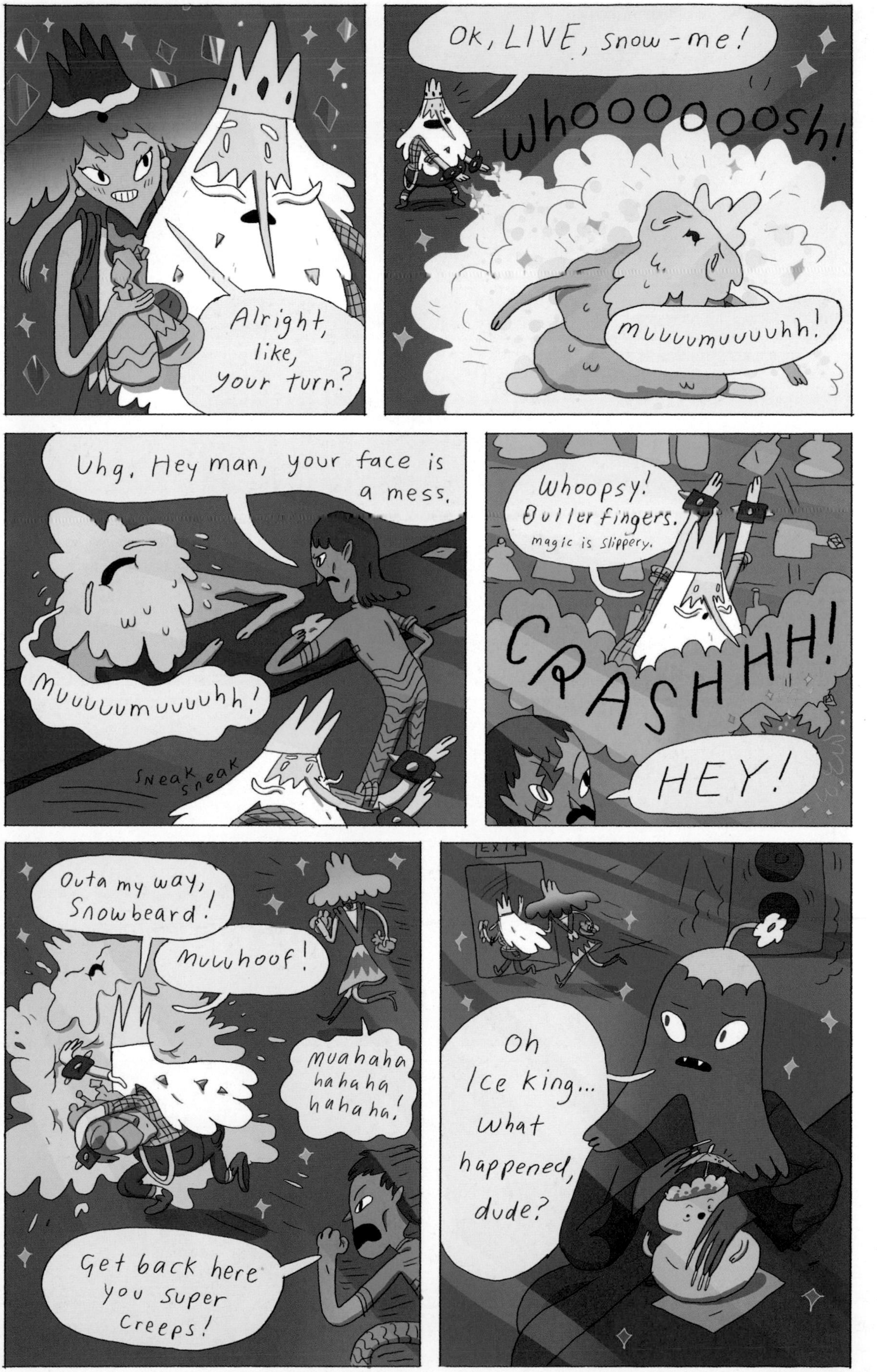

Alright, like, your turn?
Ok, LIVE, snow-me!
Whoooooosh!
muuuumuuuuhh!
Uhg. Hey man, your face is a mess.
Muuuumuuuuhh!
sneak sneak
Whoopsy! Butter fingers. magic is slippery.
CRASHHH!
HEY!
Outa my way, Snowbeard!
Muuhoof!
muahaha hahaha hahaha!
Get back here you super creeps!
EXIT
Oh Ice King... what happened, dude?

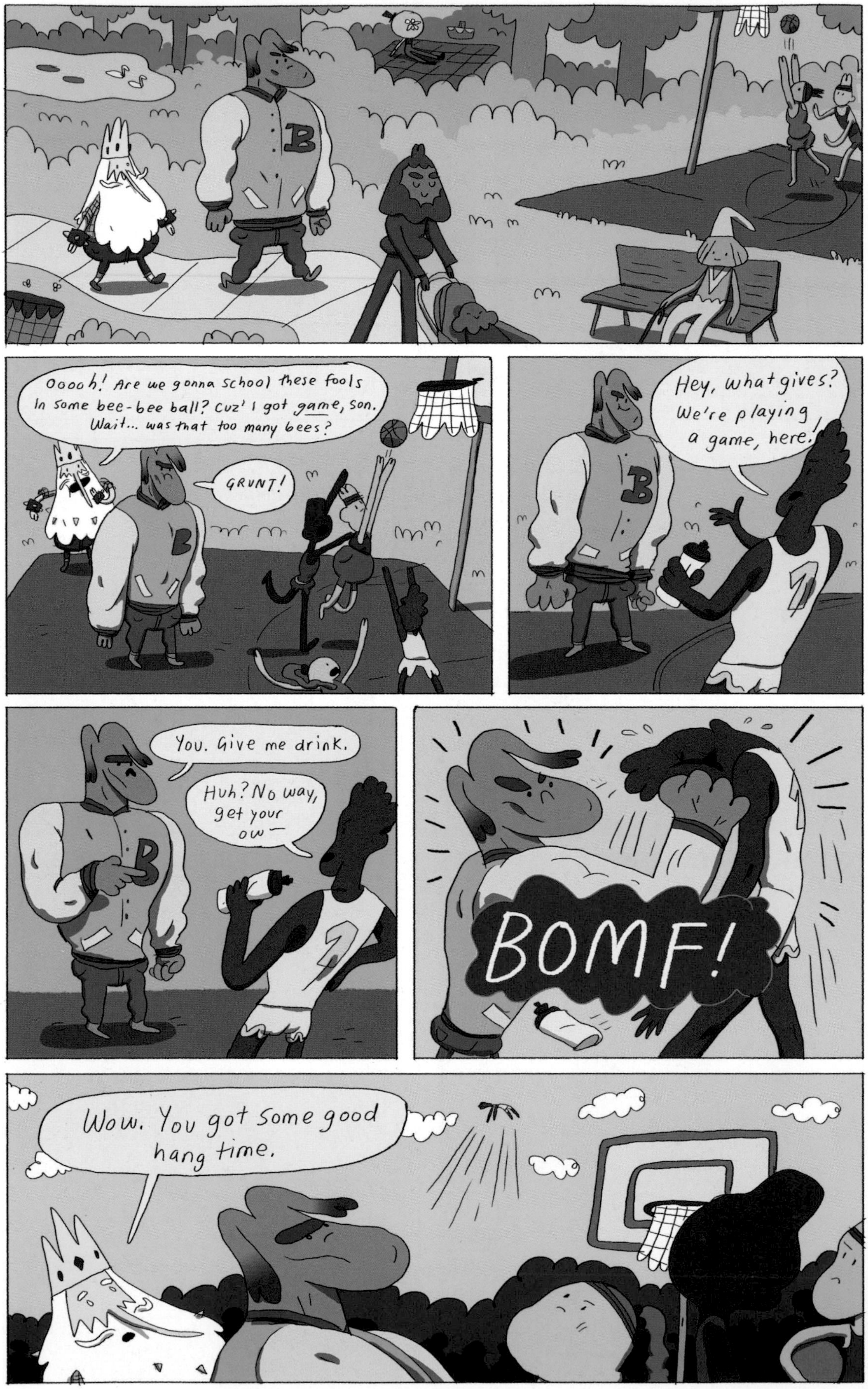

Ooooh! Are we gonna school these fools in some bee-bee ball? Cuz' I got game, son. Wait... was that too many bees?
GRUNT!
Hey, what gives? We're playing a game, here!
You. Give me drink.
Huh? No way, get your ow—
BOMF!
Wow. You got some good hang time.

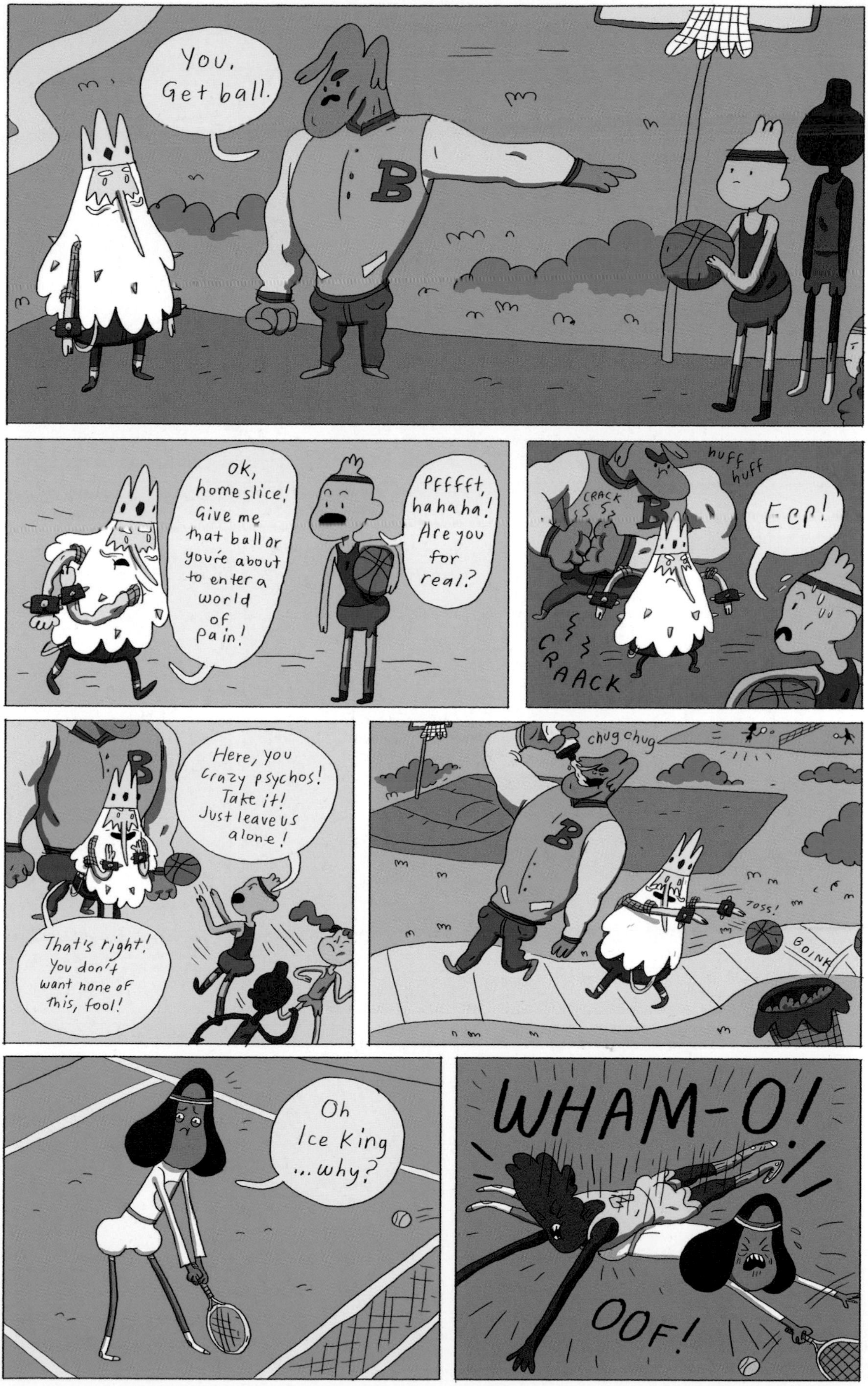
You. Get ball.
Ok, home slice! Give me that ball or you're about to enter a world of pain!
Pfffft, hahaha! Are you for real?
CRACK
CRAACK
huff huff
Eep!
Here, you crazy psychos! Take it! Just leave us alone!
That's right! You don't want none of this, fool!
chug chug
TOSS!
BOINK
Oh Ice King ...why?
WHAM-O!
OOF!

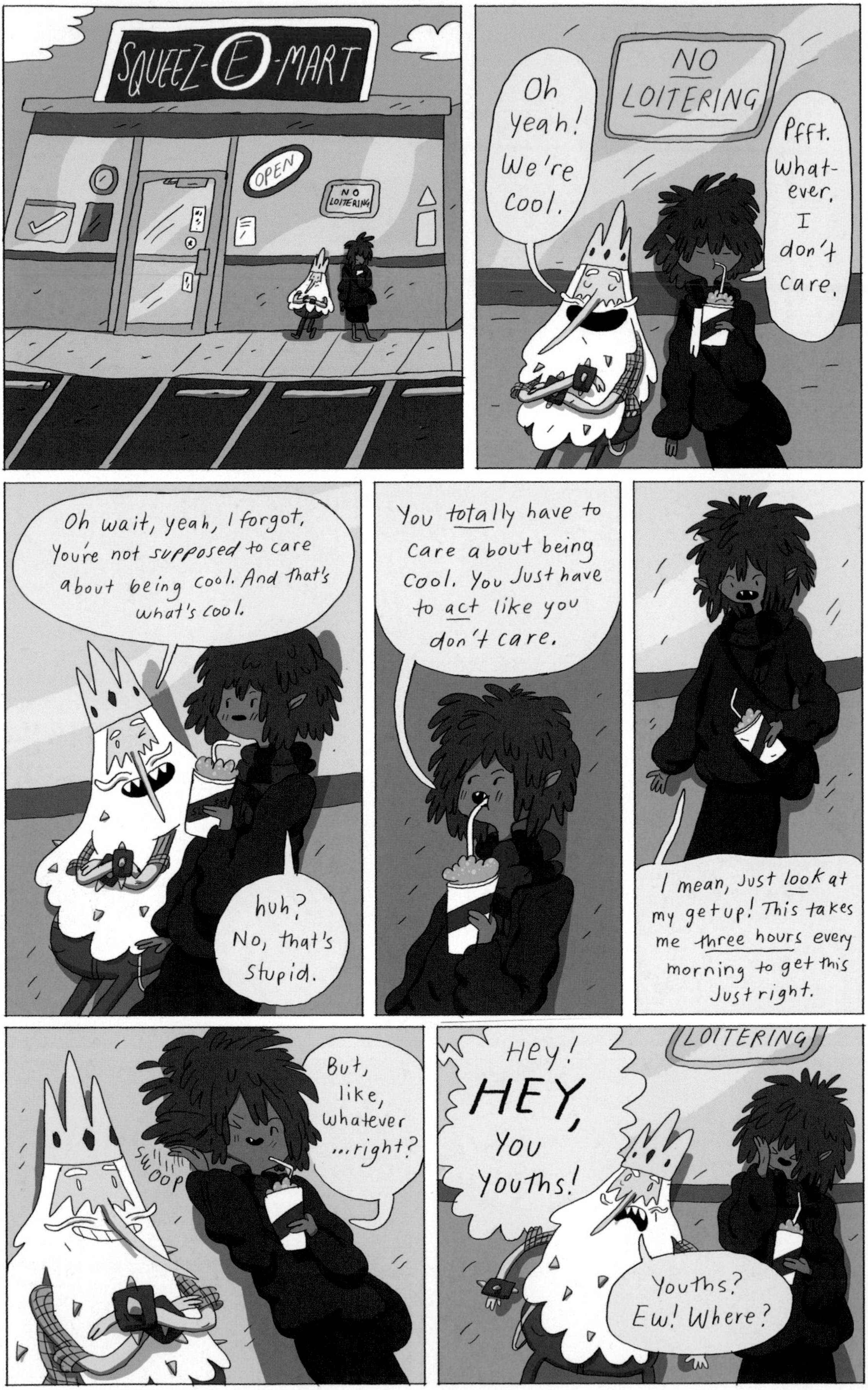
SQUEEZ-E-MART
OPEN
NO LOITERING
NO LOITERING
Oh yeah! We're cool.
Pfft. whatever. I don't care.
Oh wait, yeah, I forgot. You're not supposed to care about being cool. And that's what's cool.
huh? No, that's stupid.
You totally have to care about being cool. You just have to act like you don't care.
I mean, just look at my getup! This takes me three hours every morning to get this just right.
SWOOP
But, like, whatever ...right?
LOITERING
Hey! HEY, You Youths!
Youths? Ew! Where?

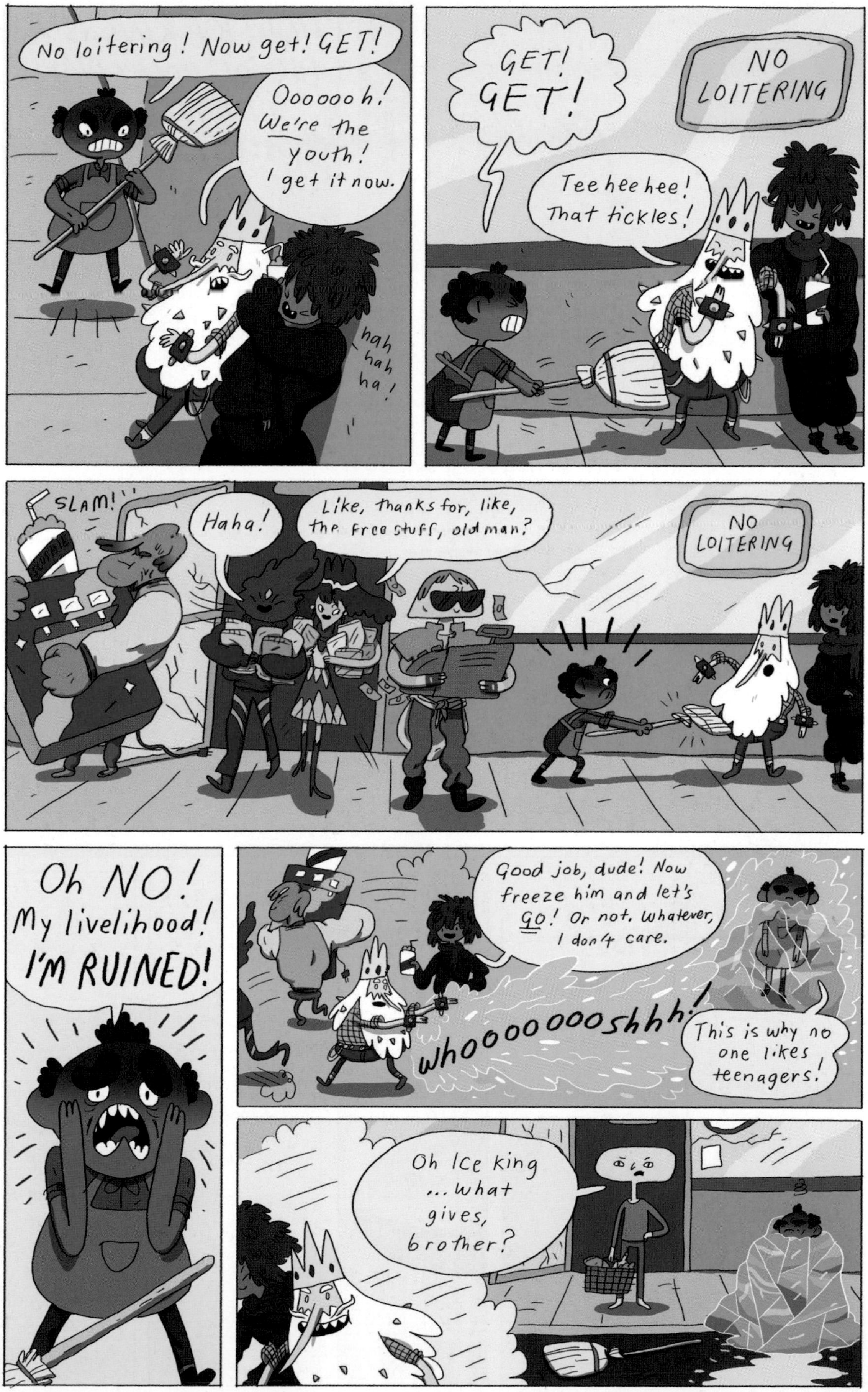

No loitering! Now get! GET!
Ooooooh! We're the youth! I get it now.
hah hah ha!
GET! GET!
NO LOITERING
Tee hee hee! That tickles!
SLAM!
Haha!
Like, thanks for, like, the free stuff, old man?
NO LOITERING
Oh NO! My livelihood! I'M RUINED!
Good job, dude! Now freeze him and let's GO! Or not. Whatever, I don't care.
whoooooooshhh!
This is why no one likes teenagers!
Oh Ice King ...what gives, brother?

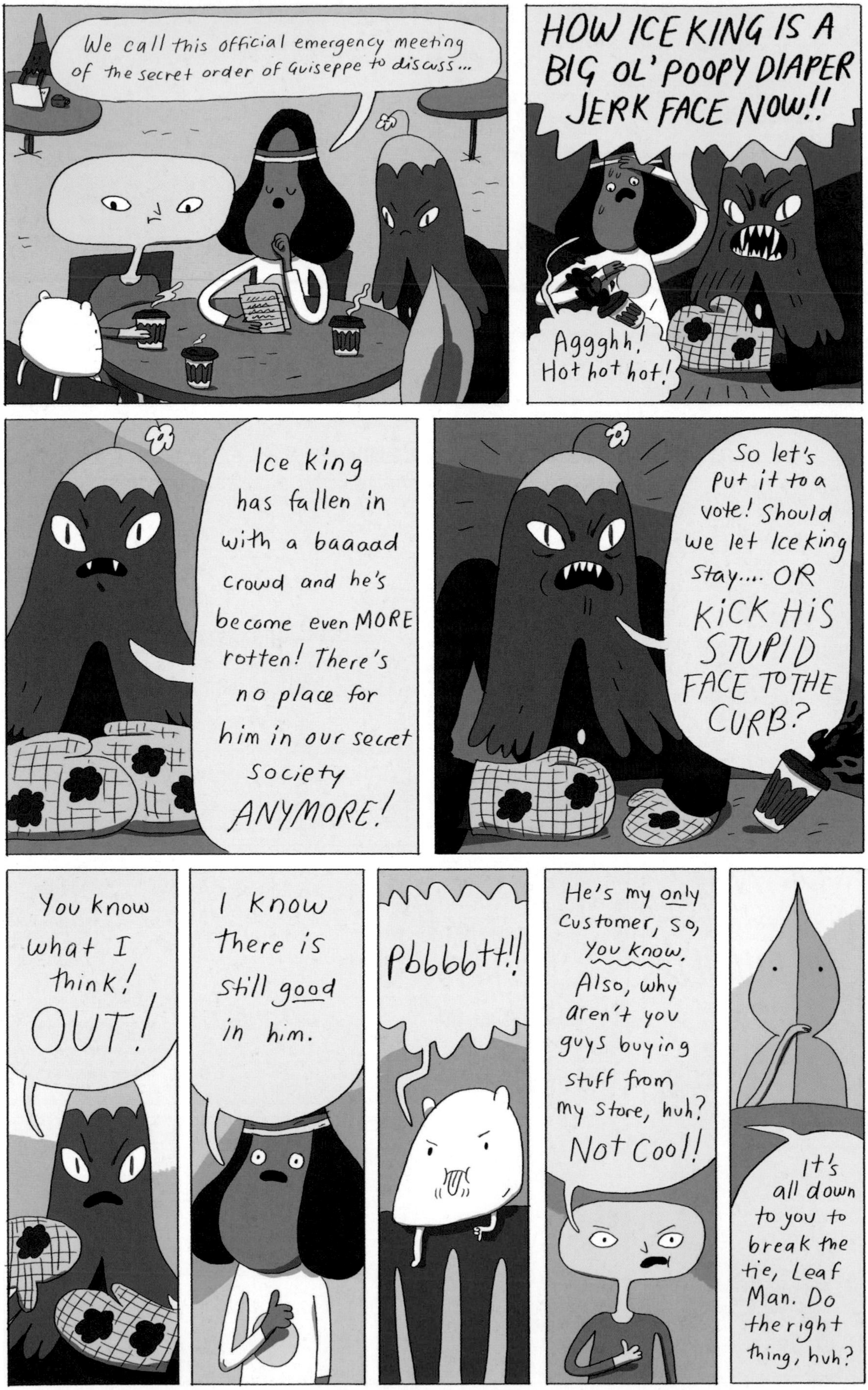
We call this official emergency meeting of the secret order of Guiseppe to discuss...
HOW ICE KING IS A BIG OL' POOPY DIAPER JERK FACE NOW!!
Aggghh! Hot hot hot!
Ice king has fallen in with a baaaad crowd and he's become even MORE rotten! There's no place for him in our secret society ANYMORE!
So let's put it to a vote! Should we let Ice King stay.... OR KICK HIS STUPID FACE TO THE CURB?
You know what I think! OUT!
I know there is still good in him.
Pbbbbtt!!
He's my only customer, so, you know. Also, why aren't you guys buying stuff from my store, huh? Not Cool!
It's all down to you to break the tie, Leaf Man. Do the right thing, huh?

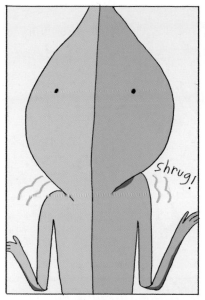

shrug!

What? Are you kidding me?!

HEY! Cool it, buddy!

AGGHHHH! WHY does this keep happening?!

Wha-huh?

BOOP!

Haha, OK, we'll let him stay. Dang, you're persuasive, Leaf Man.

WINK

But if he's gonna stay, we need to do something about his new attitude and his new "friends." So here's what we're gonna do.... pssst psssst pssst...

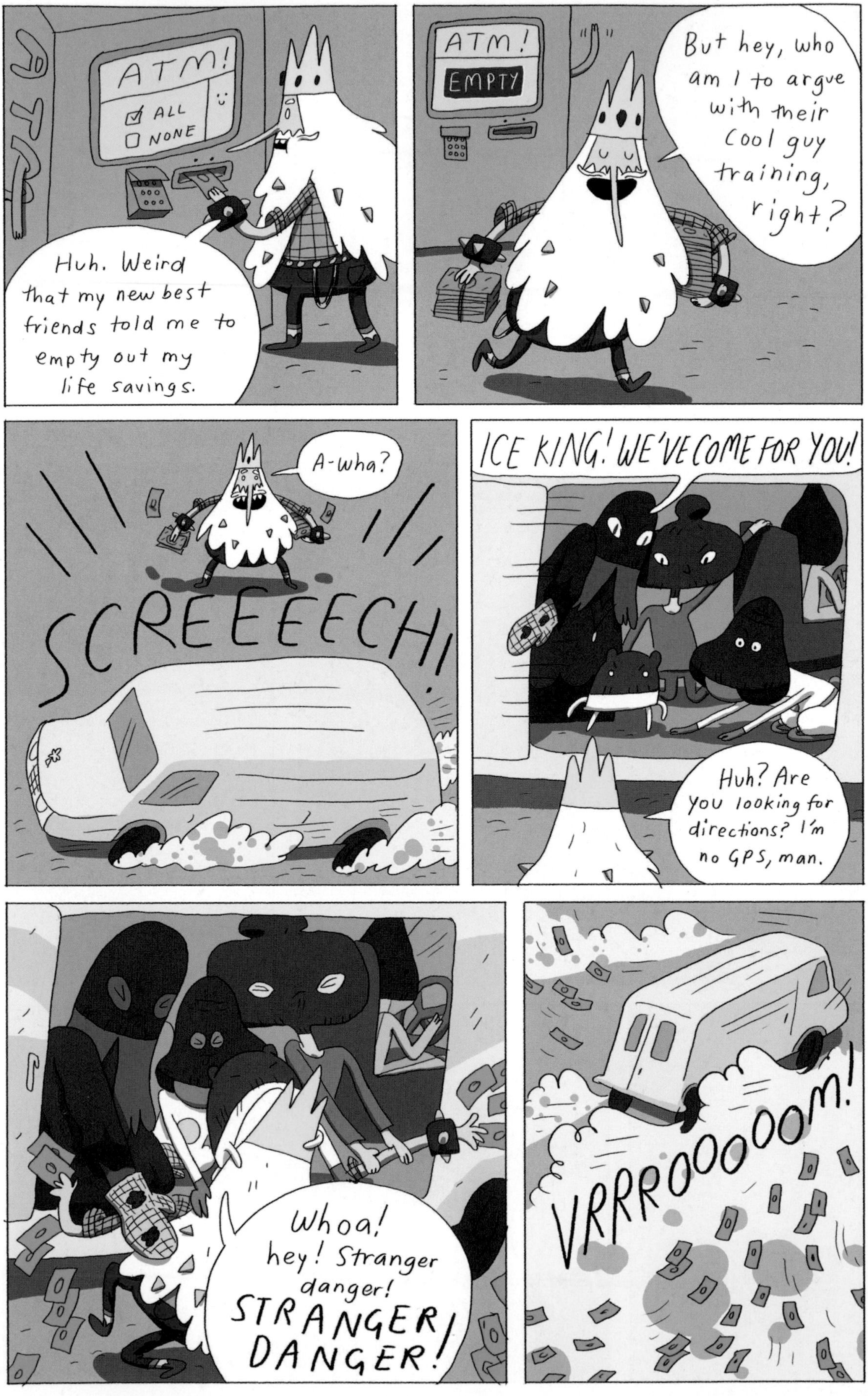
ATM!
ALL
NONE
Huh. Weird that my new best friends told me to empty out my life savings.
ATM!
EMPTY
But hey, who am I to argue with their cool guy training, right?
A-wha?
SCREEEECH!
ICE KING! WE'VE COME FOR YOU!
Huh? Are you looking for directions? I'm no GPS, man.
Whoa! hey! Stranger danger! STRANGER DANGER!
VRRROOOOOM!

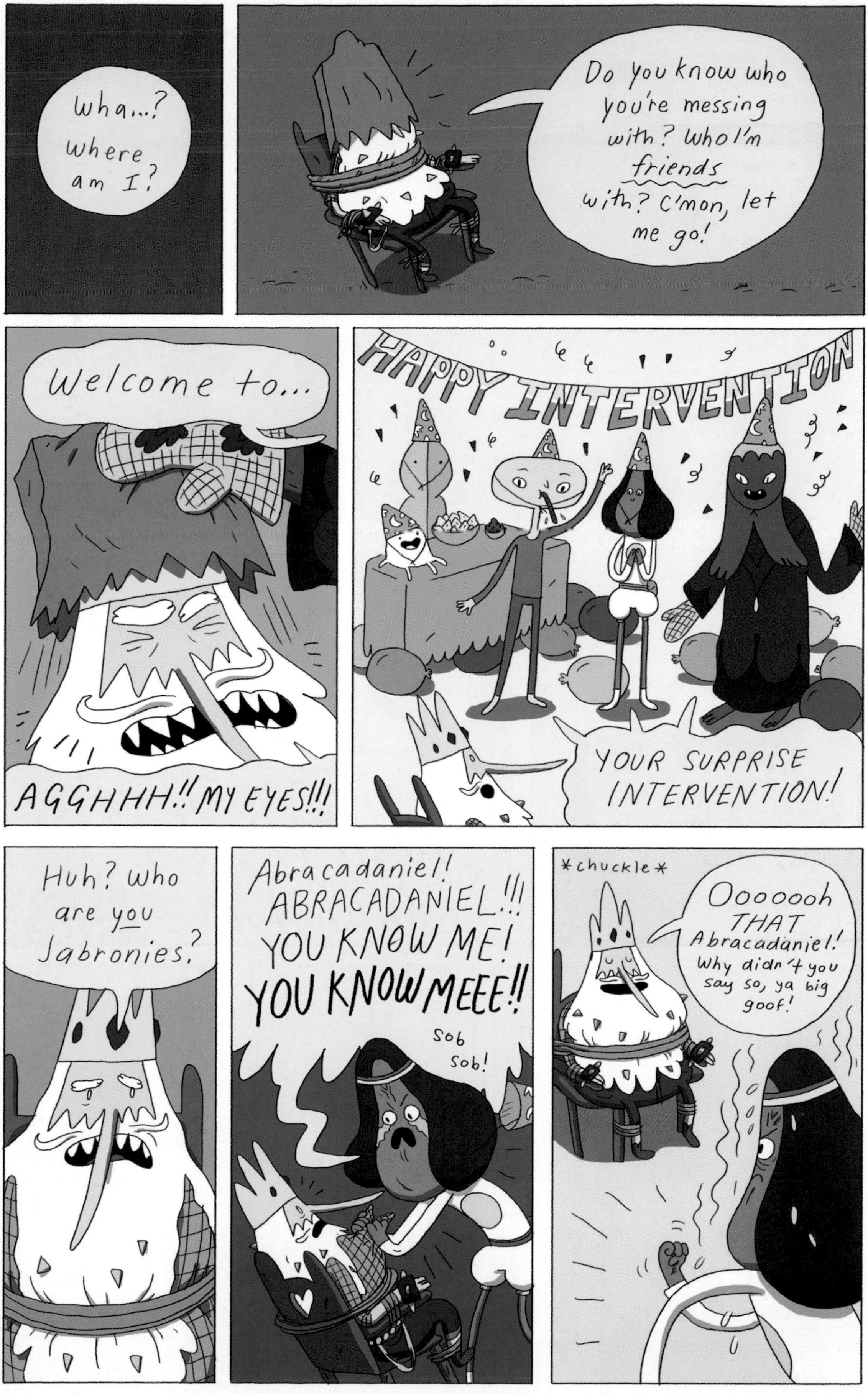
Wha...? where am I?
Do you know who you're messing with? Who I'm friends with? C'mon, let me go!
Welcome to...
AGGHHH!! MY EYES!!!
HAPPY INTERVENTION
YOUR SURPRISE INTERVENTION!
Huh? Who are you Jabronies?
Abracadaniel! ABRACADANIEL!!! YOU KNOW ME! YOU KNOW MEEE!!
Sob sob!
chuckle
Ooooooh THAT Abracadaniel! Why didn't you say so, ya big goof!

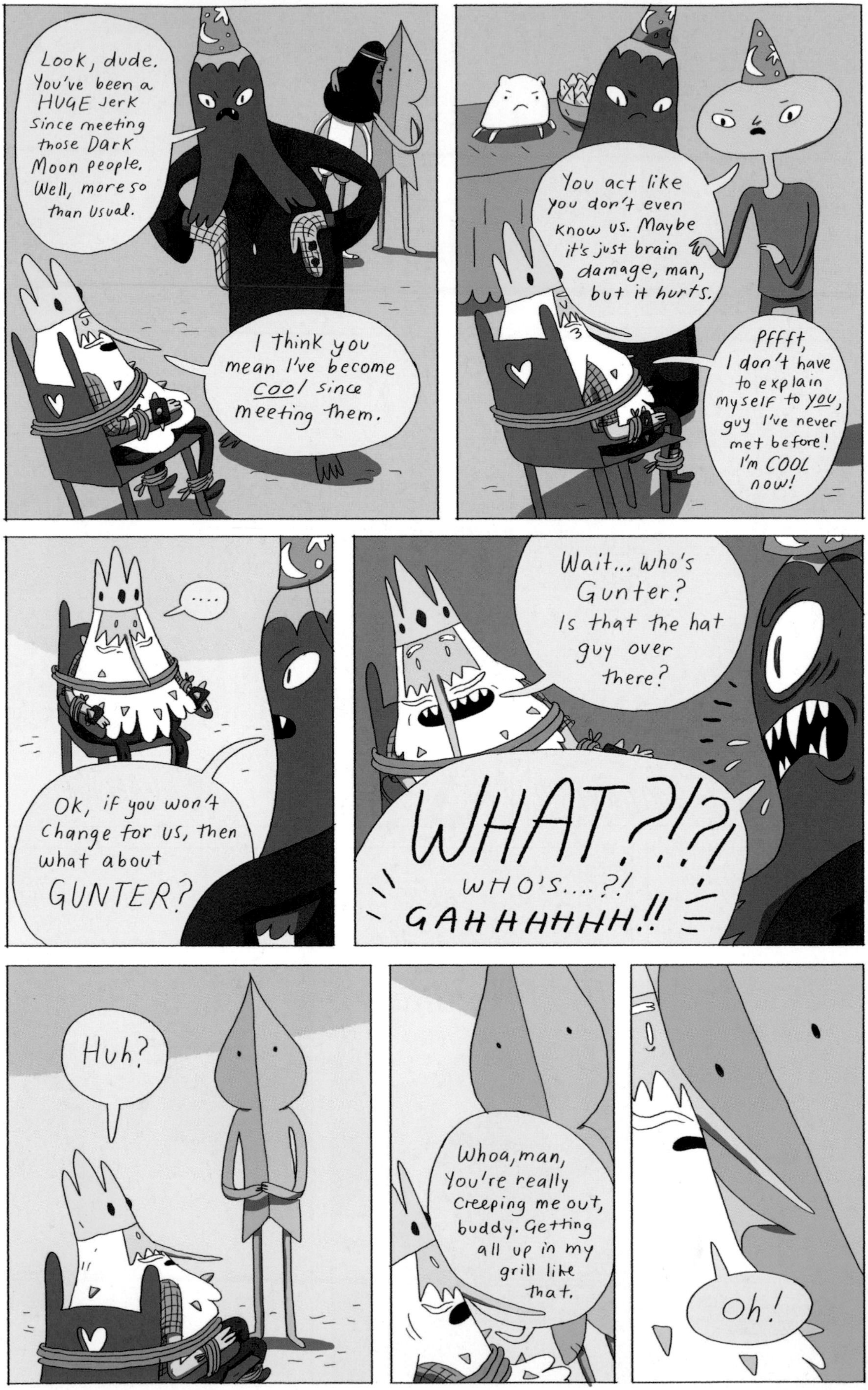

Look, dude. You've been a HUGE jerk since meeting those Dark Moon people. Well, more so than usual.
I think you mean I've become cool since meeting them.
You act like you don't even know us. Maybe it's just brain damage, man, but it hurts.
Pffft, I don't have to explain myself to you, guy I've never met before! I'm COOL now!
....
Ok, if you won't change for us, then what about GUNTER?
Wait... who's Gunter? Is that the hat guy over there?
WHAT?!?! WHO'S....?! GAHHHHHH!!
Huh?
Whoa, man, You're really creeping me out, buddy. Getting all up in my grill like that.
Oh!

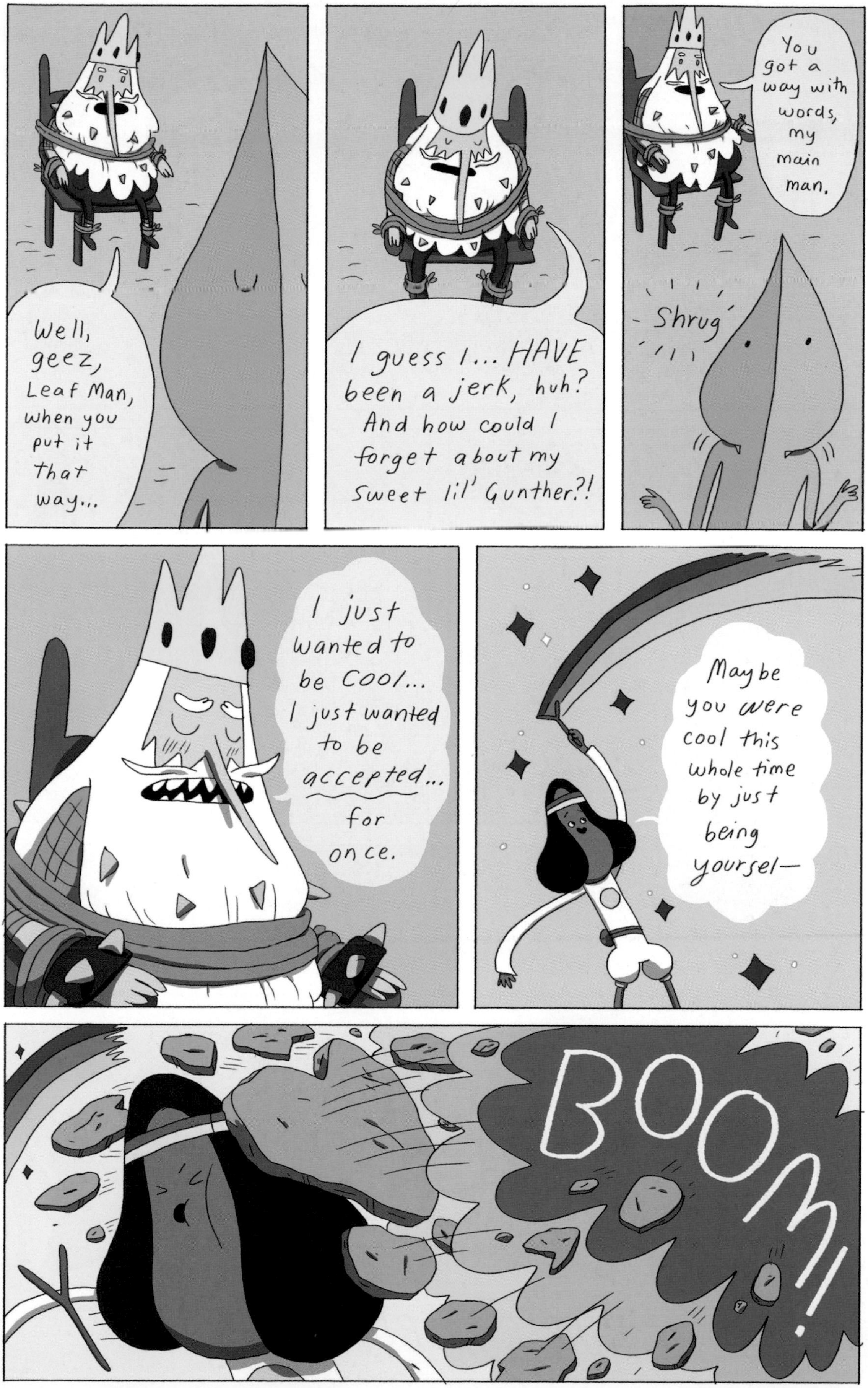
Well, geez, Leaf Man, when you put it that way...
I guess I... HAVE been a jerk, huh? And how could I forget about my sweet lil' Gunther?!
You got a way with words, my main man.
Shrug
I just wanted to be cool... I just wanted to be accepted... for once.
Maybe you were cool this whole time by just being yoursel—
BOOM!!

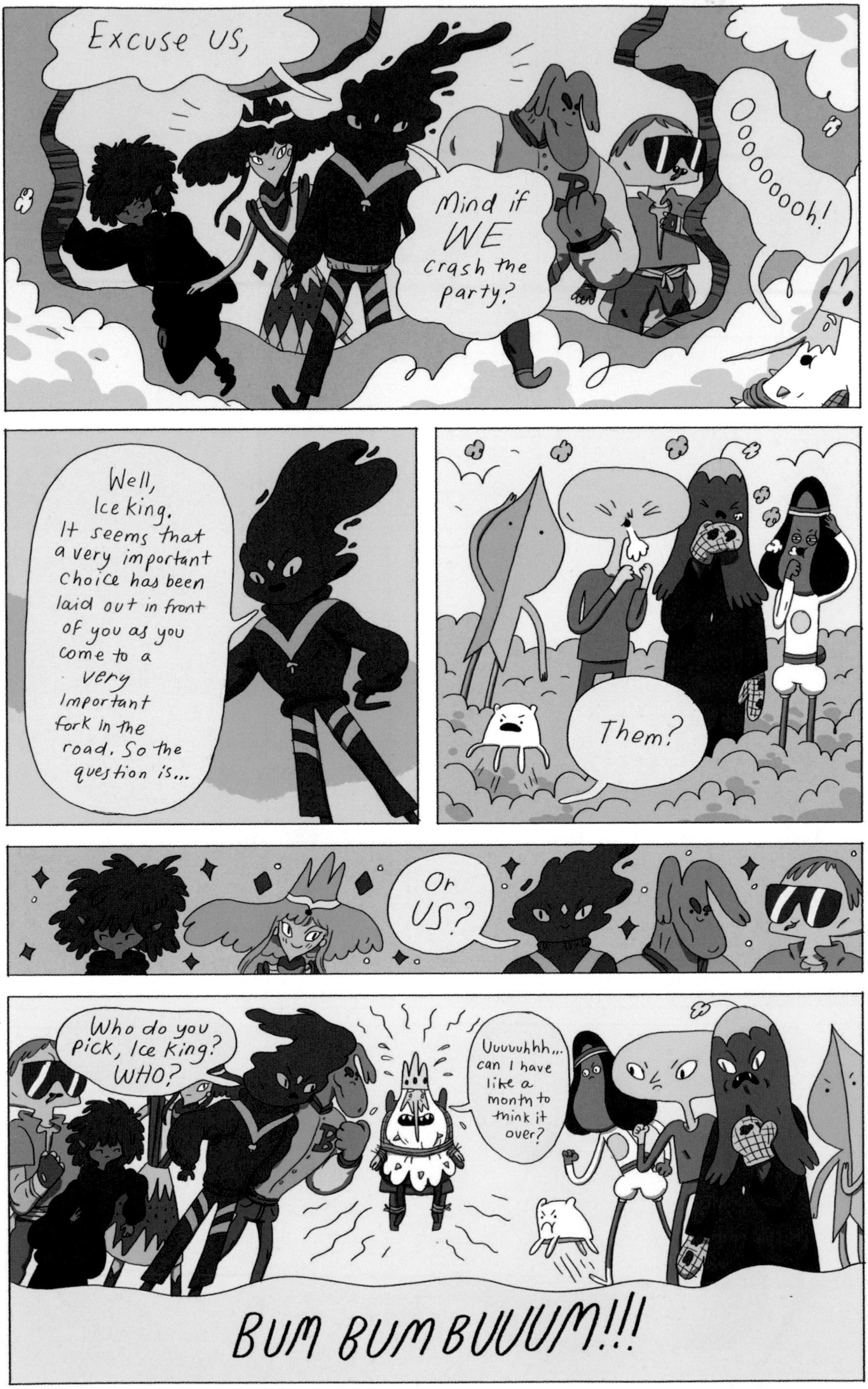
Excuse US,
Mind if WE crash the party?
Ooooooooh!
Well, Ice King. It seems that a very important choice has been laid out in front of you as you come to a very important fork in the road. So the question is...
Them?
Or US?
Who do you pick, Ice King? WHO?
Uuuuuhhh... can I have like a month to think it over?
BUM BUM BUUUM!!!

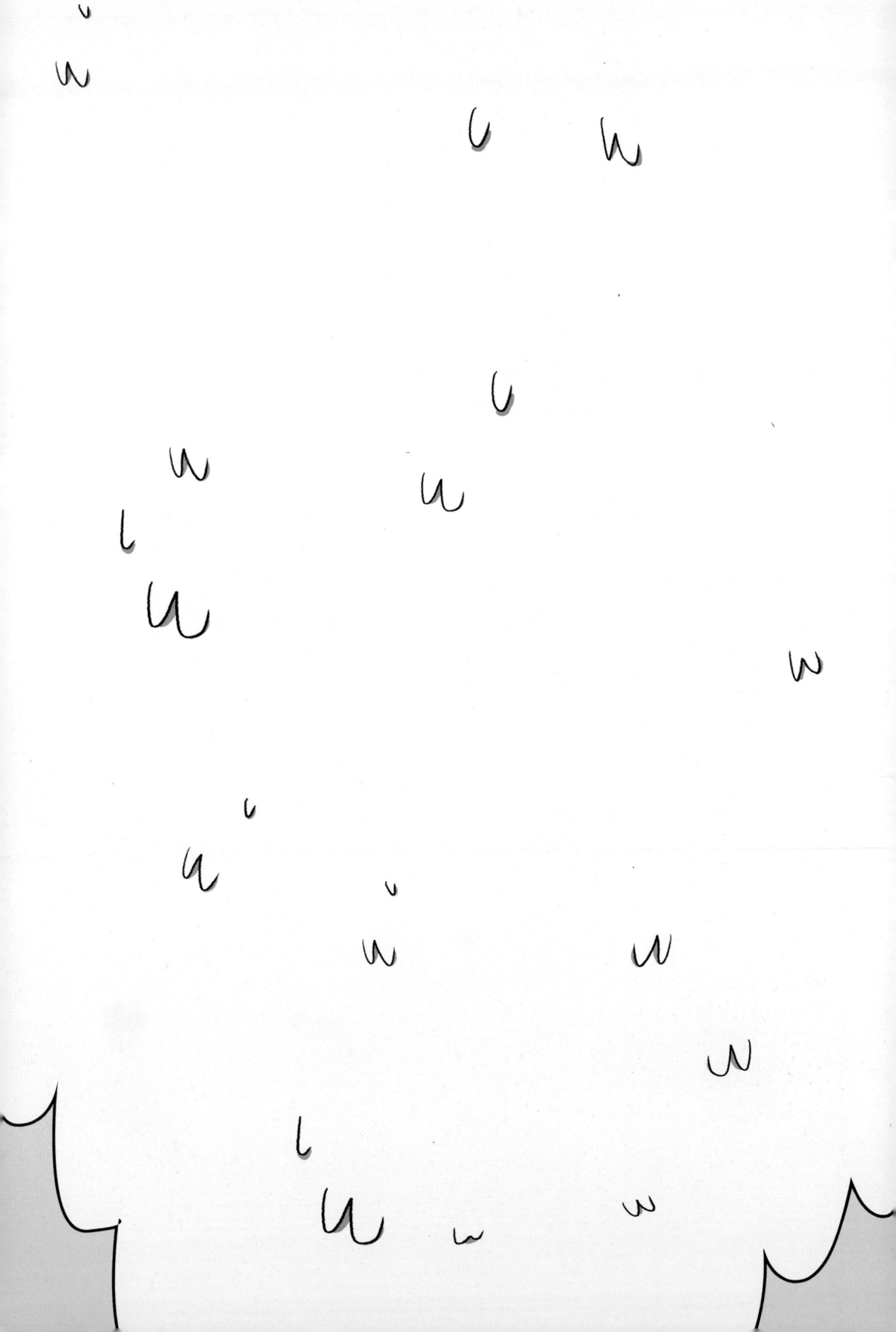

CHAPTER
FOUR

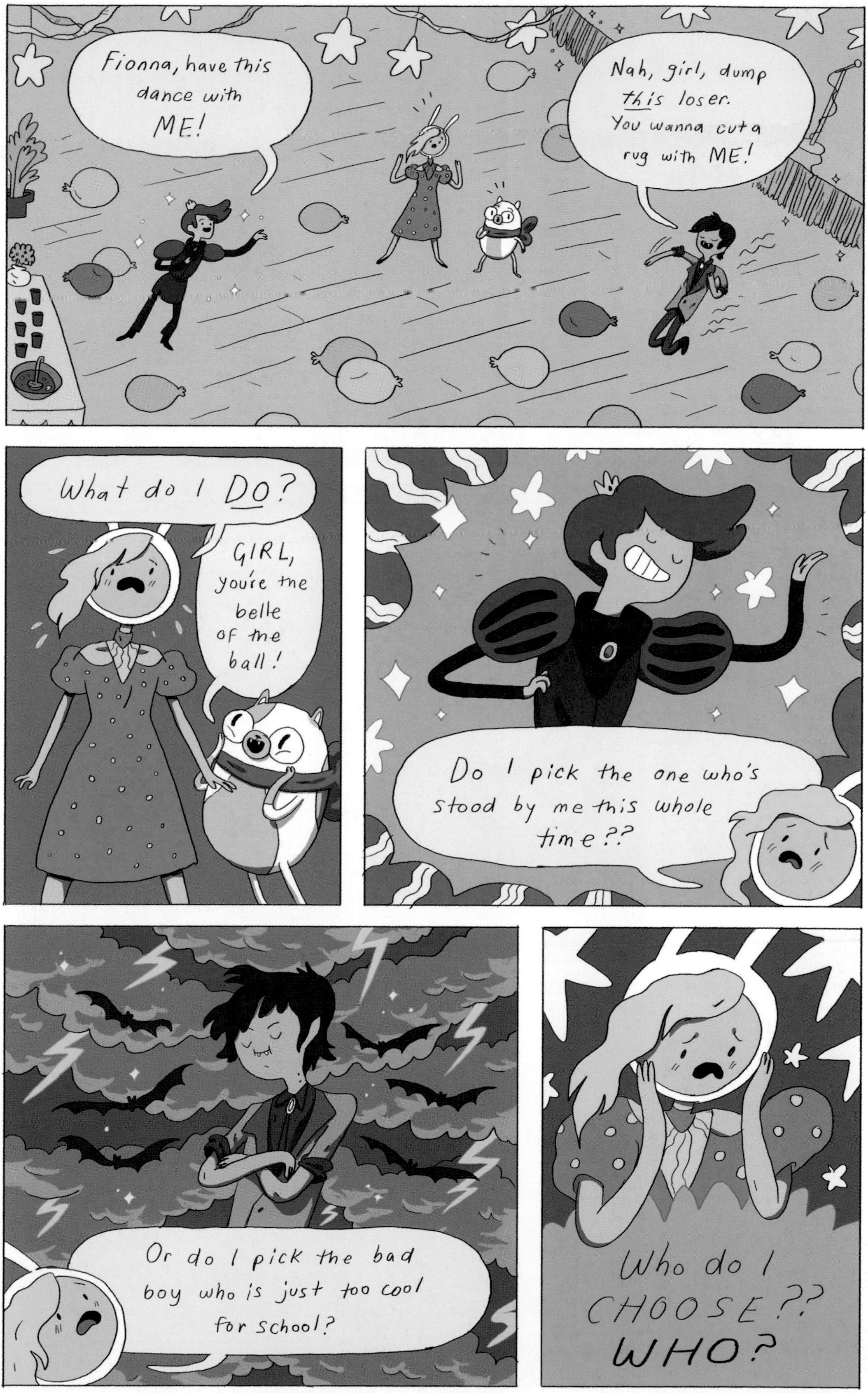

Fionna, have this dance with ME!
Nah, girl, dump this loser. You wanna cut a rug with ME!
What do I DO?
GIRL, you're the belle of the ball!
Do I pick the one who's stood by me this whole time??
Or do I pick the bad boy who is just too cool for school?
Who do I CHOOSE?? WHO?

Who do I CHOOSE?? WHO???

Come, Ice King, and pick a side.

Yeah, we've been standing like this for a while. My knees are killing me, man!

Pick a side NOW!

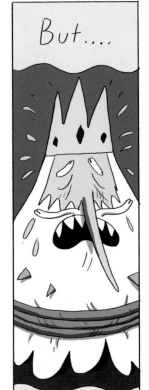

But....

...but there's pros and cons to booooooth!

Do I go old school with my original crew?

Or give in to the cool side, and hang out with these tough mama-jammas?

COOOOLL

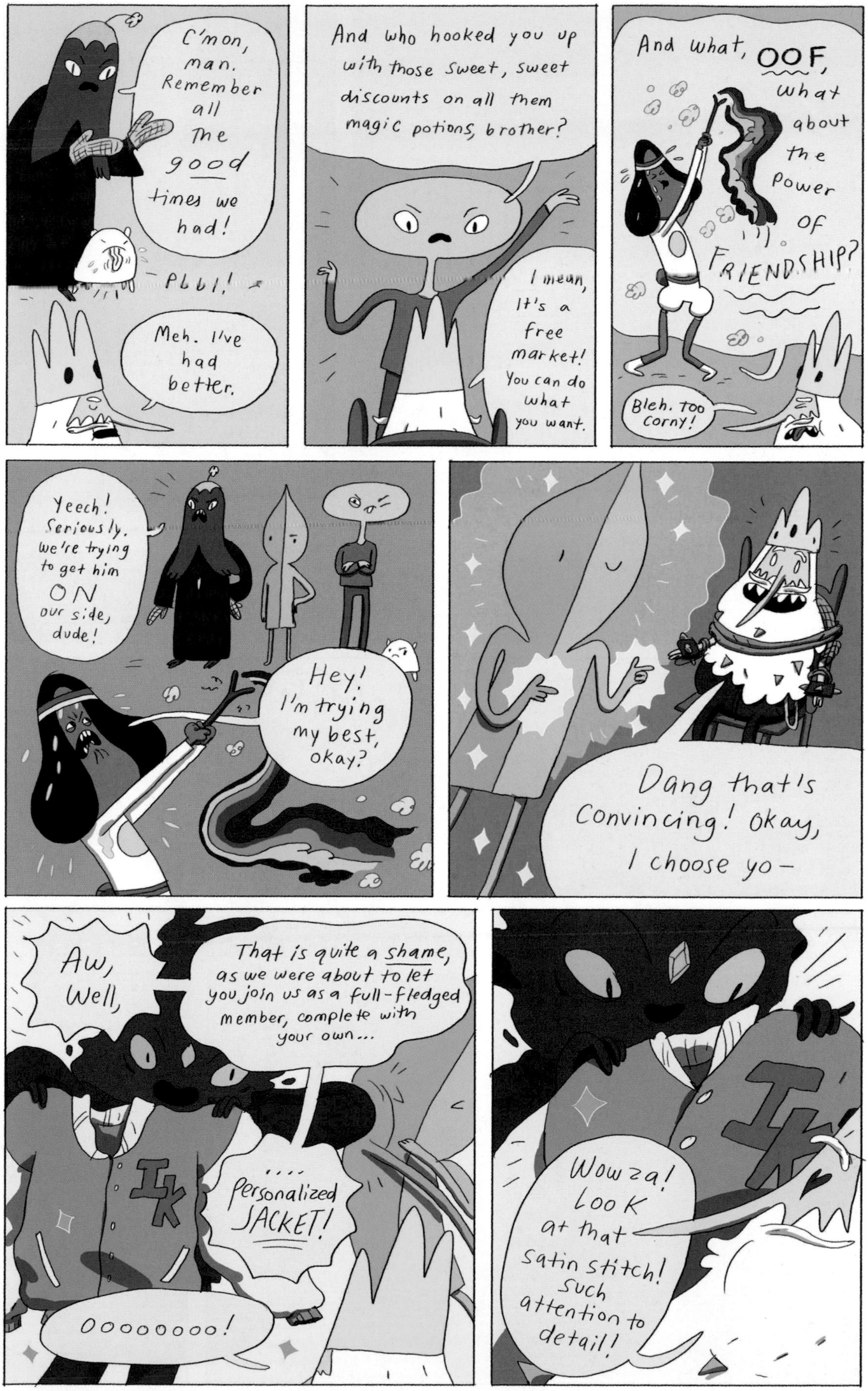
C'mon, man. Remember all the good times we had!
PLLL!
Meh. I've had better.
And who hooked you up with those sweet, sweet discounts on all them magic potions, brother?
I mean, it's a free market! You can do what you want.
And what, OOF, what about the power of FRIENDSHIP?
Bleh. Too corny!
Yeech! Seriously. We're trying to get him ON our side, dude!
Hey! I'm trying my best, okay?
Dang that's convincing! Okay, I choose yo—
Aw, Well,
That is quite a shame, as we were about to let you join us as a full-fledged member, complete with your own...
....Personalized JACKET!
OOOOOOOO!
Wowza! Look at that satin stitch! Such attention to detail!

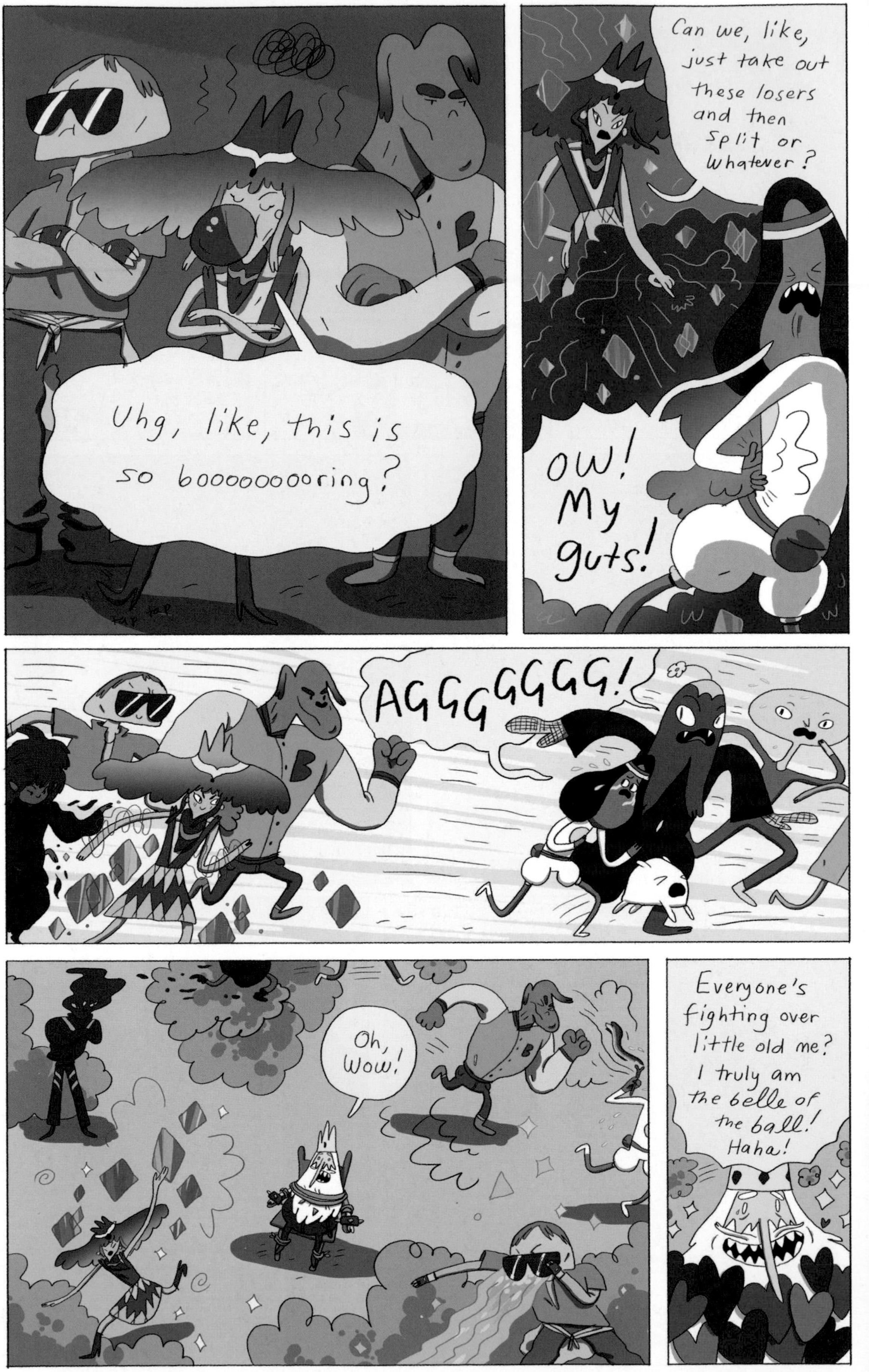
Uhg, like, this is so boooooooooring?
tap tap
Can we, like, just take out these losers and then split or whatever?
OW! My guts!
AGGGGGGG!
Oh, Wow!
Everyone's fighting over little old me? I truly am the belle of the ball! Haha!

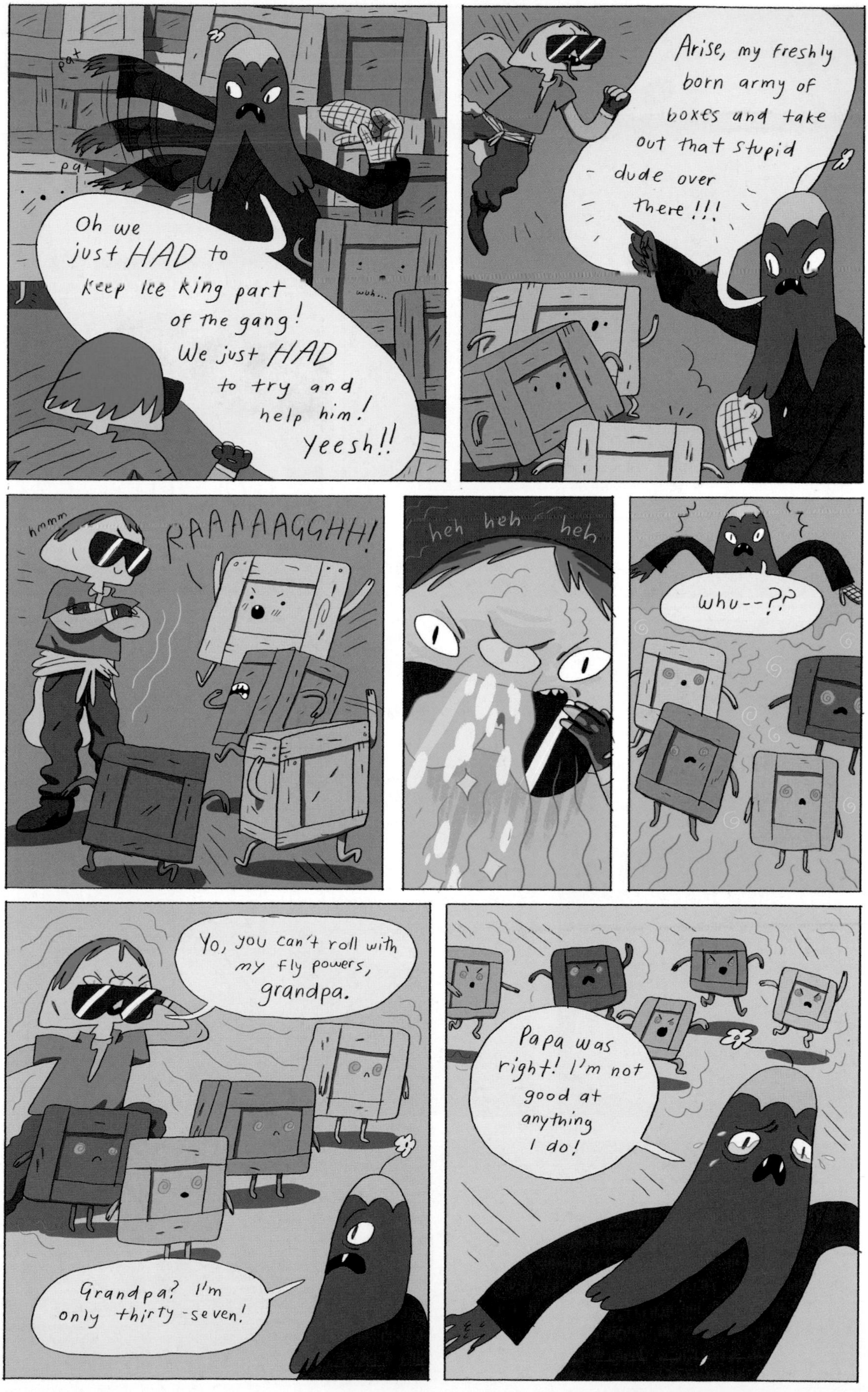
pat
pat
Oh we just HAD to keep Ice King part of the gang! We just HAD to try and help him! Yeesh!!
wuh...
Arise, my freshly born army of boxes and take out that stupid dude over there!!!
hmmm
RAAAAAGGHH!
heh heh heh
whu--?!?
Yo, you can't roll with my fly powers, grandpa.
Grandpa? I'm only thirty-seven!
Papa was right! I'm not good at anything I do!

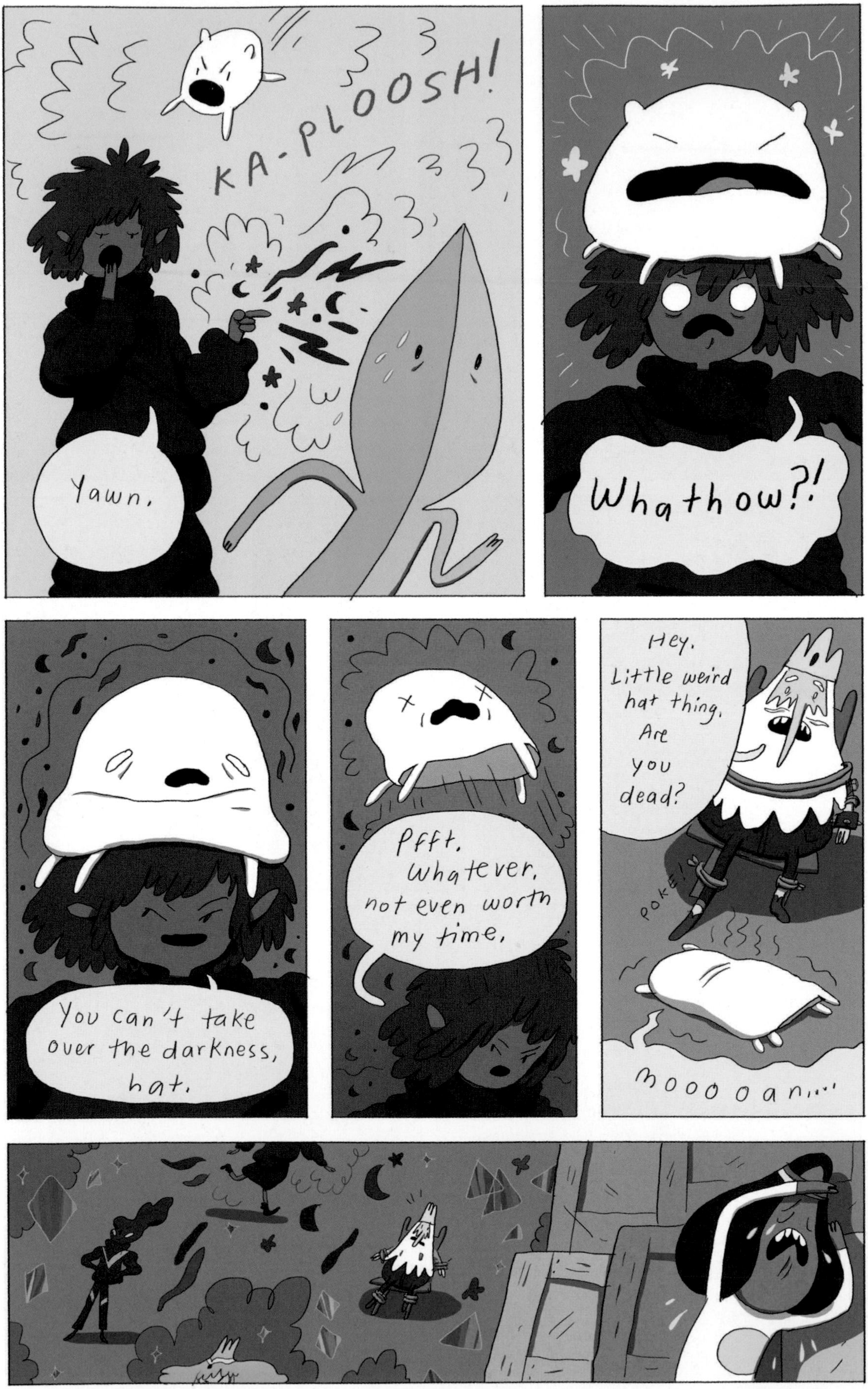
KA-PLOOSH!
Yawn.
Whathow?!
You can't take over the darkness, hat.
Pfft. Whatever. not even worth my time.
Hey. Little weird hat thing. Are you dead?
POKE
Moooo oan....

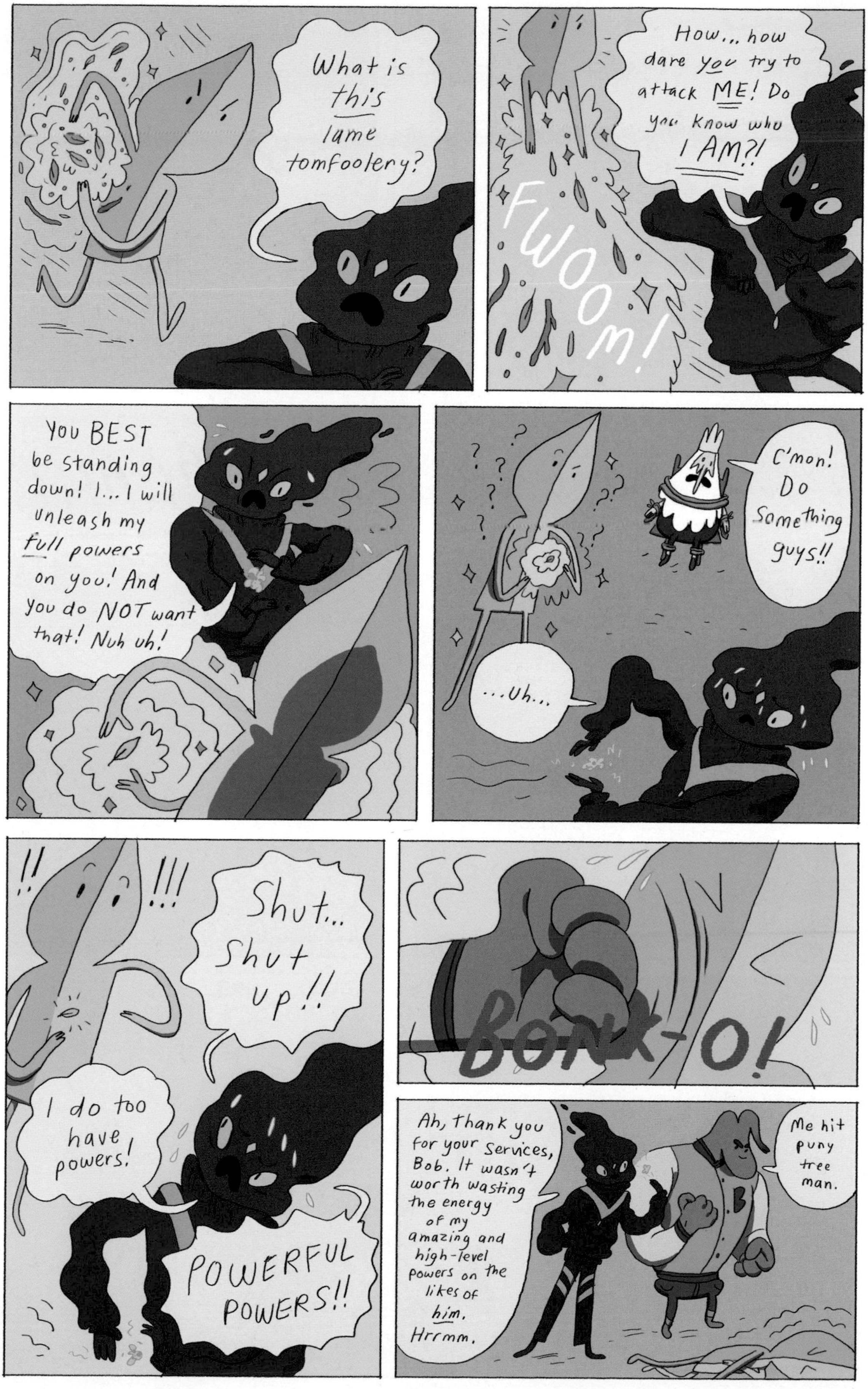

What is this lame tomfoolery?
How... how dare you try to attack ME! Do you know who I AM?!
FWOOM!
You BEST be standing down! I... I will unleash my full powers on you! And you do NOT want that! Nuh uh!
C'mon! Do Something guys!!
...Uh...
!!
!!!
Shut... Shut up!!
I do too have powers!
POWERFUL POWERS!!
BONK-O!
Ah, thank you for your Services, Bob. It wasn't worth wasting the energy of my amazing and high-level powers on the likes of him. Hrrmm.
Me hit puny tree man.

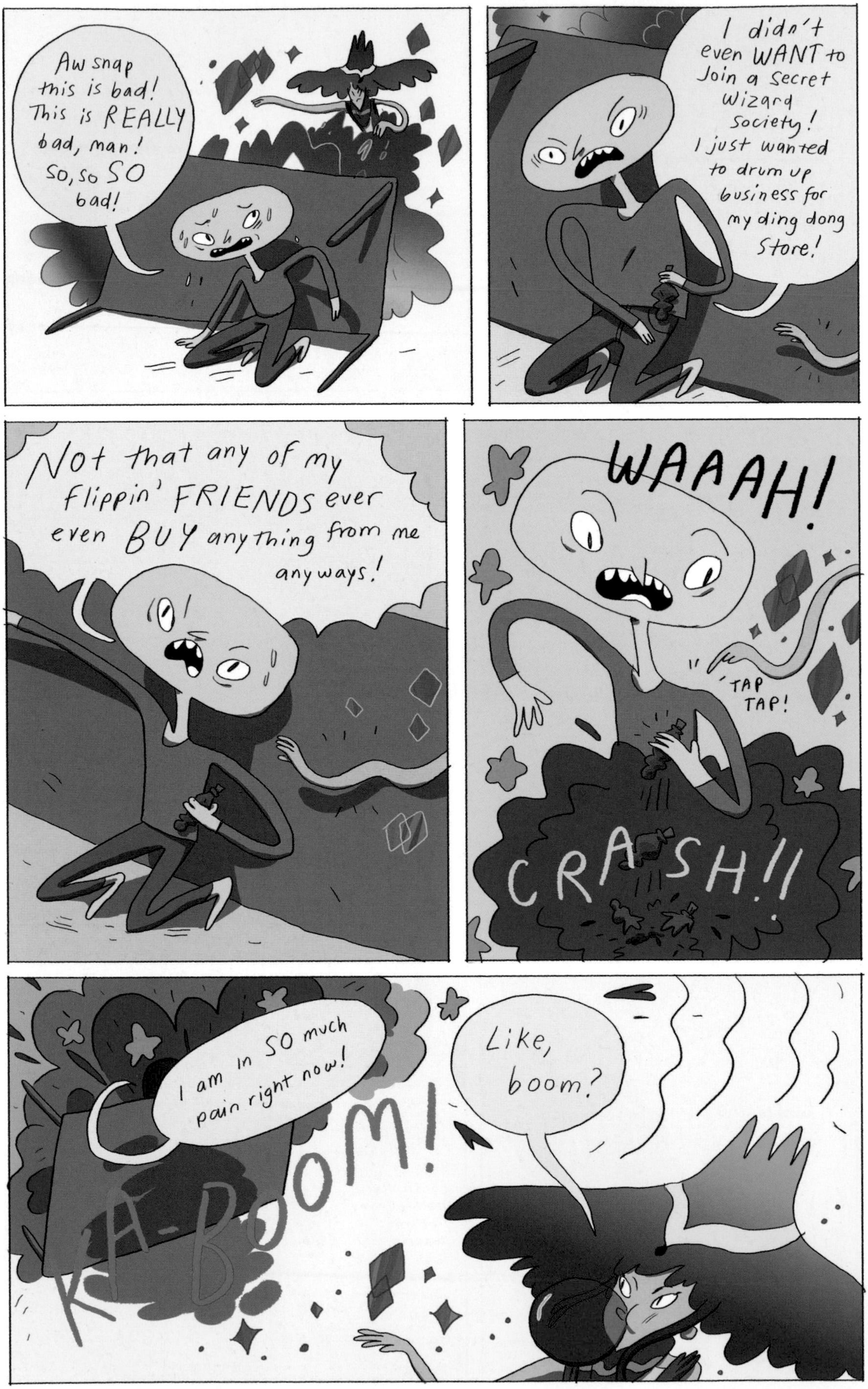
Aw snap this is bad! This is REALLY bad, man! So, so SO bad!
I didn't even WANT to Join a Secret Wizard Society! I just wanted to drum up business for my ding dong Store!
Not that any of my Flippin' FRIENDS ever even BUY anything from me anyways!
WAAAH!
TAP TAP!
CRASH!!
I am in SO much pain right now!
KA-BOOM!
Like, boom?

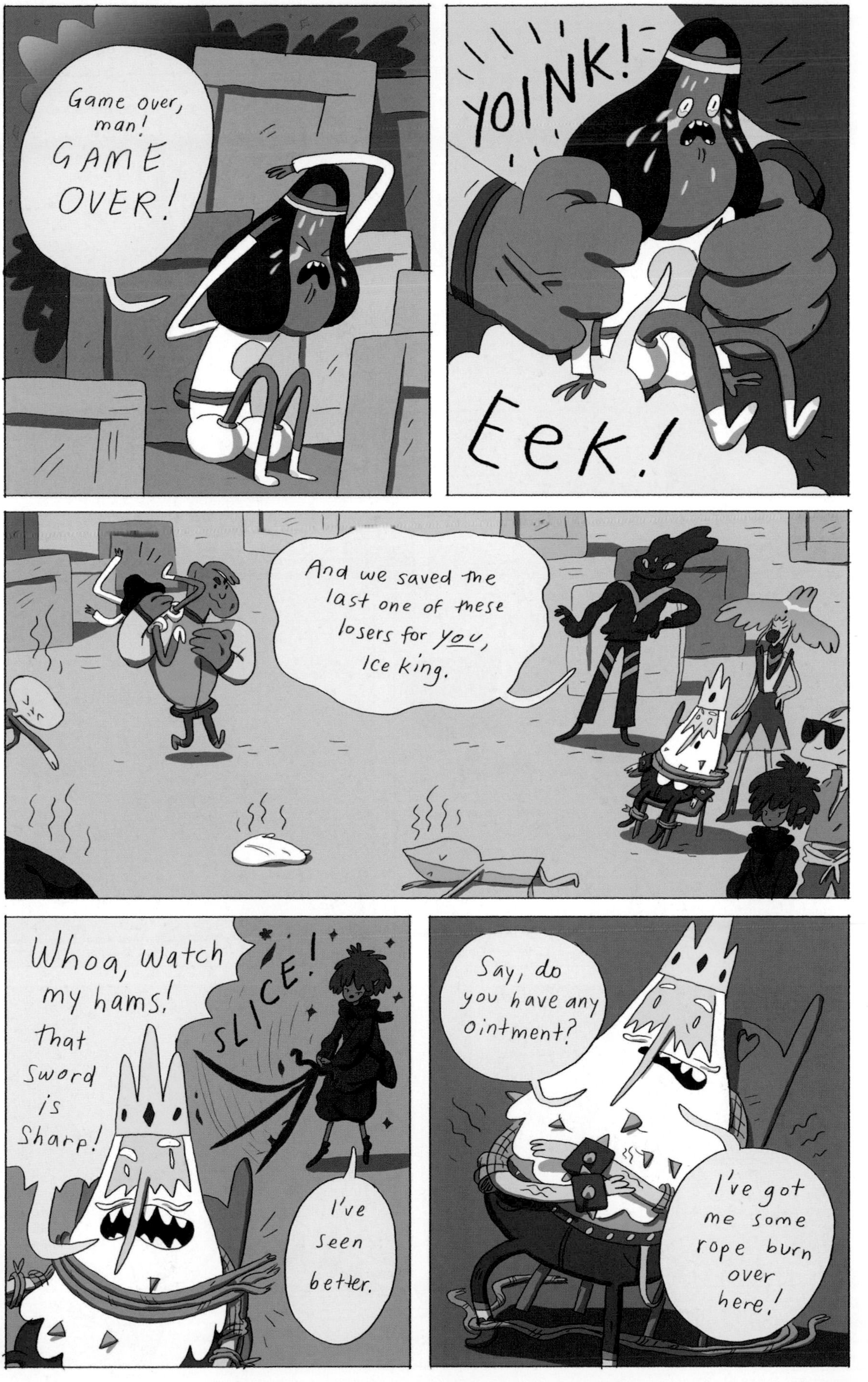
Game over, man! GAME OVER!
YOINK!
Eek!
And we saved the last one of these losers for you, Ice King.
Whoa, watch my hams! that sword is Sharp!
SLICE!
I've seen better.
Say, do you have any ointment?
I've got me some rope burn over here!

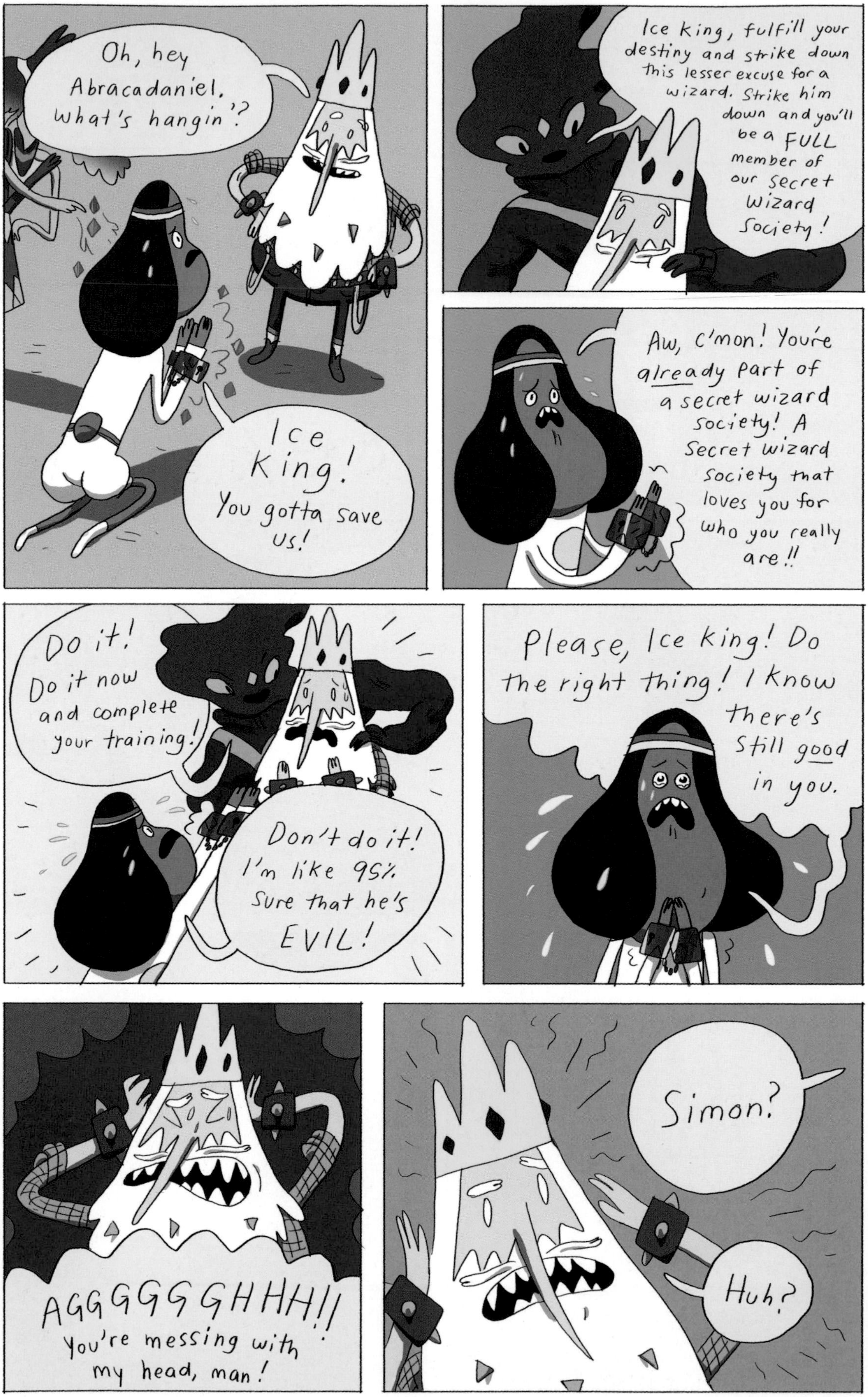
Oh, hey Abracadaniel, what's hangin'?
Ice King! You gotta save us!
Ice King, fulfill your destiny and strike down this lesser excuse for a wizard. Strike him down and you'll be a FULL member of our secret wizard society!
Aw, c'mon! You're already part of a secret wizard society! A secret wizard society that loves you for who you really are!!
Do it! Do it now and complete your training!
Don't do it! I'm like 95% sure that he's EVIL!
Please, Ice King! Do the right thing! I know there's still good in you.
AGGGGGGHHH!! You're messing with my head, man!
Simon?
Huh?

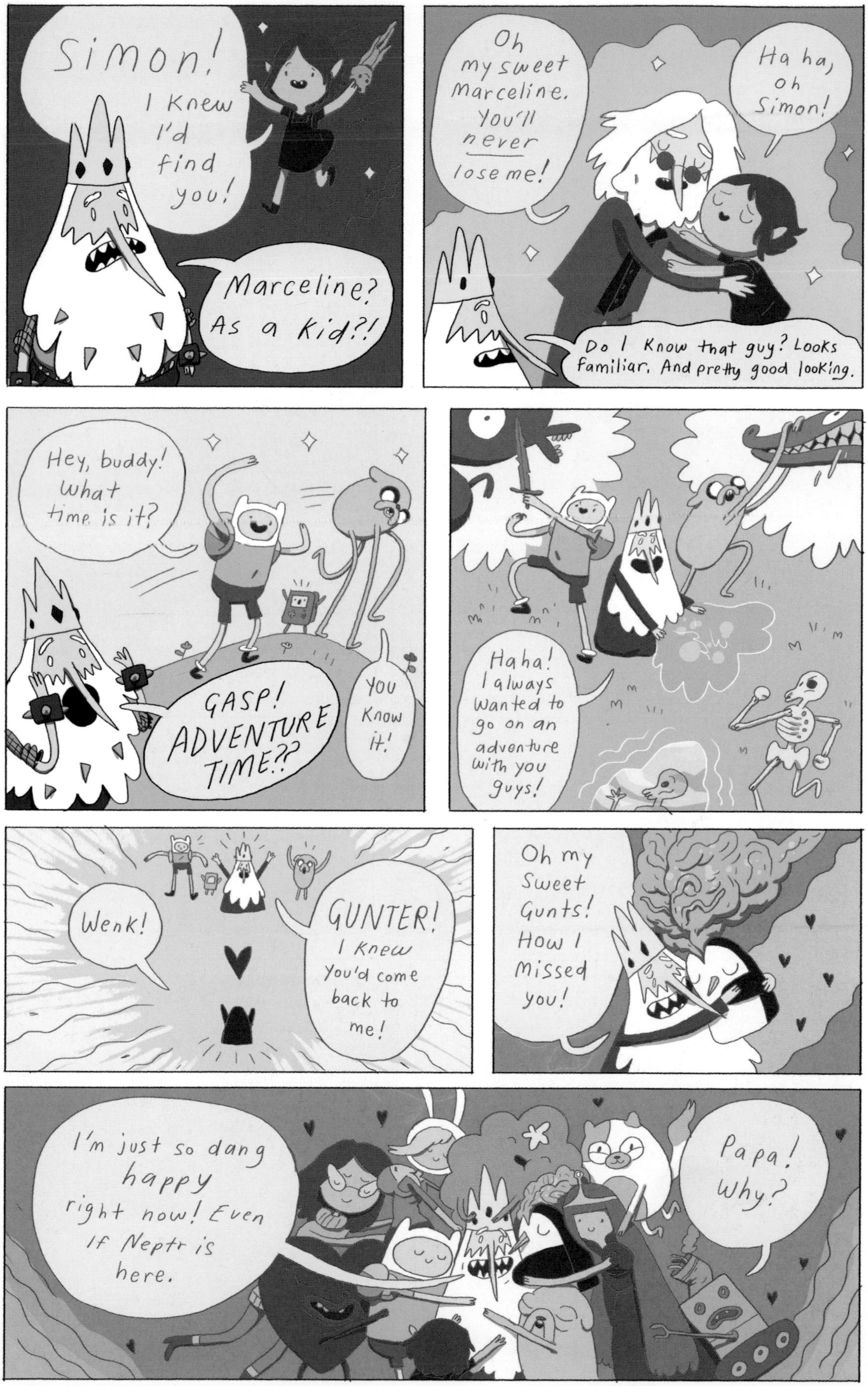

Simon! I knew I'd find you!
Marceline? As a kid?!
Oh my sweet Marceline. You'll never lose me!
Ha ha, oh Simon!
Do I know that guy? Looks familiar. And pretty good looking.
Hey, buddy! What time is it?
GASP! ADVENTURE TIME??
You know it!
Haha! I always wanted to go on an adventure with you guys!
Wenk!
GUNTER! I knew you'd come back to me!
Oh my sweet Gunts! How I missed you!
I'm just so dang happy right now! Even if Neptr is here.
Papa! Why?

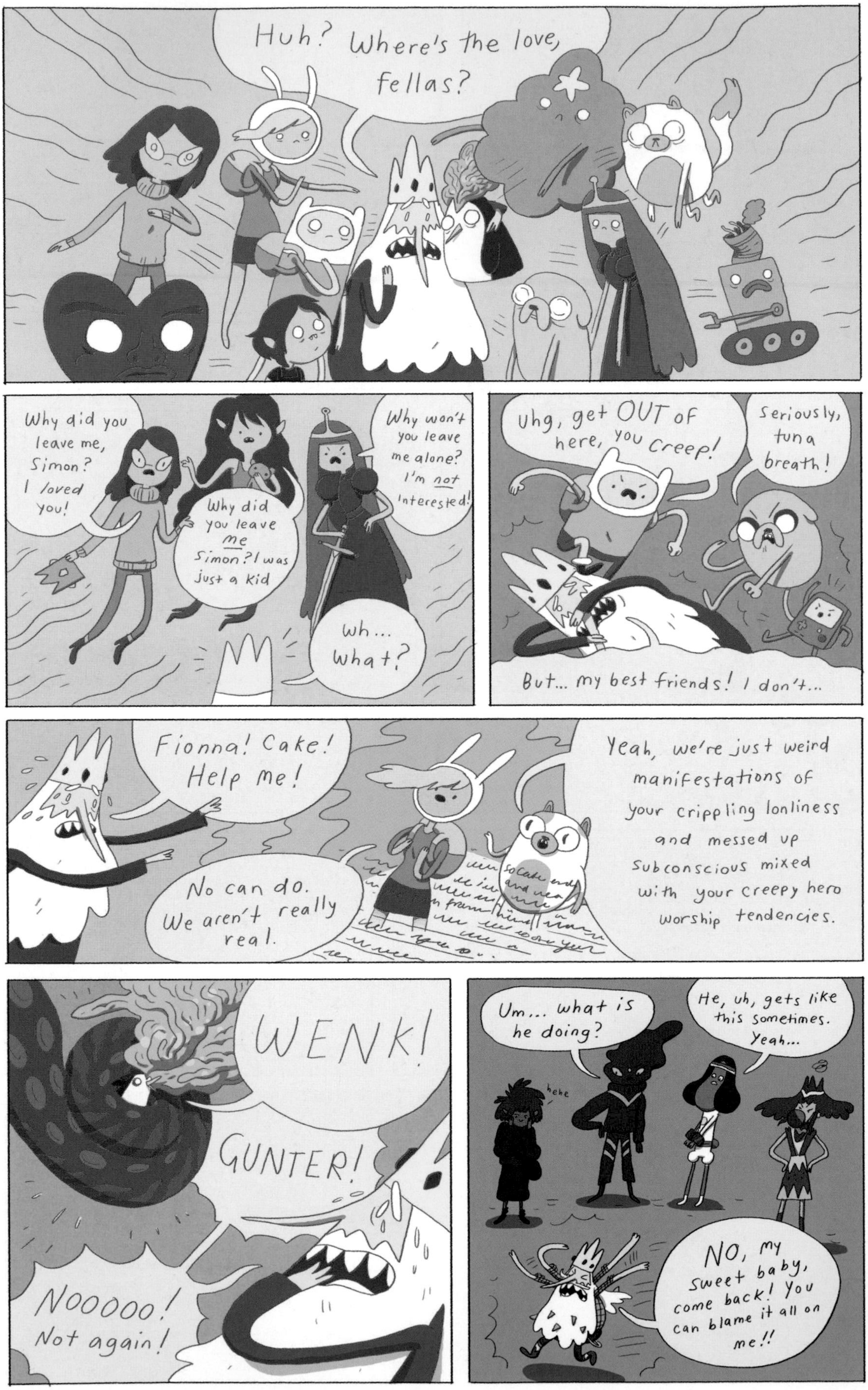

Huh? Where's the love, fellas?
Why did you leave me, Simon? I loved you!
Why did you leave me Simon?! I was just a kid
Why won't you leave me alone? I'm not interested!
wh... what?
Uhg, get OUT of here, you creep!
Seriously, tuna breath!
But... my best friends! I don't...
Fionna! Cake! Help me!
No can do. We aren't really real.
Yeah, we're just weird manifestations of your crippling lonliness and messed up subconscious mixed with your creepy hero worship tendencies.
WENK!
GUNTER!
NOOOOO! Not again!
Um... what is he doing?
He, uh, gets like this sometimes. Yeah...
hehe
NO, my sweet baby, come back! You can blame it all on me!!

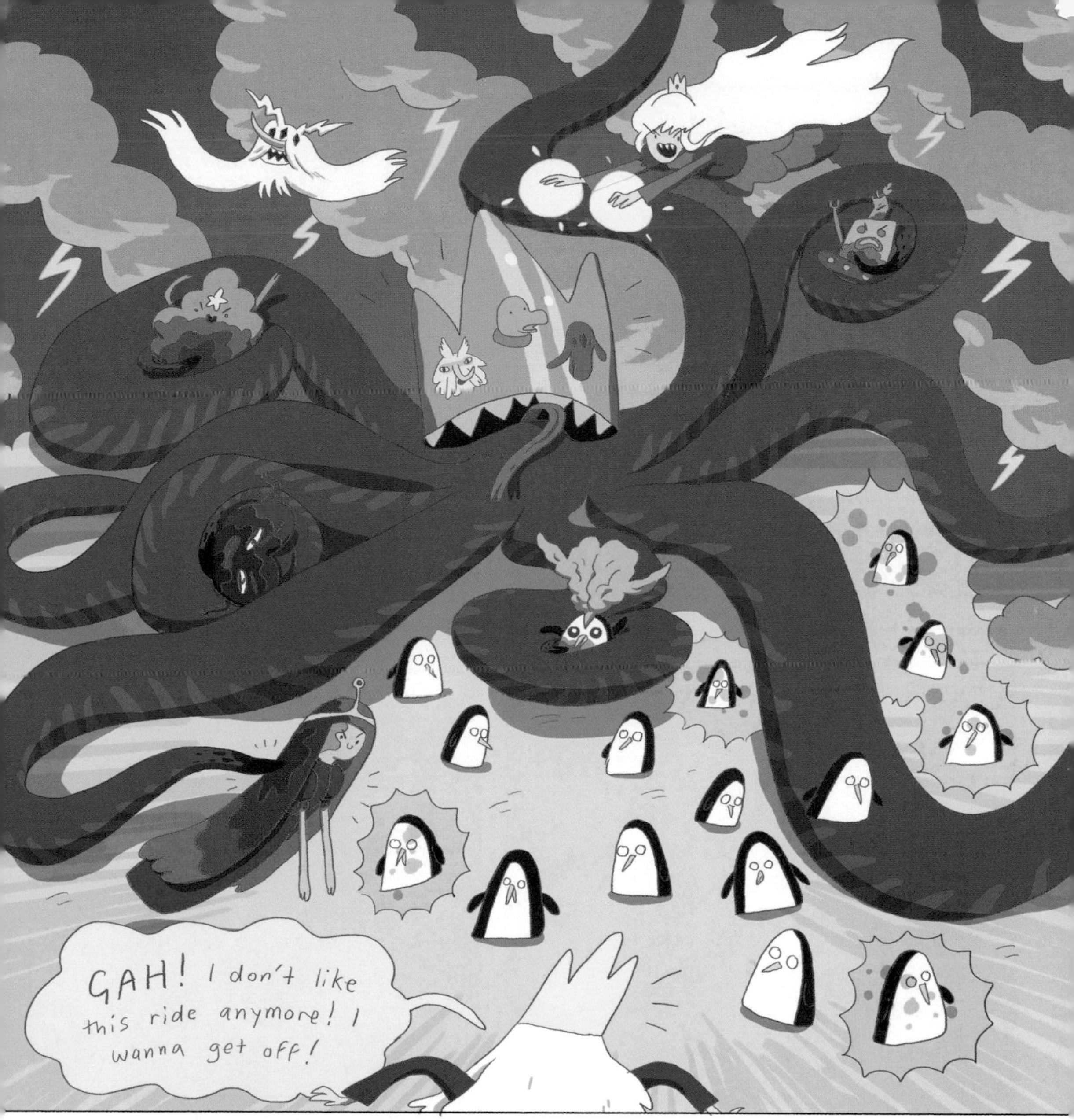
GAH! I don't like this ride anymore! I wanna get off!

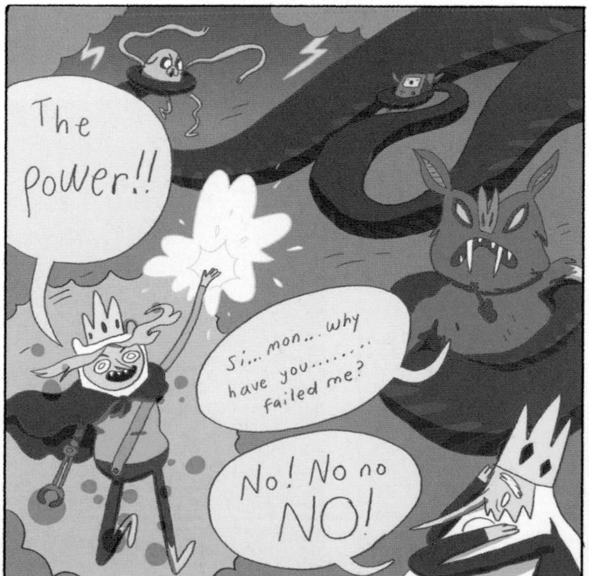
The power!!
Si... mon... why have you........ failed me?
No! No no NO!

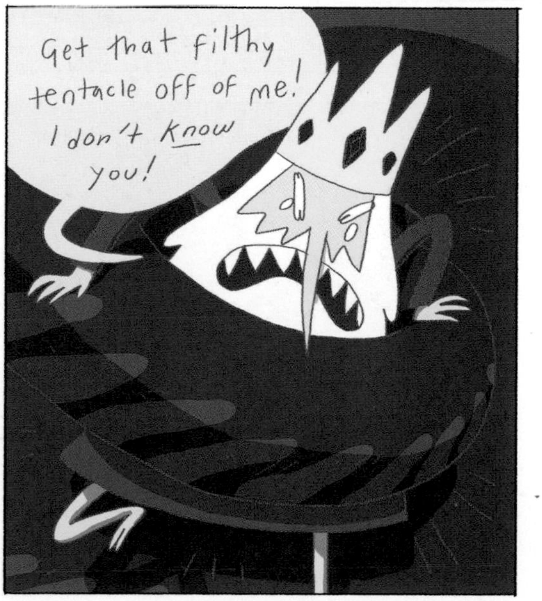
Get that filthy tentacle off of me! I don't know you!

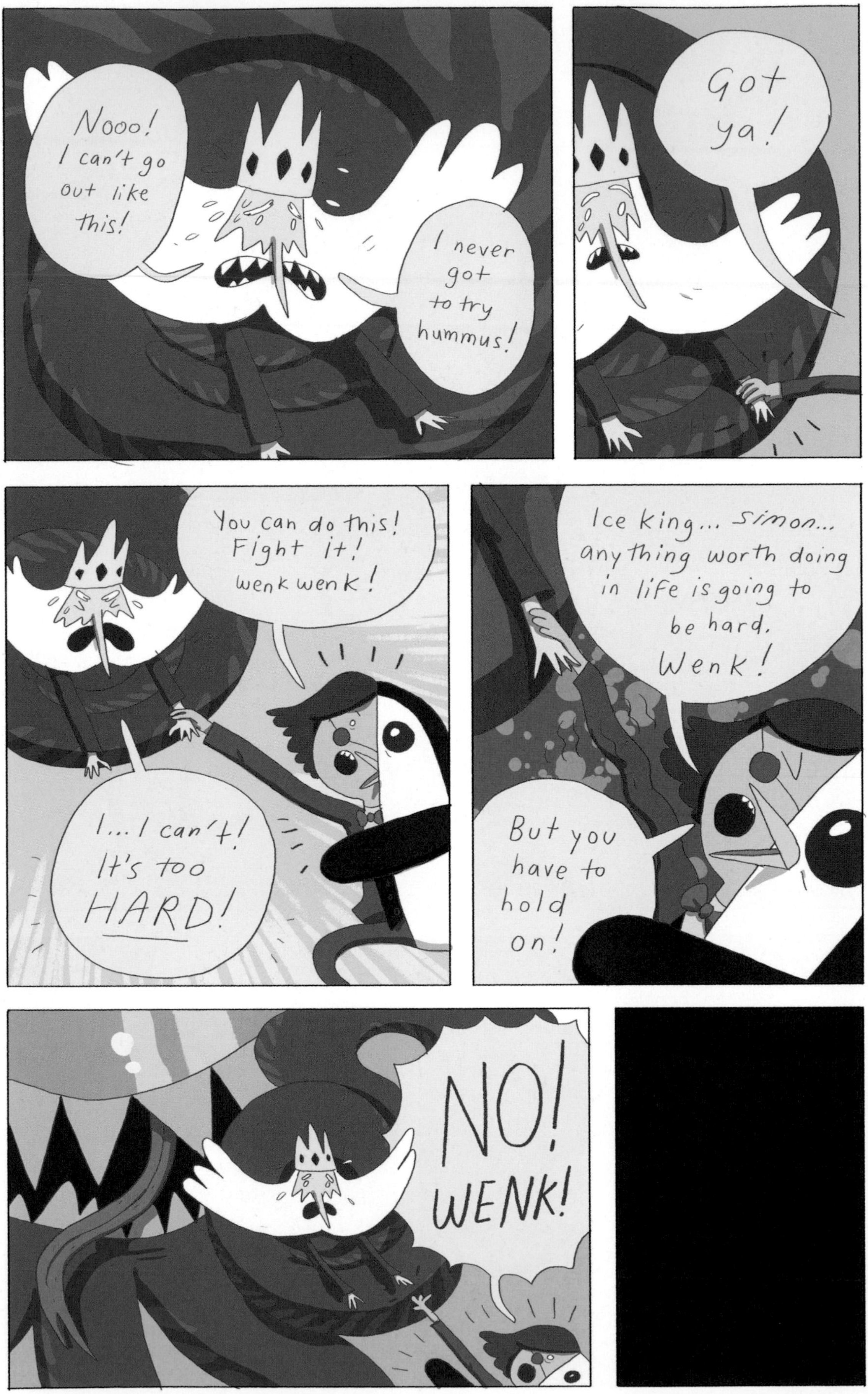
Nooo! I can't go out like this!
I never got to try hummus!
Got ya!
You can do this! Fight it! wenk wenk!
I... I can't! It's too HARD!
Ice king... simon... anything worth doing in life is going to be hard. Wenk!
But you have to hold on!
NO! WENK!

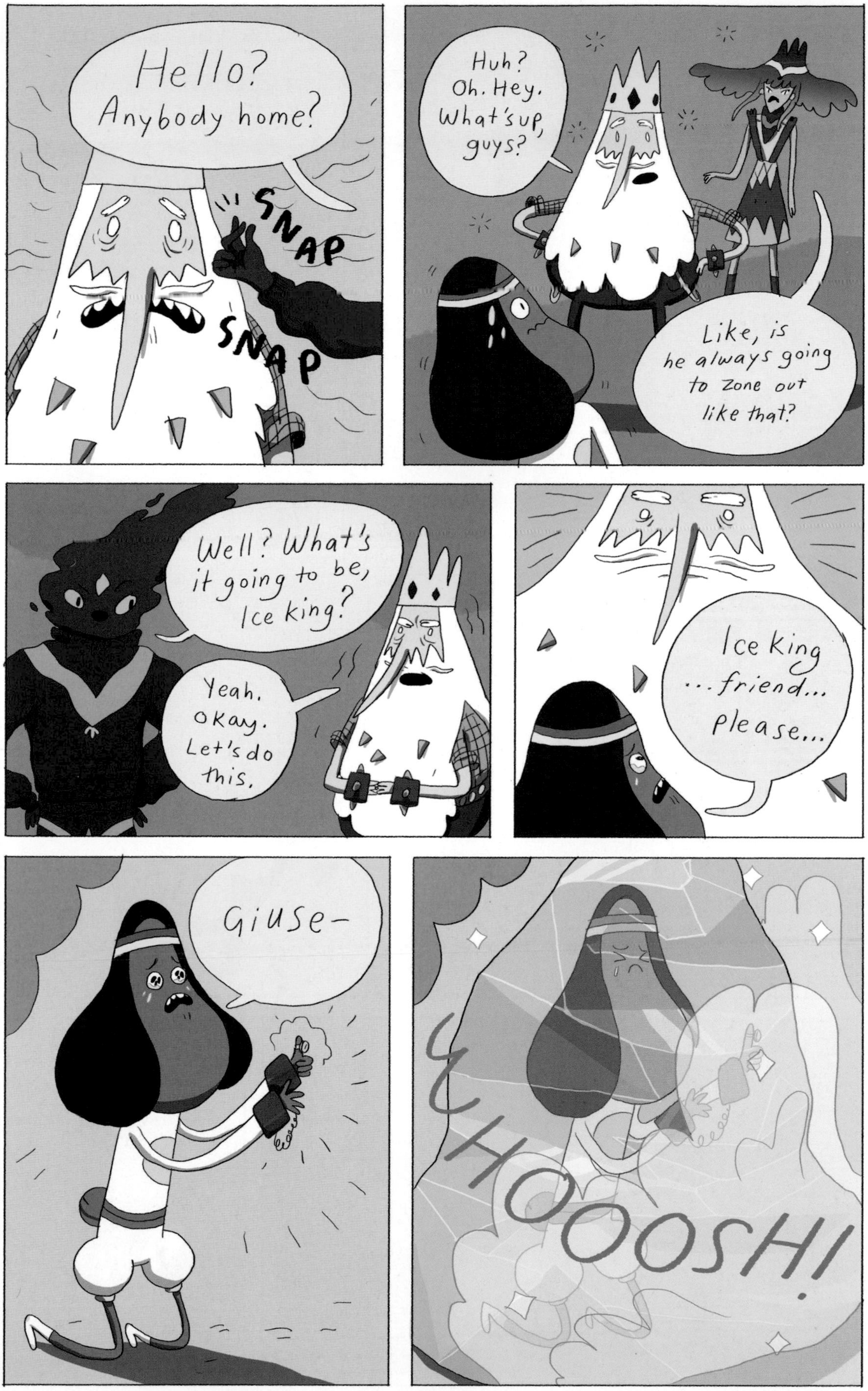
Hello? Anybody home?
SNAP
SNAP
Huh? Oh. Hey. What's up, guys?
Like, is he always going to zone out like that?
Well? What's it going to be, Ice King?
Yeah. Okay. Let's do this.
Ice King ...friend... please...
Giuse-
WHOOOSH!

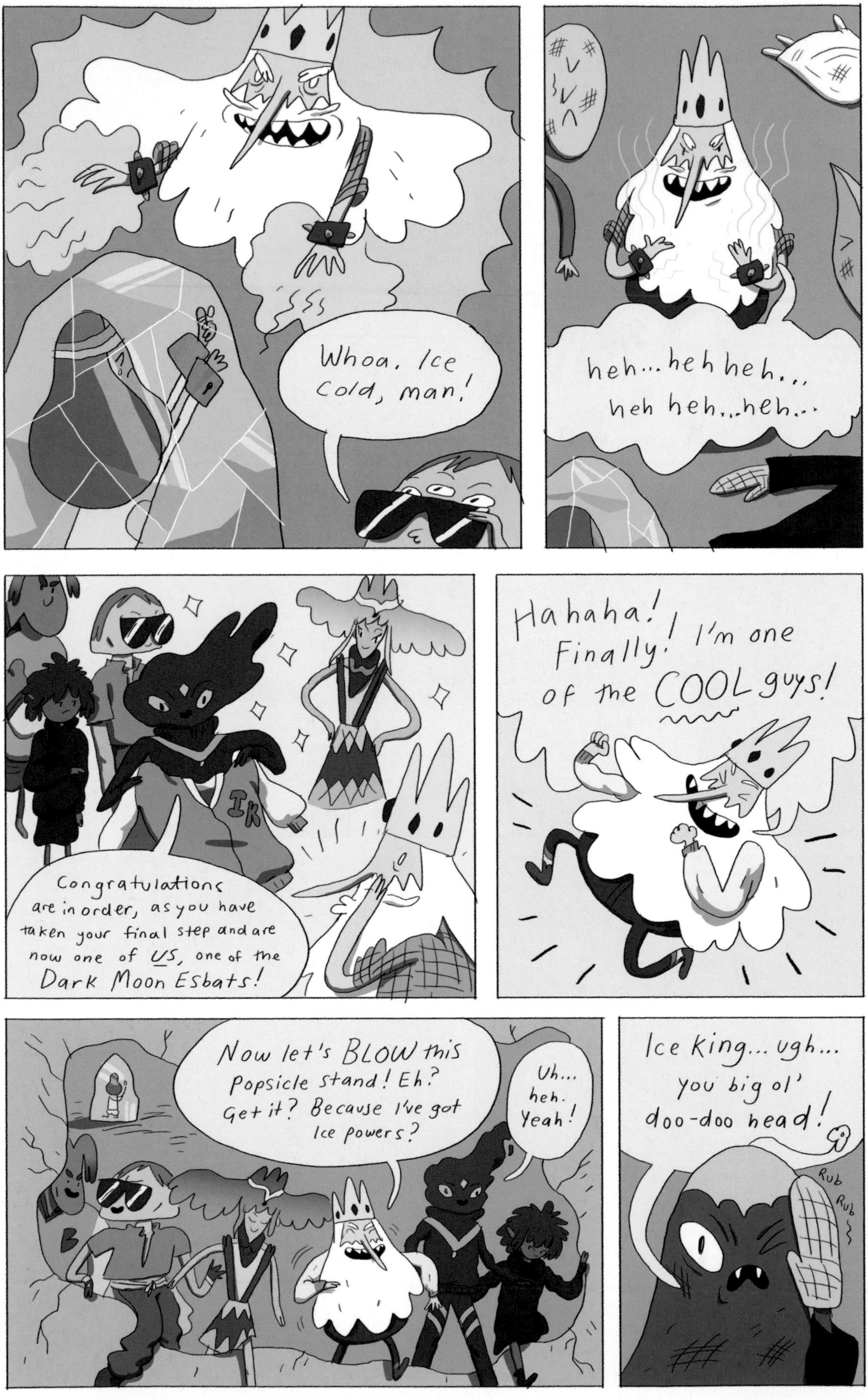

Whoa. Ice cold, man!
heh... heh heh... heh heh... heh...
Congratulations are in order, as you have taken your final step and are now one of US, one of the Dark Moon Esbats!
Hahaha! Finally! I'm one of the COOL guys!
Now let's BLOW this popsicle stand! Eh? Get it? Because I've got ice powers?
Uh... heh. Yeah!
Ice King... ugh... you big ol' doo-doo head!
Rub
Rub

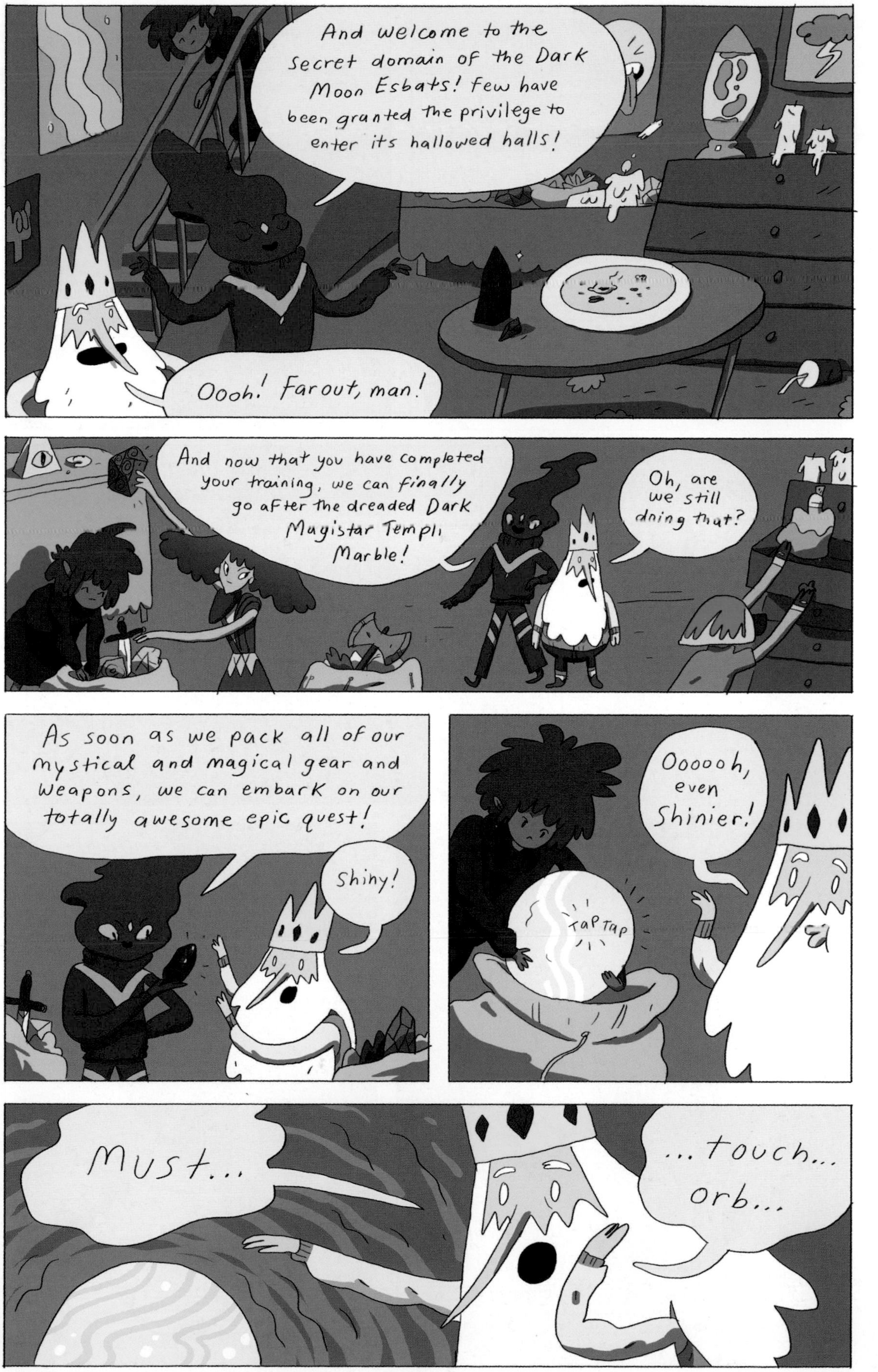
And welcome to the secret domain of the Dark Moon Esbats! Few have been granted the privilege to enter its hallowed halls!
Oooh! Far out, man!
And now that you have completed your training, we can finally go after the dreaded Dark Magistar Templi Marble!
Oh, are we still doing that?
As soon as we pack all of our mystical and magical gear and weapons, we can embark on our totally awesome epic quest!
Shiny!
Oooooh, even Shinier!
TAP TAP
Must...
...touch... orb...

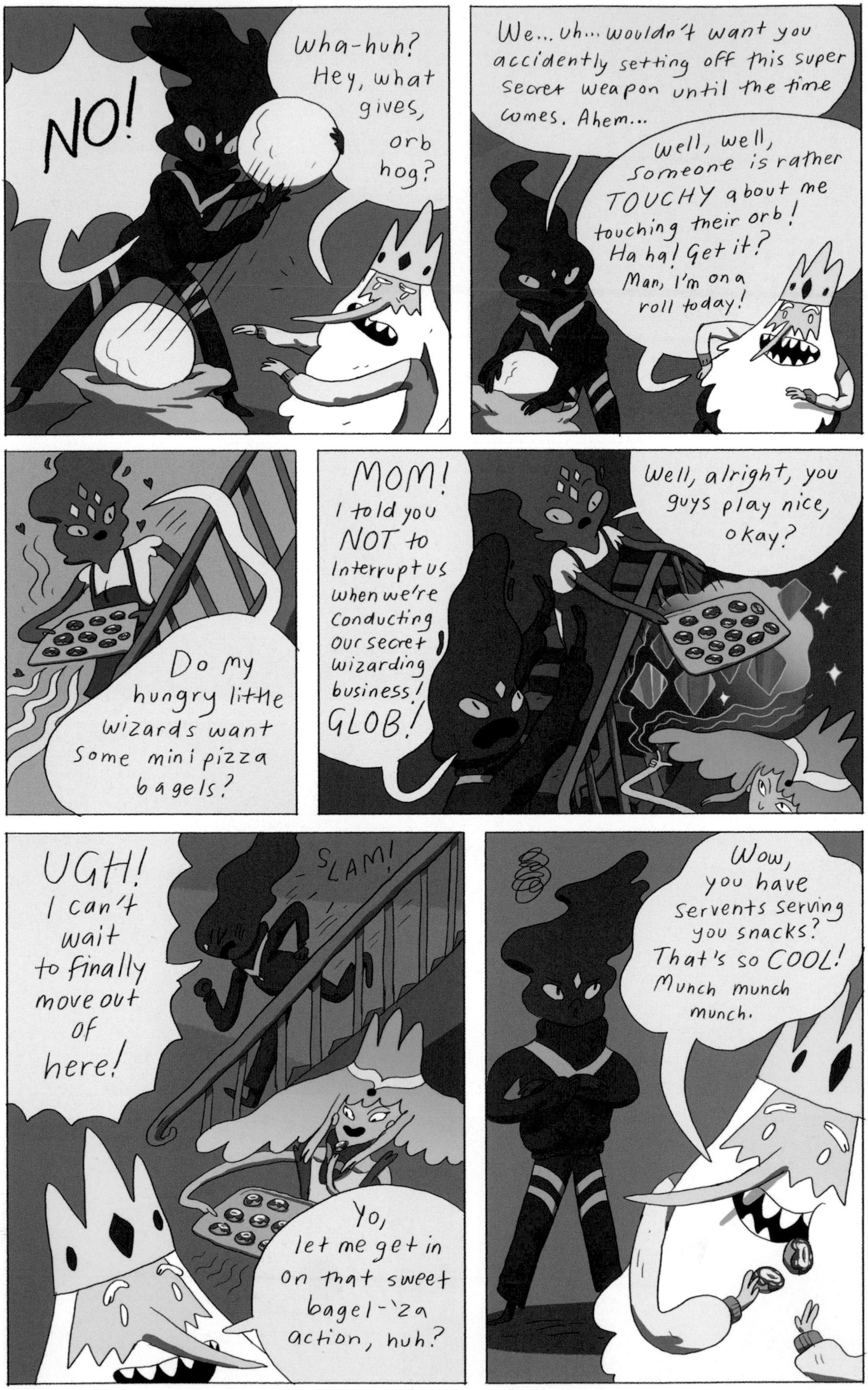
NO!
Wha-huh? Hey, what gives, orb hog?
We...uh...wouldn't want you accidently setting off this super secret weapon until the time comes. Ahem...
Well, well, Someone is rather TOUCHY about me touching their orb! Ha ha! Get it? Man, I'm on a roll today!
Do my hungry little wizards want some mini pizza bagels?
MOM! I told you NOT to Interrupt us when we're Conducting our secret wizarding business! GLOB!
Well, alright, you guys play nice, okay?
UGH! I can't wait to finally move out of here!
SLAM!
Yo, let me get in on that sweet bagel-'za action, huh?
Wow, you have servents serving you snacks? That's so COOL! Munch munch munch.

Come, my Dark Moon Esbats! Let us go and finally take down the Dark Magistar Templi Marble and claim our GLORY!

So, uh, we take a right at the fork ... I guess?

Hrmm.

Flip

Flip

Oh! A left at the fork. Hey, give me a break, I never earned that merit badge, okay?

So what's up with this Marble guy? Like, what's his bag, man?

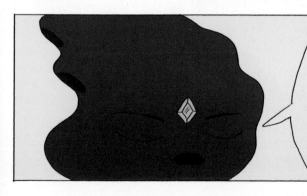

The legend, the myth, of the wizard known as Marble began hundreds and hundreds of thousands of moons ago. Or so the story goes.

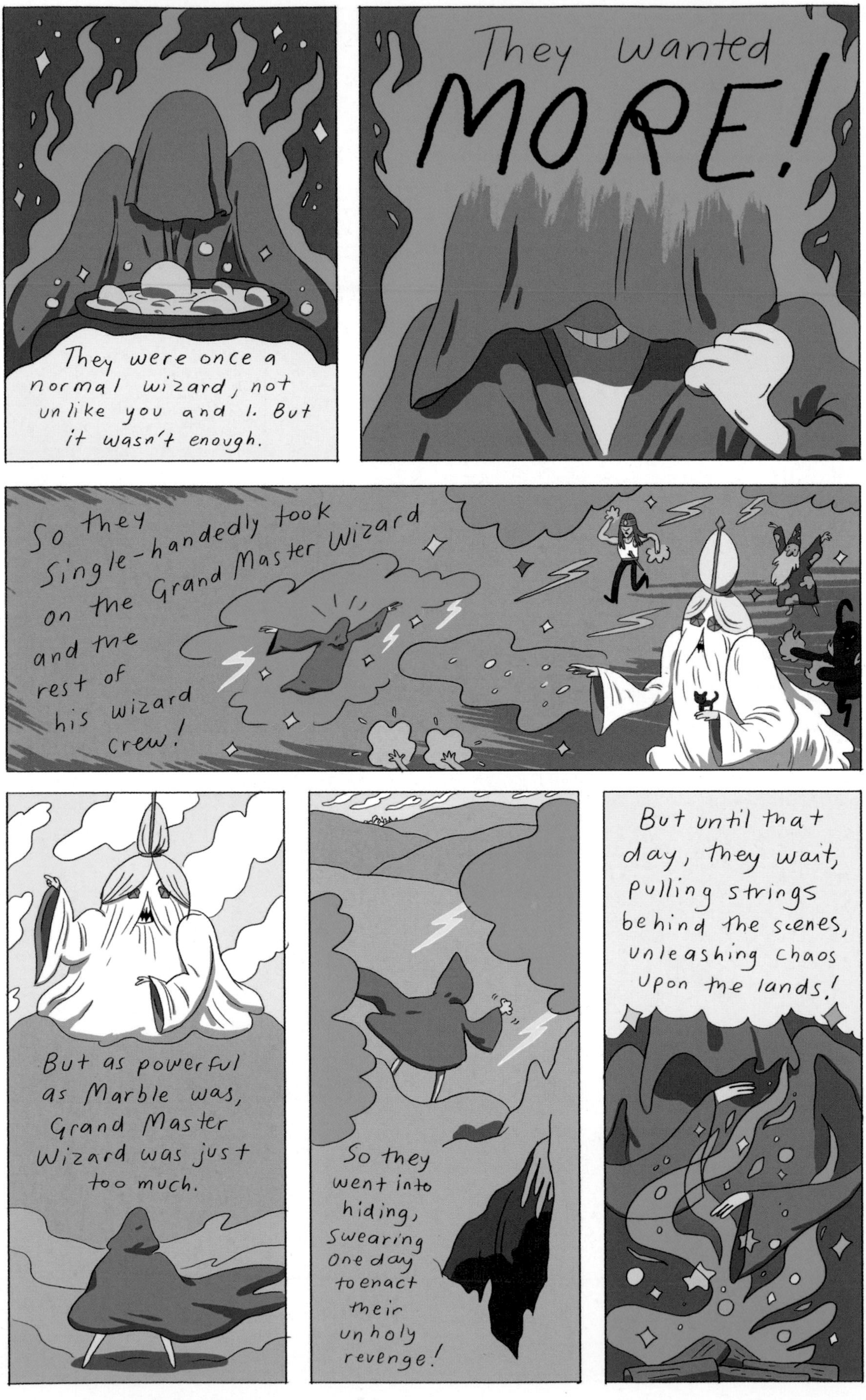
They were once a normal wizard, not unlike you and I. But it wasn't enough.
They wanted MORE!
So they single-handedly took on the Grand Master Wizard and the rest of his wizard crew!
But as powerful as Marble was, Grand Master Wizard was just too much.
So they went into hiding, swearing one day to enact their unholy revenge!
But until that day, they wait, pulling strings behind the scenes, unleashing chaos upon the lands!

And over the centuries MANY wizards tried to seek them out and make a name for themselves. And they have all failed or met their DOOM!

But not us! NOT the Dark Moon Esbats!

According to this map, this _should_ be the entrance.

Aw man!

You've gotta be kidding me.

Lame, yo!

Ugh! We came all this way and it's NOT the home of the Dark Magistar Templi Marble! I wasted five wizard bucks on that piece of junk map!

GO AWAY! seriously!

NOT the home of Dark Magistar Templi Marble!

Ain't no evil wizards here! Nuh uh!

SCRAM!

hmm... Wait a second...

Hey! Guys! Wait up!

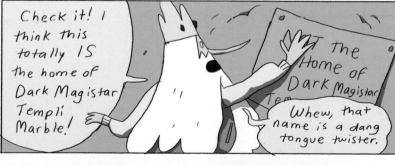

Check it! I think this totally IS the home of Dark Magistar Templi Marble!

The Home of Dark Magistar Tem

Whew, that name is a dang tongue twister.

Whoa, outta sight, Ice King!

Yeah. Good job. Or whatever.

Hey, sometimes it takes a madman to catch a madman.

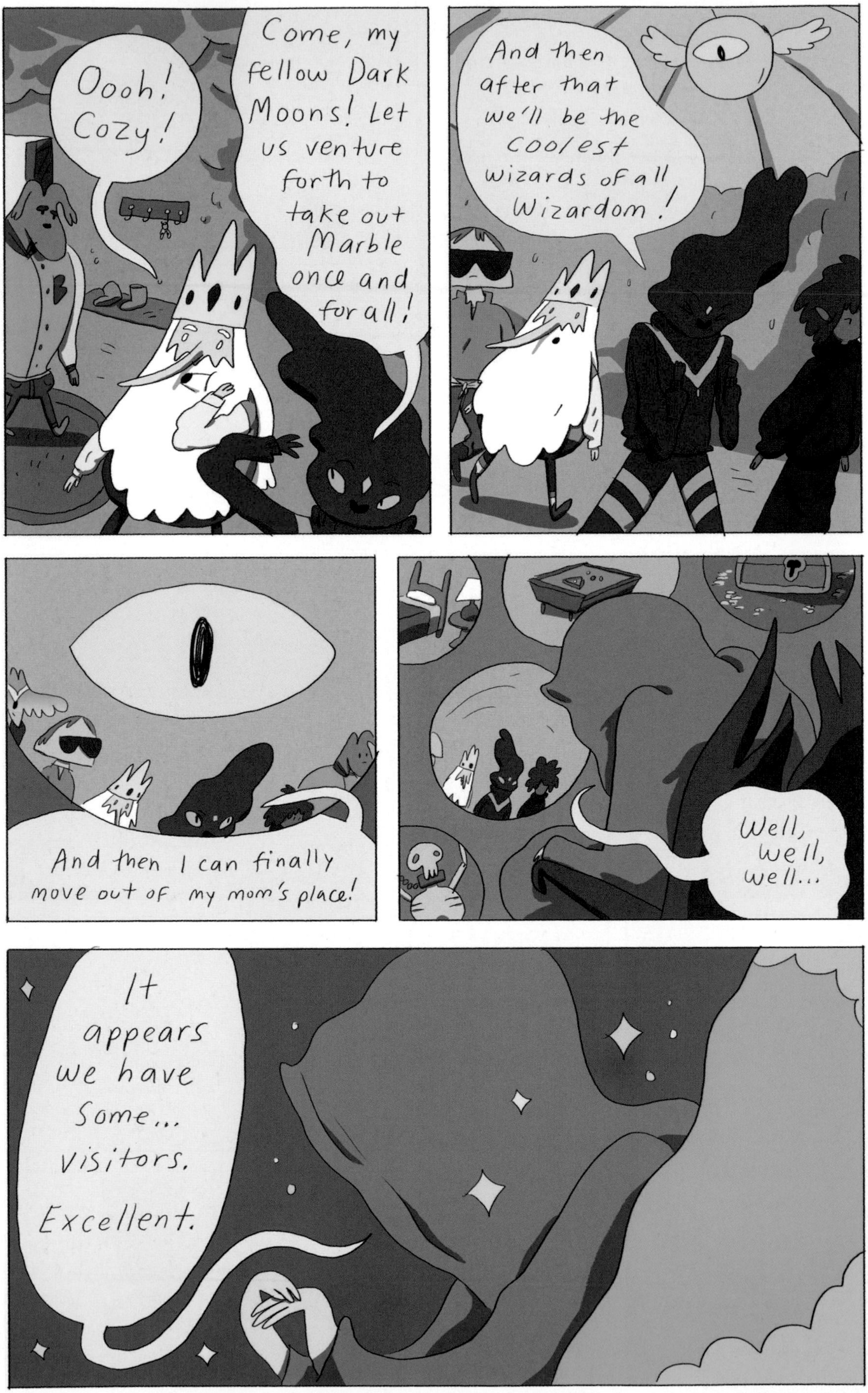
Oooh! Cozy!
Come, my fellow Dark Moons! Let us venture forth to take out Marble once and for all!
And then after that we'll be the coolest wizards of all Wizardom!
And then I can finally move out of my mom's place!
Well, well, well...
It appears we have some... visitors.
Excellent.

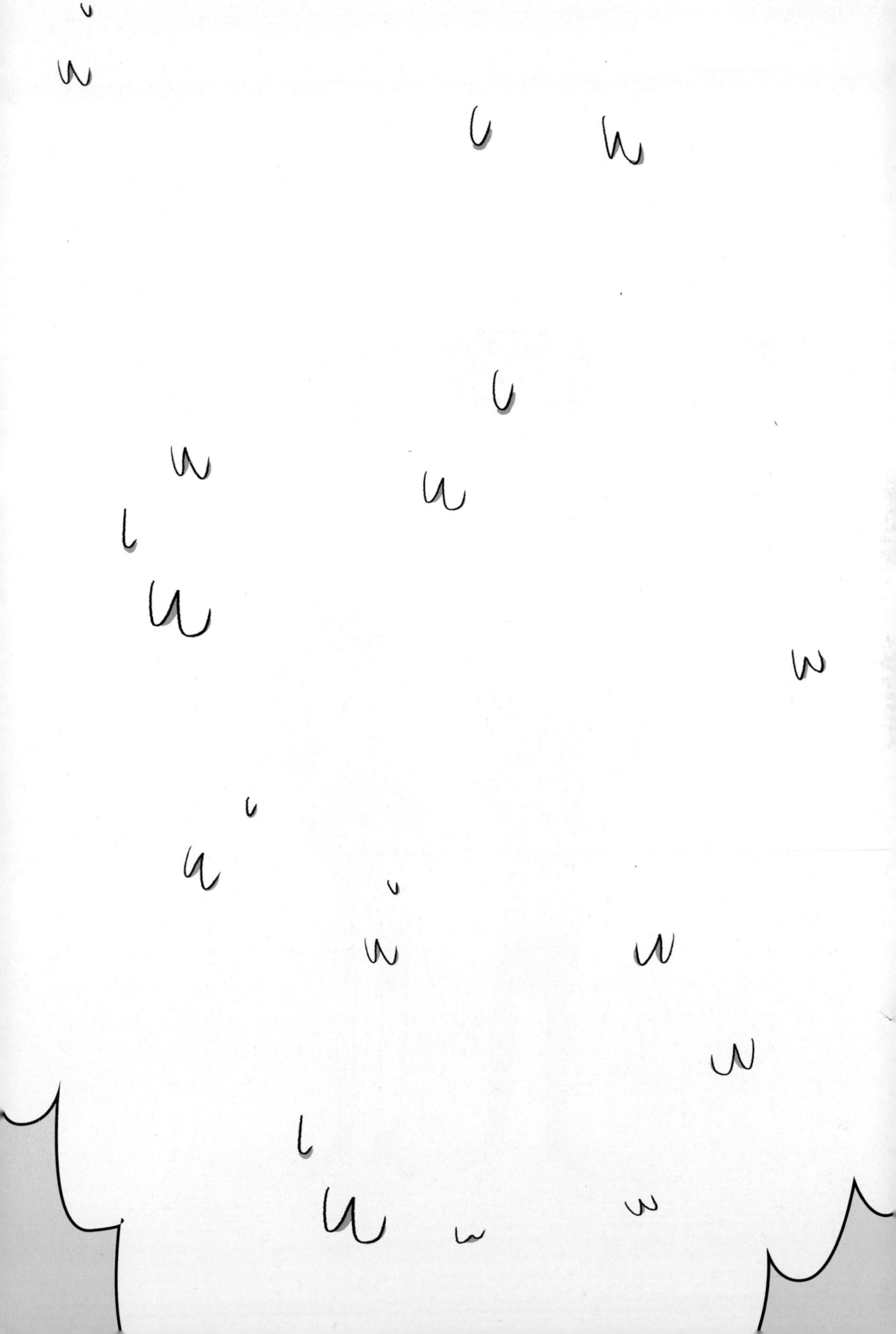

CHAPTER
FIVE

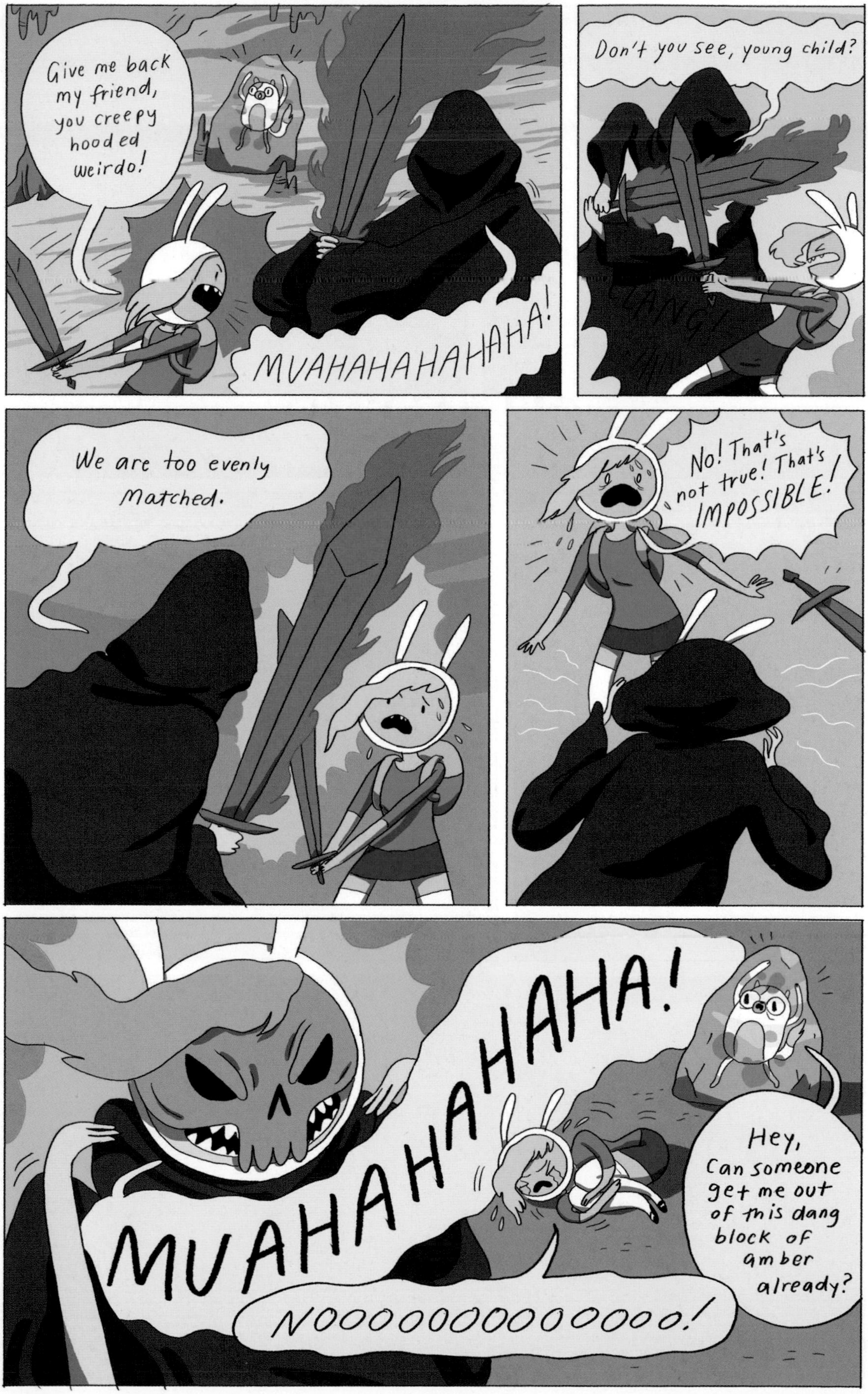
Give me back my friend, you creepy hooded weirdo!
MUAHAHAHAHAHA!
Don't you see, young child?
We are too evenly matched.
No! That's not true! That's IMPOSSIBLE!
MUAHAHAHAHAHAHA!
NOOOOOOOOOOOOOO!
Hey, can someone get me out of this dang block of amber already?

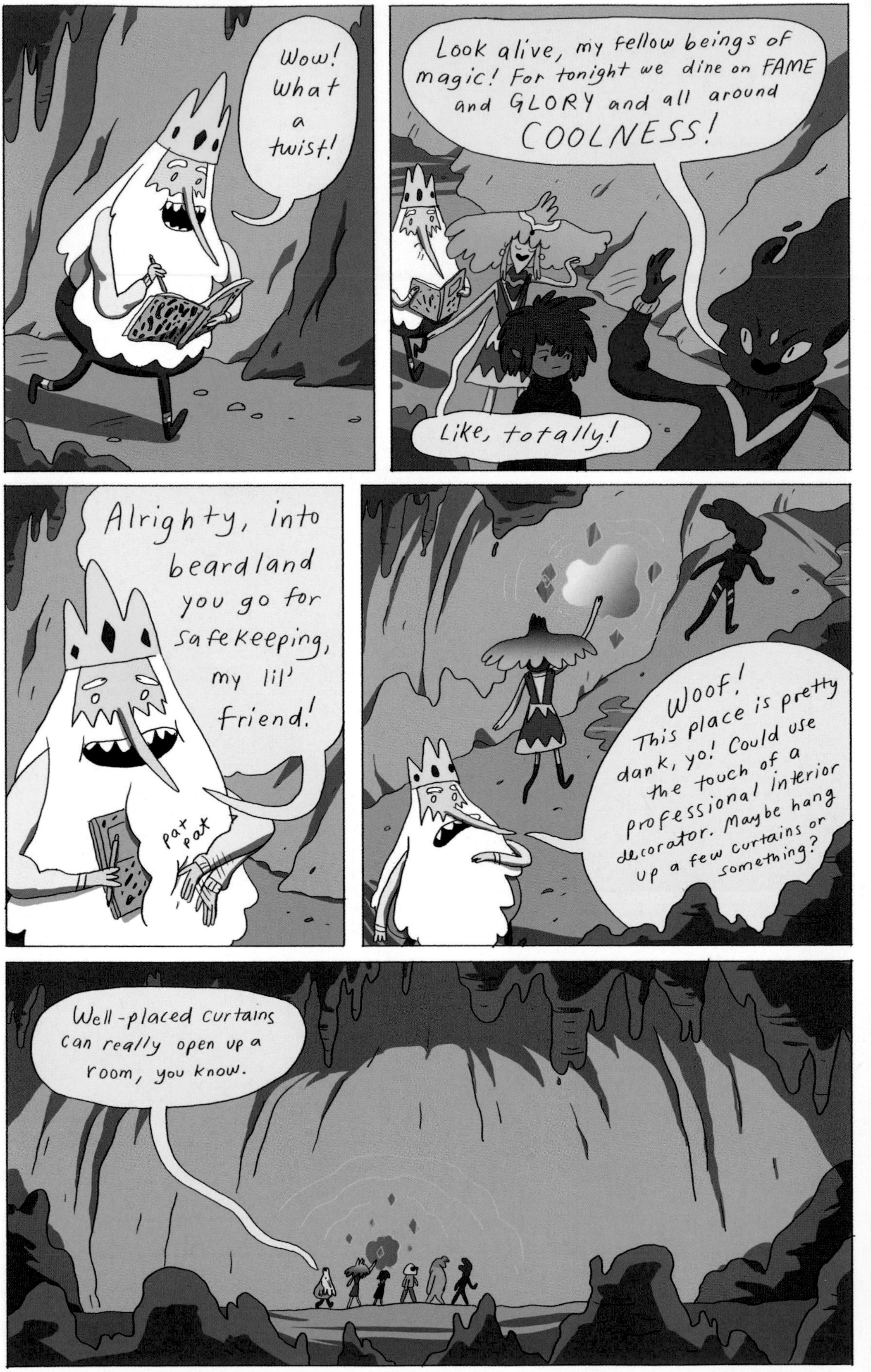
Wow! What a twist!
Look alive, my fellow beings of magic! For tonight we dine on FAME and GLORY and all around COOLNESS!
Like, totally!
Alrighty, into beardland you go for safekeeping, my lil' friend!
pat pat
Woof! This place is pretty dank, yo! Could use the touch of a professional interior decorator. Maybe hang up a few curtains or something?
Well-placed curtains can really open up a room, you know.

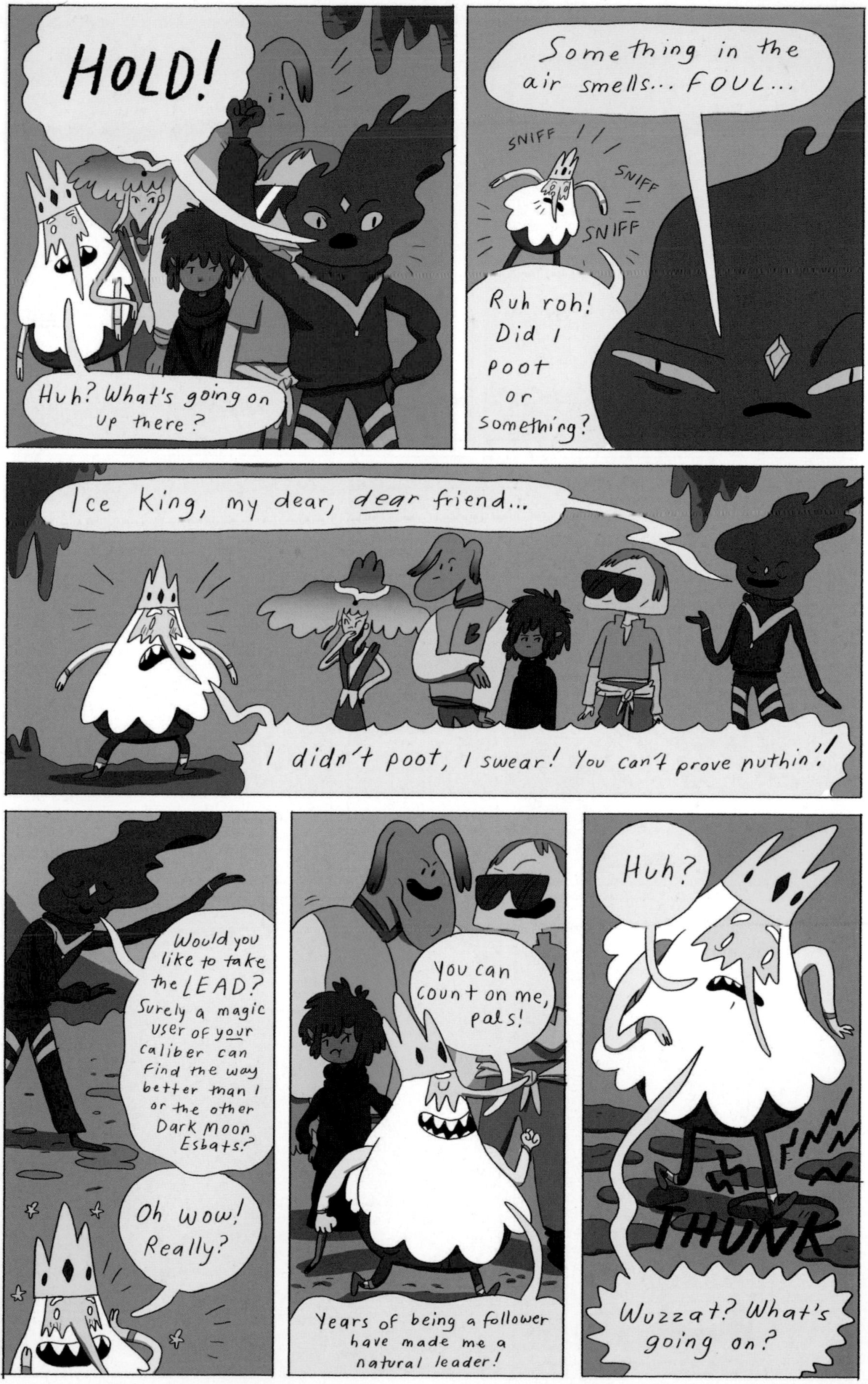
HOLD!
Huh? What's going on up there?
Something in the air smells... FOUL...
SNIFF
SNIFF
SNIFF
Ruh roh! Did I poot or something?
Ice King, my dear, dear friend...
I didn't poot, I swear! You can't prove nuthin'!
Would you like to take the LEAD? Surely a magic user of your caliber can find the way better than I or the other Dark Moon Esbats?
Oh wow! Really?
You can count on me, pals!
Years of being a follower have made me a natural leader!
Huh?
THUNK
Wuzzat? What's going on?

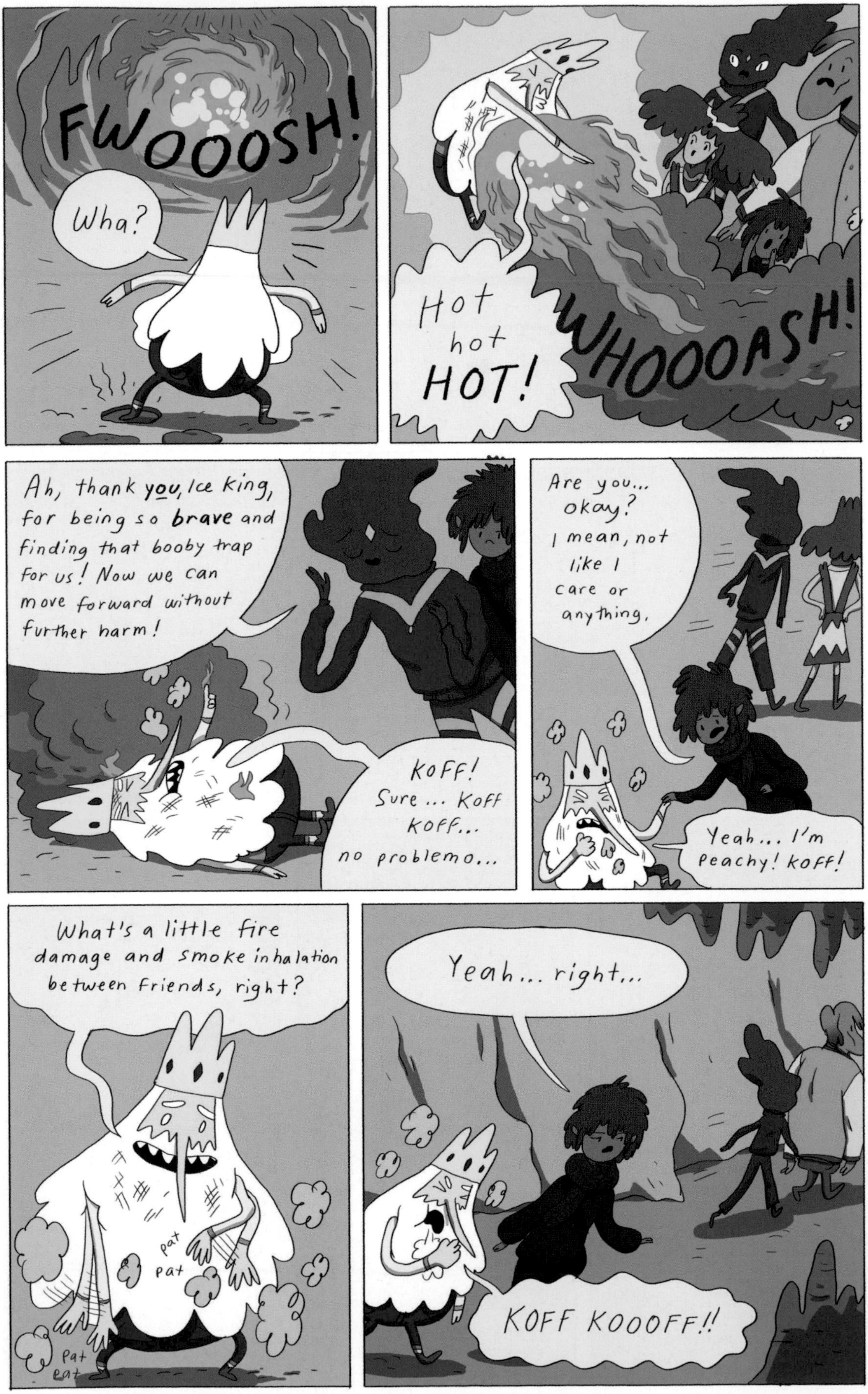
FWOOOOSH!
Wha?
Hot hot HOT!
WHOOOOASH!
Ah, thank you, Ice King, for being so brave and finding that booby trap for us! Now we can move forward without further harm!
KOFF! Sure... KOFF KOFF... no problemo...
Are you... okay? I mean, not like I care or anything.
Yeah... I'm peachy! KOFF!
What's a little fire damage and smoke inhalation between friends, right?
pat
pat
pat
pat
Yeah... right...
KOFF KOOOFF!!

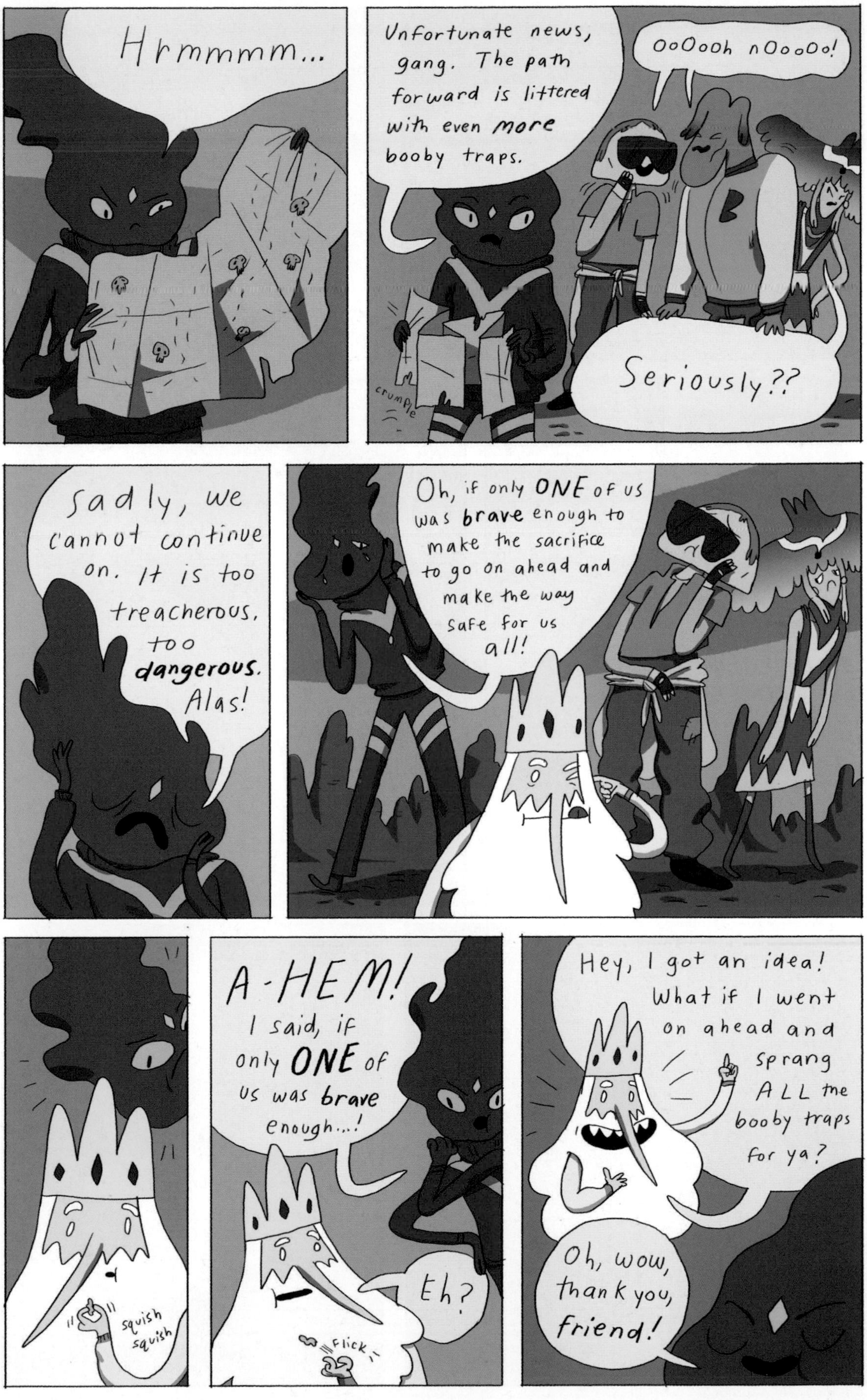
Hrmmmm...
Unfortunate news, gang. The path forward is littered with even more booby traps.
OoOooh nOooOo!
crumple
Seriously??
Sadly, we cannot continue on. It is too treacherous, too dangerous. Alas!
Oh, if only ONE of us was brave enough to make the sacrifice to go on ahead and make the way safe for us all!
squish squish
A-HEM! I said, if only ONE of us was brave enough...!
Eh?
Flick
Hey, I got an idea! What if I went on ahead and sprang ALL the booby traps for ya?
Oh, wow, thank you, friend!

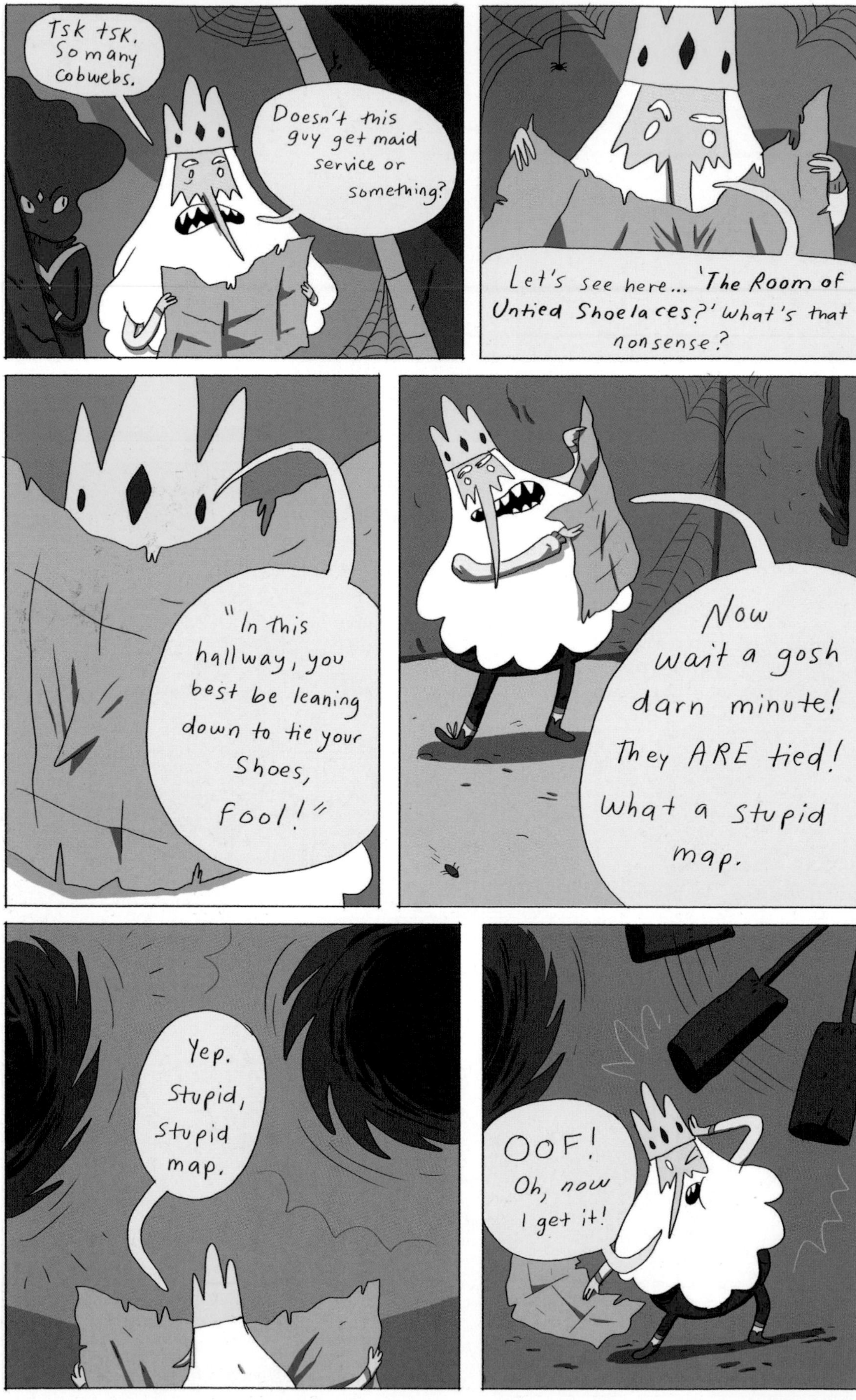
Tsk tsk. So many cobwebs.
Doesn't this guy get maid service or something?
Let's see here... 'The Room of Untied Shoelaces?' What's that nonsense?
"In this hallway, you best be leaning down to tie your shoes, fool!"
Now wait a gosh darn minute! They ARE tied! What a stupid map.
Yep. Stupid, stupid map.
OOF! Oh, now I get it!

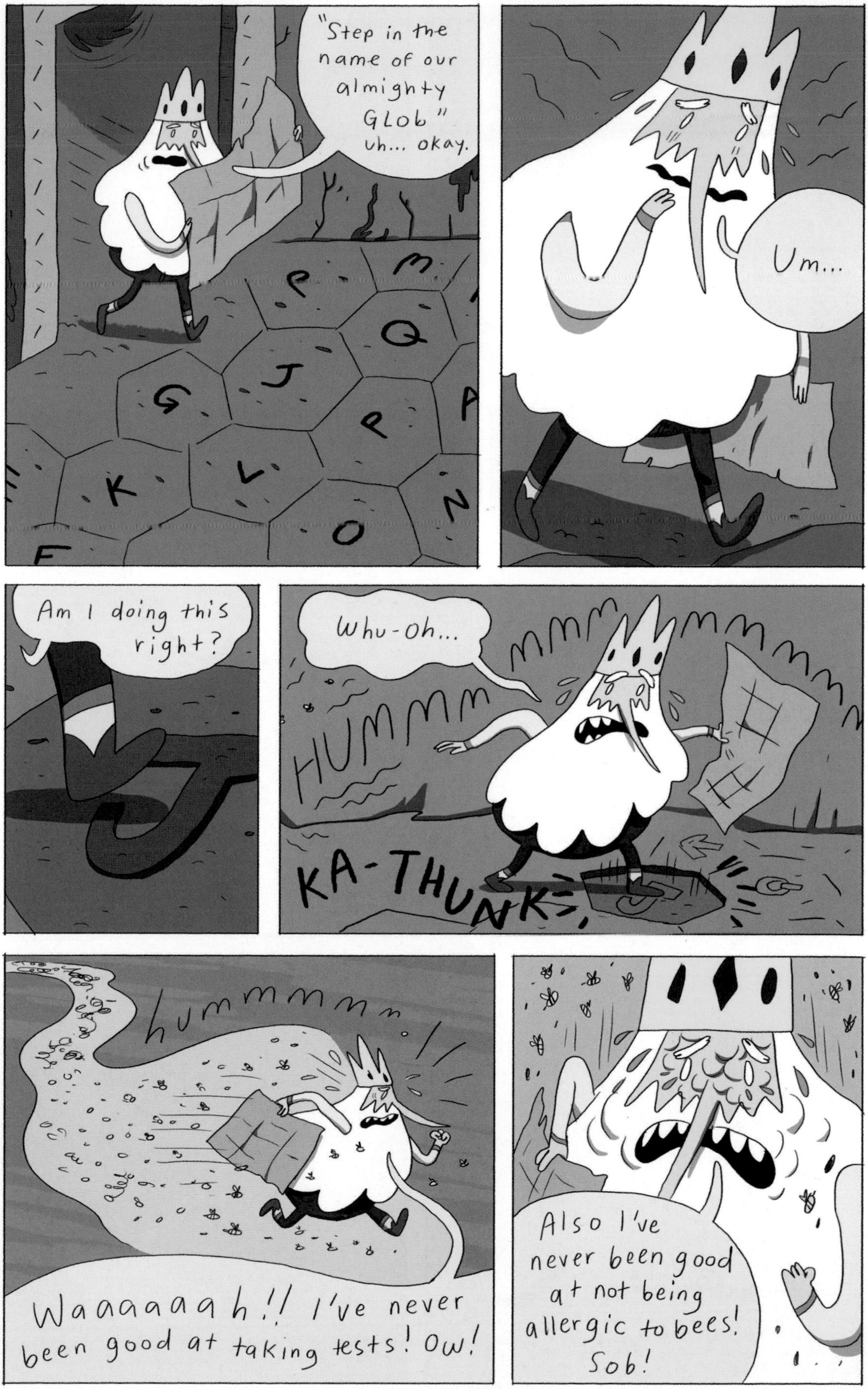
"Step in the name of our almighty GLOB" uh... okay.
Um...
Am I doing this right?
Whu-oh...
HUMMMMMMMMMMMMMM
KA-THUNK
hummmmmm
Waaaaaah!! I've never been good at taking tests! Ow!
Also I've never been good at not being allergic to bees! Sob!

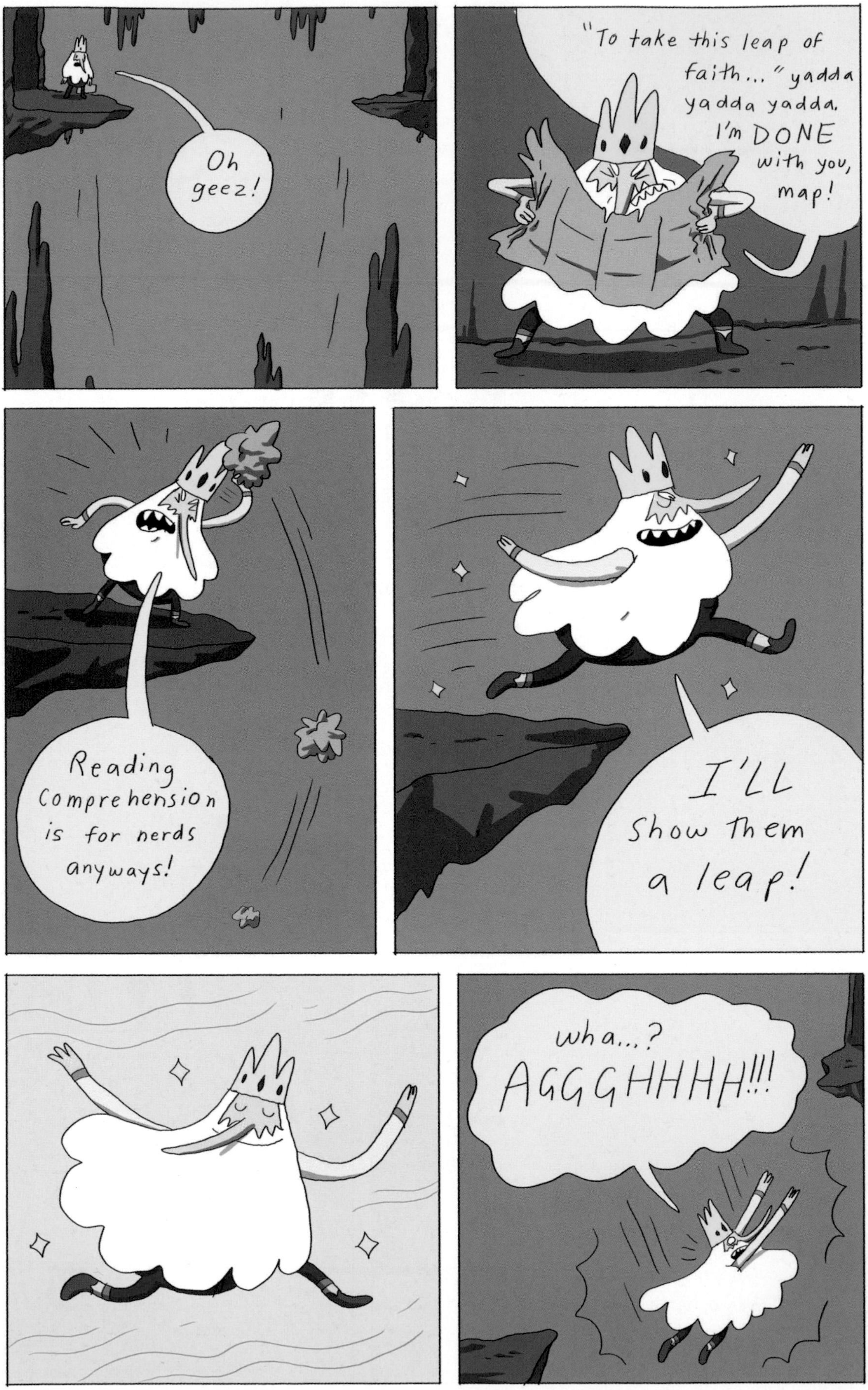
Oh geez!
"To take this leap of faith..." yadda yadda yadda. I'm DONE with you, map!
Reading comprehension is for nerds anyways!
I'LL show them a leap!
wha...? AGGGHHHH!!!

WHAAAA!
AAAAAAAAAAA!
KLUNK
Uhg. I wish I remembered I could fly before I hit the bottom. pfft. What a day. I blame the map.
PUSH THE BUTTON TO EXTEND THE BRIDGE, DUMMY.
Ooooh!
Most excellent work, Ice King!
Rub Rub
Ice Man good.
Yeah... don't mention it...

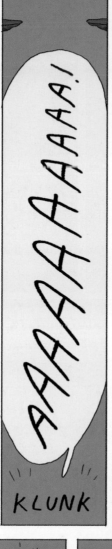

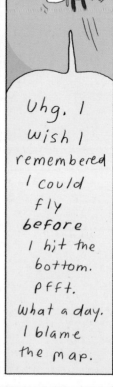

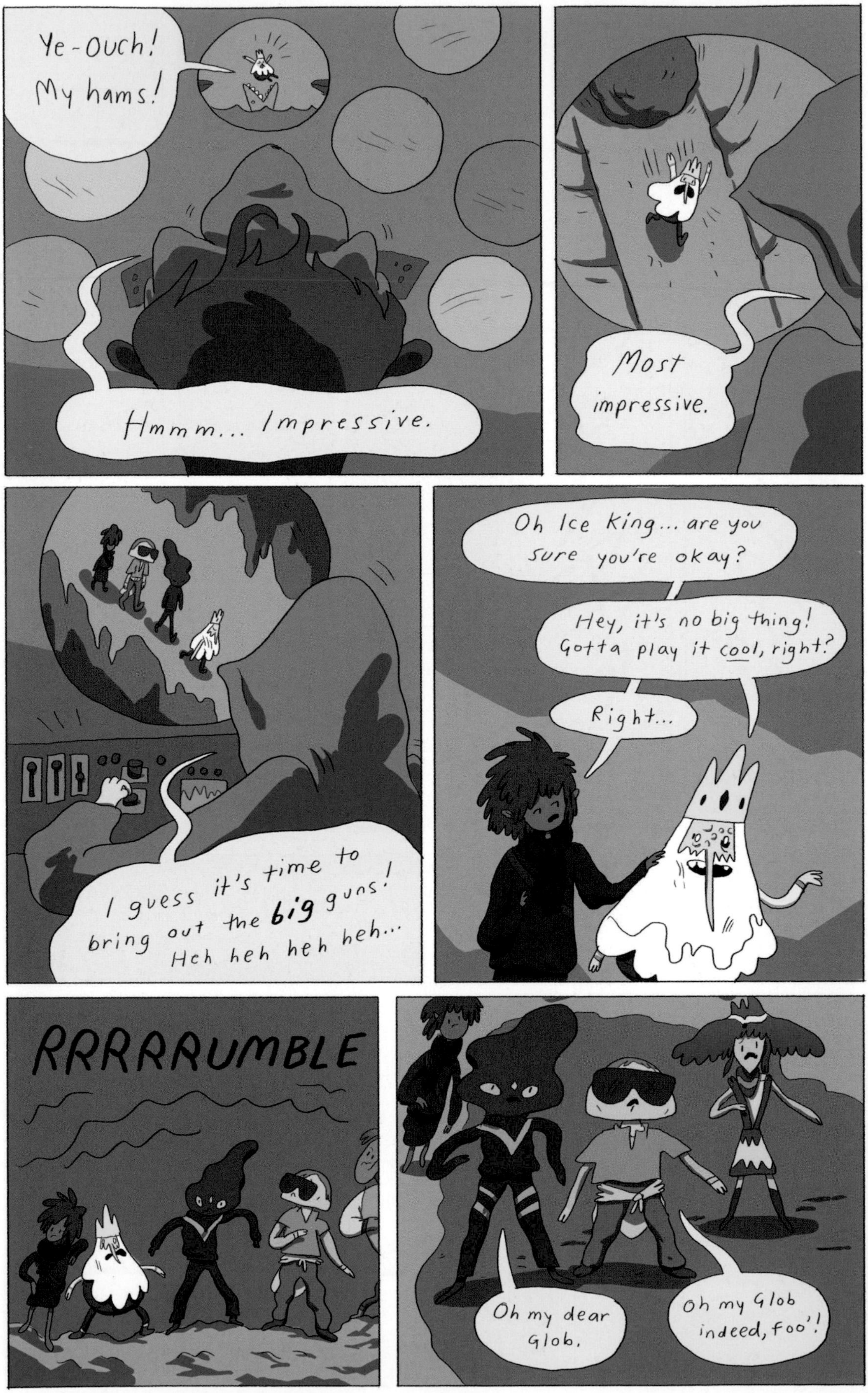
Ye-Ouch! My hams!
Hmmm... Impressive.
Most impressive.
I guess it's time to bring out the big guns! Heh heh heh heh...
Oh Ice King... are you sure you're okay?
Hey, it's no big thing! Gotta play it cool, right?
Right...
RRRRRUMBLE
Oh my dear Glob.
Oh my Glob indeed, foo'!

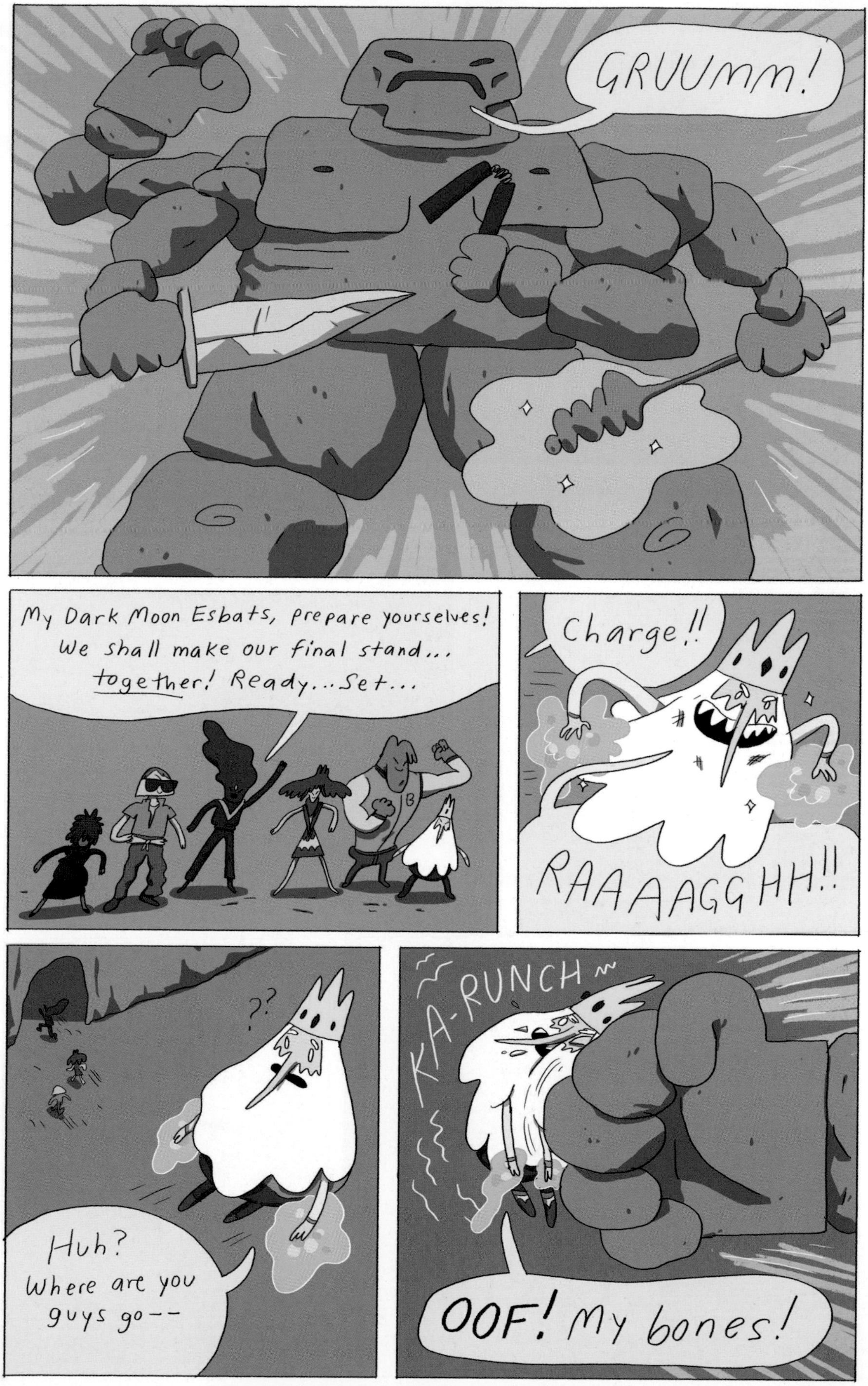
GRUUMM!
My Dark Moon Esbats, prepare yourselves! We shall make our final stand... together! Ready...Set...
Charge!!
RAAAAGGHH!!
Huh? Where are you guys go--
KA-RUNCH
OOF! My bones!

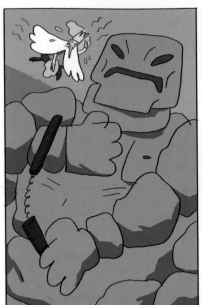

We... We can't just leave him like this!

Alistair! We must stick to the PLAN! Unless you want to take his place? Hmm?

Yeah, like, don't be, like, a buzzkill, or whatever? 'Kay?

Good strategy! I'll tire him out while you guys go get help!

GRUM!

OOF!

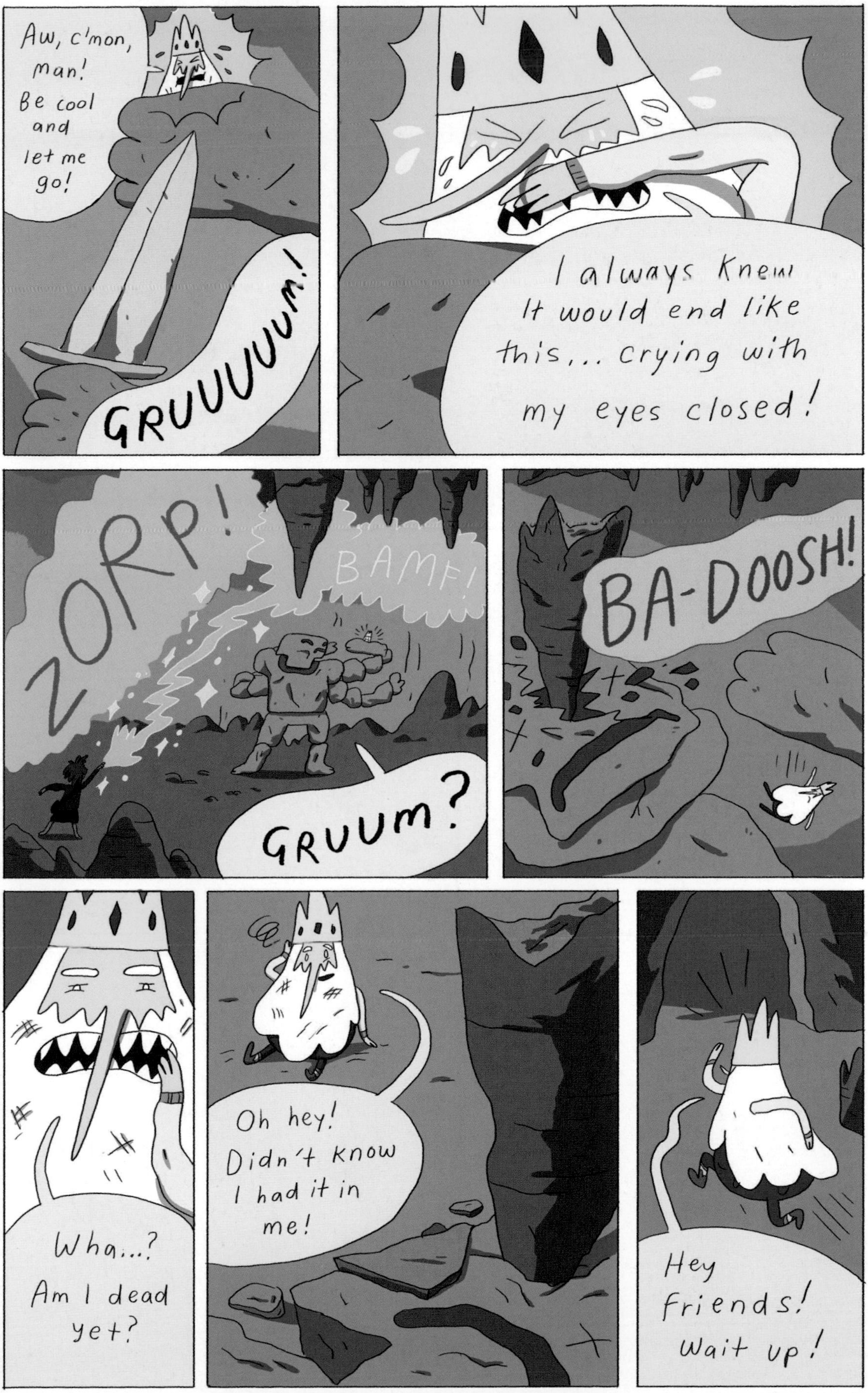
Aw, c'mon, man! Be cool and let me go!
GRUUUUUM!
I always knew it would end like this... crying with my eyes closed!
ZORP!
BAMF!
GRUUM?
BA-DOOSH!
Wha...? Am I dead yet?
Oh hey! Didn't know I had it in me!
Hey friends! Wait up!

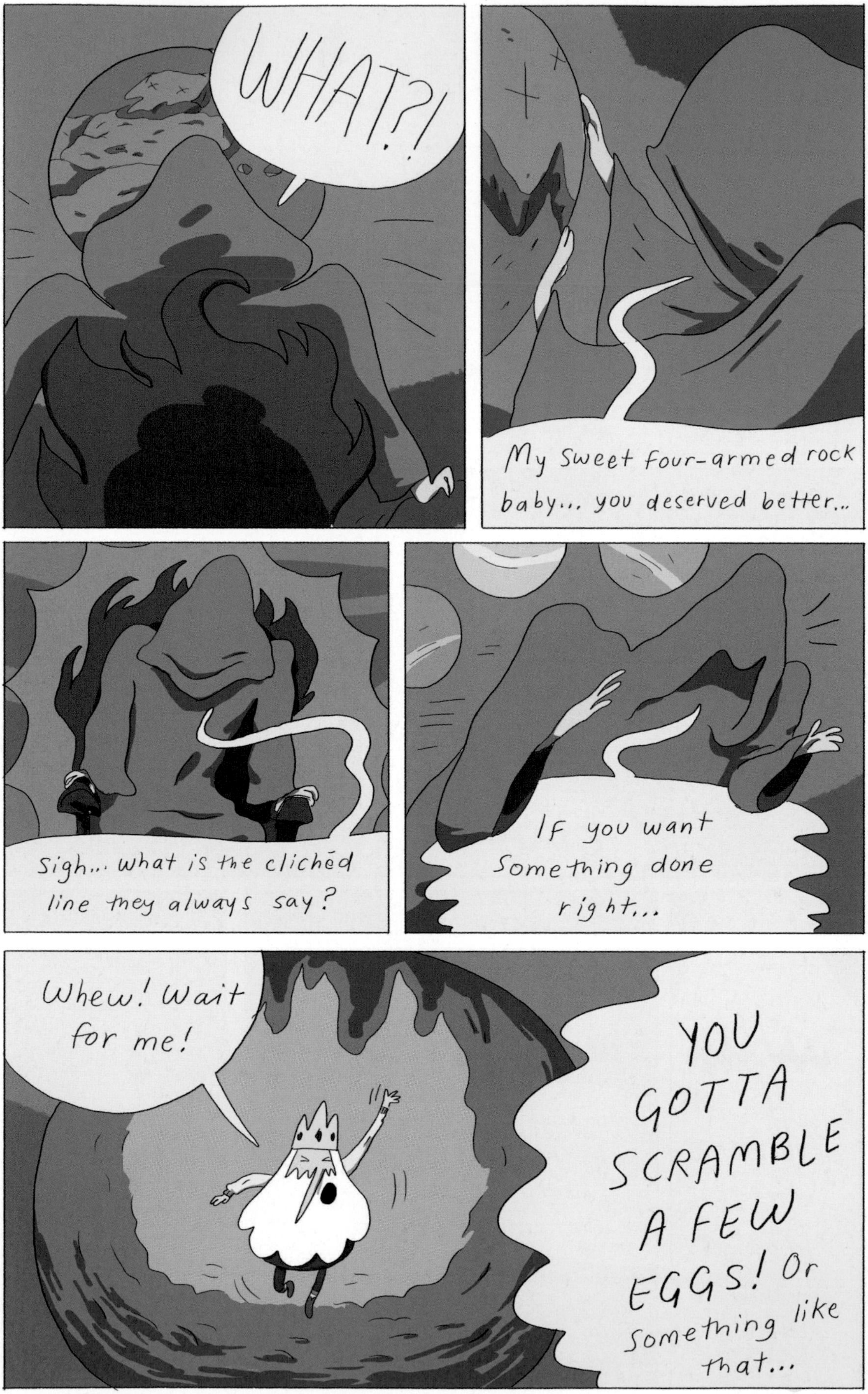
WHAT?!
My sweet four-armed rock baby... you deserved better...
Sigh... what is the clichéd line they always say?
If you want something done right...
Whew! Wait for me!
YOU GOTTA SCRAMBLE A FEW EGGS! Or something like that...

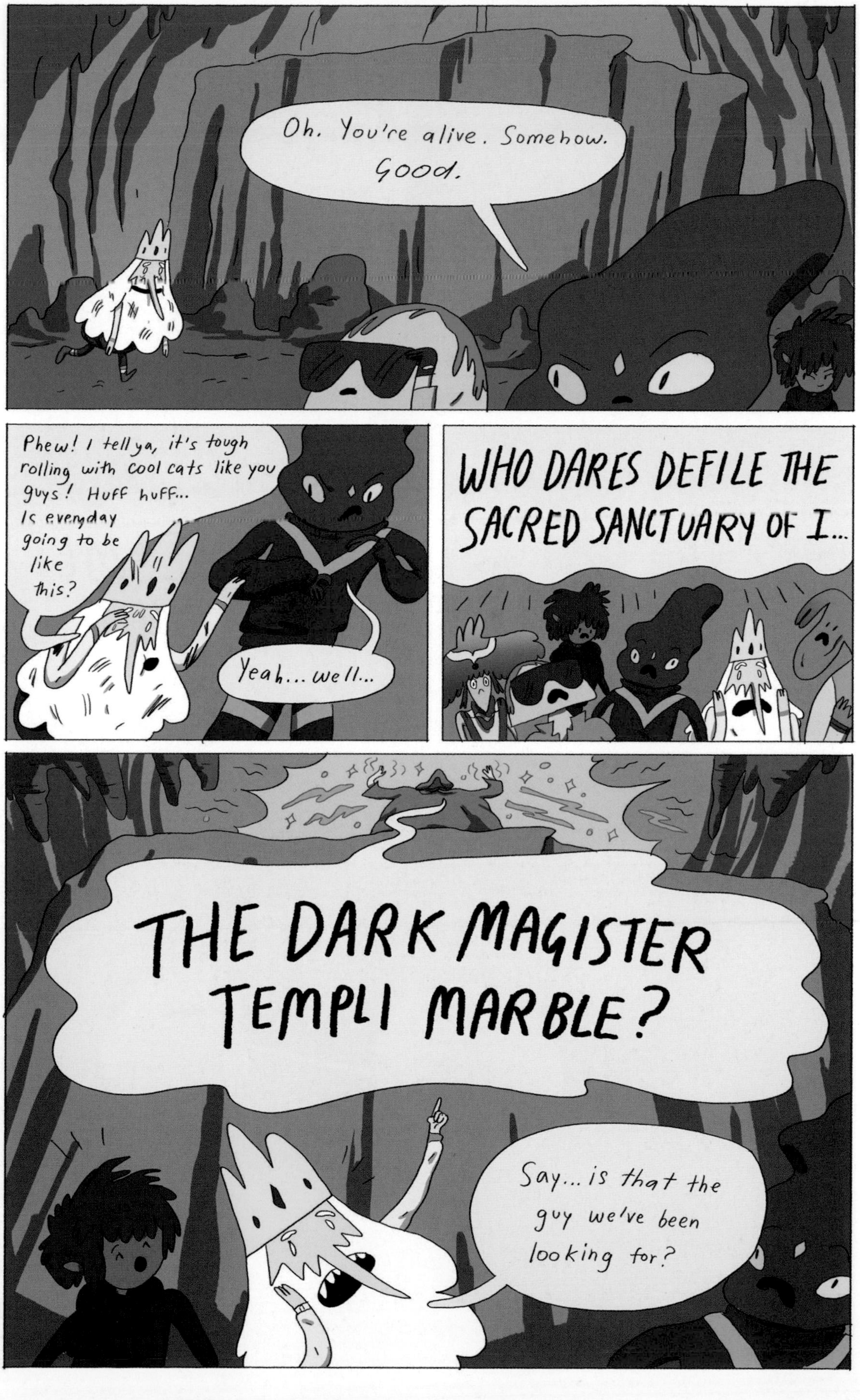
Oh. You're alive. Somehow. Good.
Phew! I tell ya, it's tough rolling with cool cats like you guys! Huff huff... Is everyday going to be like this?
Yeah... well...
WHO DARES DEFILE THE SACRED SANCTUARY OF I...
THE DARK MAGISTER TEMPLI MARBLE?
Say... is that the guy we've been looking for?

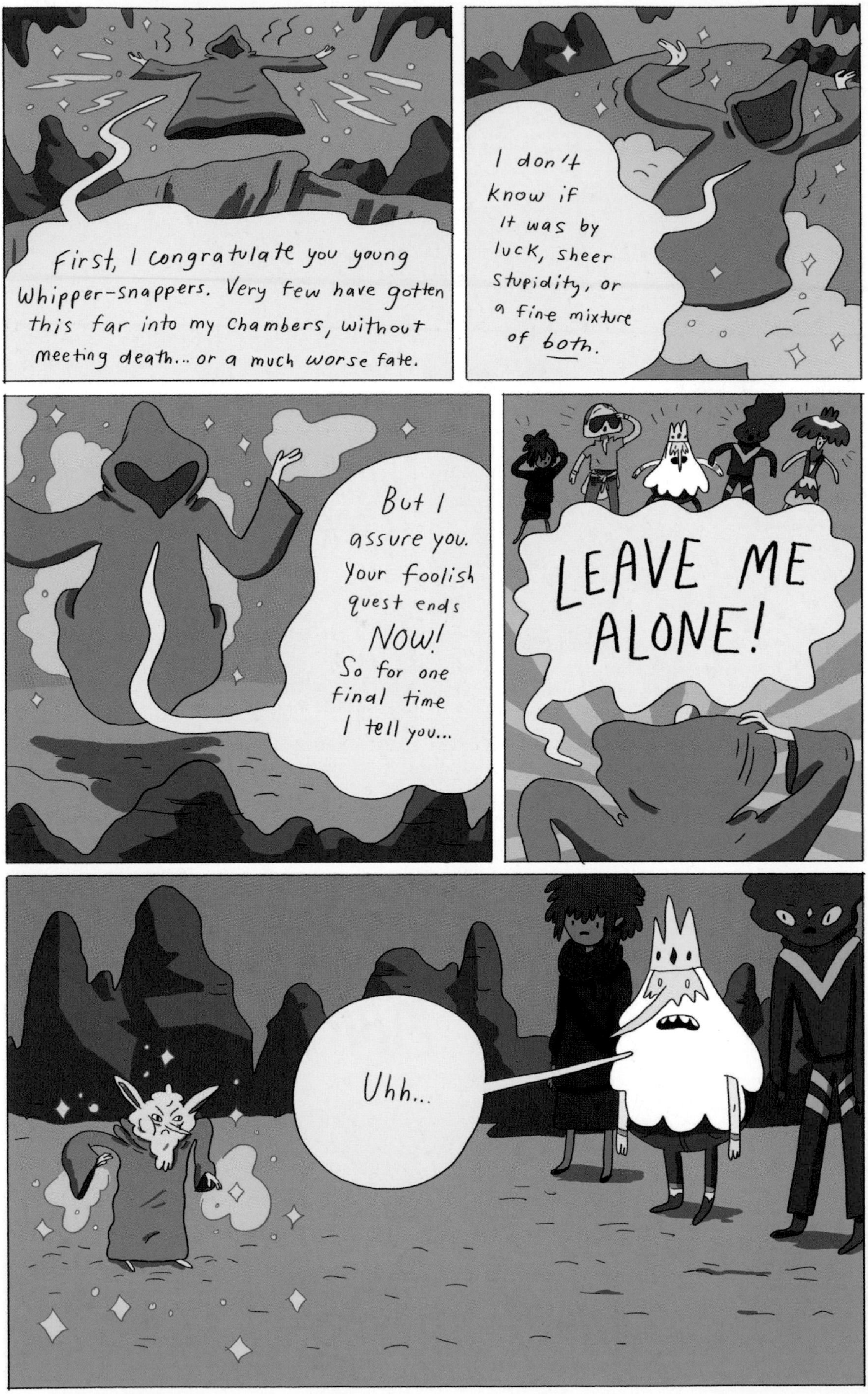
First, I congratulate you young Whipper-snappers. Very few have gotten this far into my chambers, without meeting death... or a much worse fate.
I don't know if it was by luck, sheer stupidity, or a fine mixture of both.
But I assure you. Your foolish quest ends NOW! So for one final time I tell you...
LEAVE ME ALONE!
Uhh...

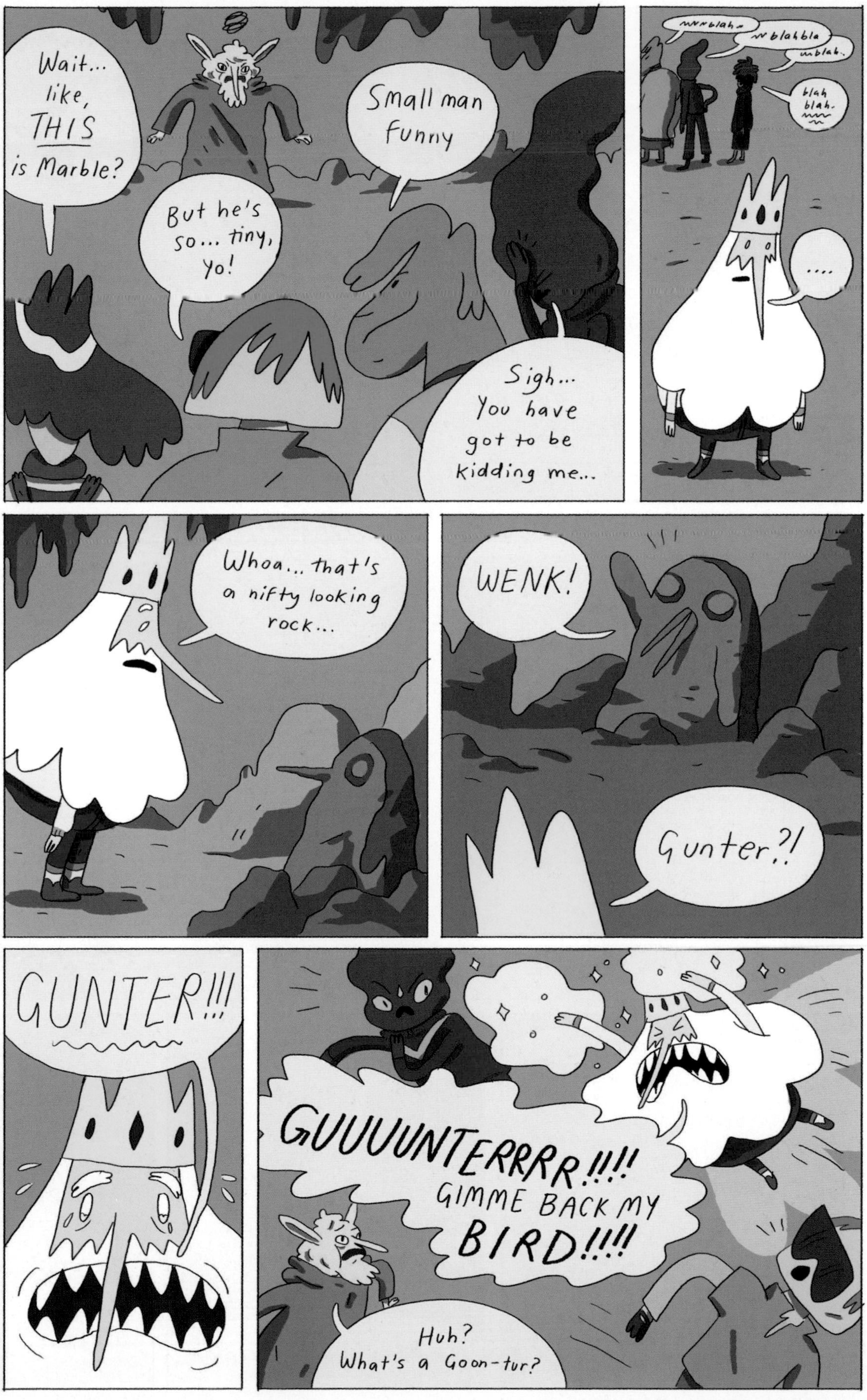
Wait... like, THIS is Marble?
But he's so... tiny, yo!
Small man funny
Sigh... You have got to be kidding me...
blah blah blabla blah.
blah blah.
....
Whoa... that's a nifty looking rock...
WENK!
Gunter?!
GUNTER!!!
GUUUUNTERRRR!!!! GIMME BACK MY BIRD!!!!
Huh? What's a Goon-tur?

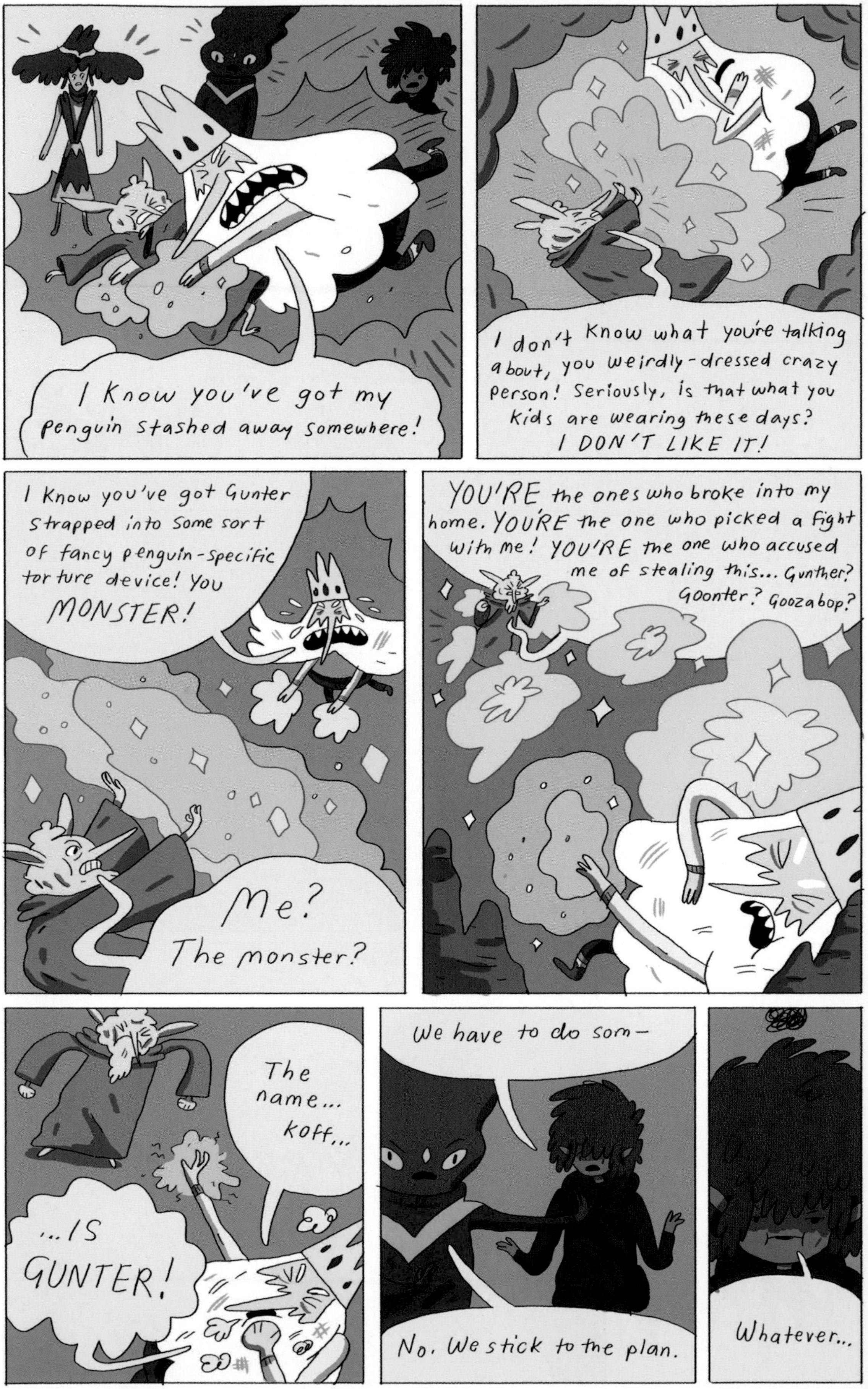
I Know you've got my penguin stashed away somewhere!
I don't Know what you're talking about, you weirdly-dressed crazy person! Seriously, is that what you kids are wearing these days? I DON'T LIKE IT!
I Know you've got Gunter strapped into some sort of fancy penguin-specific torture device! You MONSTER!
Me? The monster?
YOU'RE the ones who broke into my home. YOU'RE the one who picked a fight with me! YOU'RE the one who accused me of stealing this... Gunther? Goonter? Goozabop?
The name... koff...
...IS GUNTER!
We have to do som—
No. We stick to the plan.
Whatever...

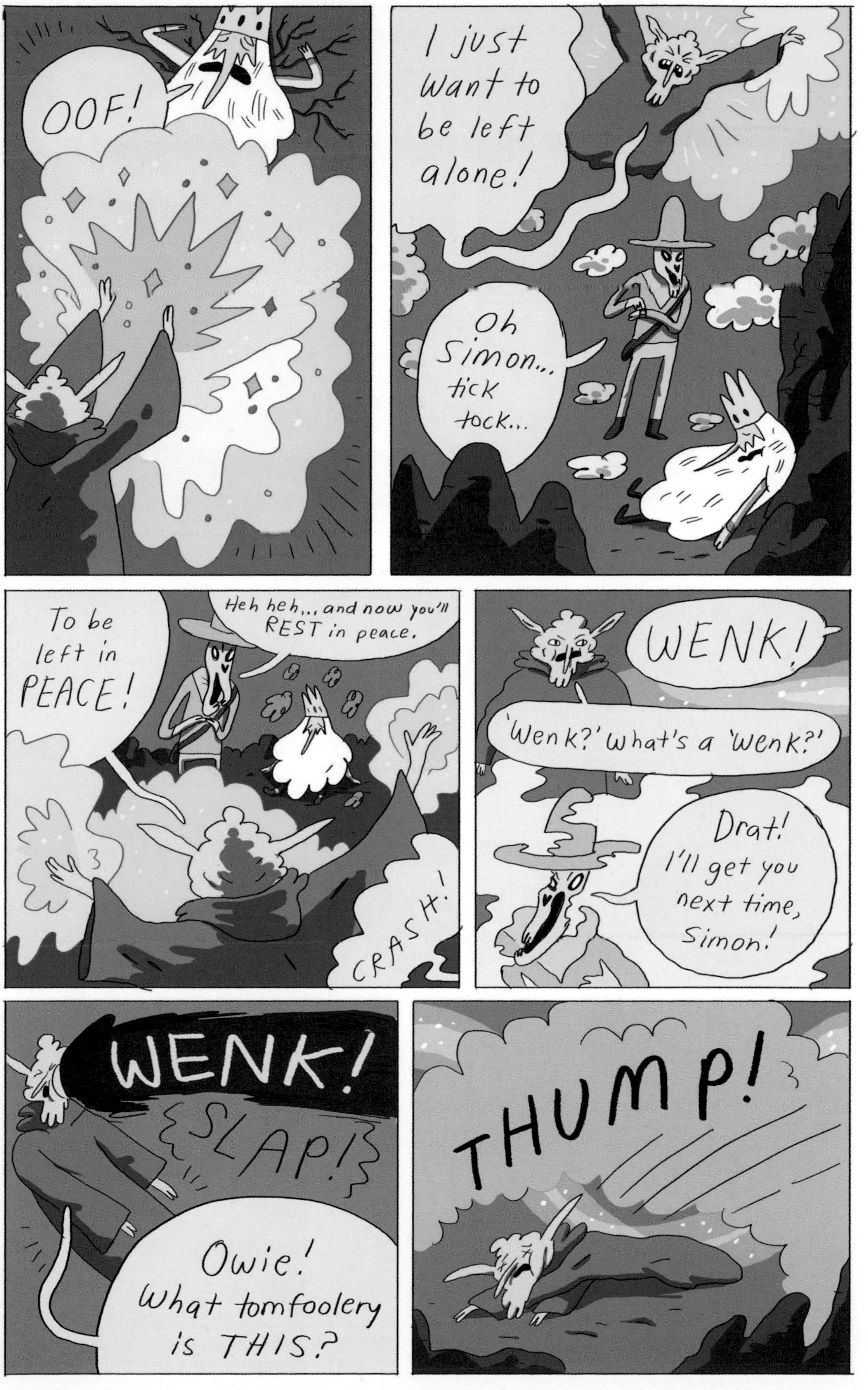
OOF!
I just want to be left alone!
Oh Simon... tick tock...
To be left in PEACE!
Heh heh... and now you'll REST in peace.
CRASH!
WENK!
'Wenk?' What's a 'wenk?'
Drat! I'll get you next time, Simon!
WENK!
SLAP!
Owie! What tomfoolery is THIS?
THUMP!

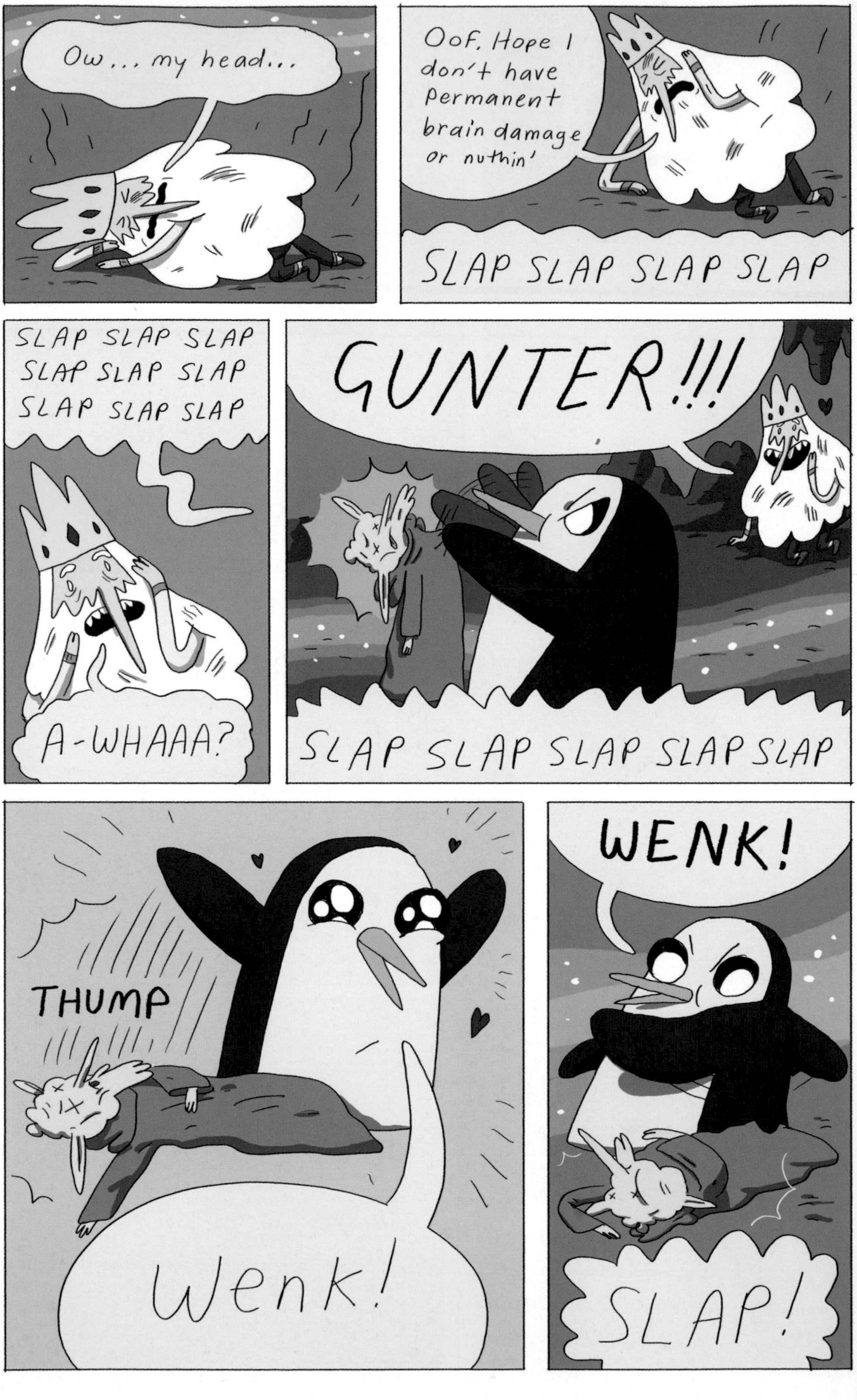

Ow... my head...
Oof. Hope I don't have permanent brain damage or nuthin'
SLAP SLAP SLAP SLAP
SLAP SLAP SLAP SLAP SLAP SLAP SLAP SLAP SLAP
A-WHAAA?
GUNTER!!!
SLAP SLAP SLAP SLAP SLAP
THUMP
Wenk!
WENK!
SLAP!

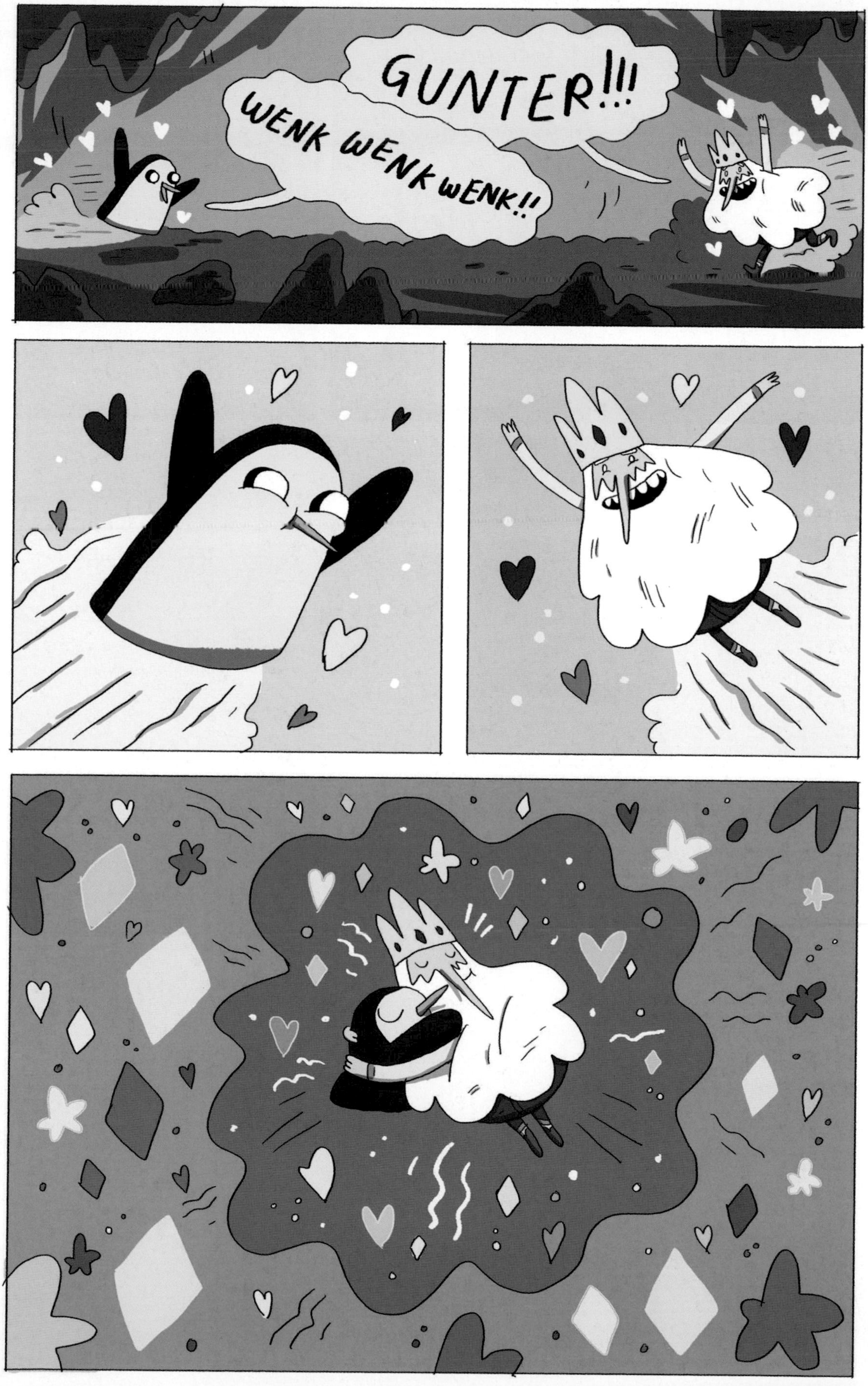
GUNTER!!!
WENK WENK WENK!!

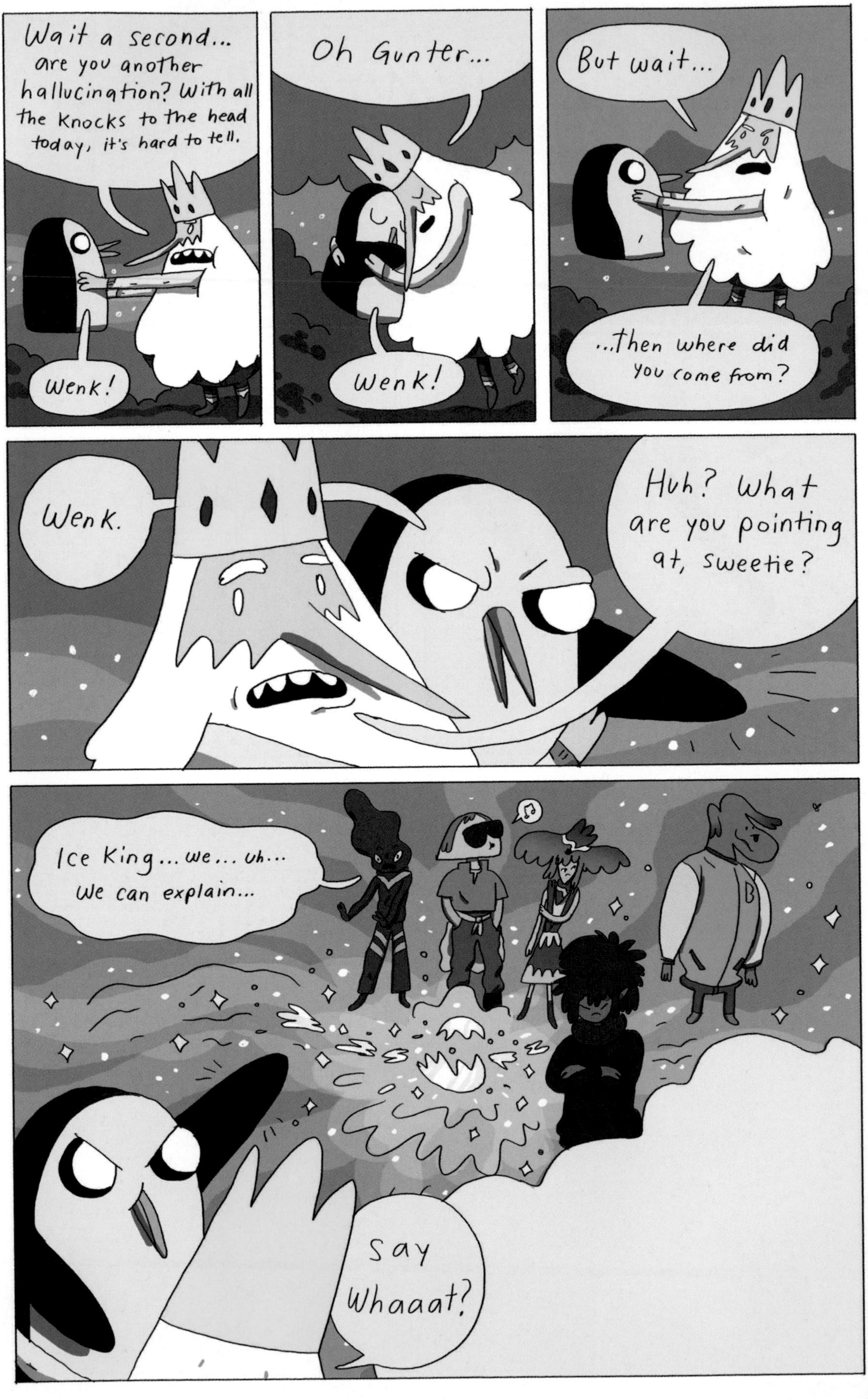
Wait a second... are you another hallucination? With all the knocks to the head today, it's hard to tell.
Wenk!
Oh Gunter...
Wenk!
But wait...
...then where did you come from?
Wenk.
Huh? What are you pointing at, sweetie?
Ice King... we... uh... we can explain...
Say Whaaat?

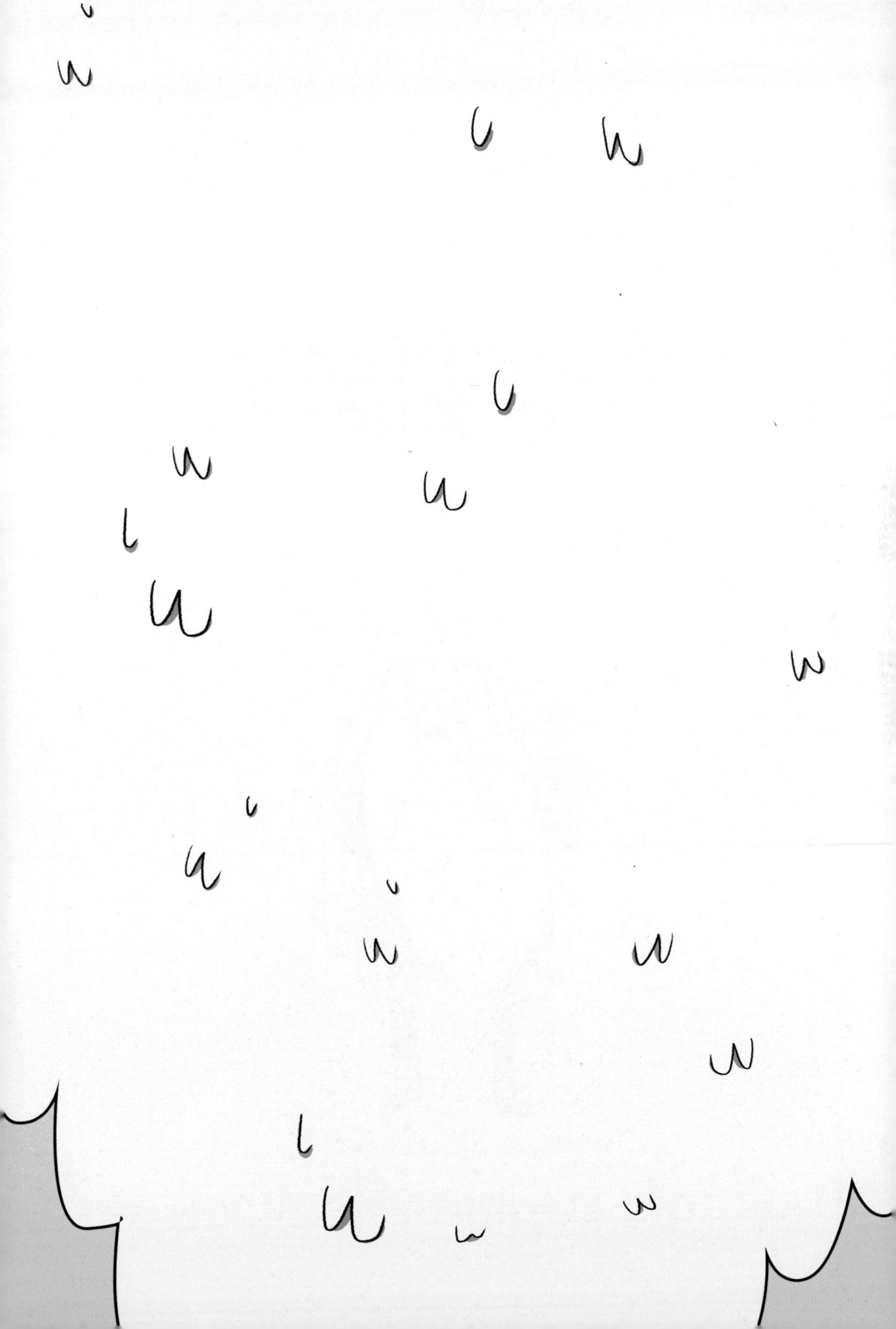

CHAPTER
SIX

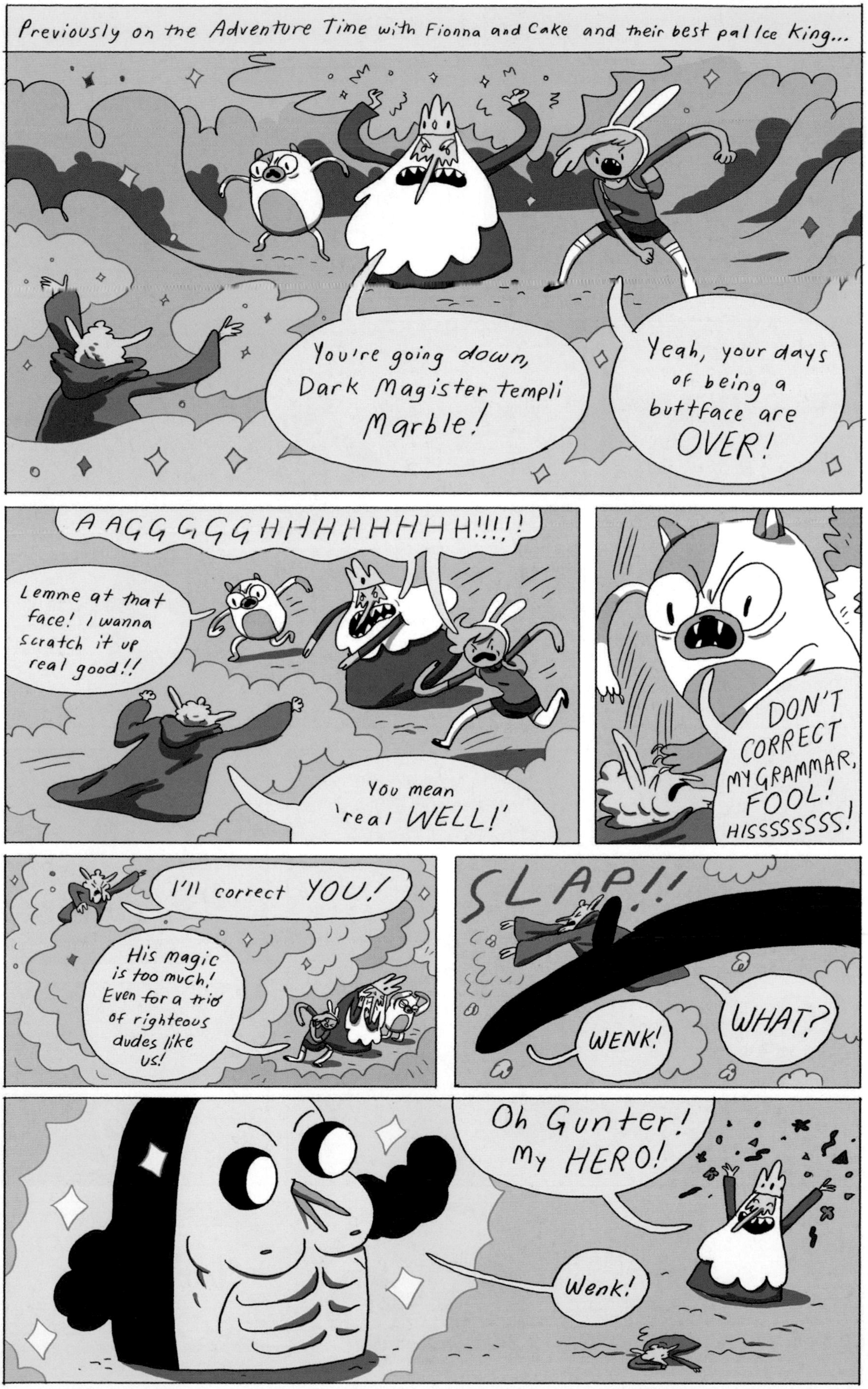
Previously on the Adventure Time with Fionna and Cake and their best pal Ice King...
You're going down, Dark Magister templi Marble!
Yeah, your days of being a buttface are OVER!
AAGGGGGHHHHHHHH!!!!!
Lemme at that face! I wanna scratch it up real good!!
You mean 'real WELL!'
DON'T CORRECT MY GRAMMAR, FOOL! HISSSSSSSS!
I'll correct YOU!
His magic is too much! Even for a trio of righteous dudes like us!
SLAP!!
WENK!
WHAT?
Oh Gunter! My HERO!
Wenk!

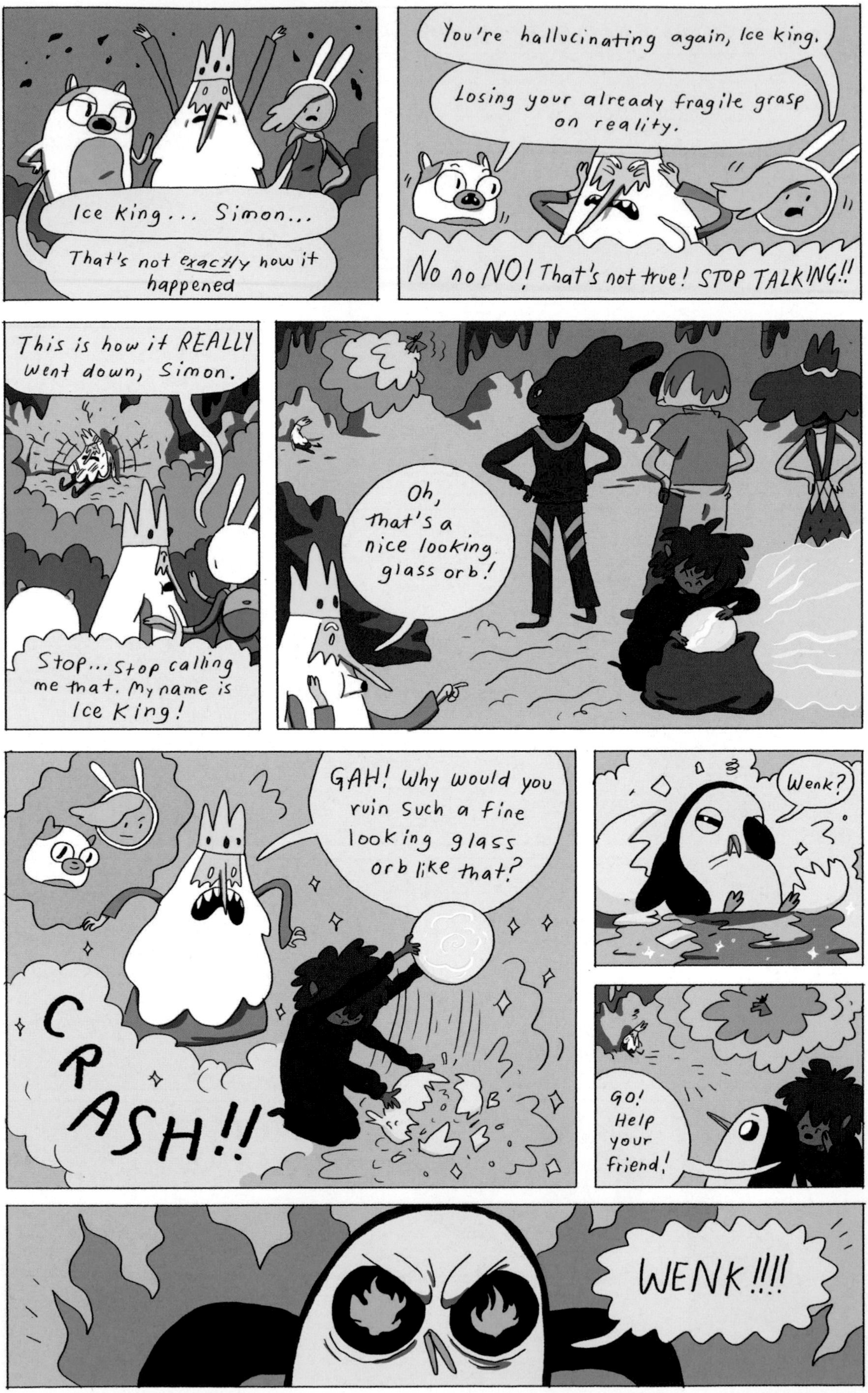
Ice King... Simon...
That's not exactly how it happened
You're hallucinating again, Ice King.
Losing your already fragile grasp on reality.
No no NO! That's not true! STOP TALKING!!
This is how it REALLY went down, Simon.
Stop... Stop calling me that. My name is Ice King!
Oh, that's a nice looking glass orb!
GAH! Why would you ruin such a fine looking glass orb like that?
CRASH!!
Wenk?
GO! Help your friend!
WENK!!!!

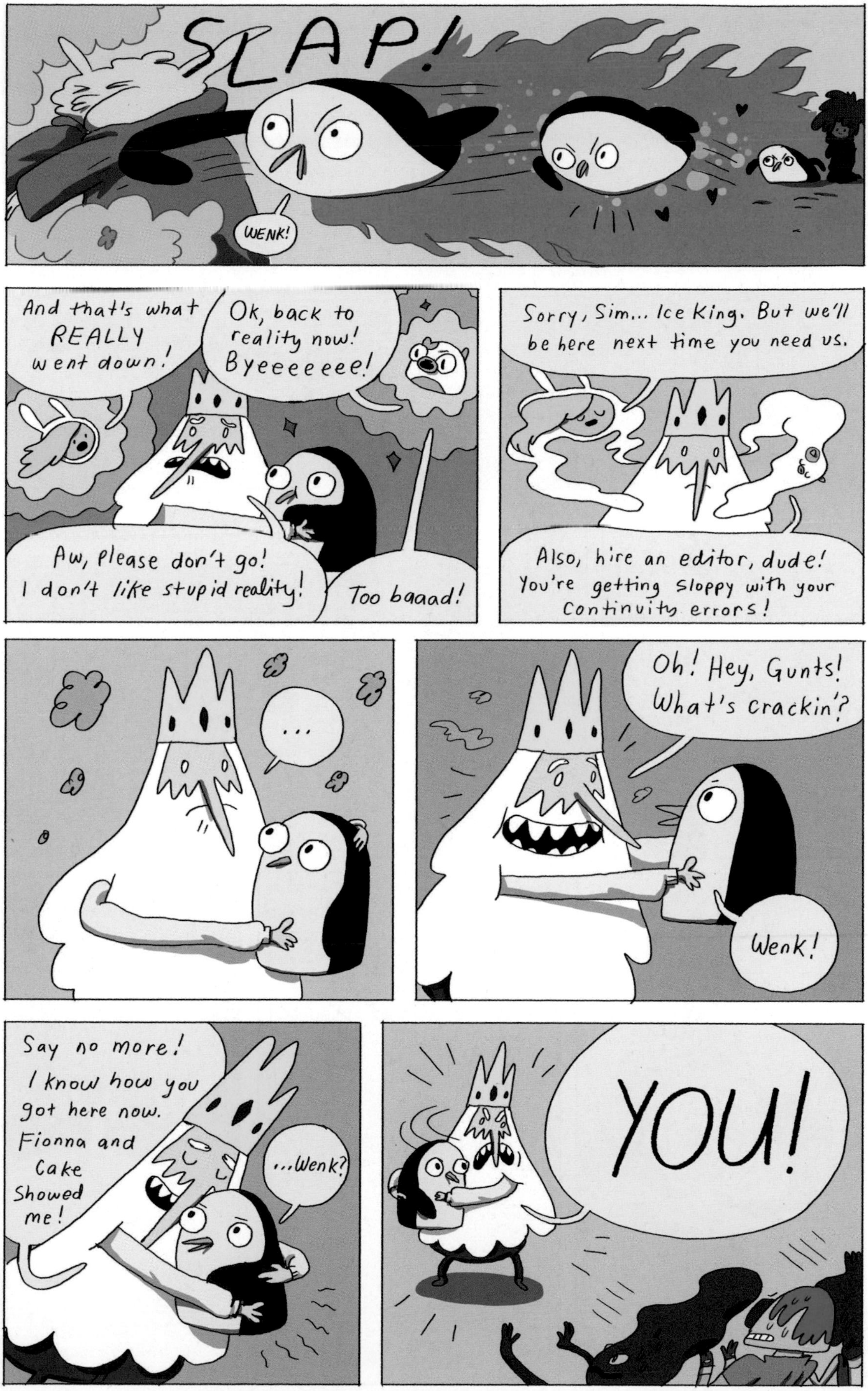
SLAP!
WENK!
And that's what REALLY went down!
Ok, back to reality now! Byeeeeeee!
Aw, please don't go! I don't like stupid reality!
Too baaad!
Sorry, Sim... Ice King. But we'll be here next time you need us.
Also, hire an editor, dude! You're getting sloppy with your continuity errors!
...
Oh! Hey, Gunts! What's crackin'?
Wenk!
Say no more! I know how you got here now. Fionna and Cake showed me!
...Wenk?
YOU!

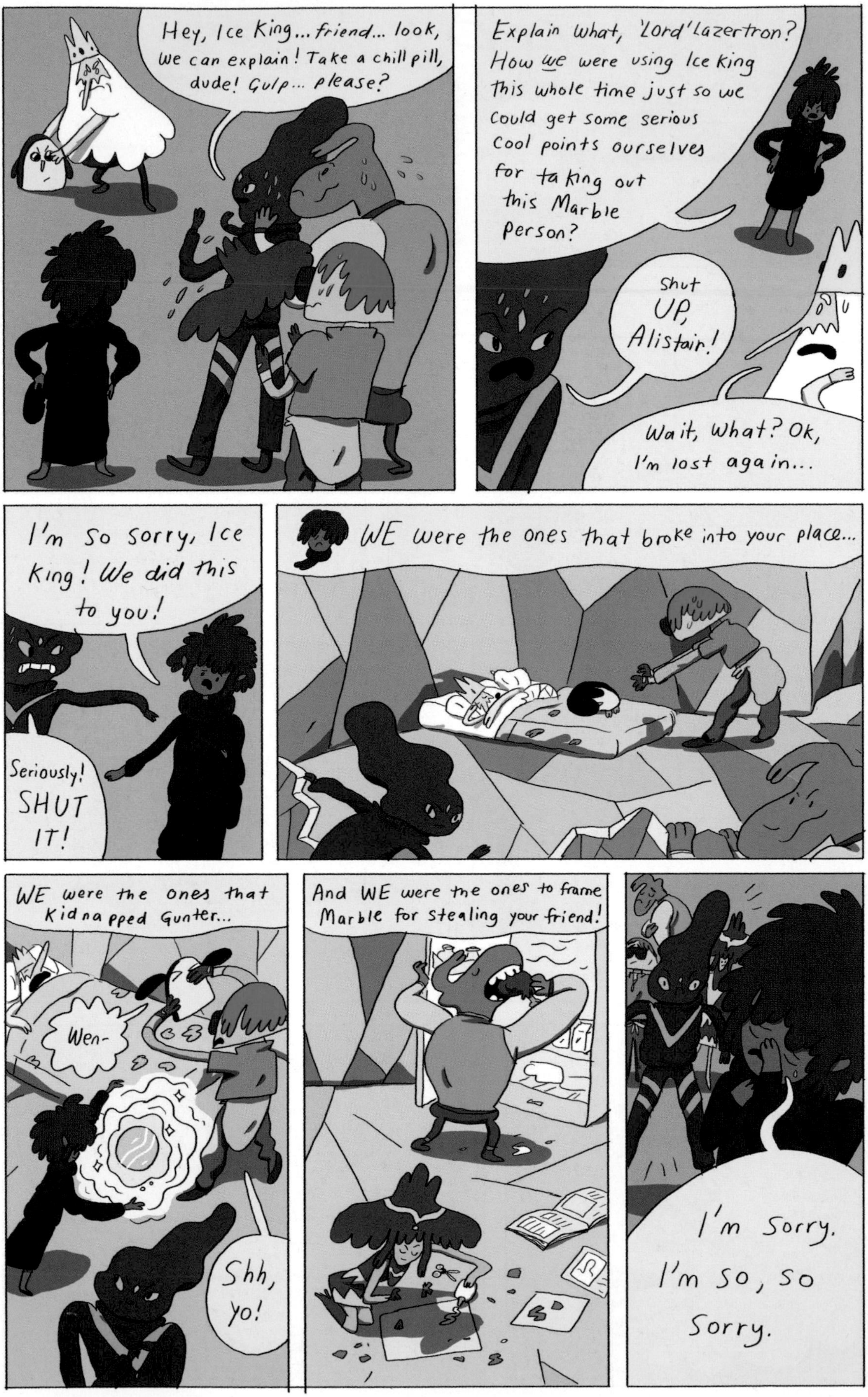
Hey, Ice King... friend... look, we can explain! Take a chill pill, dude! Gulp... please?
Explain what, 'Lord' Lazertron? How we were using Ice King this whole time just so we could get some serious cool points ourselves for taking out this Marble person?
Shut UP, Alistair!
Wait, what? Ok, I'm lost again...
I'm so sorry, Ice King! We did this to you!
Seriously! SHUT IT!
WE were the ones that broke into your place...
WE were the ones that kidnapped Gunter...
Wen-
Shh, yo!
And WE were the ones to frame Marble for stealing your friend!
I'm sorry. I'm so, so sorry.

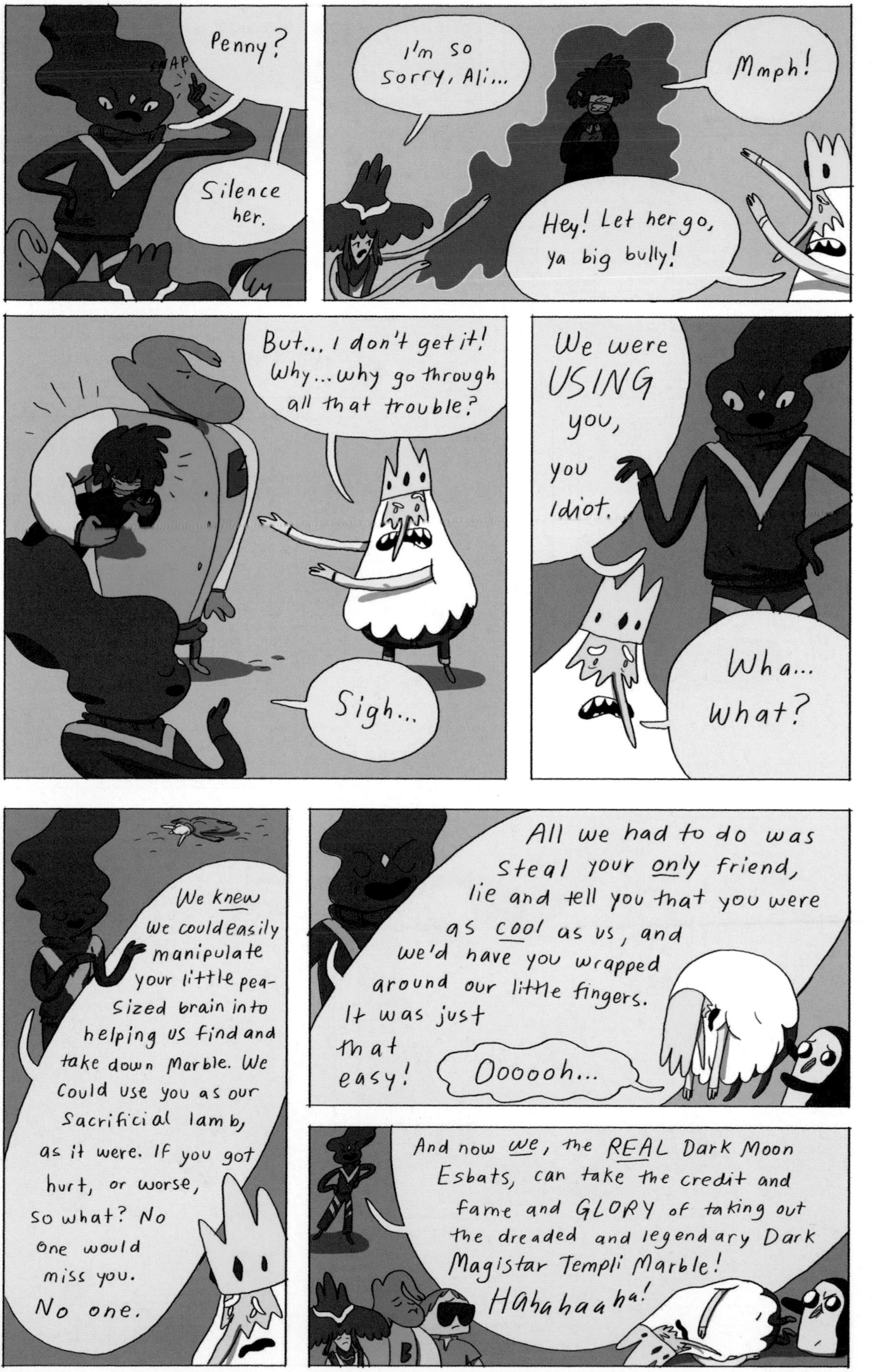
SNAP
Penny?
Silence her.
I'm so sorry, Ali...
Mmph!
Hey! Let her go, ya big bully!
But... I don't get it! Why... why go through all that trouble?
Sigh...
We were USING you, you idiot.
Wha... what?
We knew we could easily manipulate your little pea-sized brain into helping us find and take down Marble. We could use you as our sacrificial lamb, as it were. If you got hurt, or worse, so what? No one would miss you. No one.
All we had to do was steal your only friend, lie and tell you that you were as cool as us, and we'd have you wrapped around our little fingers. It was just that easy!
Oooooh...
And now we, the REAL Dark Moon Esbats, can take the credit and fame and GLORY of taking out the dreaded and legendary Dark Magistar Templi Marble! Hahahaaha!

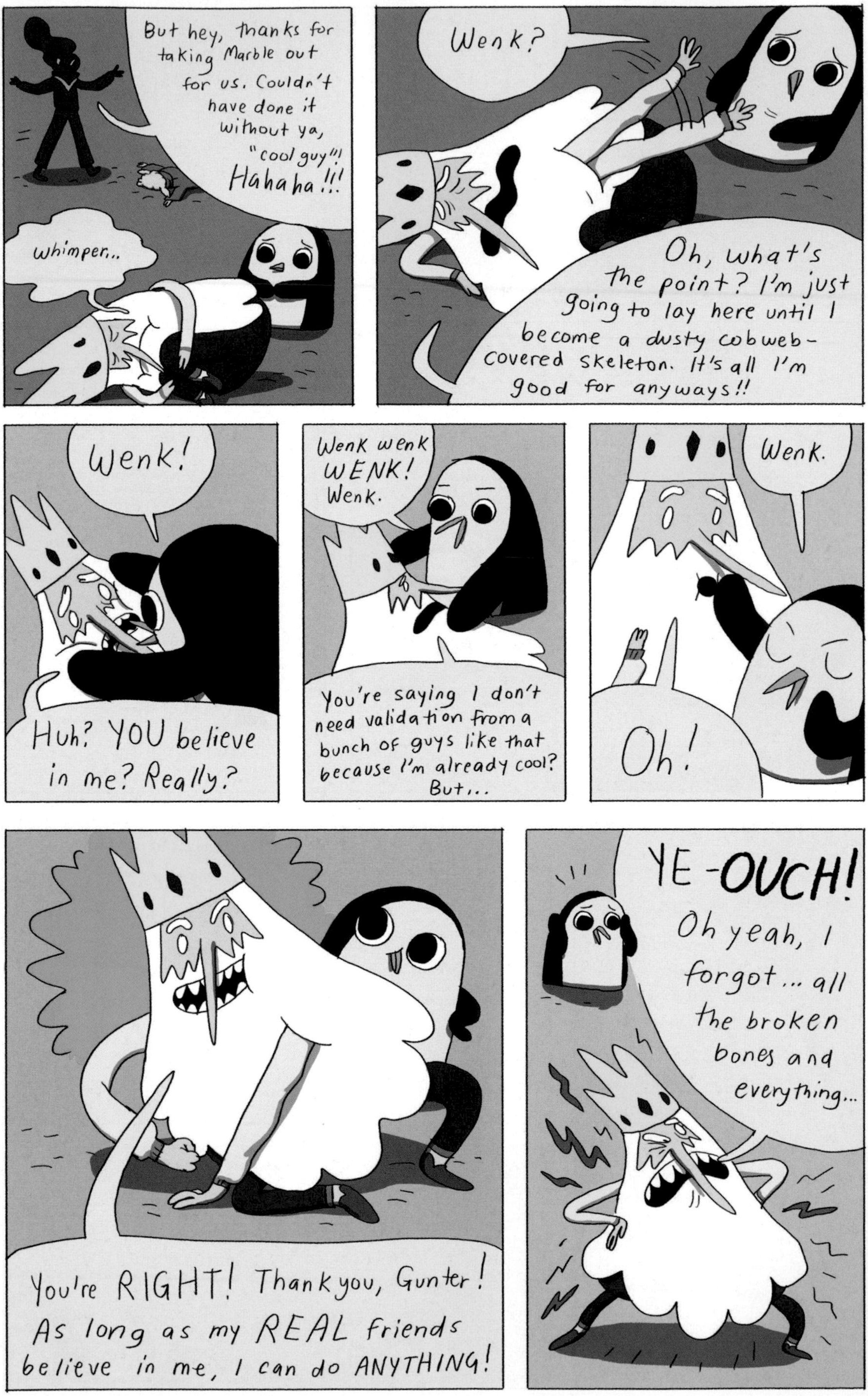

But hey, thanks for taking Marble out for us. Couldn't have done it without ya, "cool guy"!! Hahaha!!!
whimper...
Wenk?
Oh, what's the point? I'm just going to lay here until I become a dusty cobweb-covered skeleton. It's all I'm good for anyways!!
Wenk!
Huh? YOU believe in me? Really?
Wenk wenk WENK! Wenk.
You're saying I don't need validation from a bunch of guys like that because I'm already cool? But...
Wenk.
Oh!
You're RIGHT! Thank you, Gunter! As long as my REAL friends believe in me, I can do ANYTHING!
YE-OUCH! Oh yeah, I forgot... all the broken bones and everything...

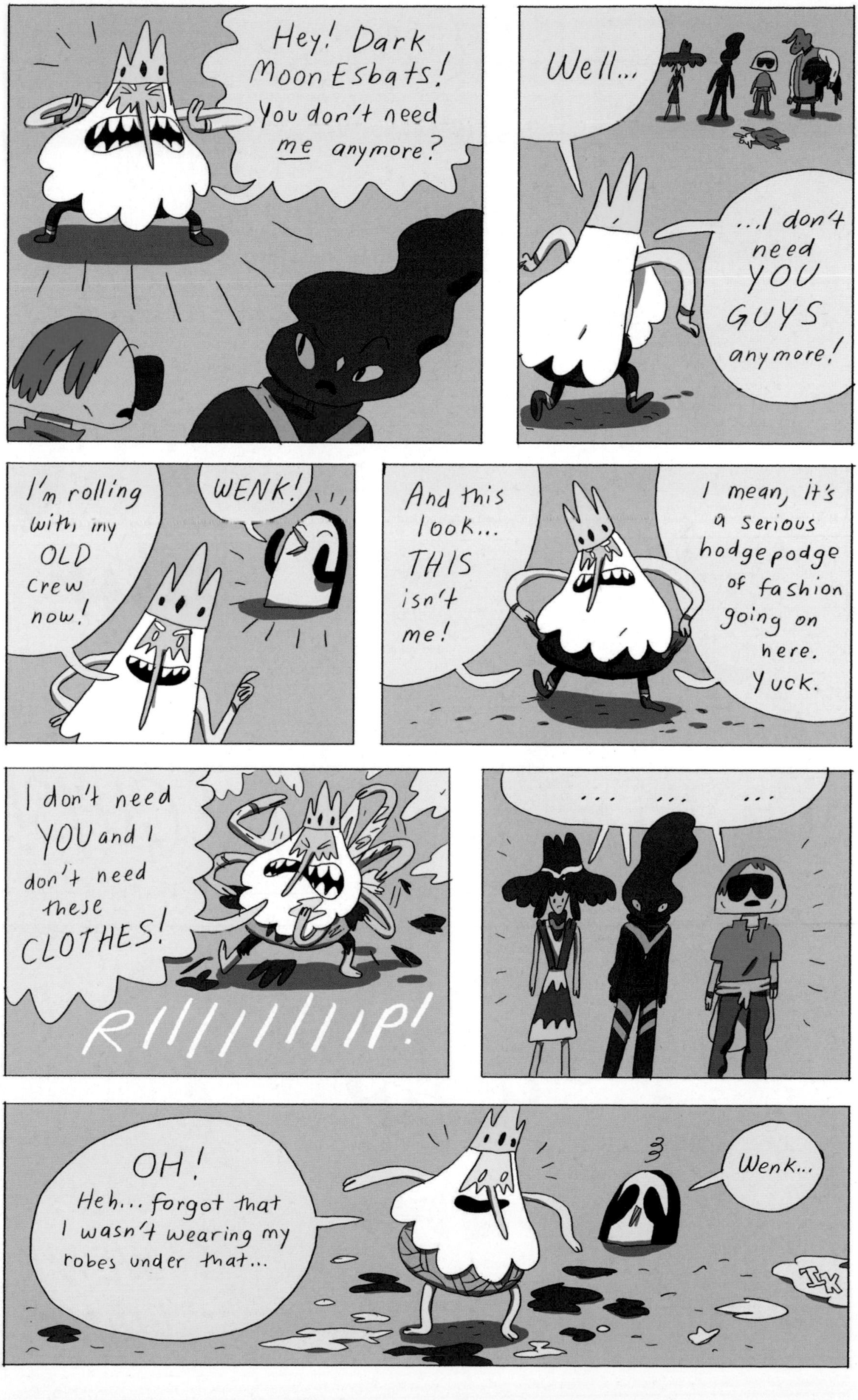
Hey! Dark Moon Esbats! You don't need me anymore?
Well...
...I don't need YOU GUYS anymore!
I'm rolling with my OLD crew now!
WENK!
And this look... THIS isn't me!
I mean, it's a serious hodgepodge of fashion going on here. Yuck.
I don't need YOU and I don't need these CLOTHES!
RIIIIIIIIP!
... ...
OH! Heh... forgot that I wasn't wearing my robes under that...
Wenk...

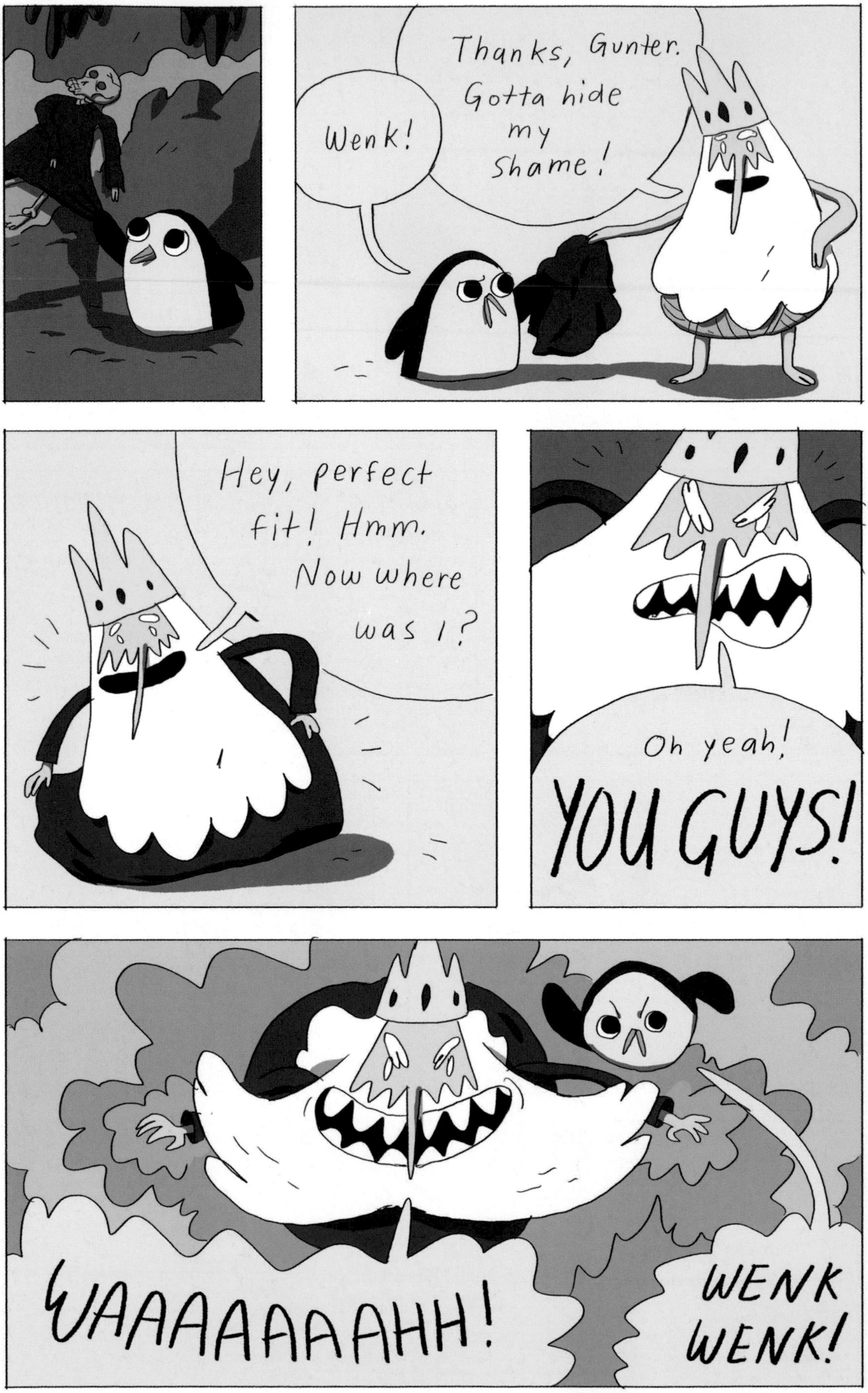
Thanks, Gunter. Gotta hide my Shame!
Wenk!
Hey, perfect fit! Hmm. Now where was I?
Oh yeah!
YOU GUYS!
WAAAAAAAAHH!
WENK WENK!

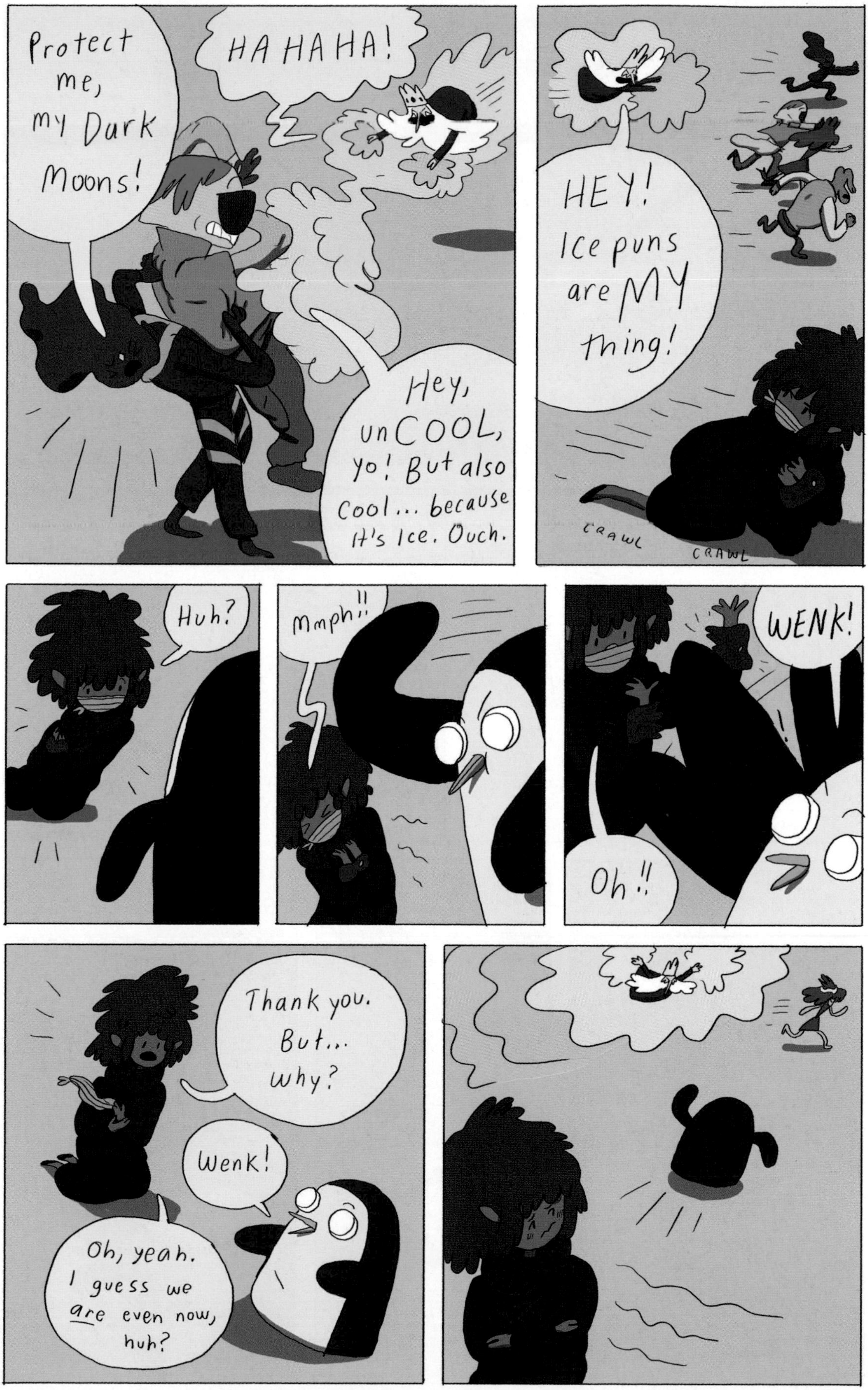
Protect me, my Dark Moons!
HAHAHA!
Hey, unCOOL, yo! But also cool... because it's ice. Ouch.
HEY! Ice puns are MY thing!
CRAWL
CRAWL
Huh?
Mmph!!
WENK!
Oh!!
Thank you. But... why?
Wenk!
Oh, yeah. I guess we are even now, huh?

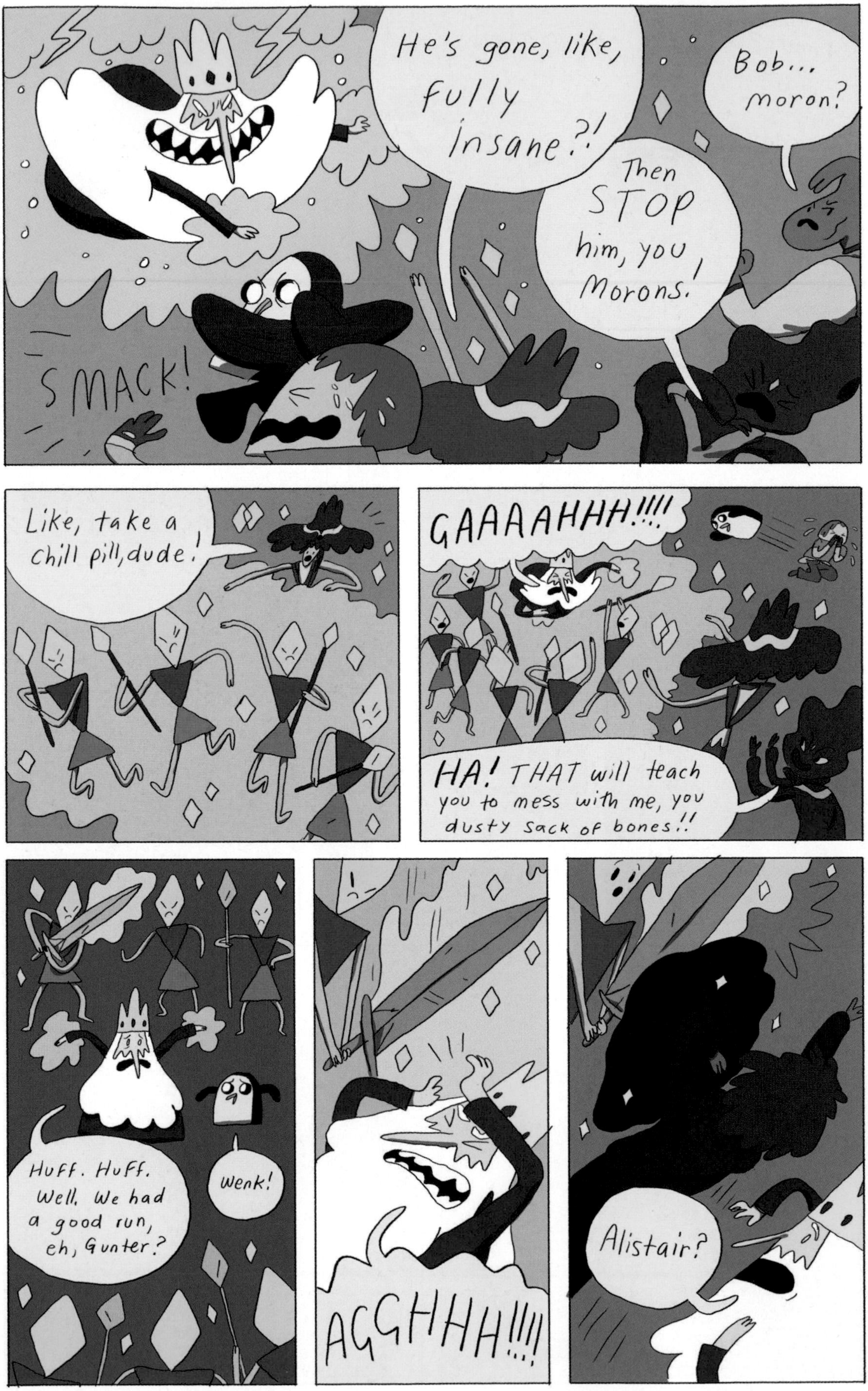
He's gone, like, fully insane?!
Bob... moron?
Then STOP him, you morons!
SMACK!
Like, take a chill pill, dude!
GAAAAHHH!!!!
HA! THAT will teach you to mess with me, you dusty sack of bones!!
Huff. Huff. Well. We had a good run, eh, Gunter?
Wenk!
AGGHHH!!!!
Alistair?

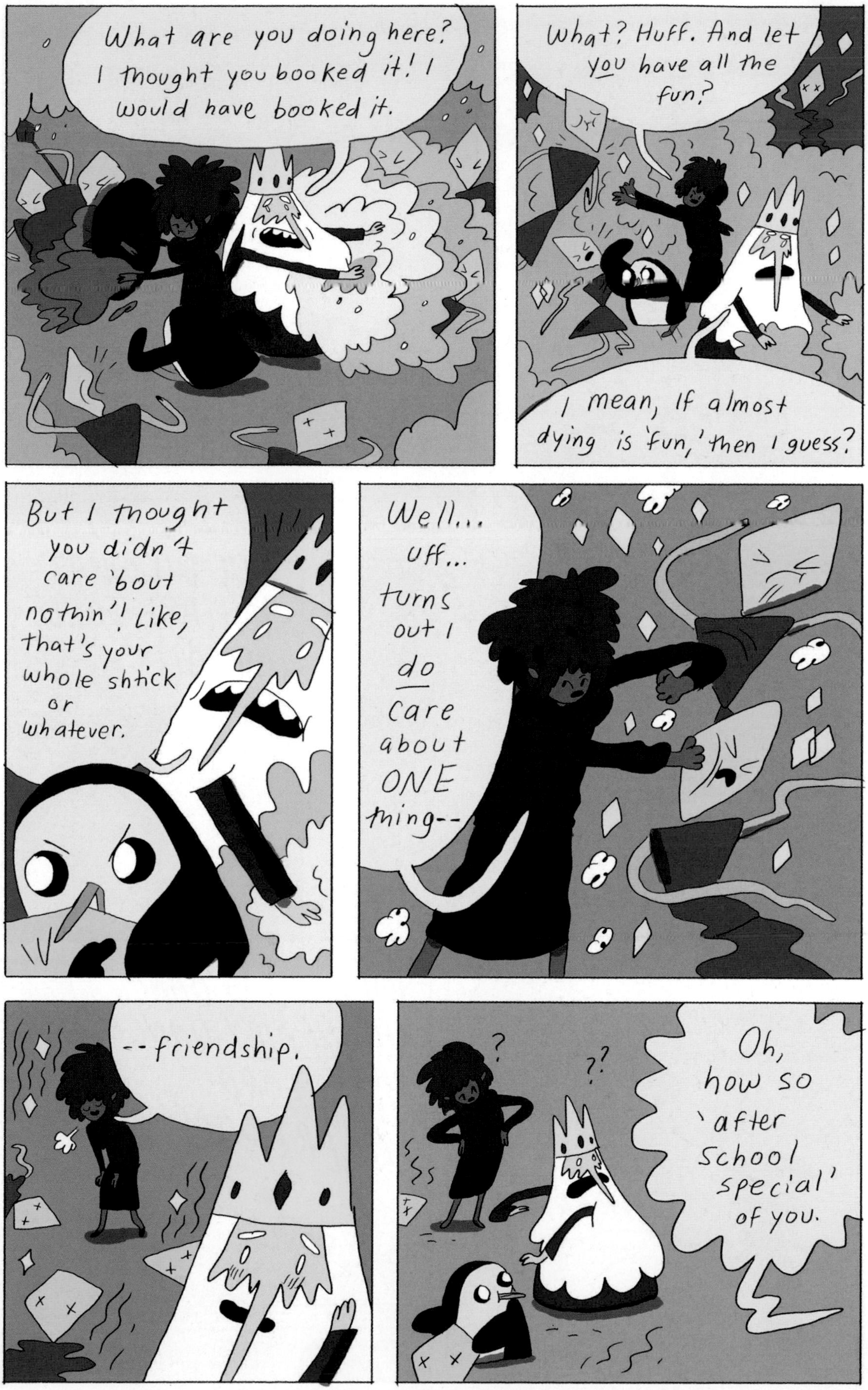
What are you doing here? I thought you booked it! I would have booked it.
What? Huff. And let you have all the fun?
I mean, If almost dying is 'fun,' then I guess?
But I thought you didn't care 'bout nothin'! Like, that's your whole shtick or whatever.
Well... uff... turns out I do care about ONE thing--
--friendship.
?
??
Oh, how so 'after school special' of you.

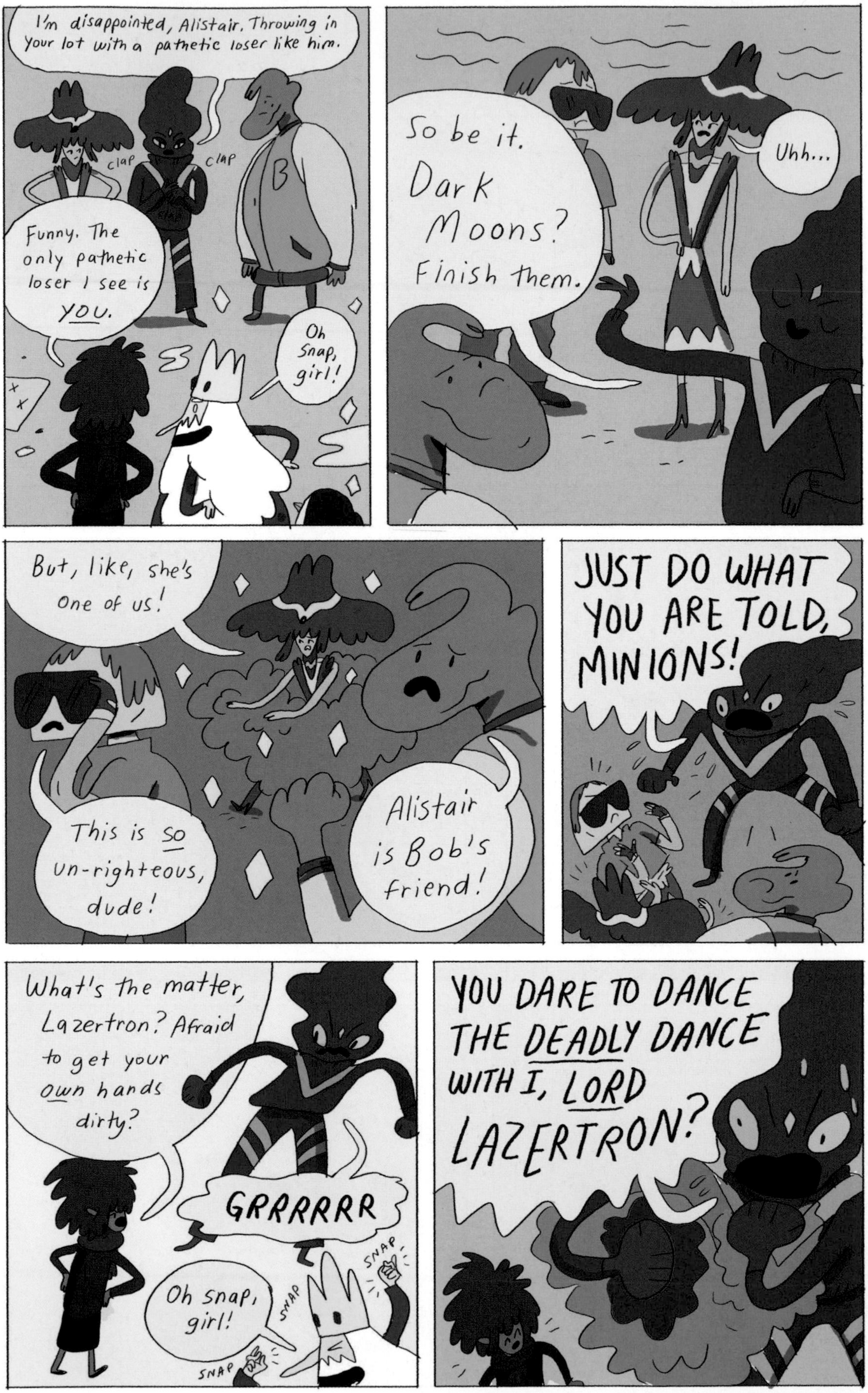
I'm disappointed, Alistair. Throwing in your lot with a pathetic loser like him.
CLAP
CLAP
Funny. The only pathetic loser I see is YOU.
Oh snap, girl!
So be it. Dark Moons? Finish them.
Uhh...
But, like, she's one of us!
This is SO un-righteous, dude!
Alistair is Bob's friend!
JUST DO WHAT YOU ARE TOLD, MINIONS!
What's the matter, Lazertron? Afraid to get your own hands dirty?
GRRRRRR
Oh snap, girl!
SNAP
SNAP
SNAP
YOU DARE TO DANCE THE DEADLY DANCE WITH I, LORD LAZERTRON?

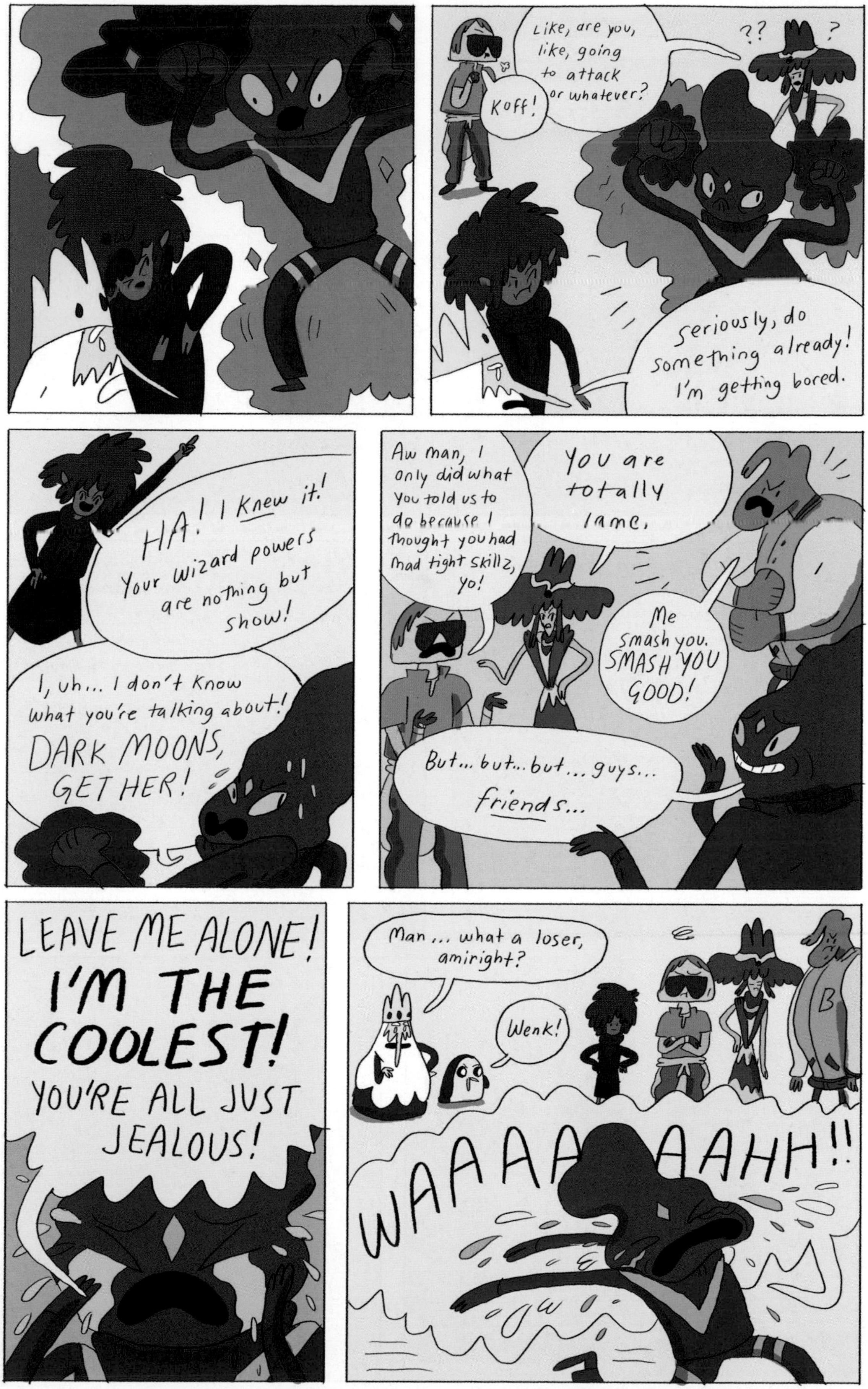
Like, are you, like, going to attack or whatever?
Koff!
??
?
Seriously, do something already! I'm getting bored.
HA! I knew it! Your wizard powers are nothing but show!
I, uh... I don't know what you're talking about! DARK MOONS, GET HER!
Aw man, I only did what you told us to do because I thought you had mad tight skillz, yo!
You are totally lame.
Me smash you. SMASH YOU GOOD!
But... but... but... guys... friends...
LEAVE ME ALONE! I'M THE COOLEST! YOU'RE ALL JUST JEALOUS!
Man... what a loser, amiright?
Wenk!
WAAAAAAAHH!!

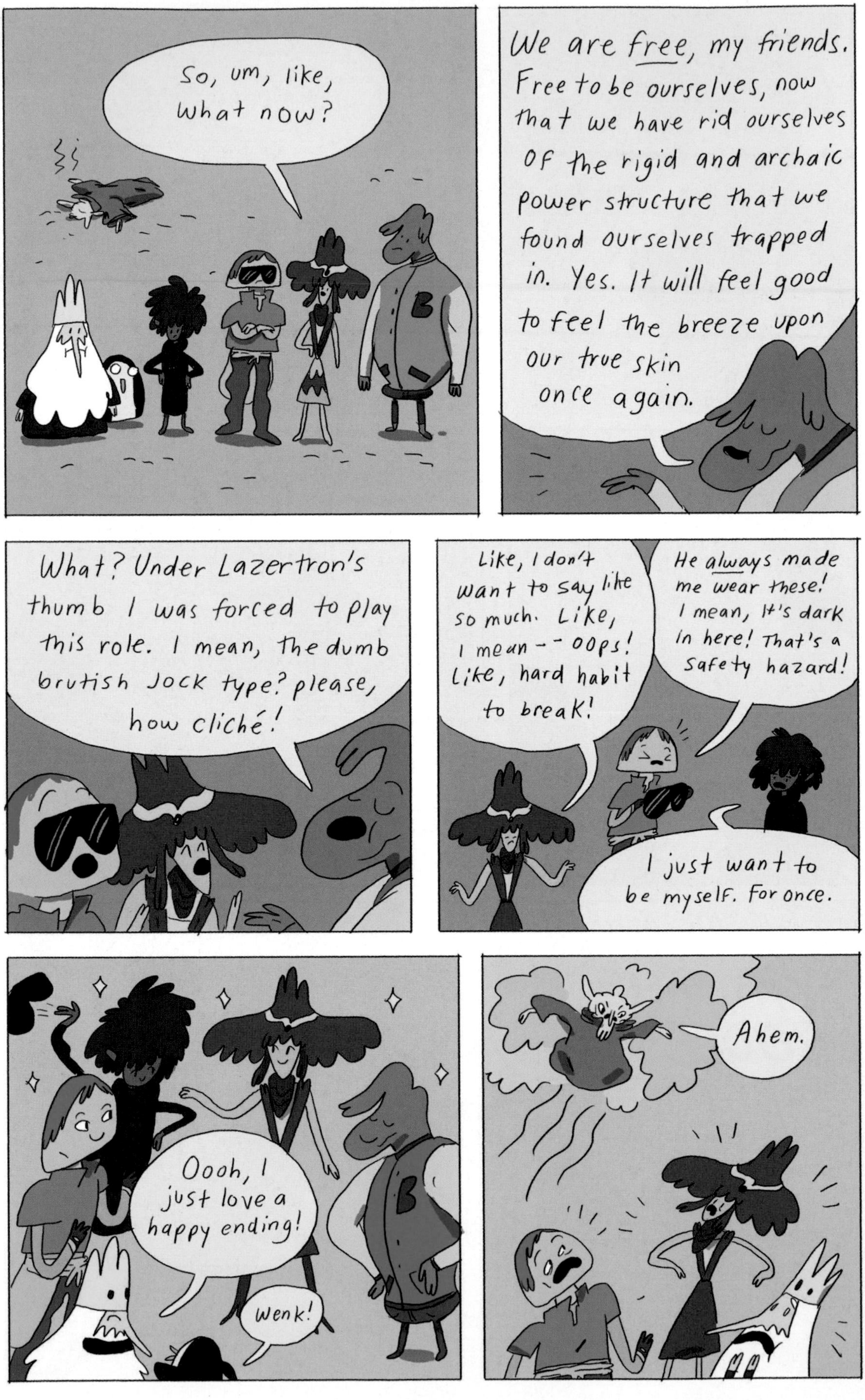
So, um, like, what now?
We are free, my friends. Free to be ourselves, now that we have rid ourselves of the rigid and archaic power structure that we found ourselves trapped in. Yes. It will feel good to feel the breeze upon our true skin once again.
What? Under Lazertron's thumb I was forced to play this role. I mean, the dumb brutish jock type? please, how cliché!
Like, I don't want to say like so much. Like, I mean-- oops! Like, hard habit to break!
He always made me wear these! I mean, it's dark in here! That's a safety hazard!
I just want to be myself. For once.
Oooh, I just love a happy ending!
Wenk!
Ahem.

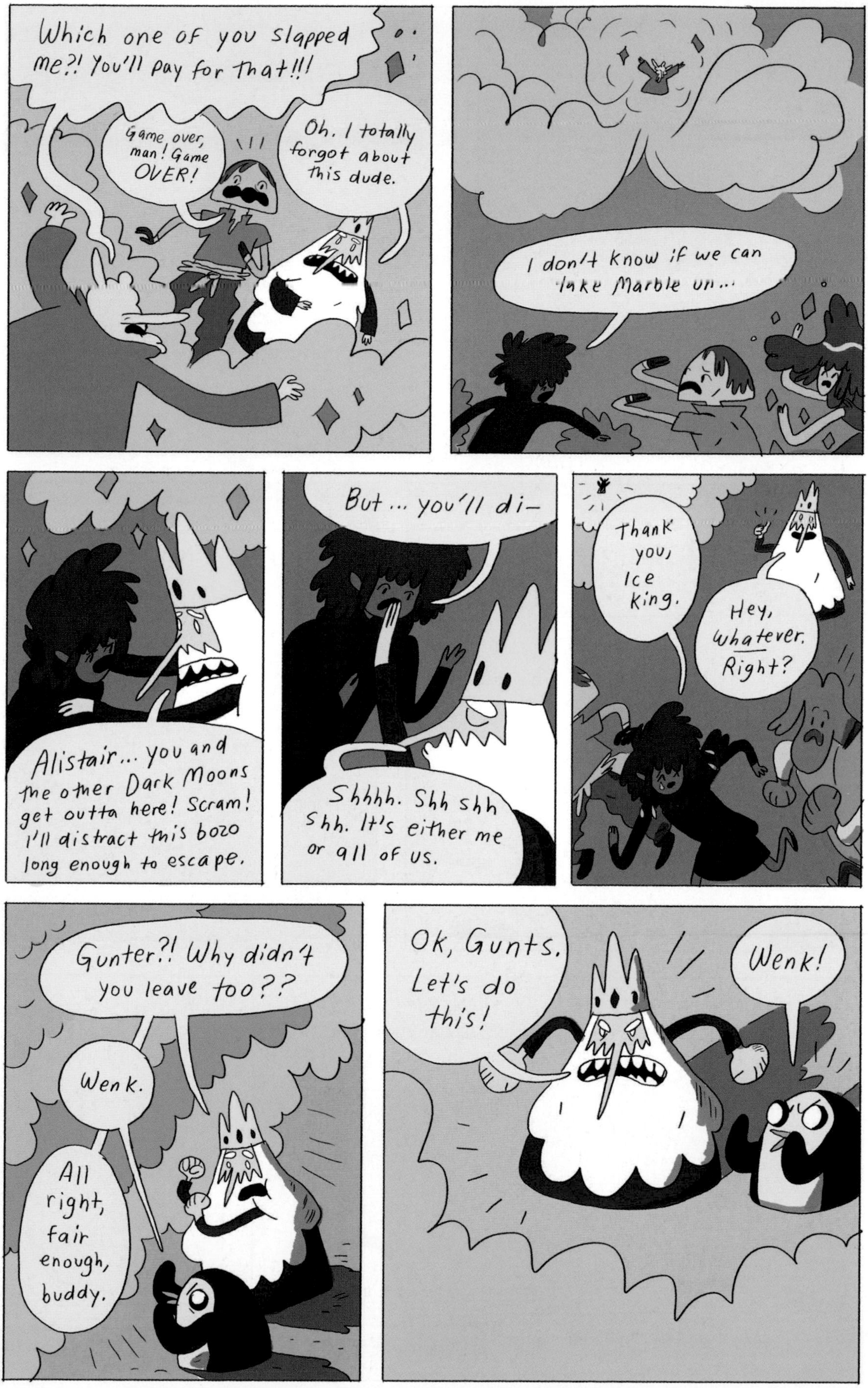
Which one of you slapped me?! You'll pay for that!!!
Game over, man! Game OVER!
Oh. I totally forgot about this dude.
I don't know if we can take Marble on...
Alistair... you and the other Dark Moons get outta here! Scram! I'll distract this bozo long enough to escape.
But... you'll di—
Shhhh. Shh shh shh. It's either me or all of us.
Thank you, Ice King.
Hey, whatever. Right?
Gunter?! Why didn't you leave too??
Wenk.
All right, fair enough, buddy.
Ok, Gunts. Let's do this!
Wenk!

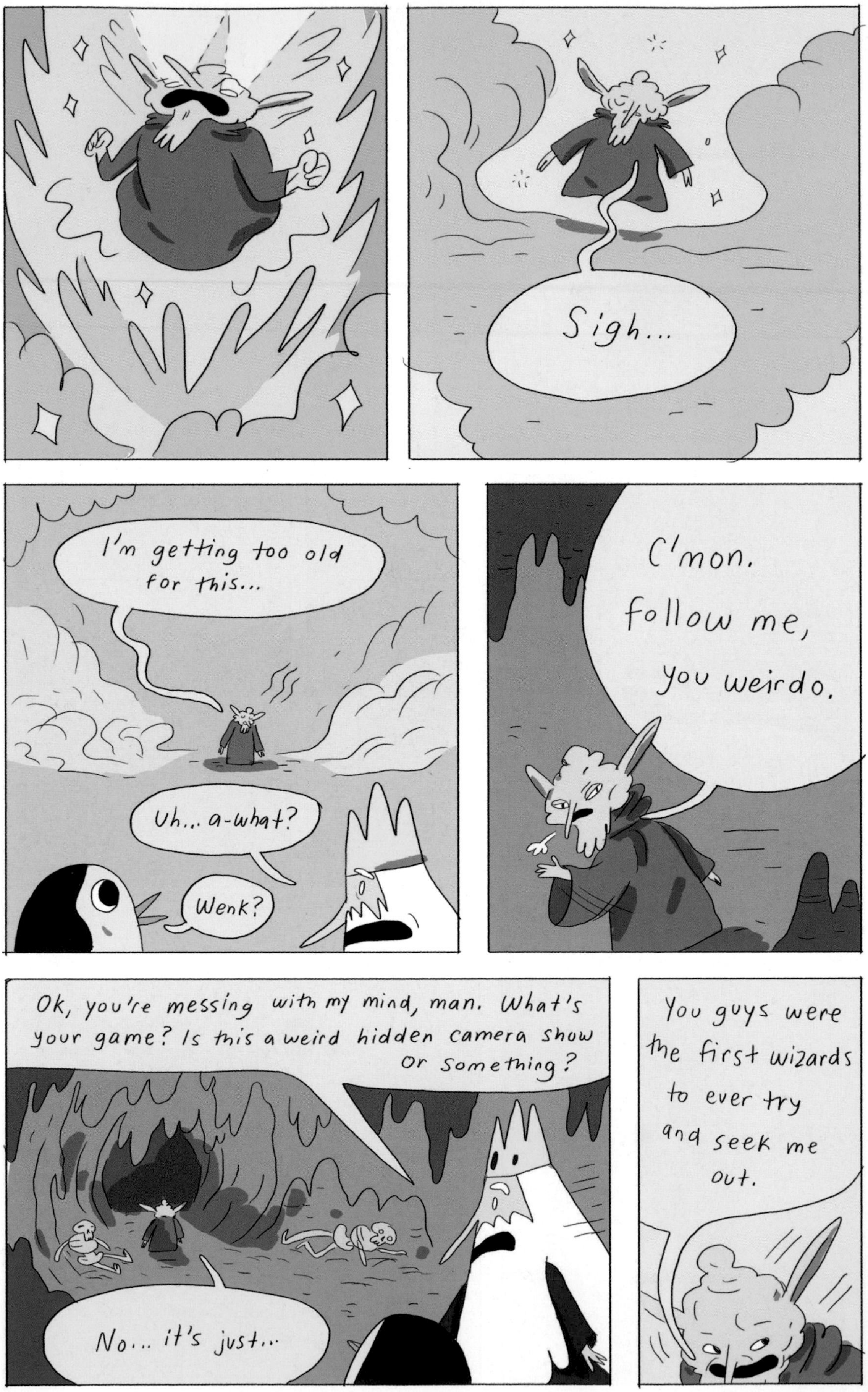
Sigh...
I'm getting too old for this...
Uh... a-what?
Wenk?
C'mon. follow me, you weirdo.
Ok, you're messing with my mind, man. What's your game? Is this a weird hidden camera show or something?
No... it's just...
You guys were the first wizards to ever try and seek me out.

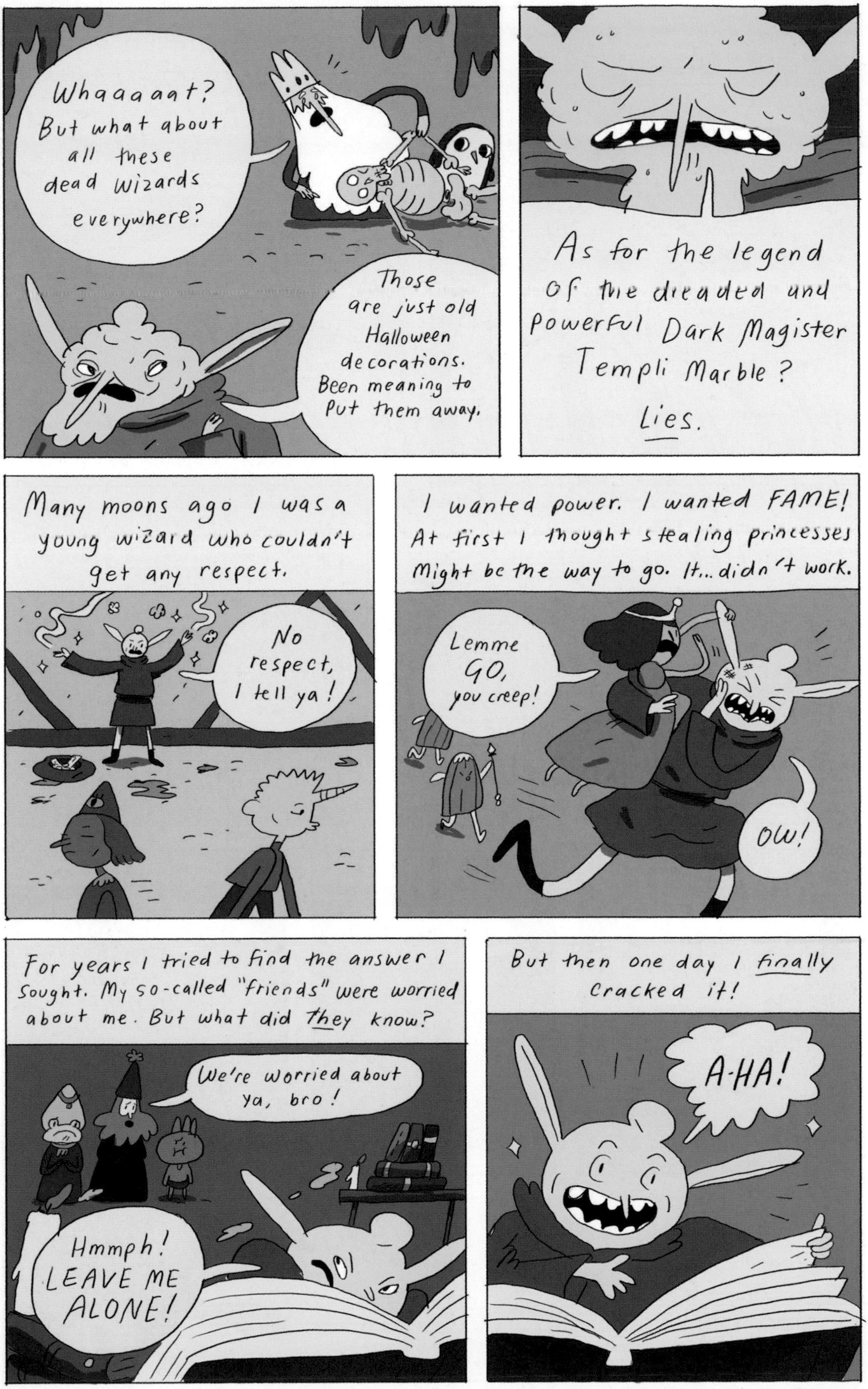
Whaaaaat? But what about all these dead wizards everywhere?
Those are just old Halloween decorations. Been meaning to put them away.
As for the legend of the dreaded and powerful Dark Magister Templi Marble? Lies.
Many moons ago I was a young wizard who couldn't get any respect.
No respect, I tell ya!
I wanted power. I wanted FAME! At first I thought stealing princesses might be the way to go. It... didn't work.
Lemme GO, you creep!
OW!
For years I tried to find the answer I sought. My so-called "friends" were worried about me. But what did they know?
We're worried about ya, bro!
Hmmph! LEAVE ME ALONE!
But then one day I finally cracked it!
A-HA!

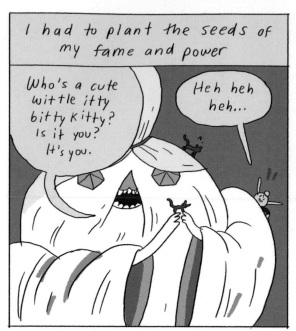

I had to plant the seeds of my fame and power

Who's a cute wittle itty bitty kitty? Is it you? It's you.

Heh heh heh...

FEEL THE WRATH OF THE DARK MAGISTER TEMPLI MARBLE!!! (tell everyone you know)!

Hahaha!

Huh? Is someone there?

Now all I had to do was flee and let my legend grow and bloom

So I waited.

Haha, this is a good plan!

And waited

Any day now...

But no one came.

You know what? Screw the rest of the world! Who needs 'em! BAH!

But finally! people came! So it really wasn't a life fully wasted!

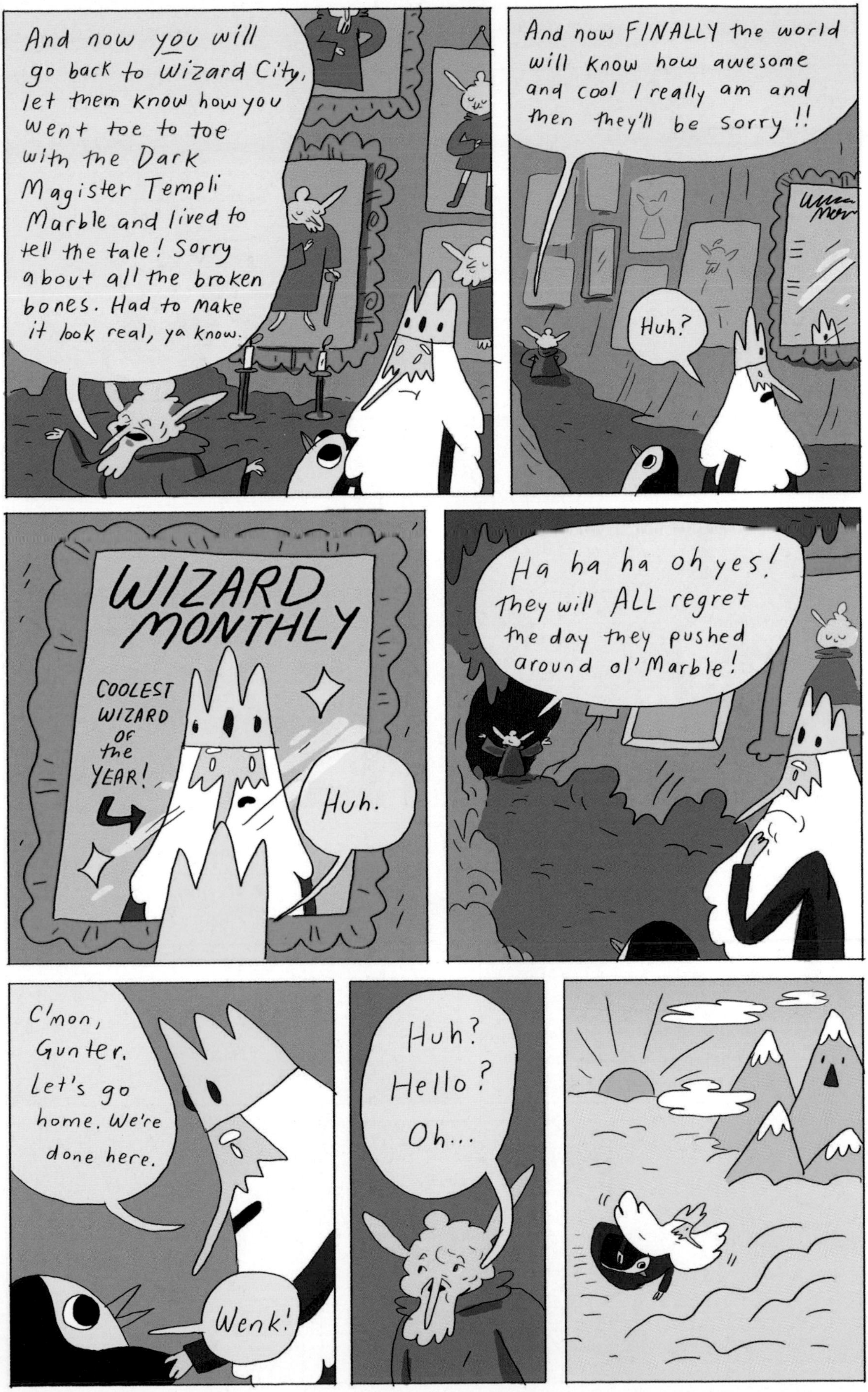
And now you will go back to Wizard City, let them know how you went toe to toe with the Dark Magister Templi Marble and lived to tell the tale! Sorry about all the broken bones. Had to make it look real, ya know.
And now FINALLY the world will know how awesome and cool I really am and then they'll be sorry!!
Huh?
WIZARD MONTHLY
COOLEST WIZARD OF the YEAR!
Huh.
Ha ha ha oh yes! They will ALL regret the day they pushed around ol' Marble!
C'mon, Gunter. Let's go home. We're done here.
Wenk!
Huh? Hello? Oh...

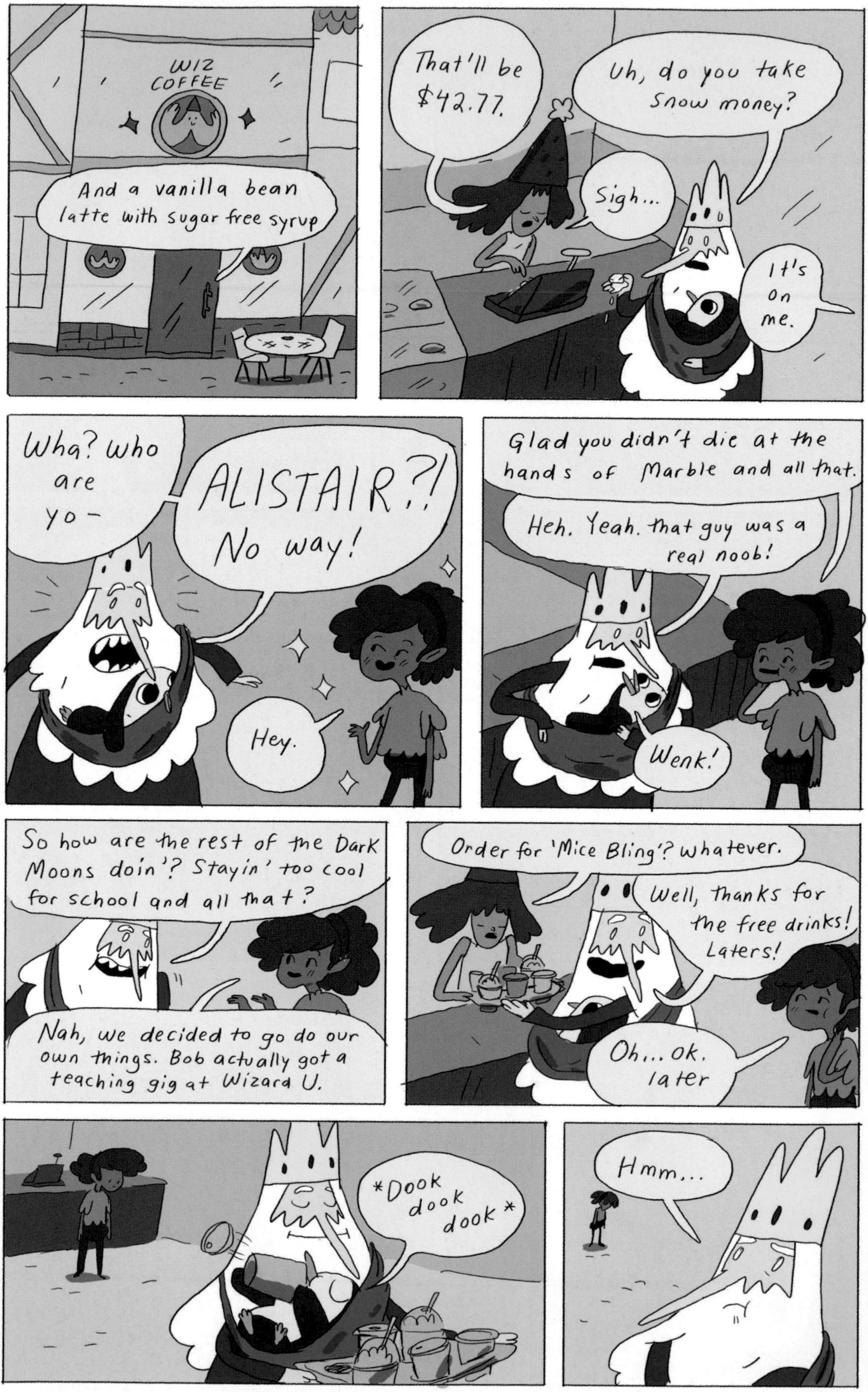
WIZ COFFEE
And a vanilla bean latte with sugar free syrup
That'll be $42.77.
Uh, do you take Snow money?
Sigh...
It's on me.
Wha? who are yo-
ALISTAIR?! No way!
Hey.
Glad you didn't die at the hands of Marble and all that.
Heh. Yeah. that guy was a real noob!
Wenk!
So how are the rest of the Dark Moons doin'? Stayin' too cool for school and all that?
Nah, we decided to go do our own things. Bob actually got a teaching gig at Wizard U.
Order for 'Mice Bling'? whatever.
Well, thanks for the free drinks! Laters!
Oh... ok. later
Dook dook dook
Hmm...

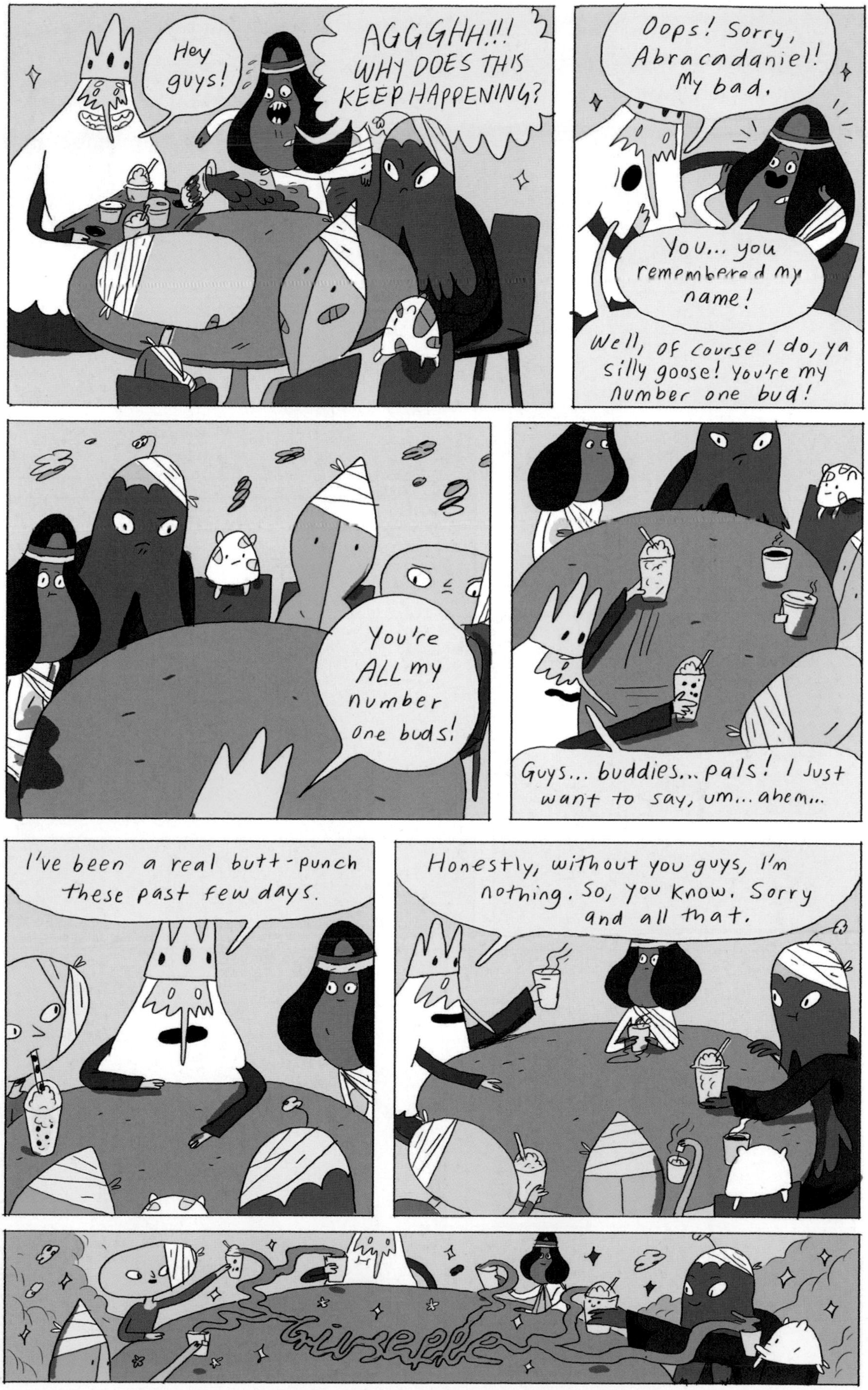
Hey guys!
AGGGHH!!! WHY DOES THIS KEEP HAPPENING?
Oops! Sorry, Abracadaniel! My bad.
You... you remembered my name!
Well, of course I do, ya silly goose! You're my number one bud!
You're ALL my number one buds!
Guys... buddies... pals! I just want to say, um... ahem...
I've been a real butt-punch these past few days.
Honestly, without you guys, I'm nothing. So, you know. Sorry and all that.
Grizzelle

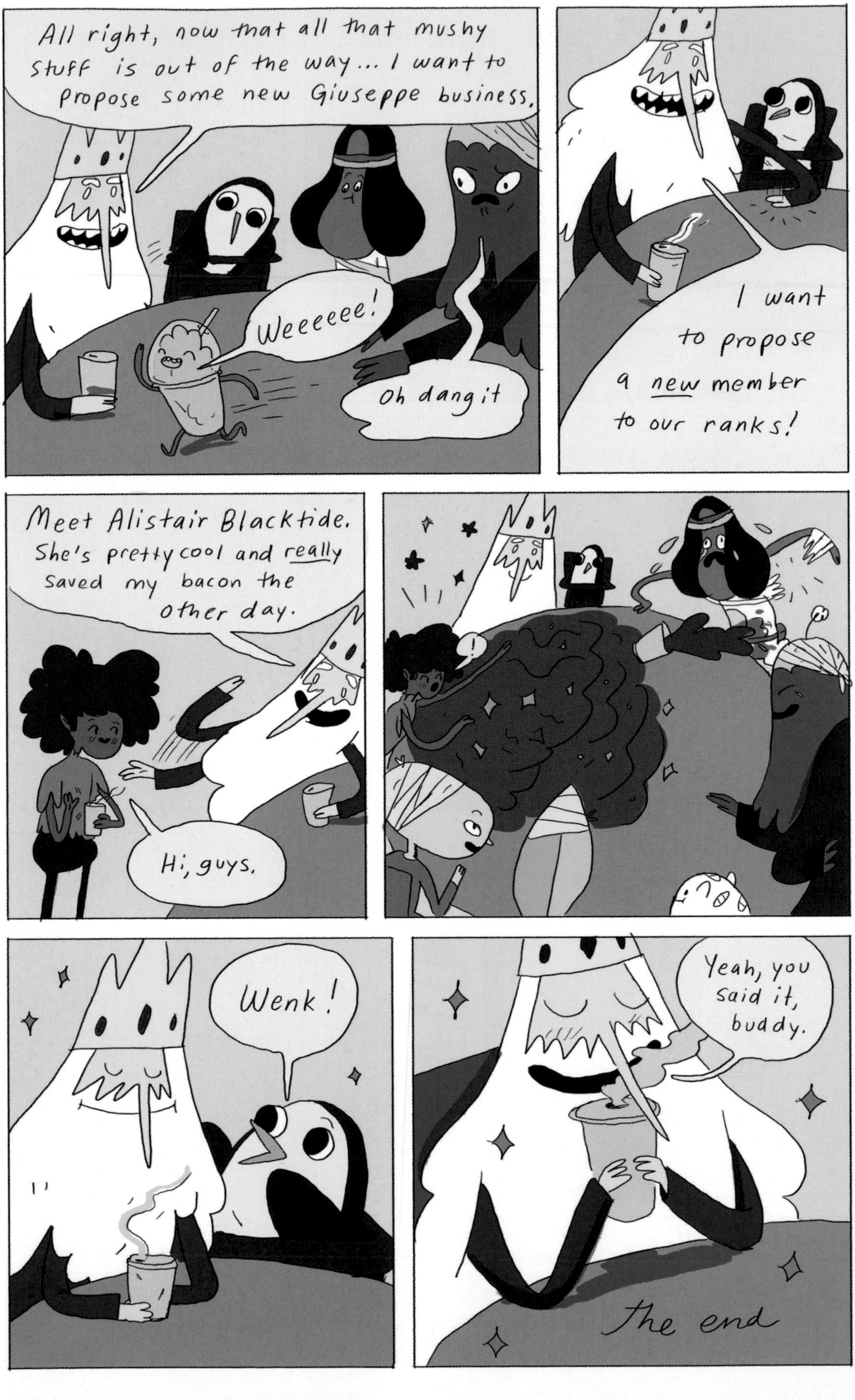
All right, now that all that mushy stuff is out of the way... I want to propose some new Giuseppe business.
Weeeeee!
Oh dang it
I want to propose a new member to our ranks!
Meet Alistair Blacktide. She's pretty cool and really saved my bacon the other day.
Hi, guys.
Wenk!
Yeah, you said it, buddy.
the end

COVER
GALLERY

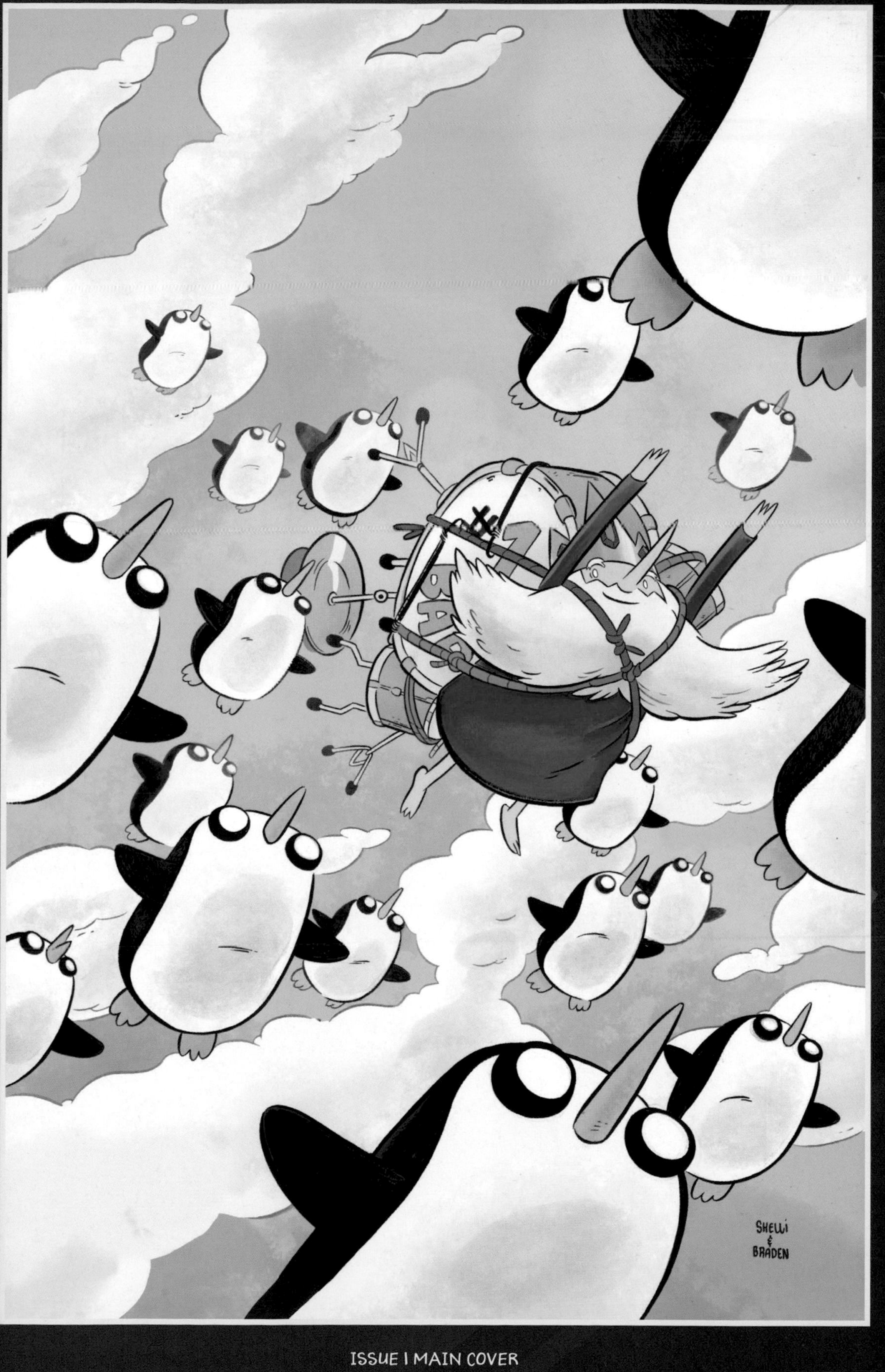
SHELLI
&
BRADEN

ISSUE 1 MAIN COVER
SHELLI PAROLINE & BRADEN LAMB

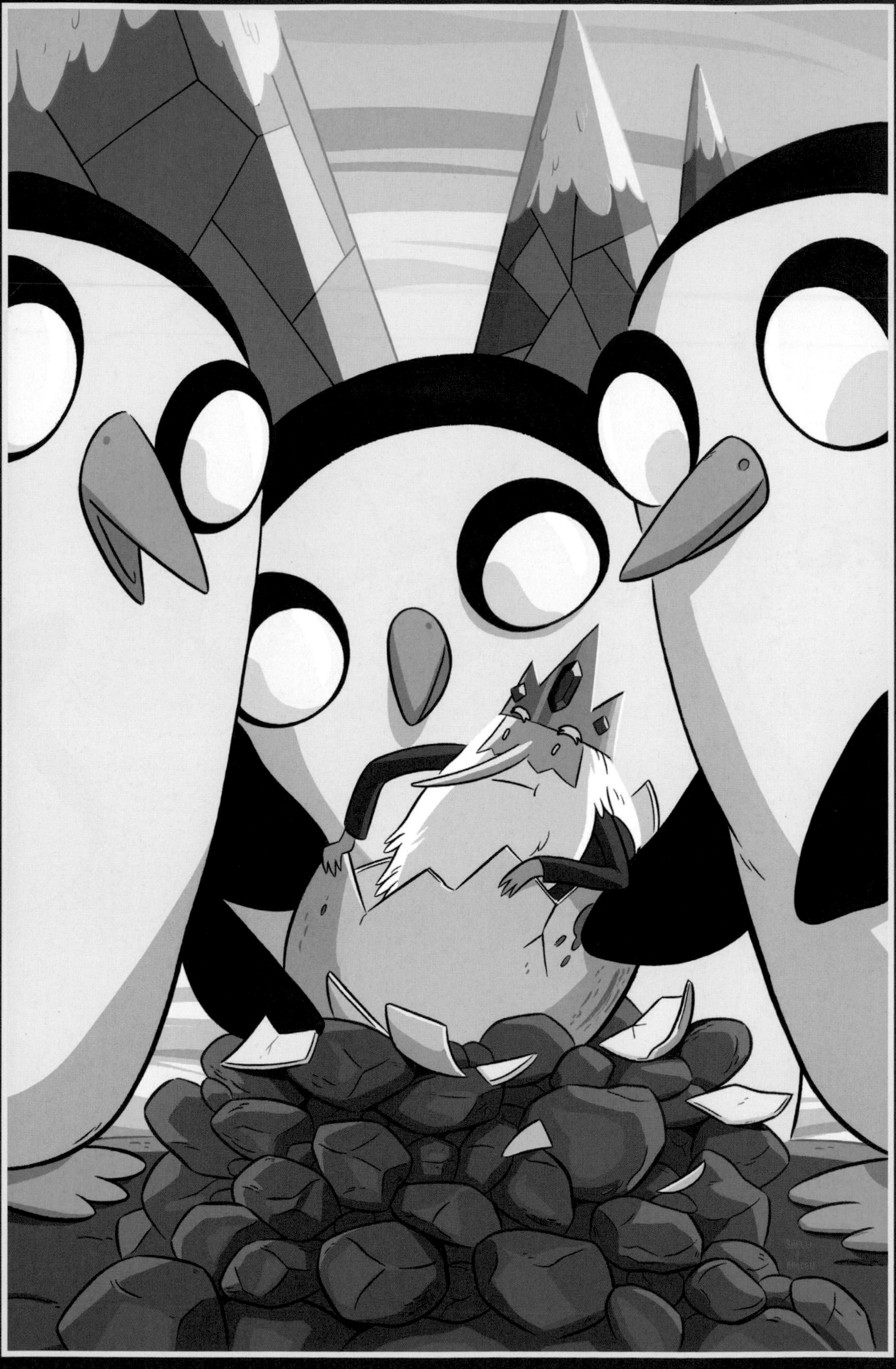

ISSUE 2 MAIN COVER
SHELLI PAROLINE & BRADEN LAMB

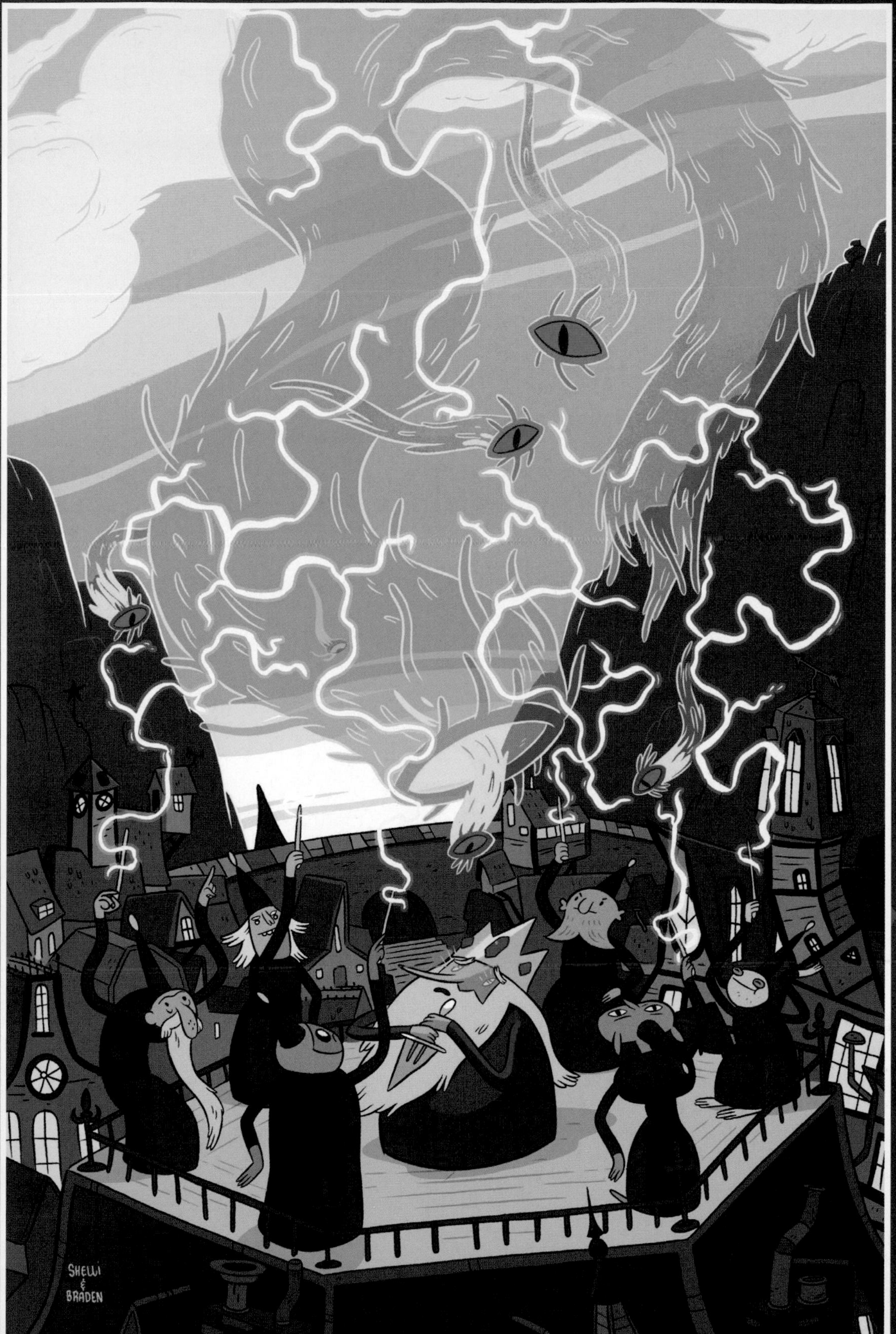
SHELLI
&
BRADEN

ISSUE 3 MAIN COVER

SHELLI PAROLINE & BRADEN LAMB

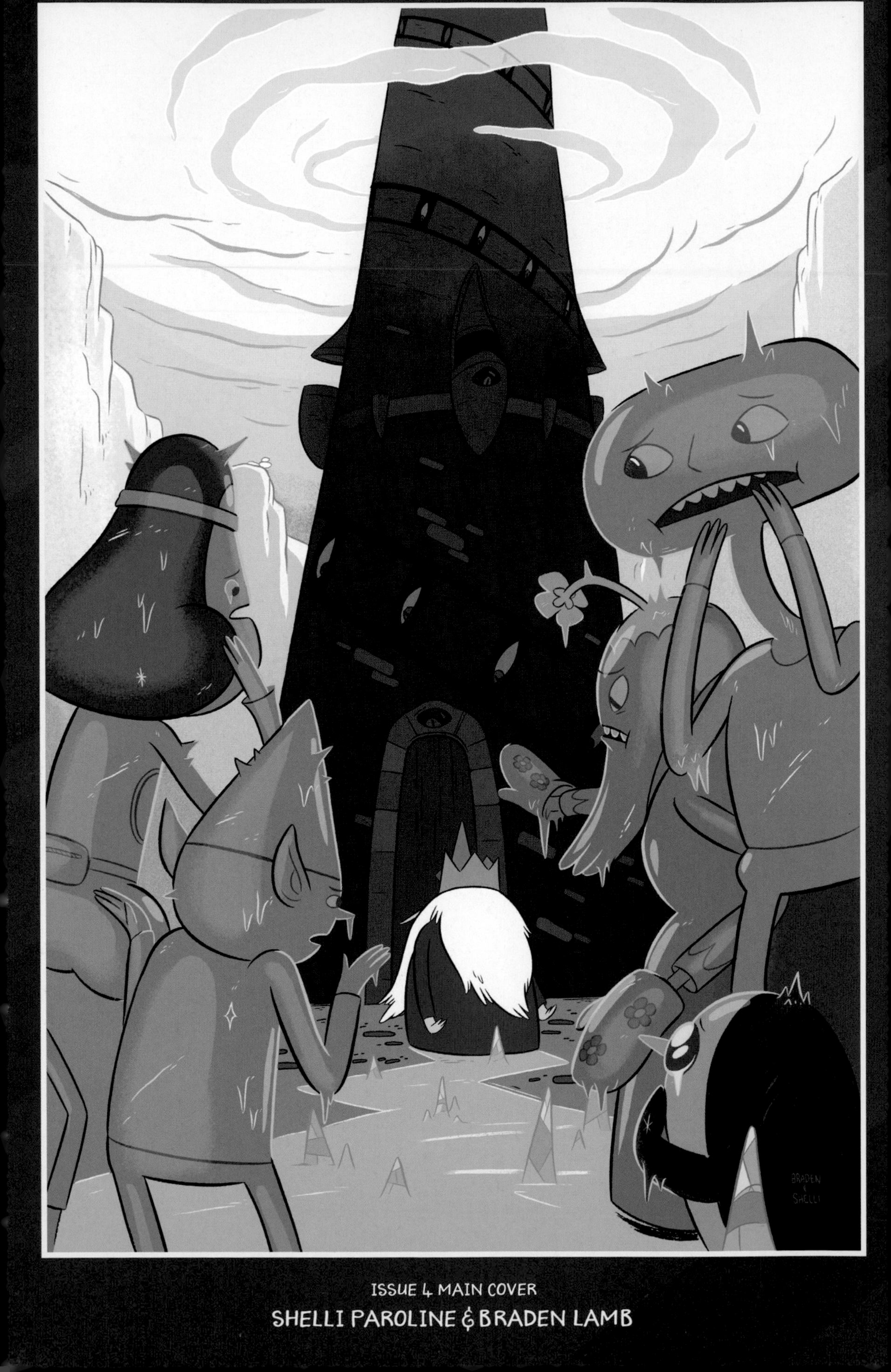
BRADEN & SHELLI

ISSUE 4 MAIN COVER

SHELLI PAROLINE & BRADEN LAMB

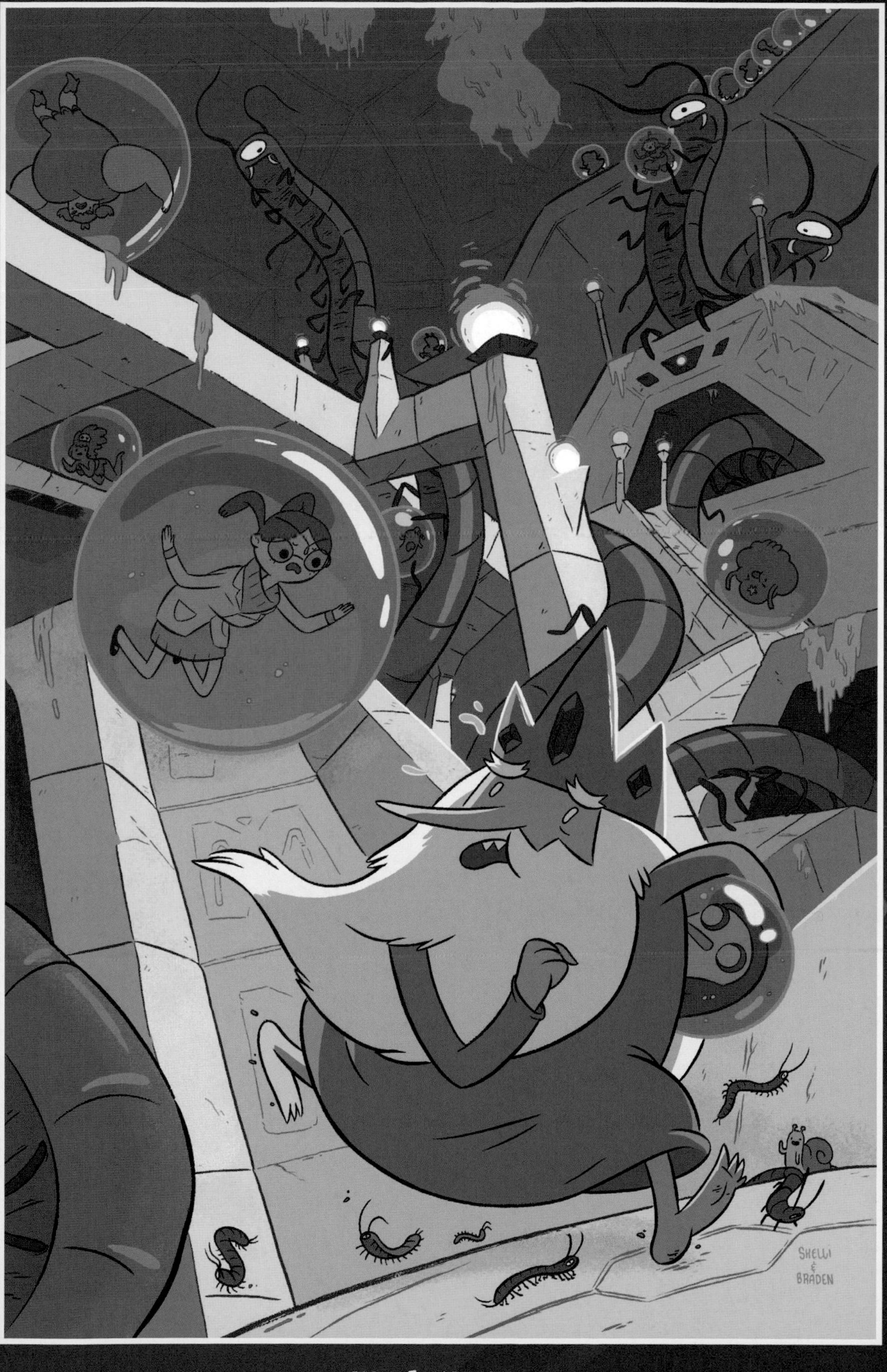
SHELLI
&
BRADEN

ISSUE 5 MAIN COVER

SHELLI PAROLINE & BRADEN LAMB

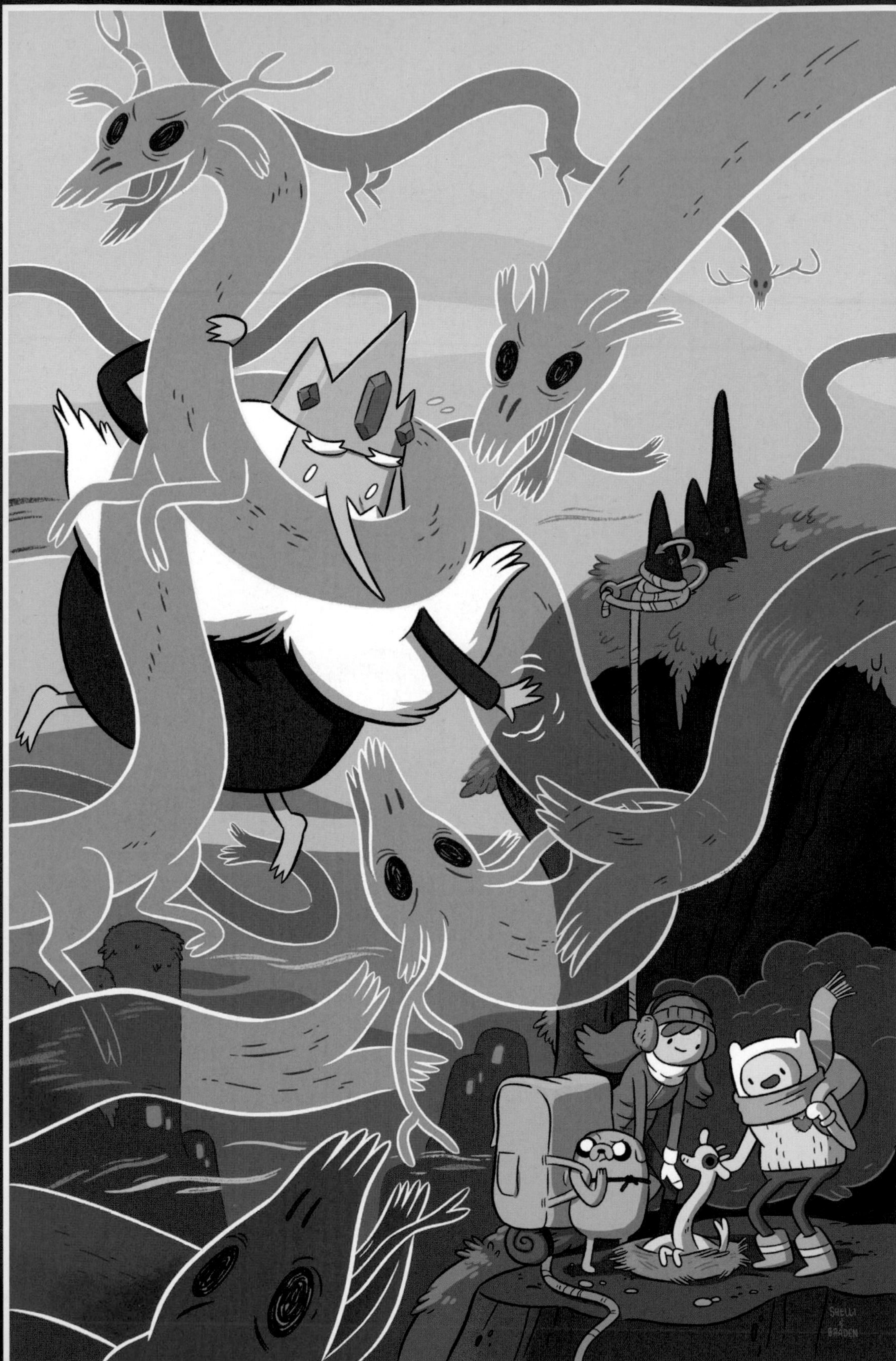
SHELLI & BRADEN

ISSUE 6 MAIN COVER
SHELLI PAROLINE & BRADEN LAMB

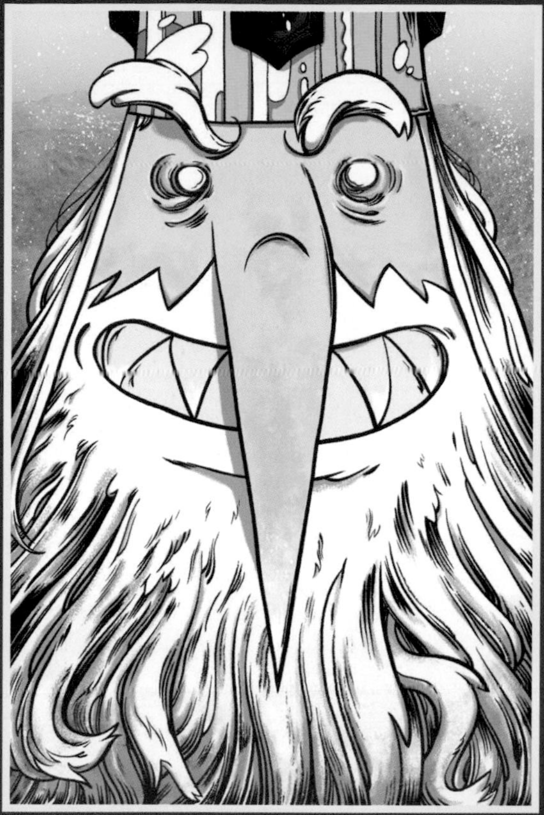

ISSUE 1 SUBSCRIPTION COVER
WYETH YATES

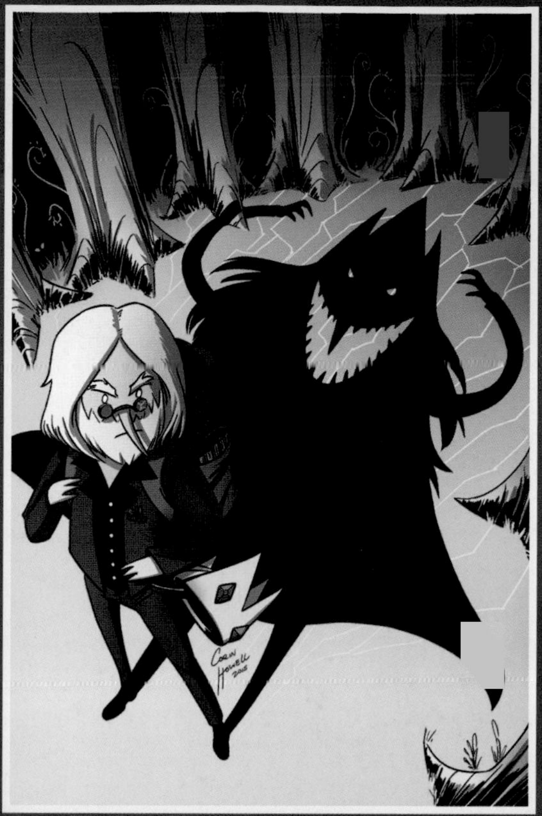

ISSUE 1 VARIANT COVER
CORIN HOWELL

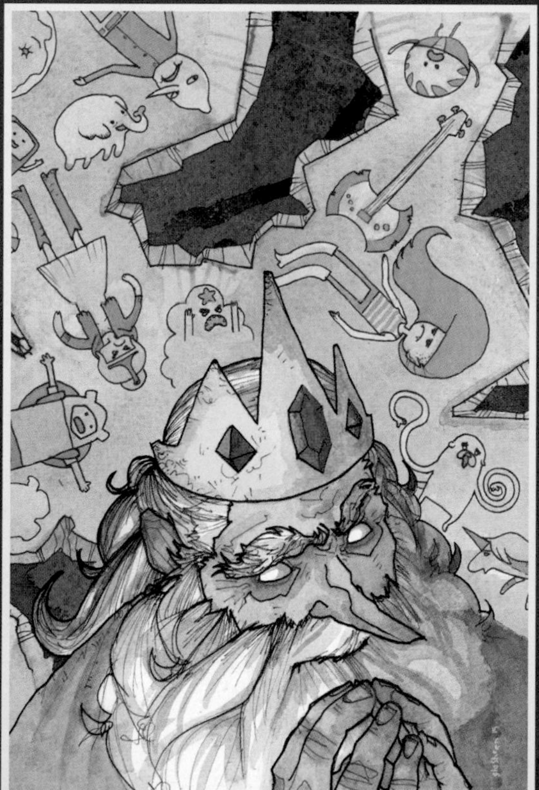

ISSUE 1 FRIED PIE EXCLUSIVE COVER
KATE GLASHEEN

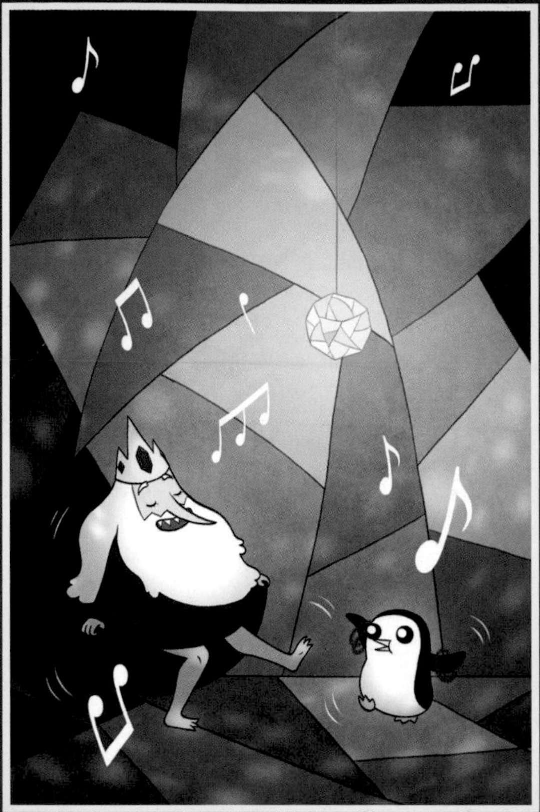

ISSUE 1 NEWBURY COMICS EXCLUSIVE COVER
SARAH SEARLE

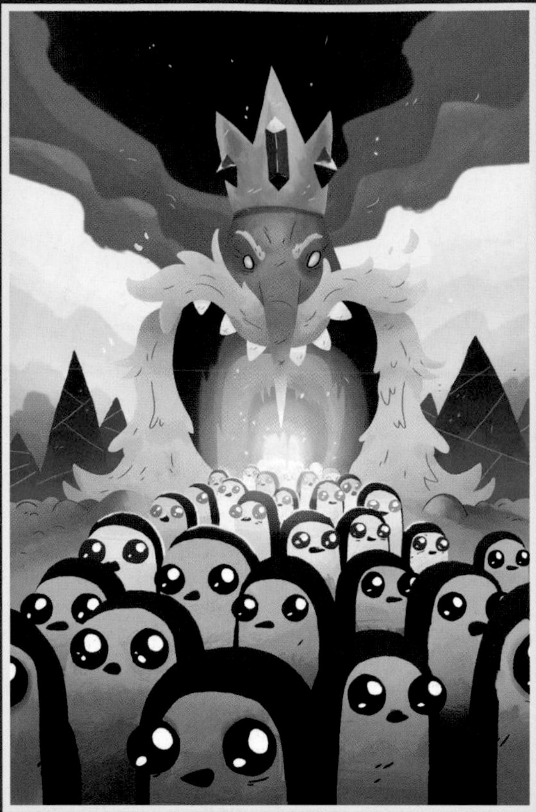

ISSUE 2 SUBSCRIPTION COVER
JOEY McCORMICK

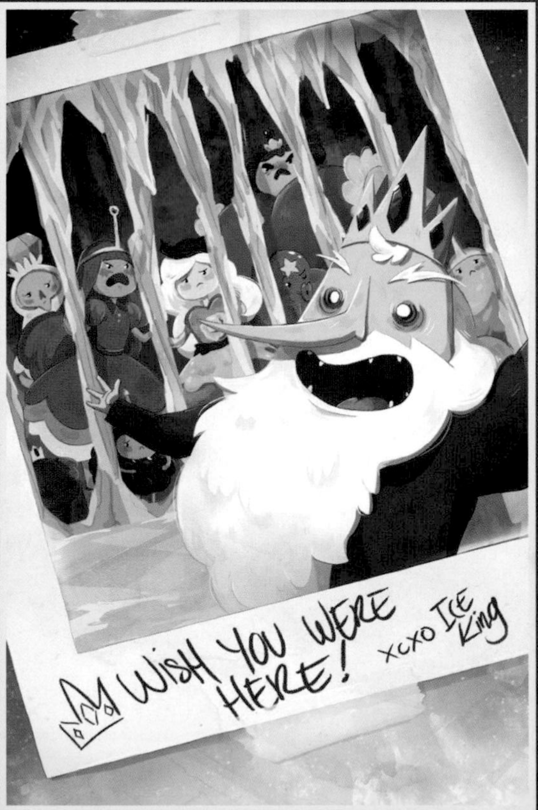
WISH YOU WERE HERE!
XOXO ICE King

ISSUE 2 VARIANT COVER
CHRYSTIN GARLAND

ISSUE 3 SUBSCRIPTION COVER
KATIE O'NEILL

ISSUE 3 VARIANT COVER
DEREK FRIDOLFS

ISSUE 4 SUBSCRIPTION COVER
LEIGH LUNA

ISSUE 4 VARIANT COVER
NICK SUMIDA

ISSUE 5 SUBSCRIPTION COVER
MICHEL FALARDEAU

ISSUE 5 VARIANT COVER
ABIGAIL DELA CRUZ

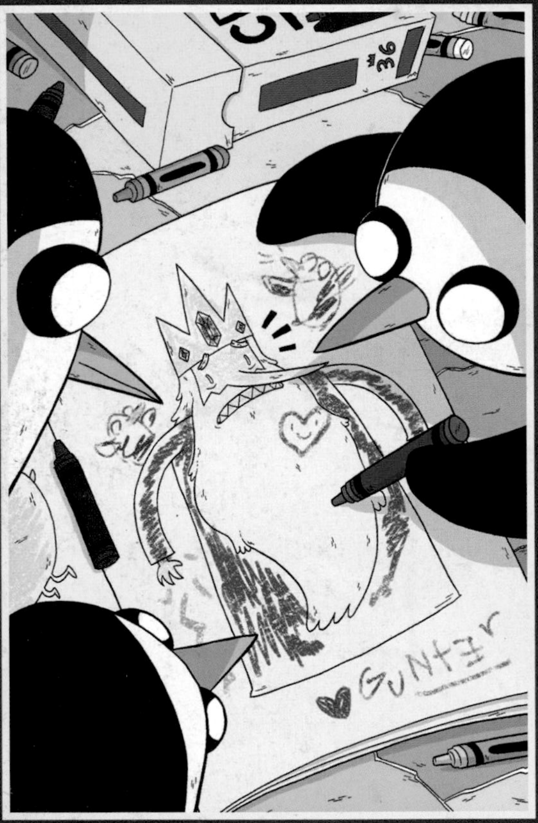
36
GUNTER

ISSUE 6 SUBSCRIPTION COVER
PRANAS NAUJOKAITIS

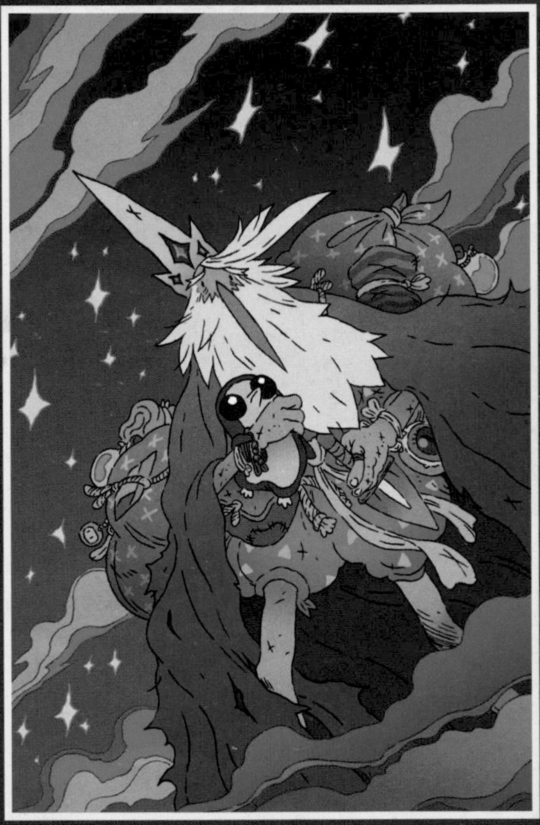

ISSUE 6 VARIANT COVER
GUILLAUME SINGELIN